Teri Wilson is a novelist for Mills & Boon. She is the author of *Unleashing Mr. Darcy*, now a Hallmark Channel Original Movie. Teri is also a contributing writer at HelloGiggles.com, a lifestyle and entertainment website founded by Zooey Deschanel that is now part of the *People* magazine, *TIME* magazine and *Entertainment Weekly* family. Teri loves books, travel, animals and dancing every day. Visit Teri at www.teriwilson.net or on Twitter, @TeriWilsonauthr.

The Drake Diamonds

TERI WILSON

MILLS & BOON

First Published in Great Britain 2019
by Mills & Boon, an imprint of HarperCollins*Publishers*
1 London Bridge Street, London, SE1 9GF

THE DRAKE DIAMONDS © 2019 Harlequin Books S. A.

His Ballerina Bride © 2016 Teri Wilson
The Princess Problem © 2017 Teri Wilson
It Started with a Diamond © 2017 Teri Wilson

ISBN: 978-0-263-27476-9

0219

MIX
Paper from
responsible sources

FSC
www.fsc.org
FSC® C007454

HIS BALLERINA BRIDE

TERI WILSON

For the classic-movie lovers out there who dream of little black dresses, diamonds and breakfast on Fifth Avenue.

"People will stare. Make it worth their while."

—Harry Winston

Chapter One

They say diamonds are a girl's best friend. Ophelia Rose had a tendency to disagree. Strongly.

Not that Ophelia had anything against diamonds per se. On the contrary, she adored them. Just two months ago, she'd earned an entire college degree in diamonds. Gemology, technically. Every piece of jewelry she'd designed for her final independent study project featured a diamond as its centerpiece. They were something of a pet jewel of hers. So naturally, working at Drake Diamonds was her dream job. It was her dream job *now*, anyway. Now that all vestiges of her former life had pretty much vanished.

Now that she'd been forced to start over.

She still loved diamonds. In truth, only *certain* diamonds had been getting on her nerves of late. Diamonds of the engagement variety. The level of stress that those particular gems were causing her was enough to make her seriously question their best-friend status. Unfortunately, engagement diamonds were something of an occupational hazard for someone who worked on the tenth floor of Drake Diamonds.

Ophelia pasted on a smile and focused on the glittering jewels in the display case before her and the way they dazzled beneath the radiant store lights. *Breathe. Just breathe.*

"This is the one. Princess cut. It's perfect for you…" The man sitting across from Ophelia slipped a 2.3-carat solitaire onto the ring finger of the woman sitting beside him and cooed, "…princess."

"Oh, stop. You're going to make me cry again," his fiancée said, gazing at the diamond on her hand. Sure enough, a lone tear slipped down her cheek.

Ophelia slid a box of rose-scented tissues toward the princess.

In the course of a typical workday, Ophelia went through at least two boxes of tissues. Twice that many on the weekend, along with countless flutes of the finest French champagne and dozens of delicate petits fours crafted to look like the distinctive Drake Diamonds blue gift box crowned with its signature white ribbon. Because shopping for an engagement ring at Drake Diamonds was an experience steeped in luxury, as it had been since 1830.

Her current customers couldn't have cared less about the trappings, particularly the edible ones. Their champagne flutes were nearly full and the petits fours completely untouched. Ophelia was fairly certain the only things they wanted to consume were each other.

It made her heart absolutely ache.

Six months had passed since Ophelia's diagnosis. She'd had half a year to accept her fate, half a year to come to terms with her new reality. She'd never be the girl with the diamond on her finger. She'd never be the bride-to-be. Multiple sclerosis was a serious, chronic illness, one that had altered every aspect of her existence. It had been difficult enough to let this uninvited guest turn her life upside down. She wouldn't let it do the same to someone else. That much she could control.

She couldn't dictate a lot of things about her new life. But her single status was one of them. And she was perfectly fine with it. She had enough on her plate with work, volunteering at the animal shelter and staying as healthy as possible. Not to mention coping with everything she'd left behind.

Still.

Being reminded on a daily basis of what she would never have was getting old.

"Look at that. It's a perfect fit." She smiled at the happy couple, and her throat grew tight. "Shall I wrap it for you?"

"Yes, please." The besotted man's gaze never left his betrothed. "In one of those fancy blue boxes?"

Ophelia nodded. "Of course. It's my pleasure."

She gathered the ring and the petits fours—which the bride declared were in flagrant violation of her wedding diet—and padded across the plush blue carpet of the sales floor toward the gift-wrap room. After dropping off the diamond ring, where it would be boxed, wrapped and tied with a bridal-white bow, she made her way to the kitchen to dispose of the tiny cakes.

She stopped and stared at the counter and the endless rows of pristine silver plates and champagne flutes. Once her current customers left, she'd be passing out another pair of fancy desserts. Another duo of champagne glasses. To yet another couple madly in love.

I can't keep doing this.

This wasn't the plan. The plan was to work in jewelry design, to sketch and create the pieces in those glittering display cases. Catering to the lovesick was definitely *not* the plan.

She knew she should be grateful. She had to start somewhere. As far as the sales team went, working on the tenth floor in Engagements was the most coveted position in the building. She simply needed to bide her time until she could somehow show upper management what she could do, and get transferred to the design department.

One day at a time. I can do this.

She could totally do it. But maybe all those happily engaged couples would be easier to stomach with a little cake.

Why not? No one was looking. Everyone was on the sales floor.

Ophelia had never been much of a rule breaker. She'd never broken *any* rules, come to think of it. Funny how being the good girl all her life hadn't stopped her world from falling apart. Life wasn't fair. She should have known that by now.

She closed her eyes and bit into one of the petits fours. As it melted in her mouth, she contemplated the healing powers of sugar and frosting. Cake might not be the best thing for the body, but at the moment, it was doing wonders for her battered soul.

Finally, she'd uncovered the one good thing about no longer being a professional ballet dancer. Cake. She couldn't remember the last time she'd had a bite of the sweet dessert. Not even on her birthday.

"My God, where have you been all my life?" she whispered.

"Excuse my tardiness," a sultry male voice said in return.

Oh, God.

Ophelia's eyes flew open.

Much to her dismay, the bemused retort hadn't come from the petit four. It had come from her boss. Artem Drake, in the flesh. His tuxedo-clad, playboy flesh.

"Mr. Drake." Her throat grew tight.

What was he even doing here? No one at Drake Diamonds had laid eyes on him since he'd inherited the company from his father. Unless the photos of him on *Page Six* counted.

And good grief. He was a thousand times hotter in person than he was on the internet. How was that even possible?

Ophelia took in his square chin, his dark, knowing gaze and the hint of a dimple in his left cheek, and went a little bit weak in the knees. The fit of his tuxedo was impeccable. As was the shine of his patent leather shoes. But it was the look on his face that nearly did her in. Like the cat who got the cream.

The man was decadence personified.

She swallowed. With great difficulty. "This isn't what it looks like."

She couldn't be seen eating one of the Drake petits fours. They were for customers, not employees. Not to mention the mortification of being caught moaning suggestively at a baked good. She dropped it like a hot potato. It landed between them on the kitchen floor with a splat. A crumb bounced onto the mirror surface of one of Artem's shoes.

What on *earth* was she doing?

He glanced down and lifted a provocative brow. Ophelia's insides went all fluttery. Perfect. She'd already made an idiot of herself and now she was borderline swooning over an eyebrow. Her *boss's* eyebrow.

"Oh, good," he said, his deep voice heavily laced with amusement. "Thanks for clearing that up. For a minute, I thought I'd stumbled upon one of my employees eating the custom-made, fifteen-dollars-per-square-inch snacks that we serve our customers."

Those petits fours were fifteen dollars apiece? That seemed insane, even for Drake Diamonds. They were good, but they weren't that good.

Ophelia glanced at the tiny cake at her feet, and her stomach growled. Okay, maybe they were that good. "Um…"

"So what's the story, then? Are you a runaway fiancée hiding in my kitchen?" His gaze flitted to the floor again. "Are those pretty feet of yours getting cold?"

"A fiancée? Me? No. Definitely not." Once upon a time, yes. But that, like so many other things, had changed. "I mean, no. Just…no."

Stop talking. She was making things so much worse, but she couldn't seem to think straight.

Those pretty feet of yours…

"So you do work for me, then?" He crossed his arms and leaned against the kitchen counter, the perfect picture of elegant nonchalance.

What was he doing, wearing a tux at ten in the morning, anyway? On a weekday, no less. Was this some kind of billionaire walk of shame?

Probably. She thought about the countless photos she'd seen of him with young, beautiful women on his arm. Sometimes two or three at a time. *Walk of shame. Definitely.*

"I do," she said. I do. *I do.* Wedding words. Her neck went instantly, unbearably hot. She cleared her throat. "I work in Engagements."

The corner of his lips twitched. So he thought that was funny, did he? "And your name is?"

"Ophelia." She paused. "Ophelia Rose." At least she had her wits about her enough to identify herself by her actual, real last name and not the stage name she'd been using for the last eight years. Out of everything in her life that had changed, no longer calling herself Ophelia Baronova had been the most difficult to accept. As if that person really, truly no longer existed.

She doesn't.

Ophelia bit her lower lip to keep it from trembling.

Artem Drake crossed his arms. "I suppose that makes me your boss."

This was getting weird.

"Come now, Ophelia Rose. Don't look so sad. I'm not going to fire you for biting into temptation." One corner of Mr. Drake's perfect mouth lifted into a half grin. "Literally."

Clearly, he knew a thing or two about temptation. How was it possible for a man to so fully embody sex?

"Good." She forced a smile. Being fired hadn't actually crossed her mind, although she supposed it should have. It was just kind of difficult to take Artem seriously, since he hadn't darkened the door of Drake Diamonds in the entire time she'd worked there. But if he thought the sadness behind her eyes was because she was afraid of him, so be it. That was fine. Better, actually. She wasn't about to bare her messed-up soul to her employer.

Her employer...

When would she have another opportunity to talk to Artem Drake one-on-one? Never, probably. Because she sure wasn't planning on sneaking off to the kitchen anymore. And who knew when he'd show up again? She had to make the most of this moment. If she didn't, she'd regret it. Just as soon as she went back out on the sales floor among all those engaged couples.

It was now or never.

But maybe she should scrape the cake off the floor first.

Artem Drake was having difficulty wrapping his mind around the fact that the goddess of a woman who'd just dropped to her knees in front of him worked for him. But to be fair, the concept of anyone in this Fifth Avenue institution answering to him was somewhat laughable.

Granted, his last name was on the front of the building. And the gift bags. And those legendary blue boxes. But he'd never had much to do with running the place. That had been his father's job. And now that his father was gone, the responsibility should fall on the shoulders of his older brother, Dalton. Dalton lived and breathed Drake Diamonds. Dalton spent so much time here that he had a foldout sofa in his office. Hell, Artem didn't even *have* an office.

Nor did he have any idea how much those silly little cakes cost. He'd pulled a number out of thin air. And now he'd nearly made the goddess cry. Maybe he was cut out to run the place, after all. His dad had loved making people cry.

Besides, *goddess* wasn't quite the right word. There was something ethereal about her. Delicate. Unspeakably graceful. She had a neck made for diamonds.

Which sounded exactly like something his father would say.

"Stand up," Artem said, far more harshly than he'd intended. But if she didn't get up off her knees, he wouldn't have any hope of maintaining an ounce of professional behavior.

She finished dabbing at the mess with a napkin and stood, her motions so effortlessly fluid that the air around her seemed to dance. "Yes, sir."

He rather liked the *sir* business. But he needed to do

what he'd come here to do and get the hell out of this place. He pushed away from the counter and straightened his cuff link. Singular. One of them had managed to go missing since the symphony gala the night before. Maybe he'd pick up a new pair on his way out. *After* he'd waved the proverbial white flag in his brother's face.

He cleared his throat. "While this has been interesting, to say the least, I have some business to attend to. And I'm sure you have work to do, as well."

Could he sound more ridiculous? *I have some business to attend to. And I'm sure you have work to do, as well.* He'd never spoken like that in his life. Dalton, yes. All the time. That's probably how he spoke to his girlfriends.

"Wait," Ophelia blurted, just as he took a step toward the door. "Please, Mr. Drake. Sir."

He turned. "Yes, Miss Rose?"

"I'd like to schedule a meeting with you. At your convenience, of course." She lifted her chin, and her neck seemed to lengthen.

God, that neck. Artem let his gaze travel down the length of it to the delicate dip between her collarbones. A diamond would look exquisite nestled right there, set off by her perfect porcelain skin. Artem had never seen such a beautiful complexion on a woman. She almost looked as though she'd never set foot outdoors. Like she was crafted of the purest, palest marble. Like she belonged in a museum rather than here. What in God's name was she doing working behind a jewelry counter, anyway?

He lifted his gaze back to her face, and her cheeks went rosebud pink. "A meeting? With me?"

He'd heard worse ideas.

"Yes. A business meeting," she said crisply. "I have some design ideas I'd like to present. I know I work in sales at the moment, but I'm actually a trained gemologist."

Artem wasn't sure why he found this news so surprising, but he did. Few people surprised him. He wished more of them did. Ophelia Rose was becoming more intriguing by the minute.

She was also his *employee*, at least for the next ten minutes or so. He shouldn't be thinking about her neck. Or the soft swell of her breasts beneath the bodice of the vintage sea-foam dress she wore. Or what her delicate bottom would feel like in the palms of his hands. He shouldn't be thinking about any of the images that were currently running through his mind.

"A gemologist? Really?" he said, somehow keeping his gaze fixed on her face. God, he deserved a medal for such restraint.

She nodded. "I've have a degree from the New York School of Design. I graduated with honors."

"Then congratulations are in order. Perhaps even a celebration." He just couldn't help himself. "With cake."

Her blush deepened a shade closer to crimson. "Honestly, I'd rather have that meeting. Just half an hour of your time to show you my designs. That's all I need."

She was determined. He'd give her that. Determined and oh-so-earnest.

And rather bold, now that he thought about it. He

had, after all, just walked in on her shoving cake in her mouth. Cake meant for lovebirds prepared to drop thousands of dollars for a Drake diamond. She had a ballsy streak. Sexy, he mused.

Artem wondered how much he was paying her. He hadn't a clue. "I'm sorry, but I can't."

She took a step closer to him, and he caught a whiff of something warm and sweet. Vanilla maybe. She smelled like a dessert, which Artem supposed made perfect sense. "Can't or won't?"

He shrugged. "I guess you could say both."

She opened her lovely mouth to protest, and Artem held up a hand to stop her. "Miss Rose, before you waste any more of your precious time, there's something you should know. I'm resigning."

She went quiet for a beat. A beat during which Artem wondered what had prompted him to tell this total stranger his plans before he'd even discussed them with his own flesh and blood. He blamed it on his hangover. Or possibly the sad, haunted look in Ophelia's blue eyes. Eyes the color of Kashmir sapphires.

It didn't seem right to let her think he could help her when he'd never even see her again.

"Resigning?" She frowned. "But you can't resign. This is Drake Diamonds, and you're a Drake."

Not the right Drake. "I'm quitting my family business, not my family." Although the thought wasn't without its merits, considering he'd never truly been one of them. Not the way Dalton and their sister, Diana, had.

"But your father left you in charge." Her voice had gone as soft as feathers. *Feathers.* A bird. That's what she reminded him of—a swan. A stunning, sylphlike swan. "That matters."

He shook his head. She had no clue what she was talking about, and he wasn't about to elaborate. He'd already said too much. And frankly, it was none of her business. "I assure you, this is for the best. I might add that it's also confidential."

"Oh, I won't tell anyone."

"I know you won't." He pointed at the petit four that she'd scraped up off the floor, still resting in her palm. "You'll keep my secret, and I'll keep yours. Does that sound fair, princess?"

His news wouldn't be a secret for long, anyway. Dalton's office was right down the hall. If Artem hadn't heard Ophelia's sensual ode to cake and made this spontaneous detour, the deed would already be done.

He'd enjoyed toying with her, but now their encounter had taken a rather vexing turn. As much as he liked the thought of half an hour behind closed doors with those lithe limbs and willowy grace, the meeting she so desperately wanted simply wasn't going to happen. Not with him, anyway.

Maybe Dalton would meet with her. Maybe Artem would suggest it. *I quit. Oh, and by the way, one of the sales associates wants to design our next collection...*

Maybe not.

"Okay, then. It was nice meeting you, Mr. Drake." She offered him her free hand, and he took it. "I'm so very sorry for your loss."

That last part came out as little more than a whisper, just breathy enough for Artem to know that Ophelia

Rose with the sad sapphire eyes knew a little something about loss herself.

"Thank you." Her hand felt small in his. Small and impossibly soft.

Then she withdrew her hand and squared her shoulders, and the fleeting glimpse of vulnerability he'd witnessed was replaced with the cool confidence of a woman who'd practically thrown cake at him and then asked for a meeting to discuss a promotion. There was that ballsy streak again. "One last thing, Mr. Drake."

He suppressed a grin. "Yes?"

"Don't call me princess."

Chapter Two

"Really, Artem?" Dalton aimed a scandalized glance at Artem's unbuttoned collar and loosened bow tie. "That penthouse where you live is less than three blocks away. You couldn't be bothered to go home and change before coming to work?"

Artem shrugged and sank into one of the ebony wing chairs opposite Dalton's desk. "Don't push it. I'm here, aren't I?"

Present and accounted for. Physically, at least. His thoughts, along with his libido, still lingered back in the kitchen with the intriguing Miss Rose.

"At long last. It's been two months since Dad died. To what do we owe the honor of your presence?" Dalton twirled his pen, a Montblanc. Just like the one their father had always used. It could have been the same one, for all Artem knew. That would have been an appropriate bequest.

Far more appropriate than leaving Artem in charge of this place when he'd done nothing more than pass out checks and attend charity galas since he'd been on the payroll.

The only Drake who spent less time in the building than he did was their sister, Diana. She was busy training for the Olympic equestrian team with her horse, which was appropriately named Diamond.

Artem narrowed his gaze at his brother. "I've been busy."

"Busy," Dalton said flatly. "Right. I think I remember reading something about that in *Page Six*."

"And here I thought you only read the financial pages. Don't tell me you've lowered yourself to reading *Page Six*, brother."

"I have to, don't I? How else would I keep apprised of your whereabouts?" The smile on Dalton's face grew tight.

A dull ache throbbed to life in Artem's temples, and he remembered why he'd put off this meeting for as long as he had. It wasn't as if he and Dalton had ever been close, but at least they'd managed to be cordial to one another while their father was alive. Now it appeared the gloves were off.

The thing was, he sympathized with Dalton. Surely his older brother had expected to be next in line to run the company. Hell, everyone had expected that to be the case.

He didn't feel too sorry for Dalton, though. He was

about to get exactly what he wanted. Besides, Artem would *not* let Dalton ruin his mood. He'd had a pleasant enough evening at the symphony gala, which had led to a rather sexually satisfying morning.

Oddly enough, though, it had been the unexpected encounter with Ophelia Rose that had put the spring in his step.

He found her interesting. And quite lovely. She would have made it almost tolerable to come to work every day, if he had any intention of doing such a thing. Which he didn't.

"Has it occurred to you that having the Drake name in the papers is good PR?" Artem said blithely.

"PR. Is that what they're calling it nowadays?" Dalton rolled his eyes.

It took every ounce of Artem's self-restraint not to point out how badly his brother needed to get laid. "I didn't come here to discuss my social life, Dalton. As difficult as you might find it to believe, I'm ready to discuss business."

Dalton nodded. Slowly. "I'm glad to hear that, brother. Very glad."

He'd be even happier once Artem made his announcement. So would Artem. He had no desire to engage in this sort of exchange on a daily basis. He was a grown man. He didn't need his brother's input on his lifestyle. And he sure as hell didn't want to sit behind a desk all day at a place where he'd never been welcomed when his father had been alive.

According to the attorneys, his father had changed the provisions of his will less than a week before he'd died. One might suppose senility to be behind the change, if not for the fact that his dad had been too stubborn to lose his mind. Shrewd. Cold. And sharp as a tack until the day he passed.

"Listen," Artem said. "I don't know why Dad left me in charge. It's as much of a mystery to me as it is to you."

"Don't." Dalton shook his head. "It doesn't matter. What's done is done. You're here. That's a start. I've had Dad's office cleaned out. It's yours now."

Artem went still. "What?"

Dalton shrugged one shoulder. "Where else are you going to work?"

Artem didn't have an answer for that.

Dalton continued, "Listen, it's going to take a few days to get you up to speed. We have one pressing matter, though, that just can't wait. If you hadn't rolled in here by the end of the week, I was going to beat down your door at the Plaza and insist you talk to me."

Whatever the pressing matter was, Artem had a feeling that he didn't want to hear about it. He didn't need to. It wasn't his problem. This idea that he would actually run the company was a joke.

"Before the heart attack…" Dalton's voice lost a bit of its edge.

The change in his composure was barely perceptible, but Artem noticed. He'd actually expected his brother to be more of a mess. Dalton, after all, had been the jewel in their father's crown. He'd been a son, whereas Artem had been a stranger to the Drakes for the first five years of his life.

"...Dad invested in a new mine in Australia. I didn't even know about it until last week." Dalton raised his brows, as if Artem had something to say.

Artem let out a laugh. "Surely you're not suggesting that he told *me* about it."

His brother sighed. "I suppose not, although I wish he had. I wish someone had stopped him. It doesn't matter, anyway. What's done is done. The mine was a bust. It's worthless, and now it's put the business in a rather precarious position."

"Precarious? Exactly how much did he spend on this mine?"

Dalton took too long to answer. He exhaled a slow, measured breath and finally said, "Three billion."

"Three billion dollars." Artem blinked. That was a lot of money. An astronomical amount, even to a man who lived on the eighteenth floor of the Plaza and flew his own Boeing business jet, which, ironically enough, Artem used for pleasure far more than he did for business. "The company has billions in assets, though. If not trillions."

"Yes, but not all those assets are liquid. With the loss from the mine, we're sitting at a twenty-five million dollar deficit. We need to figure something out."

We. Since when did any of the Drakes consider Artem part of a *we*?

He should just get up and walk right out of Dalton's office. He didn't owe the Drakes a thing.

Somehow, though, his backside remained rooted to the spot. "What about the diamond?"

"*The* diamond? The *Drake* diamond?" Dalton shook

his head. "I'm going to pretend I didn't hear that. I know you're not one for sentimentality, brother, but even you wouldn't suggest that we sell the Drake diamond."

Actually, he would. "It's a rock, Dalton. A pretty rock, but a rock nonetheless."

Dalton shook his head so hard that Artem thought it might snap clear off his neck. "It's a piece of history. Our family name was built on that rock."

Our family name. Right.

Artem cleared his throat. "How much is it worth?"

"It doesn't matter, because we're not selling it."

"How much, Dalton? As your superior, I demand that you tell me." It was a low blow. Artem would have liked to think that a small part of him didn't get a perverse sort of pleasure from throwing his position in Dalton's face, but it did. So be it.

"Fifty million dollars," Dalton said. "But I repeat, it's not for sale, and it never will be."

Never.

If Artem had learned one thing since becoming acquainted with his father—since being "welcomed" into the Drake fold—it was that *never* was an awfully strong word. "That's not your call, though, is it, brother?"

Ophelia hadn't planned on stopping by the animal shelter on the way home from work. She had, after all, already volunteered three times this week. Possibly four. She'd lost count.

She couldn't go home yet, though. Not after the day she'd had. Dealing with all the happily engaged couples was bad enough, but she was growing accustomed to it. She didn't have much of a choice, did she? But the unexpected encounter with Artem Drake had somehow thrown her completely off-kilter.

It wasn't only the embarrassment of getting caught inhaling one of the fifteen dollar petits fours that had gotten her so rattled. It was him. Artem.

Mr. Drake. Not Artem. He's your boss, not your friend. Or anything else.

He wasn't even her boss anymore, she supposed. Which was for the best. Obviously. She hadn't exactly made a glowing first impression. Now she could start over with whoever took his place. So really, there was no logical reason for the acute tug of disappointment she'd felt when he'd told her about his plans to resign. None whatsoever.

There was also no logical reason that she'd kept looking around all afternoon for a glimpse of him as he exited the building. Nor for the way she'd gone all fluttery when she'd caught a flash of tuxedoed pant leg beyond the closing elevator doors after her shift had ended. It hadn't been Artem, anyway. Just another, less dashing man dressed to the nines.

What was her problem, anyway? She was acting as though she'd never met a handsome man before. Artem Drake wasn't merely handsome, though. He was charming.

Too charming. Dangerously so.

Ophelia had felt uncharacteristically vulnerable in the presence of all that charm. Raw. Empty. And acutely aware of all that she'd lost, all that she'd never have.

She couldn't go home to the apartment she'd inherited from her grandmother. She couldn't spend another evening sifting through her grandmother's things—the grainy black-and-white photographs, her tattered pointe shoes. Her grandmother had been the only family that Ophelia had known since the tender age of two, when a car accident claimed the lives of her parents. Natalia Baronova had been more than a grandparent. She'd been Ophelia's world. Her mother figure, her best friend and her ballet teacher.

She'd died a week before Ophelia's diagnosis. As much as Ophelia had needed someone to lean on in those first dark days, she'd been grateful that the great Natalia Baronova, star ballerina of Ballet Russe de Monte Carlo in the 1940s and '50s, died without the knowledge that her beloved granddaughter would never dance again.

"Ophelia?" Beth, the shelter manager, shook her head and planted her hands on her hips as Ophelia slipped off her coat and hung it on one of the pegs by the door. "Again? I didn't see your name on the volunteer schedule for this evening."

"It's not. But I thought you could use an extra pair of hands." Ophelia flipped through the notebook that contained the animals' daily feeding schedule.

"You know better than anybody we always need help around here, but surely you have somewhere else to be on a Friday night."

Nowhere, actually. "You know how much I enjoy spending time with the animals." Plus, the shelter was now caring for a litter of eight three-week-old kittens that had to be bottle-fed every three hours. The skimpy volunteer staff could barely keep up, especially now that the city was blanketed with snow. People liked to stay home when it snowed. And that meant at any given moment, one of the kittens was hungry.

Beth nodded. "I know, love. Just be careful. I'd hate for you to ruin that pretty dress you're wearing."

The dress had belonged to Ophelia's grandmother. In addition to mountains of dance memorabilia, she'd left behind a gorgeous collection of vintage clothing. Like the apartment, it had been a godsend. When she'd been dancing, Ophelia had lived in a leotard and tights. Most days, she'd even worn her dance clothes to school, since she'd typically had to go straight from rehearsal to class at the New York School of Design. She couldn't very well show up to work at Drake Diamonds dressed in a wraparound sweater, pink tights and leg warmers.

Neither could she simply go out and buy a whole new work wardrobe. Between her student loan bills and the exorbitant cost of the biweekly injections to manage her MS, she barely made ends meet. Plus there were the medical bills from that first, awful attack, before she'd even known why the vision out of her left eye sometimes went blurry or why her fingers occasionally felt numb. Sometimes she left rehearsal with such crippling fatigue she felt as if she were walking through Jell-O. She'd blamed it on the stress of dealing with her grandmother's recent illness. She'd blamed it on the rigorous physical demands of her solo role in the company production of *Giselle*. Mostly, though, she'd simply ignored her symptoms because she couldn't quite face the prospect that something was seriously wrong.

Then one night she'd fallen out of a pirouette. Onstage, midperformance. The fact that she'd been unable to peel herself off the floor had only made matters worse.

And now she'd never perform again.

Sometimes, in her most unguarded moments, Ophelia found herself pointing her toes and moving her foot in the familiar, sweeping motion of a rond de jambe. Then she'd close her eyes and remember the sickening thud as she'd come down on the wooden stage floor. She'd remember the pitying expressions on the faces of her fellow dancers and the way the crimson stage curtains had drawn closed on the spectacle with a solemn hush. Her career, her life, everything she'd worked for, had ended with that whisper of red velvet.

She had every reason to be grateful, though. She had a nice apartment in Manhattan. She had clothes on her back and a job. She'd even had the forethought to enroll in school while she'd been dancing, because she'd known that the day would come when she'd be unable to dance for a living. She just hadn't realized that day would come so soon. She'd thought she'd had time. So much time. Time to dance, time to love, time to dream.

She'd never planned on spending her Friday nights feeding kittens at an animal shelter, but it wasn't such a bad place to be. She actually enjoyed it quite a bit.

"I'll be careful, Beth. I promise." Ophelia draped a towel over the front of her dress and reached into the cabinet above a row of cat enclosures for a bottle and a fresh can of kitten formula.

As she cracked the can open and positioned it over the tiny bottle, her gaze flitted to the cage in the corner. Her hand paused midpour when she realized the wire pen was empty.

"Where's the little white kitten?" she asked, fighting against the rapidly forming lump in her throat.

"She hasn't been adopted, if that's what you're wondering." Beth cast her a knowing glance. "She's getting her picture taken for some charity thing."

"Oh." Ophelia hated herself for the swell of relief that washed over her. The shelter's mission was to find homes for all their animals, after all. Everyone deserved a home. And love. And affection.

The lump in her throat grew tenfold. "That's too bad."

"Is it?" Beth lifted a sardonic brow.

Ophelia busied herself with securing the top on the bottle and lifting one of the squirming kittens out of the pen lined with a heating pad that served as a makeshift incubator. "Of course it is."

She steadfastly refused to meet Beth's gaze, lest she give away her true feelings on the matter, inappropriate as they were.

But there was no fooling Beth. "For the life of me, I don't know why you won't just adopt her. Don't get me wrong—I appreciate your help around here. But I have a sneaky suspicion that the reason you came by tonight has more to do with visiting your fluffy friend than with feeding our hungry little monsters. You're besotted with that cat."

"And you're exaggerating." The orange kitten in Ophelia's hand mewed at a volume that belied its tiny size. Ophelia nestled the poor thing against her chest, and it began suckling on the bottle at once. "Besides, I told you. I can't have a pet. My apartment doesn't allow them."

It was a shameless lie. But how else was she supposed to explain her reluctance to adopt an animal she so clearly adored?

The truth was that she'd love to adopt the white Persian mix. She'd love coming home to the sound of its dainty feet pattering across the floor of her empty apartment. If the cat could come live with her, Ophelia would let it sleep at the foot of her bed, and feed it gourmet food from a can. If…

But she couldn't do it. She was in no condition to let anyone depend on her for their survival. Not even an animal. She was a ticking time bomb with an unknown deadline for detonation.

Ophelia braced herself for an ardent sales pitch. Beth obviously wasn't buying the excuses she'd manufactured. Fortunately, before Beth went into full-on lecture mode, they were interrupted by none other than the adorable white cat they'd been discussing. The snow-white feline entered the room in the arms of a statuesque woman dressed in a glittering, sequined floor-length dress.

Ophelia was so momentarily confused to see a woman wearing an evening gown at the animal shelter that at first she didn't seem to notice that the sequin-clad Barbie was also on the arm of a companion. And that companion was none other than Artem Drake.

Him.

Again? Seriously?

She could hardly believe her eyes. What on earth was he doing here?

For some ridiculous reason, Ophelia's first instinct was to hide. She didn't want to see him again. Especially here. Now. When he had a glamorous supermodel draped all over him and Ophelia was sitting in a plastic chair, chest covered in stained terry cloth while she bottle-fed a yelping orange tabby. And, oh, God, he was dressed in another perfect tuxedo. Had the man come strutting out of the womb in black tie?

She wondered what he'd look like in something more casual, a pair of soft faded jeans, maybe. Shirtless. Heck, as long as she was fantasizing, bottomless. Then she wondered why, exactly, she was wondering about such things.

"My, my, who do we have here?" Artem tilted his head.

Ophelia had been so busy dreaming of what he had going on beneath all that sleek Armani wool that she'd neglected to make herself invisible. Super.

"Um…" She struggled for something to say as his gaze dropped to her chest. Her nipples went tingly under his inspection, until she realized he was looking at the kitten, not her. Of course.

Why, oh, why hadn't she gone straight home after work?

He lifted his gaze so that he was once again looking her directly in the eyes. "Miss Rose, we meet again."

"You two know each other?" Beth asked, head swiveling back and forth between Ophelia and Artem.

Ophelia shook her head and centered all her concentration on not being attracted to him, while the orange kitten squirmed against her chest. "No, not really," she said.

"Why, yes. Yes, we do," Artem said at that exact instant.

The grin on his face was nothing short of suggestive. Or maybe that was just his default expression. Resting playboy face.

Heat pooled in her center, much to her mortification and surprise. She couldn't remember the last time she'd experienced anything remotely resembling desire. Unless this morning in the kitchen of Drake Diamonds counted. Which, if she was being honest, it most definitely did.

Beth frowned. Artem's date lifted an agitated brow.

Ophelia clarified the matter before Ms. Supermodel got the wrong idea and thought she was one of his sexual conquests, which no doubt were plentiful. "We've met. But we don't actually know one another." *Not at all*.

Artem directed his attention toward Beth and, by way of explanation, said, "Miss Rose works for me."

Worked, past tense, since he'd resigned from his family's business. Who did that, anyway?

"Drake Diamonds." Beth nodded. "Of course. Ophelia's told me all about it. I'm sure I don't need to tell you what a treasure you've found in her. She's one of our best volunteers. Such a hard worker."

"A hard worker," Artem echoed, with only a subtle hint of sarcasm in his smoky voice. Then, presumably to ensure that Ophelia knew he hadn't forgotten about her indiscretion in the kitchen, he flashed a wink in her direction. "Quite."

The wink floated through her in a riot of awareness. *He's not flirting with you. He's goading you.* There was a difference. Right?

Beth continued gushing, oblivious to Artem's sarcastic undertones. "I don't know what we'd do without her. She's such a cat lover, here almost every night of the week. Weekends, too."

So now she sounded like a lonely cat lady. Perfect. "Beth, I'm sure Mr. Drake isn't here to hear about my volunteer work." Again, why exactly *was* he here?

"Oh, sorry. Of course he isn't. Mr. Drake, thank you so much for the generous donation on behalf of your family, as well as for being photographed with one of our charges. Having your picture in the newspaper with one of the animals will definitely bring attention to our cause." Beth beamed at Artem.

So he'd given a donation to the shelter. A *generous* donation…and right when Ophelia had been wishing for something that would make him seem less appealing. Thank goodness she'd no longer be running into him at work. He was too…too *much*.

"My pleasure," Artem said smoothly, and ran a manly hand over the white kitty still nestled in his date's arms.

Ophelia's kitty.

Not hers, technically. Not hers at all. But that didn't stop the sting of possessiveness she felt as she watched the cat being cuddled by someone else. And not just *any*one else. Someone who was clearly on a date with Artem Drake.

It shouldn't have mattered, but it did. Very much.

"That's actually Ophelia's favorite cat you have there." Beth smiled.

"She's awfully sweet," Artem's date cooed.

Ophelia felt sick all of a sudden. What if Artem's companion adopted it? *Her* cat? She took a deep breath and fought against the image that sprang to her mind of the woman and Artem in the back of a stretch limo with the white kitten nestled between them. Did everything in life have to be so unfair?

"Is it now?" Artem slid his gaze toward Ophelia. "Your favorite?"

She nodded. There was no sense denying it, especially since she had that odd transparent feeling again. Like he could see straight into her heart.

"I keep insisting Ophelia should adopt her." An awkward smile creased Beth's face. Artem's date still had a firm grip on the kitten. Clearly, Beth was hinting that Ophelia needed to speak now or forever hold her peace.

She needed to get out of here before she did something monumentally stupid like snatch the kitten out of the woman's arms.

"I should be going." Ophelia stood and returned the tiny orange kitten to the incubator. "It was lovely seeing you again, Mr. Drake. Beth."

She nodded at Artem's date, whose name she still didn't know, and kept her gaze glued to the floor so she wouldn't have to see the kitten purring away in the woman's arms.

Artem ignored Ophelia's farewell altogether and looked right past her, toward Beth. "How much is the kitten? I'd like to purchase it for Miss Rose."

What?

"That would be delightful, Mr. Drake. The adoption fee is fifty dollars, but of course we'll waive it for one of our generous donors." Beth beamed.

Artem plucked the kitten out of his date's arms. Ophelia had to give the woman credit; she didn't hesitate to hand over the cat, but kept a firm grip on Artem's bicep. Ophelia felt like reassuring her. *He's all yours.* She wasn't going home with her former boss.

Nor was she going home with the kitten. "Mr. Drake, I need to have a word with you. *Alone.*"

Beth weaved her arm around Artem's date's elbow and peeled her away. "Come with me, dear. I'll give you a tour of our facility."

Beth gave Ophelia a parting wink as she ushered the woman out the door toward the large kennels. Surely she wasn't trying to play matchmaker. That would have been absurd. Then again, everything about this situation was absurd.

Ophelia crossed her arms and glared at Artem. "What do you think you're doing?"

He shrugged. "Buying you a cat. Consider it an early Christmas bonus. You're welcome, by the way."

"No." She shook her head.

Was he insane? And did he have to stand there, looking so unbelievably hot in that tuxedo, while he stroked the kitten like he was Mr. December in a billionaires-with-baby-animals wall calendar?

"No?" His blue eyes went steely. Clearly, he'd never heard such a sentiment come out of a woman's mouth before.

"No. Thank you. It's a generous gesture, but…" She glanced at the kitten. Big mistake. Her delicate little nose quivered. She looked impossibly helpless and tiny snuggled against Artem's impressive chest. How was Ophelia supposed to say no to that face? How was she supposed to say no to *him*? She cleared her throat. "…but no."

He looked distinctly displeased.

Let him be angry. Ophelia would never even see him again. *That's what you thought this morning, too.* She lifted her chin. "I really should be going. And you should get back to your date."

"My date?" He smiled one of those suggestive smiles again, and Ophelia's insides went instantly molten. Damn him. "Is that what this is about? You're not jealous, are you, Miss Rose?"

Yes. To her complete and utter mortification, she was. She'd been jealous since he'd waltzed through the door with another woman on his arm. What had gotten into her?

She rolled her eyes. "Hardly."

"I'm not quite sure I believe you."

Ophelia sighed. "Why are you doing this?"

"What exactly is it that I'm doing?"

"Being nice." She swallowed. She felt like crying all of a sudden, and she couldn't. If she did, she might not ever stop. "Trying to buy me a cat."

He shrugged. "The cat needs a home, and you like her. Why shouldn't you have her?"

There were so many reasons that even if Ophelia wanted to list them all, she wouldn't have known where to start. "I told you. I can't."

Artem angled his head. "Can't or won't?"

He'd thrown back at her her own words from their encounter at Drake Diamonds, which made Ophelia bite back a smile. The man was too charming for his own good. "Mr. Drake, as much as I'd love to, I cannot adopt that cat."

He took a step closer to her, so close that Ophelia suddenly had trouble taking a breath, much less forming a valid argument for not taking the kitten she so desperately wanted. Then he reached for her hand, took it in his and placed it on the supple curve of the cat's spine.

The kitty mewed in recognition, and Artem moved their linked hands through her silky soft fur in long, measured strokes. Ophelia had to bite her lip to keep from crying. Why was he doing this? Why did he care?

"She likes you," he said. And as if he could read her mind, he added, "Something tells me you two need each other. You come here nearly every day. You want this kitten. You need her, but you won't let yourself have her. Why not?"

Because what would happen if Ophelia had another attack?

No, not *if.* When. Her illness was officially called relapsing-remitting MS, characterized by episodic, clearly defined attacks, each one more neurologically devastating than the last. Ophelia never knew when the next one would come. A year from now? A month? A day? What would she do with the cat then, when she was too sick to care for it?

The kitten purred, and the sensation vibrated warmth through Ophelia's hand, still covered with Artem's. God, this was tortuous. She jerked her hand away. "Mr. Drake, I—"

Before she could say another word of protest, he cut her off. "I'll adopt the cat. You take care of her for me, and I'll give you your meeting," he said.

His voice had lost any hint of empathy. He sounded angry again, as if she'd forced him into making such a suggestion.

"My meeting?" She swallowed. It would have been an offer too good to be true, if it were possible. Thank God it wasn't. "And how are you going to arrange such a meeting, now that you no longer work at Drake Diamonds?"

"I'm a Drake, remember?" As if she could forget. "And there's been a change of plans. I do, in fact, still work there."

"Oh," she said, stunned. "I don't understand."

He offered no explanation, just handed her the kitten.

She held out her arms without thinking. What was happening? She hadn't agreed to his ludicrous proposition, had she? "Wait. If you didn't resign, what does that mean, exactly?"

"It means I'm still your boss." He turned on his heel and brushed past her toward the kennels. He was leaving, just like that? He paused with his hand on the door.

"Take that cat home with you, Miss Rose. I trust I'll see you tomorrow in my office?"

She couldn't let him manipulate her like this. At best, it was unprofessional. At worst…well, she didn't even want to contemplate the worst-case scenario. She could not take the kitten, no matter how much she wanted to. Even temporarily. She couldn't be Artem Drake's cat sitter. She absolutely couldn't.

He stood there staring at her with his penetrating gaze, as if they were engaged in some sort of sexy staring contest.

One that Ophelia had no chance of winning.

"Fine."

Chapter Three

Artem arrived at Drake Diamonds the next morning before the store even opened, which had to be some kind of personal record. He couldn't remember the last time he'd been there during off-hours. If he ever had.

Dalton, on the other hand, had been making a regular practice of it for most of his life. In recent years, for work. Naturally. But back when they'd been teenagers, when Dalton had been more human and less workaholic robot, Artem's brother had gotten caught with a girlfriend in the middle of the night, in the middle of the first-floor showroom, in flagrante delicto.

It remained Artem's favorite story about his brother, even if it marked the moment when he'd discovered that Dalton had been the only Drake heir who'd been entrusted with a key to the family business while still in prep school.

He wished it hadn't mattered. But it had. In truth, it still did, even though those feelings had nothing to do with the business itself.

He'd never had any interest in hanging around the shop on Fifth Avenue. To the other Drakes, it was a shrine. To the world, it was a historic institution. Drake Diamonds had been part of the Manhattan landscape since its crowded, busy streets teemed with horse-drawn carriages. To young Artem, it had always simply been his father's workplace.

And now it was his. Same building, same office, same godforsaken desk.

What was he doing? Dalton didn't need him. Not really. Wasn't his brother in a better position to save the company? Dalton was the one familiar with the ins and outs of the business. His bedroom in Lenox Hill was probably wallpapered with balance sheets.

All Dalton's life, he'd worn his position as a Drake like a mantle, whereas to Artem it had begun to feel like a straitjacket. Now that his father was gone, there was no reason why he couldn't simply shrug it off and move on with his life. In addition to his recent promotion, he'd been left a sizable inheritance. Sizable enough that he could walk away from his PR position with the company and never again have his photo taken at another dull social event if he so chose. There was no reason in the world he should willingly get out of bed at an ungodly predawn hour so he could walk to the store and sit behind his father's desk.

Yet here he was, climbing out of the back of his black town car on the corner of Fifth Avenue and Fifty-seventh Street.

He told himself that his decision to stay on as CEO, at least temporarily, had nothing to do with Ophelia. Because that would be preposterous.

Yes, she was lovely. Beyond lovely, with her fathomless eyes, hair like spun gold and her willowy, fluid grace. And yes, he'd lost more sleep than he cared to admit thinking about what it would feel like to have those impossibly graceful legs wrapped around his waist as he buried himself inside her.

Her simplest gestures utterly beguiled him. Innocent movements, like the turn of her wrist, made him want to do wholly inappropriate things. He wanted to wrap his fingers around her wrists like a diamond cuff bracelet, pin her arms over her head and trace the exquisite length of her neck with his tongue. He wanted that more than he'd wanted anything in a long, long time.

Artem was no stranger to passion. He'd experienced desire before, but not like this. Nothing like this.

He found it frustrating. And quite baffling, particularly when he found himself doing things like sitting behind a desk, adopting animals and dismissing a perfectly good date, choosing instead to go home and get in bed before midnight. Alone.

His temples throbbed as he stepped out of the car and caught a glimpse of himself in the reflection of the storefront window. He'd dressed the part of CEO in a charcoal Tom Ford suit, paired with a smooth silk tie in that dreadful Drake Diamond blue. *Who are you?*

"Good morning, Mr. Drake." The store's doorman greeted him with a tip of his top hat and a polite smile.

Standing on the sidewalk in the swirling snow, clad in a Dickensian overcoat and Drake-blue scarf, the doorman almost looked like a throwback to the Victorian era. Probably because the uniforms had changed very little since the store first opened its doors. Tradition ruled at Drake Diamonds, even down to how the doormen dressed.

"Good morning." Artem nodded and strode through the door.

He made his way toward the elevator on the opposite side of the darkened showroom, his footsteps echoing on the gleaming tile floor. Then his gaze snagged on the glass showcase illuminated by a radiant spotlight to his right—home to the revered Drake Diamond.

He paused. Against its black velvet backdrop, the diamond almost appeared to be floating. The most brilliant star, shining in the darkest of nights.

He walked slowly up to the showcase, inspecting the glittering yellow stone mounted at the center of a garland necklace of white diamonds. Upon its discovery in a South African mine in the late 1800s, it had been the third largest yellow diamond in the world. Artem's great-great-great-great-great-grandfather bought it on credit before it had even been properly cut. Then he'd had it shaped and set in Paris—in a tiara of all things—before bringing it to New York and putting it on display in his new Fifth Avenue jewelry store. People had come from all over the country to see the breathtaking diamond. That single stone had put old man Drake's little jewelry business on the map.

Would it really be so bad to let it go? Drake Diamonds was world famous now. Sure, tourists still flocked to the store and pressed their faces to the glass to get a glimpse of the legendary diamond. But would things really change if it were no longer here?

He glanced at the plaque beneath the display case. It gave the history of the diamond, its various settings and the handful of times it had actually been worn. The last sentence of the stone's biography proclaimed it the shining star in the Drake family crown.

Artem swallowed, then looked back up at the diamond.

Ophelia's face materialized before him. Waves of gilded hair, sparkling sapphire eyes and that lithe, swan-like neck…with the diamond positioned right at the place where her pulse throbbed with life.

He blinked, convinced he was seeing things. A mirage. A trick of the mind, like a cool pool of glistening water before a man who hasn't had a drink in years.

It was no mirage. It was her.

Standing right behind him, only inches away, with her exquisite face reflected back at him in the pristine pane of glass. And damned if that diamond didn't look as though it had been made just for her. Placed deep in the earth billions of years ago, waiting for someone to find it and slip it around her enchanting neck.

"Beautiful, isn't it?" Her blue eyes glittered beneath the radiant showroom lights, lighting designed to make gemstones shimmer and shine. Somehow she sparkled brighter than all of them.

Beautiful, indeed.

"Quite," Artem said.

She moved to stand beside him, and her reflection slipped languidly away from the necklace. "Sometimes I like to come here and look at it, especially at times like this, when the store is quiet. Before all the crowds descend. I think about what it must have been like to wear something like this, back in the days when it was actually worn. It seems almost a shame that it's become something of a museum piece, don't you think?"

"I do, actually." At the moment, it seemed criminal the diamond wasn't draped around her porcelain neck. He could see her wearing it. The necklace and nothing else. He could imagine that priceless jewel glittering between her beautiful breasts, an image as real as the snow falling outside.

He shoved his hands in his pockets before he used them to press her against the glass and take her right there against the display case until the gemstone inside fell off its pedestal and shattered into diamond dust. The very idea of it made him go instantly hard.

And that's when Artem knew.

Ophelia did, in fact, have something to do with his decision to stay on as head of Drake Diamonds. She may have had *every*thing to do with it.

He ground his teeth and glared at her. He didn't enjoy feeling out of control. About anything, but most especially about his libido. Artem was a better man than his father had been. He had to believe that.

Ophelia blinked up at him with those melancholy eyes that made his chest ache, seemingly oblivious to the self-control it required for Artem to have a simple conversation with her. "Is it true that it's only been worn by three women? Or is that just an urban myth?"

"Yes, it's true." He nodded. A Hollywood star, a ballerina back in the forties and Diana Kincaid Drake. Only three. That fact was so much a part of Drake mythology that Artem wouldn't have been able to forget it even if he'd tried.

"I see," she whispered, her eyes fixed dreamily on the diamond. She almost looked as though she were trying to see inside it, to the heart of the stone. Its history.

Then she blinked, turned her back on the necklace and focused fully on Artem, her trance broken. "About our meeting…"

"Ah, yes. Our meeting." Out of the corner of his eye, he spotted Dalton making his entrance through the store's revolving door. Artem lowered his voice, although he wasn't quite sure why. He had nothing to hide. "Shall I assume my kitten is tucked snug inside your home, Miss Rose?"

"Yes." Her cheeks went pink, and her bow lips curved into a reluctant smile.

So he'd been right. She'd wanted that kitten all along. Needed it, even though she'd acted as though he'd been forcing it on her.

He'd done the right thing. For once in his life.

"So." She cleared her throat. "Shall I make an appointment with your assistant so I can show you my designs?"

"What did you name her?" he asked.

Ophelia blinked. "I'm sorry?"

"The kitten." Somewhere in the periphery, Artem saw the curious expression on his brother's face and ignored it altogether. "Have you given her a name yet?"

"Oh." Her flush deepened a shade, as pink as primroses. "I named her Jewel."

For some reason, this information took the edge off Artem's frustration. Which made no sense whatsoever. "Then I suppose you and I have business to discuss, Miss Rose. I'll have my assistant get you the details." He gave her a parting nod and headed to the elevator, where Dalton stood waiting. Watching.

Somehow it felt as if their father was watching, too.

Ophelia stood poised on the black-and-white marble terrace while snowflakes whipped in the frosty wind. Despite the chill in the air, she hesitated.

"Welcome to the Plaza, miss." A doorman dressed in a regal uniform, complete with gold epaulettes on his shoulders, bowed slightly and pulled the door open for her with gloved hands.

A hotel. Artem Drake had summoned her to a *hotel*. Granted, the Plaza was the most exclusive hotel in Manhattan, if not the world, but still.

A hotel.

Did he think she was going to sleep with him? Surely not. She was worried over nothing. He was probably waiting for her in the tearoom or something. Although, as refined as he might be, Ophelia couldn't quite picture him taking afternoon tea.

"Thank you." She nodded politely at the doorman. After all, this wholly awkward scenario wasn't his fault. She wondered if she was supposed to tip him for opening the door for her. She had no clue.

Crossing the threshold into the grand lobby of the Plaza was like entering another world. Another decade. She felt like she'd walked into an F. Scott Fitzgerald novel. The decor was opulent, gilded with an art deco flavor reminiscent of Jay Gatsby.

Ophelia found it breathtakingly beautiful. If she'd known such a place existed less than a mile from her workplace, she would have been coming here every afternoon with her sketchbook and jotting down ideas. Drawings of geometric pieces with zigzag rows of gemstones that mirrored the glittering Baccarat chandeliers and the gold inlaid design on the gleaming tile floor.

Maybe she'd do those designs. If this meeting went as well as she hoped, maybe she'd end up with a job in the design department and she could come here and sketch to her heart's content. And maybe she'd actually see some of her designs come to fruition instead of just taking up space in her portfolio.

She tightened her grip on her slim, leather portfolio. It was Louis Vuitton. Vintage. Another treasure she'd found in her grandmother's belongings. It had been filled to bursting with old photographs from Natalia Baronova's time at the Ballet Russe de Monte Carlo. Ophelia had spent days studying those photos when she'd come home from her time in the hospital.

In the empty hours when she once would have been at company rehearsal dancing until her toes bled, she'd relived her grandmother's legendary career instead. Those news clippings, and the faded photographs with her grandmother's penciled notations on the back, had kept Ophelia going. She'd lost her health, her family, her job. Her life. All she'd had left was school and her grandmother's memories.

Ophelia had clung to those memories, studied those images until she made them her own by incorporating what she saw into her jewelry designs. The result was an inspired collection that she knew would be a success…if only someone would give her a chance and look at them.

She took a deep breath. If there was any fairness at all in the world, this would be her moment. And that *someone* would be Artem Drake.

"May I help you, miss?" A man in a pristine white dinner jacket and tuxedo pants smiled at her from behind the concierge desk.

"Yes, actually. I'm meeting someone here. Artem Drake?" She glanced toward the dazzling atrium in the center of the lobby, where tables of patrons sipped glasses of champagne and cups of tea beneath the shade of elegant palm fronds. Artem was nowhere to be seen.

She fought the sinking feeling in her stomach. *It doesn't mean anything. He could simply be running late.*

"Mr. Drake is in penthouse number nine. This key will give you elevator access to the eighteenth floor." The concierge slid a discreet black card key across the desk.

Ophelia stared at it. She'd never been so bitterly disappointed. Finally, *finally*, she'd thought she'd actually spotted a light at the end of the very dark tunnel that had become her life. But no. There was no light. Just more darkness. And a man who thought she'd meet him at a hotel on her lunch hour just to get ahead.

The irony was that's exactly what everyone in the company had thought when she'd begun dating Jeremy, the director. The other dancers had rolled their eyes whenever she'd been cast in a lead role. As if she hadn't earned it. As if she hadn't been dancing every day until her toes bled through the pink satin of her pointe shoes.

It hadn't been like that, though. She'd cared for Jeremy. And he'd cared for her, too. Or so she'd thought.

"Miss?" The concierge furrowed his brow. "Is there something else you need?"

Yes, there is. Just a glimmer of hope, if you wouldn't mind...

"No." She shook her head woodenly, and reached for the card key. "Thank you for your help."

She marched toward the elevator, her kitten heels echoing off the gold-trimmed walls of the palatial lobby. She didn't know why she was so upset. Or even remotely surprised. She'd seen all those photos of Artem in the newspaper, out every night with a different woman on his arm. Of course he'd assumed she'd want to sleep with him. She was probably the only woman in Manhattan who *didn't.*

Except she sort of did.

If she was honest with herself—painfully honest— she had to admit that the thought of sex with Artem Drake wasn't exactly repulsive. On the contrary.

She would never go through with it, of course. Not now. *Especially* not now. Not *ever.* It was just difficult to think about Artem without thinking about sex, especially since she went weak in the knees whenever he looked at her with those penetrating eyes of his. Eyes that gave her the sense that he could see straight into her aching, yearning center. Eyes that stirred chaos inside her. *Bedroom eyes.* And now she was on her way to meet him. In an actual bedroom.

Bed or no bed, she would *not* be sleeping with him.

The elevator stopped on the uppermost floor. She squared her shoulders and stepped out, prepared to search for the door to penthouse number nine.

She didn't have to look very hard. It was the only door on the entire floor.

He'd rented a hotel room that encompassed the entire floor? She rolled her eyes and wondered if all his dates got such royal treatment. Then she reminded herself that this was a business meeting, not a date.

If she had any sense at all, she'd turn around and walk directly back to Drake Diamonds. But before she could talk herself into leaving, the door swung open and she was face-to-face with Mr. Bedroom Eyes himself.

"Mr. Drake." She smiled in a way that she hoped conveyed professionalism and not the fact that she'd somehow gone quite breathless.

"My apologies, Miss Rose. I'm on the phone." He opened the door wider and beckoned her inside. "Do come in."

Ophelia had never seen such a large hotel room. She could have fit three of her apartments inside it, and it was absolutely stunning, decorated in cool grays and blues, with sleek, modern furnishings. But the most spectacular feature was its view of Central Park. Horse drawn carriages lined the curb alongside the snow-covered landscape. In the distance, ice skaters moved in a graceful circle over the pond.

Ophelia walked right up to the closest window and looked down on the busy Manhattan streets below. Everything seemed so faraway. The yellow taxicabs looked like tiny toy cars, and she could barely make out the people bundled in dark coats darting along the crowded sidewalks with their scarves trailing behind them like ribbons. Snow danced against the glass in a dizzying waltz of white, drifting downward, blanketing the city below. The effect was rather like standing inside a snow globe. Absolutely breathtaking.

"Um-hmm. I see," muttered Artem, standing a few feet behind her with his cell phone pressed against his ear.

Ophelia turned and found him watching her.

He didn't so much talk *to* whoever was on the other end as much he talked *at* them. He sounded rather displeased, but even so, he never broke eye contact with her throughout the call. "Despite the fact that this seems a rather…questionable…time to make such a donation, we must honor our commitment. I know you don't like to involve yourself with the press, brother, but think about the headlines if we backed out. Not pretty. And might I add, it would be my face they'd print a photo of alongside the negative chatter. So that's my final decision."

The person on the receiving end of his tirade was clearly Dalton. Ophelia felt guilty about overhearing such a conversation, so she averted her gaze. No sooner had she looked away than she caught sight of an enormous bed looming behind Artem.

My God, it's a behemoth.

She'd never seen such a large bed. It could have fit a dozen people.

Her face went hot, and she looked away. But as Artem wrapped up his call, her gaze kept returning to the bed and its sumptuous, creamy-white linens.

"Again, my apologies." Artem tossed his phone on the nearby sectional sofa and walked toward her. "Please, let me take your coat. Do make yourself comfortable."

She took a step out of his reach. "Mr. Drake, I'm afraid you've got the wrong impression."

"Do I?" He stopped less than an arm's length away, just close enough to send a wave of awareness crashing over her, while at the same time not quite crossing the boundary of respectability. "And what impression is that?"

"This." She waved a shaky hand around the luxurious room, trying—and failing—to avoid looking at the bed.

Artem followed her gaze. When he turned back toward her, an angry knot throbbed in his jaw. He lifted an impetuous brow. "I'm afraid I don't know what you mean, Miss Rose. Do you care to elaborate?"

"This room. And that bed." Why, oh, why, had she actually mentioned the bed? "When I said I wanted to show you my designs, that was precisely what I meant. I've no idea why you arranged to rent this ridiculous suite. The hourly rate for this room must be higher than my yearly salary. It's absurd, and thoroughly inappropriate. I have no interest in sleeping with you. None. Zero."

She really wished she hadn't stammered on the last few words. She would have preferred to sound at least halfway believable.

Artem's eyes flashed. "Are you quite finished?"

"Yes." She ordered her feet to walk straight to the door and get out of there. Immediately. They willfully disobeyed.

"I live here, Miss Rose. This is my home. I did not, as you so boldly implied, procure a rent-by-the-hour room in which to ravage you on your lunch break." He paused, glaring at her for full effect.

He lived here? In a penthouse at the Plaza?

Of course he did.

Ophelia had never been so mortified in her life. She wanted to die.

Artem took another step closer. She could see the ring of black around the dreamy blue center of his irises, a hidden hint of darkness. "For starters, if my intention was to ravage you, I would have set aside far more than an hour in which to do so. Furthermore, I'm your employer. You are my employee. Despite whatever you may have heard about my father, sleeping with the staff is not the way I intend to do business. Occasionally, the apple does, in fact, fall farther from the tree than you might imagine."

Ophelia had no idea what he was talking about, but apparently she'd touched a nerve. For the first time since setting eyes on Artem Drake—her *boss*, as he took such pleasure in pointing out time and time again—he looked less than composed. He raked an angry hand through his hair, mussing it. He almost looked like he'd just gotten out of bed.

Stop. God, what was wrong with her? She should *not* be thinking about Artem in bed. Absolutely, definitely not. Yet somehow, that was the one and only thought in her head. Artem, dark and passionate, tossing her onto the mammoth-sized bed behind him. The weight of him pressing down on her as he kissed her, entered her...

Her throat grew tight. "Good, because I have no interest whatsoever in sleeping with my boss."

Been there, done that. Got the T-shirt. Never again.

Artem narrowed his gaze at her. "So you mentioned."

Ophelia nodded. She wasn't sure she could manage to say anything without her voice betraying her. Because the more she tried to convince him that she didn't want to sleep with him, the more she actually wanted to. Assuming it was possible to want two very contradictory things at the same time.

But apparently he did *not* want to sleep with her, which was fine. No, not merely fine. It was good. She should be relieved.

Then why did she feel so utterly bereft?

"Now that we've established how ardently opposed we both are to having sex with one another—" His gaze flitted ever so briefly to her breasts, or maybe she only imagined it, since her nipples felt sensitive to the point of pain every time he looked at her "—perhaps you should show me your designs."

Her designs. The very reason she'd come here in

the first place. She swallowed around the lump in her throat. "Yes, of course."

He motioned toward the sleek, dark table in the center of the room. Ophelia opened her portfolio and carefully arranged her sketches, aware of his eyes on her the entire time. She felt every glance down to her core.

He picked up the first of her four large pages of bristol paper. "What do we have here?"

She took a deep breath. *This is it. Try not to blow it any more than you already have.* "Those are a collection of rings. I call them ballerina diamonds."

The subtlest of smiles came to his lips. "Ballerina diamonds? Why is that?"

"Each ring has a large center stone. See? That stone represents the dancer. The baguettes surrounding the center diamond are designed to give the appearance of a ballerina's tutu." She gestured around her waist, as if she were wearing one of the stiff classical tutus that she once wore onstage.

"I see." He nodded.

She allowed herself to exhale while he studied her drawings. She hadn't realized how exposed she would feel watching him go over her designs. These pieces of jewelry were personal to her. Deeply personal. They allowed her to keep a connection to her old self, her former life, in the only way she could.

She wanted him to love them just as much as she did, especially since no one in the design department at Drake Diamonds would even agree to meet with her.

"These are lovely, Miss Rose," he said. "Quite lovely."

"Thank you."

"What do we have here? A tiara? It almost looks familiar." He picked up the final page, the one she was the most nervous for him to see.

"That's intentional. It's a modernized version of the tiara that once held the Drake Diamond."

He grew very still at the mention of the infamous jewel.

Ophelia continued, "As you know, the original tiara was worn by Natalia Baronova. My collection calls for the stone to be reset in a new tiara that would honor the original one. I think it would draw a great number of people to the store. Don't you?"

He returned the sketch to the stack of papers and nodded, but Ophelia couldn't help but notice that his smile had faded.

"Mr. Drake…"

"Call me Artem," he said. "After all, we did nearly sleep together."

He winked, and once again Ophelia wished the floor of his lavish penthouse would open up and swallow her whole.

She cleared her throat. "I want to apologize. You've been nothing but kind to me, and I jumped to conclusions. It's just that I was involved with someone at work once before, and it was a mistake. A big mistake. But I shouldn't have assumed…"

Stop talking.

She was making things worse. But she wanted to be given a chance so badly that she was willing to lay everything on the line.

"Ophelia," he said, and she loved the way her name

sounded rolling off his tongue. Like music. "Stop apologizing. Please."

She nodded, but she wasn't quite finished explaining. She wanted him to understand. She *needed* him to, although she wasn't sure why. "It's just that I don't do that."

He angled his head. "What, exactly?"

"Relationships." Heat crawled up her neck and settled in the vicinity of her cheeks. "Sex."

Artem lifted a brow. "Never?"

"Never," she said firmly. "I'm not a virgin, if that's what you're thinking. It's just not something I do." *Since my diagnosis...*

Maybe she should tell him. Maybe she should just spill the beans and let him know she was sick, and that's why she'd been so adamant about not adopting the kitten. It was why she would never allow herself to sleep with him. Or anyone else. Not that she'd really wanted to...until now. Today. In this room. With him.

She should tell him. Didn't she have an obligation to be honest with her employer? To tell the truth?

Except then he'd know. He'd know everything, and he wouldn't look at her anymore the way he was looking at her now. Not like she was something to be fixed. Not like she was someone who was broken. But like she was beautiful.

She needed a man to look at her like that again. Not just any man, she realized with a pang. *This* man. Artem.

He gazed at her for a long, silent moment, as if weighing her words. When he finally spoke, his tone was measured. Serious. "A woman needs to be adored, Ophelia. She needs to be cherished, worshipped." His gaze dropped to her mouth, and she forgot how to breathe. "Touched."

And, oh, God, he was right. She'd never in her life needed so badly to be touched. Her body arched toward him, like a hothouse orchid bending toward the light of the sun. She wrapped her arms around herself, in desperate need of some kind of barrier.

"Especially a woman like you," he whispered, his eyes going dark again.

She swallowed. "A woman like me?"

Sick? Lonely?

"Beautiful," he whispered, and reached to cup her cheek with his hand.

It was the most innocent of touches, but at that first brush of Artem Drake's skin against hers, Ophelia knew she was in trouble.

So very much trouble.

Chapter Four

It took Dalton less than a minute to confirm what Artem already knew.

"These designs are exceptional." Dalton bent over the round conference table in the corner of their father's office—now Artem's office—to get a closer look at Ophelia's sketches. "Whose work did you say this was?"

Artem shifted in his chair. "Ophelia Rose."

Even the simple act of saying her name awakened his senses. He was restless, uncomfortably aroused, while doing nothing but sitting across the table from his brother looking at Ophelia's sketches. He experienced this nonsensical reaction every time she crossed his mind. It was becoming a problem. A big one.

He'd tried to avoid this scenario. Or any scenario that would put the two of them in a room together again. He really had. After their electrically charged meeting in his suite at the Plaza ten days ago, he'd kept to himself as much as possible. He'd barely stuck his head out of his office, despite the fact that every minute he spent between those wood-paneled walls, it seemed as though his father's ghost was breathing down his neck. It was less than pleasant, to say the least. It had also been the precise reason he'd chosen to meet Ophelia in his suite to begin with.

He'd needed to get out. Away from the store, away from the portrait of his father that hung behind his desk.

Away from the prying eyes of his brother and the rest of the staff, most notably his secretary, who'd been his dad's assistant for more than a decade before Artem had "inherited" her.

Not that he'd done anything wrong. Ophelia was an employee. There was no reason whatsoever why he shouldn't meet with her behind closed doors. Doing so didn't mean there was anything between them other than a professional relationship. Pure business. He hadn't crossed any imaginary boundary line.

Yet.

He'd wanted to. God, how he'd wanted to. But he hadn't, and he wouldn't. Even if keeping that promise to himself meant that he was chained to his desk from now on. He needed to be able to look at himself in the mirror and know that he hadn't become the thing he most despised.

His dad.

Of course, there was the matter of the cat. Artem supposed animal adoption wasn't part of the ordinary course of business. But he could justify that to himself easily enough. Like he'd said, the kitten had been an early Christmas bonus. A little unconventional, perhaps, but not *entirely* inappropriate.

If he'd tried to deny that he wanted her, he'd have been struck down by a bolt of lightning. Wanting Ophelia didn't even begin to cover it. He craved her. He *needed* her. His interest in her went beyond the physical. Beneath her strong exterior, there was a sadness about her that he couldn't help but identify with. Her melancholy intrigued him, touched a part of him he seldom allowed himself to acknowledge.

Any and all doubt about how badly he needed to touch her had evaporated the moment she'd told him that she didn't allow herself the pleasure of sexual companionship. Why would she share something so intimate with him? Even more important, why couldn't he stop thinking about it?

Since their conversation, he'd thought of little else.

Something was holding her back. She'd been hurt somehow, and now she thought she was broken beyond repair. She wasn't. She was magic. Hope lived in her skin. She just didn't know it yet. But Artem did. He saw it in the porcelain promise of her graceful limbs. He'd felt it in the way she'd shivered at his touch.

If he'd indeed crossed a forbidden line, it had been the moment he'd reached out and cupped her face. Something electric had passed between them then. There'd been no denying it, which was undoubtedly why she'd promptly gathered her coat and fled.

Artem had made a mistake, but it could have been worse. Far worse. The list of things he'd wanted to do to her in that hotel room while the snow beat against the windows had been endless. He'd exercised more restraint than he'd known he'd possessed. The very idea of a woman like Ophelia remaining untouched was criminal.

Regardless, it wouldn't happen again. It couldn't. And since he could no longer trust himself to have a simple conversation with Ophelia without burying his hands in her wayward hair and kissing her pink peony mouth until she came apart in his hands, he would just avoid her altogether. It was the best way. The only way.

There was just one flaw with that plan. Ophelia's jewelry designs were good. Too good to ignore. Drake Diamonds needed her, possibly as much as Artem did.

"Ophelia Rose?" Dalton frowned. "Why does that name sound familiar?"

"Because she works here," Artem said. "In Engagements."

Dalton waved a hand at the sketches of what she'd called her ballerina diamonds. "She can do *this*, and we've got her working in sales?"

"*You* have her working in sales." After all, Artem hadn't had a thing to do with hiring her. "I'd like to move her to the design team, effective immediately. I've been going over the numbers. If we can fast-track the production of a new collection, we might be able to reverse some of the financial damage that Dad did when he bought the mine."

Some. Not all.

If only they had more time…

"Provided it's a success, of course," Dalton said. "It's a risk."

"That it is." But what choice did they have? He'd already investigated auctioning off the Drake Diamond. Even if he went through with it, they needed another course of action. A proactive one that would show the world Drake Diamonds wasn't in any kind of trouble, especially not the sort of trouble they were actually in.

Over the course of the past ten days, while Artem had been actively trying to forget Ophelia, he'd been doing his level best to come up with a way to overcome the mine disaster. It had been an effective distraction. Almost.

Time and again, he'd found himself coming back to Ophelia's designs, running his hands along those creamy-white pages of cold-press drawing paper. Obviously, given the attraction he felt toward Ophelia, promoting her was the last thing he should do. Right now, he could move about the store and still manage to keep a chaste distance between them. Working closely with her was hardly an ideal option.

Unfortunately, it happened to be the *only* option.

"Let's do it," Dalton said.

In the shadow of his father's portrait, Artem nodded his agreement.

Ten days had passed since Ophelia had shown Artem her jewelry designs. Ten excruciating days, during which she'd seen him coming and going, passing her in the hall, scarcely acknowledging her presence. He'd barely even deigned to look at her. On the rare occasion when he did, he'd seemed to see right through her. And morning after morning, he kept showing up on *Page Six*. A different day, a different woman on his arm. It was a never-ending cycle. The man went through women like water.

Which made it all the more frustrating that every time Ophelia closed her eyes, she heard his voice. And all those bewitching things he'd said to her.

A woman needs to be adored, Ophelia. She needs to be cherished, worshipped.

Touched.

Ophelia had even begun to wonder if maybe he was right. Maybe she did need those things. Maybe the ache she felt every time she found herself in the company of Artem Drake was real. It certainly felt real. Every electrifying spark of arousal had shimmered as real as a blazing blue diamond.

Then she'd remembered the look on Jeremy's face when she'd told him about her diagnosis—the small, sad shake of his head, the way he couldn't quite meet her gaze. There'd been no need for him to tell her their affair was over. He'd done so, anyway.

Ophelia had sat quietly on the opposite side of his desk, barely hearing him murmur things like, *too much*, *burden* and *not ready for this*. The gravity of his words hadn't even registered until later, when she'd left his office.

Because for the duration of Jeremy's breakup speech, all Ophelia's concentration had been focused on not looking at the framed poster on the wall behind him—the company's promotional poster for the *Giselle* production, featuring Ophelia herself standing en pointe, draped in ethereal white tulle, clutching a lily. She wasn't sure if it was poetic or cruel that her final role had been the ghost of a woman who'd died of a broken heart.

That was exactly how she'd felt for the past six months. Like a ghost of a woman. Invisible. Untouchable.

But when Artem had said those things to her, when he'd reached out and cupped her face, everything had changed. His touch had somehow summoned her from the grave.

She'd embodied Giselle's resurrected spirit dancing in the pale light of the moon, without so much as slipping her foot into a ballet shoe. Her body felt more alive than it ever had before. Liquid warmth pooled in her center. Delicious heat danced through every nerve ending in her body, from the top of her head to the tips of her pointed toes. She'd been inflamed. Utterly enchanted. If she'd dared open her mouth to respond, her heart would have leaped up her throat and fallen right at Artem's debonair feet.

So she'd done the only thing she could do. The smart thing, the right thing. She'd run.

She'd simply turned around and bolted right out the door of his posh Plaza penthouse. She hadn't even bothered to collect her designs, those intricate colored pencil sketches she'd labored over for months.

She needed to get them back. She *would* get them

back. Just as soon as she could bring herself to face Artem again. As soon as she could forget him. Clearly, he'd forgotten about her.

That's what you wanted. Remember?

"Miss Rose?"

Ophelia looked up from the glass case where she'd been carefully aligning rows of platinum engagement rings against a swath of Drake-blue satin. Artem's secretary, the one who'd given her the instructions to meet him at the Plaza a week and a half ago, stood on the other side, hands crossed primly in front of her.

Ophelia swallowed and absolutely forbade herself to fantasize that she was being summoned to the hotel again. "Yes?"

"Mr. Drake has requested a word with you."

A rebellious flutter skittered up Ophelia's thighs. She cleared her throat. "Now?"

The secretary nodded. "Yes, now. In his office."

Not the hotel, his office. Right. That was good. Proper.

It required superhuman effort to keep the smile on her face from fading. "I see."

"Follow me, please."

Ophelia followed Artem's secretary across the showroom floor, around the corner and down the hall toward the corporate offices. They passed the kitchen with its bevy of petits fours atop gleaming silver plates, and Ophelia couldn't help but feel a little wistful.

She took a deep breath and averted her gaze. At least all this was about to end, and she could go back to the way things were before he'd ever walked in on her scarfing down cake. She assumed the reason for this forced march into his office was to retrieve her portfolio.

Although wouldn't it have been easier to simply have someone return it to her on his behalf? Then they wouldn't have been forced to interact with one another at all. He'd never cross Ophelia's mind again, except when Jewel purred and rubbed up against her ankles. Or when she saw him looking devastatingly hot in the society pages of the newspaper every morning. Or the other million times a day she found herself thinking of him.

"Here you go." Artem's secretary pushed open the door to his office and held it for her.

Ophelia stepped inside. For a moment she was so awestruck by the full force of Artem's gaze directed squarely at her for the first time since the Plaza that the fact they weren't alone didn't even register.

"Miss Rose," he said. For a millisecond, his focus drifted to her mouth, then darted back to her eyes.

Ophelia's limbs went languid. There was no legitimate reason to feel even the slightest bit aroused, but she did. Uncomfortably so.

She pressed her thighs together. "Mr. Drake."

He stood and waved a hand at the man sitting opposite him, whom Ophelia had finally noticed. "I'd like to introduce you to my brother, Dalton Drake."

Dalton rose from his chair and shook her hand. Ophelia had never thought Dalton and Artem looked much alike, but up close she could see a faint family resemblance. They had the same straight nose, same chiseled features. But whereas Dalton's good looks seemed wrapped in dark intensity, Artem's devil-may-care expression got under her skin. Every time.

It was maddening.

"It's a pleasure to meet you, Miss Rose," he said, in a voice oddly reminiscent of his brother's, minus the timbre of raw sexuality.

Ophelia nodded, unsure what to say.

What was going on? Why was Dalton here, and why were her sketches spread out on the conference table?

"Please, have a seat." Dalton gestured toward the chair between him and Artem.

Ophelia obediently sat down, flanked on either side by Drakes. She took a deep breath and steadfastly avoided looking at Artem.

"We've been discussing your work." Dalton waved a hand at her sketches. "You have a brilliant artistic eye. It's lovely work, Miss Rose. So it's our pleasure to welcome you to the Drake Diamonds design team."

Ophelia blinked, unable to comprehend what she was hearing.

Artem hadn't forgotten about her, after all. He'd shown her designs to Dalton, and now they were giving her a job. A real design job, one that she'd been preparing and studying for for two years. She would no longer be working in Engagements.

Something good was happening. Finally.

"Thank you. Thank you so much," she breathed, dropping her guard and fixing her gaze on Artem.

He smiled, ever so briefly, and Ophelia had to stop

herself from kissing him right on his perfect, provocative mouth.

Dalton drummed his fingers on the table, drawing her attention back to the sketches. "We'd like to introduce the new designs as the Drake Diamonds Dance collection, and we plan on doing so as soon as possible."

Ophelia nodded. It sounded too good to be true.

Dalton continued, "The ballerina rings will be the focus of the collection, as my brother and I both feel those are the strongest pieces. We'd like to use all four of your engagement designs, plus we'd like you to come up with a few ideas for companion pieces—cocktail rings and the like. For those, we'd like to use colored gemstones—emeralds or rubies—surrounded by baguettes in your tutu pattern."

This was perfect. Ophelia had once danced the Balanchine choreography for *Jewels*, a ballet divided into three parts, *Emeralds*, *Rubies* and *Diamonds*. She'd performed one of the corps roles in *Rubies*.

"Can you come up with some new sketches by tomorrow?" Artem slid his gaze in her direction, lifting a brow as her toes automatically began moving beneath the table in the prancing pattern from *Rubies'* dramatic finale.

Ophelia stilled her feet. She didn't think he'd noticed, but she felt hot under his gaze all the same. "Tomorrow?"

"Too soon?" Dalton asked.

"No." She shook her head and did her best to ignore the smirk on Artem's face, which probably meant he was sitting there imagining her typical evening plans of hanging out with kittens. "Tomorrow is fine. I do have one question, though."

"Yes, Miss Rose?" Artem leaned closer.

Too close. Ophelia's breath froze in her lungs for a moment. *Get yourself together. This is business.* "My inspiration for the collection was the tiara design. I'd hoped that would be the centerpiece, rather than the ballerina rings."

He shook his head. "We won't be going forward with the tiara redesign."

Dalton interrupted, "Not yet."

"Not ever." Artem pinned his brother with a glare. "The Drake Diamond isn't available for resetting, since soon it will no longer be part of the company's inventory."

Ophelia blinked. She couldn't possibly have heard that right.

"That hasn't been decided, Artem," Dalton said quietly, his gaze flitting to the portrait of the older man hanging over the desk.

Artem didn't bat an eye at the painting. "You know as well as I do that it's for the best, brother."

"Wait. Are you selling the Drake Diamond?" Ophelia asked. It just wasn't possible. That diamond had too much historical significance to be sold. It was a part of the company's history.

It was part of *her* history. Her grandmother had been one of only three women to ever wear the priceless stone.

"It's being considered," Artem said.

Dalton stared silently down at his hands.

"But you can't." Ophelia shook her head, vaguely aware of Artem's chiseled features settling into a stern expression of reprimand. She was overstepping and she knew it. But they couldn't sell the Drake Diamond. She had plans for that jewel, grand plans.

She shuffled through the sketches on the table until she found the page with her tiara drawing. "Look. If we reset the diamond, people will come from all over to see it. The store will be packed. It will be great for business."

Ophelia couldn't imagine that Drake Diamonds was hurting for sales. She herself had sold nearly one hundred thousand dollars in diamond engagement rings just the day before. But there had to be a reason why they were considering letting it go. Correction: Artem was considering selling the diamond. By all appearances, Dalton was less than thrilled about the idea.

Of course, none of this was any of her business at all. Still. She couldn't just stand by and let it happen. Of the hundreds of press clippings and photographs that had survived Natalia Baronova's legendary career, Ophelia's grandmother had framed only one of them—the picture that had appeared on the front page of the arts section of the *New York Times* the day after she'd debuted in *Swan Lake*. The night she'd worn the Drake Diamond.

She'd been only sixteen years old, far younger than any other ballerina who'd taken on the challenging dual role of Odette and Odile, the innocent White Swan and the Black Swan seductress. No one believed she could pull it off. The other ballerinas in the company had been furious, convinced that the company director had cast Natalia as nothing more than a public relations ploy. And he had. They knew it. She knew it. Everyone knew it.

Natalia had been ostracized by her peers on the most important night of her career. Even her pas de deux partner, Mikhail Dolin, barely spoke to her. Then on opening night, the company director had placed that diamond tiara, with its priceless yellow diamond, on Natalia's head. And a glimmer of hope had taken root deep in her grandmother's soul.

Natalia danced that night like she'd never danced before. During the curtain call, the audience rose to its feet, clapping wildly as Mikhail Dolin bent and kissed Natalia's hand. To Ophelia's grandmother, that kiss had been a benediction. One dance, one kiss, one diamond tiara had changed her life.

Ophelia still kept the photo on the mantel in her grandmother's apartment, where it had sat for as long as she could remember. Since she'd been a little girl practicing her wobbly plié, Ophelia had looked at that photograph of her grandmother wearing the glittering diamond crown and white-ribboned ballet shoes, with a handsome man kissing her hand. Her grandmother had told her the story of that night time and time again. The story, the diamond, the kiss…they'd made Ophelia believe. Just as they had Natalia.

If the Drakes sold that diamond, it would be like losing what little hope she had left.

"Is that agreeable to you, Miss Rose?" Dalton frowned. "Miss Rose?"

Ophelia blinked. What had she missed while she'd been lost in the past? "Yes. Yes, of course."

"Very well, then. It's a date." Dalton rose from his chair.

Wait. What? A date?

Her gaze instinctively flew to Artem. "Excuse me? A date?"

The set of his jaw visibly hardened. "Don't look so horrified, Ophelia. It's just a turn of phrase."

"I'm sorry." She shook her head. Maybe if she shook it hard enough, she could somehow undo whatever she'd unwittingly agreed to. "I think I missed something."

"We'll announce the new collection via a press release on Friday afternoon. You and Artem will attend the ballet together that evening and by Saturday morning, the Drake Diamond Dance collection will be all over newspapers nationwide." Dalton smiled, clearly pleased with himself. And why not? It was a perfect PR plan.

Perfectly horrid.

Ophelia couldn't go out with Artem, even if it was nothing but a marketing ploy. She definitely couldn't accompany him to the ballet, of all places. She hadn't seen a live ballet performance since she'd been one of the dancers floating across the stage.

She couldn't do it. It would be too much. Too overwhelming. Too heartbreaking. *No. Just no.* She'd simply tell them she wouldn't go. She was thankful for the opportunity, and she'd work as hard as she possibly could on the collection, but attending the ballet was impossible. It was nonnegotiable.

"That will be all, Miss Rose," Artem said, with an edge to his voice that sent a shiver up Ophelia's spine. "Until Friday."

Then he turned back to the papers on his desk. He'd finished with her. Again.

Chapter Five

Ophelia looked down at the ring clamp that held her favorite ballerina engagement design. Not a sketch. An actual ring that she'd designed and crafted herself.

It was really happening. She was a jewelry designer at Drake Diamonds, with her own office overlooking Fifth Avenue, her own drafting table and her own computer loaded with state-of-the-art 3-D jewelry design software. She hadn't used such fancy equipment since her school days, but after spending the morning getting reacquainted with the technology, it was all coming back to her. Which was a good thing, since she clearly wasn't going to get any help from the other members of the design team.

She recognized the dubious expressions on the faces of the other designers. They looked at her the same way the ballet company members had when Jeremy had chosen her as the lead in *Giselle*. Once again, everyone assumed her relationship with the boss was the reason she'd been promoted. Except this time, she had no connection with her boss whatsoever.

At least that's what she kept telling herself.

She did her best to forget about office politics. She had a job to do, after all.

In fact, she'd been so busy adapting to her new reality that she'd almost managed to forget that she was scheduled to attend the ballet with Artem on Friday night. *Almost.* The fact that she wasn't experiencing daily panic attacks in anticipation of stepping into the grand lobby of Lincoln Center was due to good old-fashioned denial. She could almost pretend their "date" wasn't actually going to happen, since Artem had gone back to keeping his distance.

She'd seen him a grand total of one time since their meeting with Dalton. Just once—late at night after the store had closed. Ophelia had stopped to look at the Drake Diamond before she'd headed home to feed Jewel. She hadn't planned on it, but as she'd crossed the darkened showroom, her gaze had been drawn toward the stone, locked away in its lonely glass case. Protected. Untouched.

She'd begun to cry, for some silly reason, as she'd gazed at the gem, then she'd looked up and spotted Artem watching from the shadows. She'd thought she had, anyway. Once she'd swept the tears from her eyes, she'd realized there had been no one else there. Just her. Alone.

Her day-to-day communication at the office was mostly with Dalton. On the occasions when Artem needed something from her, he sent his secretary, Mrs. Burns, in his stead. So when Mrs. Burns walked into Ophelia's office on Friday morning, she wasn't altogether surprised.

Until the secretary, hands clasped primly at her waist, stated the reason for her visit. "Mr. Drake would like to know what you're wearing."

The ring clamp in Ophelia's hand slipped out of her grasp and landed on the drafting table with a clatter. "Excuse me?"

Four days of nothing. No contact whatsoever, and now he was trying to figure out what she was wearing? Did he expect her to take a selfie and send it to him over the Drake Diamonds company email?

Mrs. Burns cleared her throat. "This evening, Miss Rose. He'd like to know what you're planning to wear to the ballet. I believe you're scheduled to accompany him tonight to Lincoln Center."

Oh. That.

"Yes. Yes, of course." Ophelia nodded and tried to look as though she hadn't just jumped to an altogether ridiculous assumption. *Again.*

Maybe the fact that she kept misinterpreting Artem's intentions said more about her than it did about him. It *did*, she realized, much to her mortification. It most definitely did. And what it said about her, specifically, was that she was hot for her boss. Her kitten-buying, penthouse-dwelling, tuxedo-wearing playboy of a boss.

Ugh.

She supposed she shouldn't have been surprised. After all, every woman on the island of Manhattan—and undoubtedly a good number of the men—would have willingly leaped into Artem Drake's bed. There was a big difference between the infatuated masses and Ophelia, though. They could sleep with whomever they wanted.

Ophelia could not. Not with Artem. Not with anyone. The fact that doing so would likely put her fancy new job in jeopardy was only the tip of the iceberg.

"Miss Rose?" Mrs. Burns eyed her expectantly over the top of her glasses.

Ophelia sighed. "Honestly, why does he even care what I wear?"

"Mr. Drake didn't share his reasoning with me, but I assume his logic has something to do with the fact that you're a representative of Drake Diamonds now. All eyes will be on you this evening."

All eyes will be on you.

Oh, God. Ophelia hadn't even considered the fact that she'd be photographed on Artem's arm. At the ballet, of all places. What if someone recognized her? What if they printed her stage name in the newspaper?

Then everyone would know. *Artem* would know.

She swallowed. "Mrs. Burns, do you suppose it's really necessary for me to be there?"

The older woman looked at Ophelia like she'd just sprouted an extra head. "The appearance is part of the publicity plan for the new collection. The collection that you designed."

Right. Of course it was necessary for her to go. She should *want* to be there.

The frightening thing was that part of her did want to be there. She wanted to hear the whisper of pointe shoes on the stage floor again. She wanted to smell the red velvet curtain and feel the cool kiss of air-conditioning in the wings. She wanted to wear stage makeup—dramatic black eyeliner and bright crimson lips. One last time.

She just wasn't sure her heart could take it. Not to mention the fact that she'd be revisiting her past alongside Artem. She didn't want to feel vulnerable in front of him. Nothing good could come from that.

But she didn't exactly have a choice in the matter, did she?

She did, however, have the power to deny his ridiculous request. "Tell Mr. Drake he'll know what I'm wearing when he sees me tonight. Not to worry. I'm fully capable of dressing myself in an appropriate manner for the ballet."

Artem's secretary seemed to stifle a grin. "I'll certainly pass that message along."

Of course, an hour later, Mrs. Burns was back in Ophelia's office with a second request regarding her fashion plans for the evening. Again Ophelia offered no information. She was sure she'd find something appropriate in Natalia's old things, but she couldn't think about it right now. Because thinking about it would mean it was really happening.

Then after lunch, Mrs. Burns was back a third time, with instructions for Ophelia to arrive promptly at

Artem's suite at the Plaza at seven o'clock. Drake Diamonds would send a car to pick her up a half hour prior.

Ophelia wanted to ask why on earth it was necessary to convene at his penthouse beforehand. Honestly, couldn't they just meet at Lincoln Center? But all this back and forth with Mrs. Burns was starting to get ridiculous.

Maybe one day, in addition to her office, her drafting table and her computer, Ophelia would eventually have her own secretary. Then there would be no need to communicate with Artem at all. They could simply talk to one another through their assistants. No lingering glances. No aching need in the pit of her stomach every time he looked at her. No butterflies.

Better yet, no temptation.

Artem glanced at the vintage Drake Diamonds tank watch strapped round his wrist. It read 7:05. Ophelia was late.

Brilliant.

He'd been on edge for days, and her tardiness was doing nothing to help his mood.

For once in his life, he'd exercised a modicum of self-control. He'd done the right thing. He'd kept his distance from Ophelia Rose. Other than one evening when he'd spied her looking at the Drake Diamond after hours, he hadn't allowed himself to even glance in her direction.

And he'd never been so bloody miserable.

She'd seemed so pensive standing in the dark, staring at the diamond, her face awash in a kaleidoscope of cool blues and moody violets reflected off the stone's surface. What was it about that diamond? If the prospect didn't sound so ridiculous, Artem would have believed it had cast some sort of spell over her. She'd looked so beautiful, so sad, that he'd been unable to look away as the prisms of color moved over her porcelain skin.

And when amethyst teardrops had slid down her lovely face, he'd been overcome by a primal urge to right whatever wrong had caused her sorrow. Then she'd seen him, and her expression had closed like a book. Thinking about it as he paced the expanse of his suite, he could almost hear the ruffle of pages. Poetic verse hiding itself away. Sonnets forever unread.

And now?

Now she was late. It occurred to him she might not even show. Artem Drake, stood up by his evening companion. That would be a first. It was laughable, really.

He had never felt less like laughing.

As he poured himself a drink, a knock sounded on the door. Finally.

"You're late," he said, swinging the door open.

"Am I fired?" With a slow sweep of her eyelashes, Ophelia lifted her gaze to meet his, and Artem's breath caught in this throat.

She'd gathered her blond tresses into a ballerina bun—fitting, he supposed—exposing her graceful neck and delicate shoulders, wrapped in a white fur stole tied closed between her breasts with a pearly satin bow. Her dress was blush pink, the color of ballet slippers, and flowed into a wide tulle skirt that whispered and swished as she walked toward him.

Never in his life had he gazed upon a woman who looked so timelessly beautiful.

Seeing her—here, now, in her glorious flesh—took the edge off his irritation. He felt instantly calmer somehow. This was both a good thing and a very bad one.

He shot a glance at the security guard from Drake Diamonds standing quietly in the corner of the room, and thanked whatever twist of fate had provided a chaperone for this moment. His self-control had already worn quite thin. And as stunning as he found her dress, it would have looked even better as a puff of pink on the floor of his bedroom.

"Fired? No. I'll let it slide this time." He cleared his throat. "You look lovely, Miss Rose."

"Thank you, Mr. Drake." Her voice went breathy. As soft as the delicate tulle fabric of her dress.

She'd been in the room for less than a minute, and Artem was as hard as granite. It was going to be an undoubtedly long night.

"Come," he said, beckoning her to the long dining table by the window.

Since they were already behind schedule, he didn't waste time on pleasantries. And chaperone or no chaperone, he needed to get her out of this hotel room before he did something idiotic.

"Artem?" Ophelia's eyes grew wide as she took in the assortment of jewelry carefully arranged on black velvet atop the table. A Burmese ruby choker with eight crimson, cushion-cut stones and a shimmering band of baguettes and fancy-cut diamonds. A bow-shaped broach of rose-cut and old European-cut diamonds with carved

rock crystal in millegrain and collet settings. A necklace
of single-cut diamonds alternating with baroque-shaped
emerald cabochon drops. And so on. Every square inch
of the table glittered.

Ophelia shook her head. "I don't understand. I've
never seen any of these pieces before."

"They're from the company vault," Artem explained.
"Hence the security detail." He nodded toward the
armed guard standing silently in the corner of the room.

Ophelia followed his gaze, took in the security officer and looked back up at Artem. "But you're the CEO."

"I am indeed." *CEO.* Artem was beginning to get
accustomed to the title, which in itself was cause for
alarm. This was supposed to be temporary. "Insurance
regulations require an armed guard when assets in ex-
cess of one million dollars leave the premises. Think
of him as a bodyguard for the diamonds."

The security guard gave a subtle nod of his head.

Ophelia raised a single, quizzical brow. "A million
dollars?"

"Of course, if I'd known what you'd planned on
wearing tonight, I could have selected just one appropriate item instead of transforming my suite into the
equivalent of Elizabeth Taylor's jewelry box."

"Oh." She flushed a little.

Had she been any other woman, Artem would have
suspected her coyness to be an act. A calculated, flir-
tatious maneuver. But Ophelia wasn't just any other
woman.

He'd seen her at the office. At work, she was bright,
confident and earnest. Far more talented than she re-

alized. And always so serious. Serious, with that ever-present hint of melancholy.

But whenever they were alone together, her composure seemed to slip. And by God, was it a turn-on.

Artem liked knowing he affected her in such a way. He liked knowing he was the one who'd put the pretty pink glow in her cheeks. He liked seeing her blossom like a flower. A lush peony in full bloom.

Hell, he loved it all.

"Wait." Ophelia blinked. "These aren't for me."

"Yes, Ophelia, they are. For tonight, anyway. Just a little loan from the store." He shrugged one shoulder, as if he did this sort of thing every night, for every woman he stepped out with. Which he most definitely did not. "Choose whichever one you like. More than one if you prefer."

Ophelia's hand fluttered to her neck with the grace of a thousand butterflies. "Really?"

"You're representing Drake Diamonds," he said, by way of explanation.

"I suppose I am." She gave a little tilt of her head, then there it was—the smile he'd been waiting for. More dazzling than the treasure trove of jewels at her disposal. "I think a necklace would be lovely."

She pulled at the white satin bow of her little fur jacket. At last. Artem's fingers had been itching to do that since she'd crossed the threshold. He hadn't. Obviously. The diamonds he could explain. Undressing her in any fashion would have stepped over that boundary line that he was still determined not to cross.

He wondered if his father had been at all cognizant

of that line. Had he thought, even once, about the ramifications of his actions? Or had he taken what he wanted without regard to what would happen to his family, his business, his legacy?

Artem's jaw clenched. He didn't want to think about his father. Not now. He didn't want to think about how he himself represented everything that was wrong with the great Geoffrey Drake. Artem Drake was nothing but a living, breathing mistake of the highest order.

And his father was always there, wasn't he? A larger than life presence. A ghost haunting those he'd left behind.

Artem was tired of being haunted. It was exhausting. Tonight he wanted to live.

He gave Ophelia a quiet smile. "A necklace it is, then."

Ophelia had never felt so much like Cinderella. Not even two years ago when she'd danced the lead role in the company's production of the fairy tale.

As for jewels, from the outrageously opulent selection at Artem's penthouse, she'd chosen a necklace of diamond baguettes set in platinum that wrapped all the way around her neck in a single, glittering strand. It fit almost like a choker, except in front it split into three strands, each punctuated with large, brilliant cut diamonds. The overall effect was somehow dazzling, yet delicate.

It wasn't until Artem had fastened it around her neck that he'd told her the necklace had once belonged to Princess Grace of Monaco. Ophelia had been concentrating so hard on not reacting to the warm graze of his fingertips against her skin that she'd barely registered what he'd said. Now, as she sat beside him in the sleek black limousine en route to Lincoln Center, her hand kept fluttering to her throat.

She was wearing Princess Grace's necklace. How was that even possible?

She wished her grandmother were alive to see her right now. Ordinarily, she never let herself indulge in such wishes. Natalia Baronova's heart would break if she knew about the illness that had ended her granddaughter's dance career. But wouldn't she get a kick out of seeing Ophelia dressed in one of her grandmother's vintage gowns, wearing Grace Kelly's jewelry?

She smiled and her gaze slid toward Artem, who was watching her with great intensity.

"Allow me?" he asked, reaching for the bow on her faux fur stole.

Ophelia gave him a quiet nod as he tugged on the end of the satin ribbon. He loosened the bow and opened the stole a bit. Just enough to offer a glimpse of the spectacular diamonds around her neck.

"There," he said. "That's better."

Ophelia swallowed, unable to move, unable to even breathe while he touched her. She'd dropped her guard. Only for a moment. And now…

Now he was no more than a breath away, and she could see her reflection in the cool blue of his irises. He had eyes like a tempest, and there she was, right at the center of his storm. Looking beautiful and happy. Full of life and hope. So much like her old self—the girl

who'd danced through life, unfettered and unafraid—
that she forgot all the reasons why she shouldn't kiss
this man. This man who had such a way of reminding
her of who she used to be.

Her heart pounded hard in her chest, so hard she was
certain he could hear it. She parted her lips and murmured Artem's name as she reached to cup his chiseled jaw. His eyes locked with hers and a surge of heat
shot straight to her lower body. She licked her lips, and
there was no more denying it. She wanted him to kiss
her. She wanted Artem's kiss and more. So much more.

His fingertips slid from her stole to her neck, down
her throat to her collarbone. There was a reverence in
his touch, like a blessing. And those words that had
haunted her so came flooding back.

*A woman needs to be adored, Ophelia. She needs to
be cherished, worshipped.*

"Mr. Drake, sir, we've arrived." The limo's intercom
buzzed, and the driver's voice startled some sense back
into Ophelia.

What was she *doing*?

She was letting a silly diamond necklace confuse
her and make her think something had changed when,
in fact, *nothing* had. She was still sick. And she always
would be.

"I'm sorry." She removed her hand from Artem's
face and slid across the leather seat, out of his reach. "I
shouldn't have… I'm sorry."

"Ophelia," he said, with more patience in his tone
than she'd ever heard. "It's okay."

But it wasn't okay. *She* wasn't okay.

As if she needed a reminder, Lincoln Center loomed in her periphery. Inside that building, dancers with whom she'd trained less than a year ago were getting ready to perform, winding pink ribbons around their ankles in dressing rooms filled with bouquets of red roses. Jeremy, the man who'd once asked her to marry him, was inside that building, too. Only he was no longer watching her go through her last-minute series of pliés and port de bras. He was watching someone else do those things. He was kissing someone else's cheek in the final moments before the curtain went up. Another dancer. An able-bodied girl. One who wouldn't have to be carried off the stage when she fell down because she'd lost her balance. One who could do more than three pirouettes before her vision went blurry. One who wouldn't have to give herself injections twice a week and be careful not to miss her daily 8000 IU of vitamin D.

A girl who wasn't broken.

Not that she missed Jeremy. She didn't. She'd confused her feelings for him with her love of dance. If she'd ever had a proper lover, that lover was ballet. Ballet had fed her soul. And now? Now she was starving. Her body needed to move. As did her heart. Her soul.

Artem reached for her hand, but she shook her head and fixed her gaze out the car window, where a group of paparazzi were gathered with cameras poised at the ready.

She couldn't let him touch her again. If she did, there was no telling what she'd do. She was too raw, too tender, too hungry. And Artem Drake was too...

…too *much*.

She'd just have to pretend, wouldn't she? She'd have to act as though the way he looked at her and the things he said didn't make her want to slip out of her fancy dress and slide naked into his lap right there in the back of the Drake Diamonds limousine.

Artem looked at her. Long and hard, until her hands began to shake from the effort it took to keep pretending she was fine. The driver cleared his throat, and Artem finally directed his gaze past her, toward the photographers waiting on the other side of the glass.

"Showtime," he muttered.

Yeah. Ophelia swallowed around the lump in her throat. *Showtime.*

Chapter Six

Artem smiled for the cameras. He made polite small talk. He answered questions about the press release that Dalton had issued earlier in the day announcing the new Drake Diamonds Dance collection. He did everything he always did in his capacity as public relations front man for the company.

It was business as usual. With one very big exception—this time, Ophelia stood beside him.

He'd been attending events like this one for the better part of his adult life, and rarely had he done so alone. Having a pretty woman on his arm went with the territory. Logically, Ophelia's presence shouldn't have made a bit of difference. Logic, however, had little to do with the torturous ache he felt when he placed his hand on the small of her back or cupped her elbow as they walked up the broad steps to the entrance of Lincoln Center. Logic certainly wasn't behind the surge of arousal he'd felt when he'd placed the diamonds around her graceful neck. Logic hadn't swirled between them in the back-seat of the car. That had been something else entirely. Some forbidden form of alchemy.

The fulfillment of what had nearly happened in the limousine tormented him. The kiss that wasn't even a kiss. The look in her eyes, though. That look had been as intimate as if she'd touched her lips to his. Perhaps even more so.

He could still feel the riotous beat of her pulse as he'd traced the curve of her elegant neck with his fin-gertips. Most of all, he could still see the glimmer in her sapphire eyes as she'd reached out to touch his face. Eyes filled with insatiable need. Sweet, forbidden hun-ger that rivaled the ravenous craving he'd been strug-gling against since the moment he'd caught her eating that silly cake.

God, what was wrong with him? He was a grown man. A man of experience. He shouldn't be feeling this wound up over a woman he barely knew, particularly one whom he had no business sleeping with.

On some level he loathed to acknowledge, he won-dered if what he was experiencing was in any way simi-lar to what his father had felt any of the myriad times he'd strayed. But Artem knew that wasn't the case. His father had been a selfish bastard, with little or no re-spect for his wedding vows. End of story. Artem wasn't even married, for God's sake. With good reason. He didn't have any intention of repeating the past.

Besides, this attraction he felt for Ophelia was different in every possible way. *She* was different.

Maybe it was her vulnerability that he found so intriguing. Or perhaps it was her unexpected ballsy streak. Either way, this strange pull they felt toward one another was without precedent. That much had become clear in the back of the limousine. With a single touch of her hand on his face, he'd known that she felt it, too. Whatever this was.

And now here they were, in the grand lobby of Lincoln Center, surrounded by people and cameras and blinding flashbulbs. Yet for all the distractions, Artem's senses were aware of one thing and one thing only— the whisper-thin fabric of her lovely dress beneath his hand as he guided her through the crowd. Just a fine layer of tulle between his flesh and hers.

It was enough to drive a man mad.

He somehow managed to answer a few more questions from lingering reporters before handing the usher their tickets and moving beyond the press of the crowd into the inner lobby.

"Welcome, Mr. Drake." The usher smiled, then nodded at Ophelia. "Good evening, miss."

"Thank you," she said, glancing at the ticket stubs as he passed them back to Artem.

Artem kept his hand planted on the small of her back as he led her to the lobby bar. It took every ounce of self-control he possessed not to keep that hand from sliding down, over the dainty, delectable curve of her behind, in plain view of everyone.

Get ahold of yourself.

His hand had no business on her bottom. Not here, nor anyplace else. Things were so much simpler when he could stick to the confines of his office.

Just as Artem realized he'd begun to think of the corner office as his rather than his father's, Ophelia turned to face him. Tulle billowed beneath his fingertips. He really needed to take his hands off her altogether. He would. Soon.

"I haven't even asked what we're seeing this evening. What's the repertoire?" She frowned slightly, as if trying to remember something. Like she had a catalog of ballets somewhere in her pretty head.

Artem hadn't the vaguest idea. Mrs. Burns had handed him an envelope containing the tickets as he'd walked out the door at five o'clock. He examined the ticket stubs and his jaw clenched involuntarily.

You've got to be kidding me.

"Artem?" Ophelia blinked up at him.

"Petite Mort," he said flatly.

"Petite Mort," she echoed, her cheeks going instantly pink. "Really?"

"Really." He held up the ticket stubs for inspection.

She stared at them. "Okay, then. That's certainly… interesting."

He lifted a brow.

"Petite mort means 'little death' in French," Ophelia said, with the seriousness of a reference librarian. She'd decided to tackle the awkwardness of the situation head-on, apparently. Much to Artem's chagrin, he found this attitude immensely sexy. "It's a euphemism for…"

"Orgasm." Artem was uncomfortably hard. In the champagne line at the ballet. Marvelous. "I'm aware."

What had he done to deserve this? Fate must be seriously pissed to have dealt him this kind of torturous hand. Of all the ballets…

Petite Mort.

He'd never seen this performance. In fact, he knew nothing about it. Perhaps it wasn't as provocative as it sounded.

It didn't matter. Not really. His thoughts had already barreled right where they didn't belong. Now there was no stopping them. Not when he could feel the tender warmth of Ophelia's body beneath the palm of his hand. Not when she was right there, close enough to touch. To kiss.

He looked at her, and his gaze lingered on the diamonds decorating the base of her throat. That's where he wanted to kiss her. Right there, where he could feel the beat of her pulse under his tongue. There. And elsewhere.

Everywhere.

His jaw clenched again. Harder this time. *Petite Mort.* How was he supposed to sit in the dark beside Ophelia all night and not think about touching her? Stroking her. Entering her. How could he help but envision what she looked like when she came? Or imagine the sounds she made. Cries in the dark.

How could he not dream of the myriad ways in which he might bring about *her* little death? Her *petite mort*.

"Sir?" Somewhere in the periphery of Artem's consciousness he was aware of a voice, followed by the clearing of a throat. "Mr. Drake?"

He blinked against the image in his head—Ophelia, beneath him, bare breasted in the moonlight, coming apart in his arms—and forced himself to focus on the bartender. They'd somehow already made it to the front of the line.

He forced a smile. "My apologies. My mind was elsewhere."

"Can I get you anything, sir?" The bartender slid a pair of cocktail napkins across the counter, which was strewn with items for sale. Ballet shoes, posters, programs.

Artem glanced at the *Petite Mort* program and the photograph on its cover, featuring a pair of dancers in flesh-colored bodysuits, their eyes closed and limbs entwined. His brows rose, and he glanced at Ophelia to gauge her reaction, but her gaze was focused elsewhere. She wore a dreamlike expression, as if she'd gone someplace faraway.

Artem could only wonder where.

Ophelia had to be seeing things.

The pointe shoes on display alongside the *Petite Mort* programs and collectible posters couldn't possibly be hers. Being back in the theater was messing with her head. She was suffering from some sort of nostalgia-induced delusion.

She forced herself to look away from them and focus instead on the bartender.

"I hope you enjoy the ballet this evening." He smiled at her.

He looked vaguely familiar. What if he recognized her?

She smiled in return and held her breath, hoping against hope he didn't know who she was.

"Mr. Drake?" The bartender didn't give her a second glance as he directed his attention toward Artem.

Good. He hadn't recognized her. She didn't want her past colliding with her present. It was better to make a clean break. Besides, if anyone from Drake Diamonds learned who she was, they'd also find out exactly why she'd stopped dancing. She couldn't take walking into the Fifth Avenue store and having everyone there look at her with pity.

*Every*one or a certain someone?

She pushed that unwelcome question right out of her head. She shouldn't be thinking that way about Artem. She shouldn't be caressing his face in the back of limousines, and she shouldn't be standing beside him at the ballet with his hand on the small of her back, wanting nothing more than to feel the warmth of that hand on her bare skin.

And the repertoire. *Petite Mort.*

My God.

She sneaked another glance at the pointe shoes, mainly to avoid meeting her date's penetrating gaze. And because they were there. Demanding her attention. One shoe tucked into the other like a neat satin package, wound with pink ribbon.

They could have been anyone's pointe shoes, and

most probably were. The company always sold shoes that had been worn by the ballerinas. Pointe shoes that had belonged to the principal dancers sometimes went for as much as two-fifty or three hundred dollars, which provided a nice fund-raising boost for the company.

She told herself they weren't hers. Why would her shoes be offered for sale when she was no longer performing, anyway?

Still. There was something so familiar about them. And she couldn't help noticing they were the only pair that didn't have an autograph scrawled across the toe.

Beside her, Artem placed their order. "Two glasses of Veuve Clicquot Rosé, please."

He removed his hand from her back to reach for his wallet, and she knew it had to be her imagination, but Ophelia felt strangely unmoored by the sudden loss of his touch.

He looked at her, and as always it felt as though he could see straight inside her. Could he tell how fractured she felt? How being here almost made it seem like she was becoming the old Ophelia? Ophelia Baronova. "Anything else, darling?"

Darling.

He shouldn't be calling her darling. It was almost as bad as princess, and she hated it. She hated it so much that she sort of loved it.

"The pointe shoes." With a shaky hand, she gestured toward the pastel ballet shoes. "Can I see them please?"

"Of course, miss." The bartender passed them to her while Artem watched.

If he found it odd that she wanted to hold them, he

didn't let it show. His expression was cool, impassive. As always, she had no idea what he was thinking.

And for once, Ophelia didn't care. Because the moment she touched those shoes, she knew. She *knew*. If flesh had a memory, remembrance lived in the brush of her fingertips against the soft pink satin, the familiar heaviness of the shoe's box—its stiff square toe—in the palm of her hand and the white powder that stull clung to the soles from the backstage rosin box.

Ophelia had worn these shoes.

The ones she now held were custom-made by a shoemaker at Freed of London, as all her shoes had been. A maker who knew Ophelia's feet more intimately than she knew them herself. She remembered peeling back the tissue paper from the box the shoes had come in. She'd sewn the ribbons on them with her own hands. She'd pirouetted, done arabesques in them. She'd danced in them. She'd dreamed in them. They were hers.

She glanced at Artem, who was now busy paying for the champagne, and then fixed her gaze once again on the shoes clutched to her chest. She wanted to see. She needed to be sure.

Maybe she was imagining things. Or maybe she just wanted so badly to believe, she was spinning stories out of satin. Heart pounding, she unspooled the ribbons from around the shoes. Her hands shook as she gently parted the pink material and peered inside. Penned in black ink on the insole, as secret as a diary entry, were the words she most wanted to see:

Giselle, June 1. Ophelia Baronova's final performance.

The pointe shoes in her hands were the last pair of ballet slippers she'd ever worn.

"What have you got there?" Artem leaned closer, and Ophelia was so full of joy at her fortuitous discovery that she forgot to move away.

"Something wonderful." Not until she beamed up at him did she notice the intimacy of the space between them. But even then she didn't take a backward step. She was too happy to worry about self-preservation.

For once, she wanted to live in the moment. Like she used to live.

"I'd ask you to elaborate, but I'm already convinced. Anything that puts such a dazzling smile on your face is priceless as far as I'm concerned." Without breaking eye contact, Artem slid two one-hundred-dollar bills out of his slim leather wallet and handed them to the man behind the counter. "We'll take the shoes, too."

Unlike the kitten incident, Ophelia didn't utter a word of protest. "Thank you, Artem. Thank you very much."

He pocketed his wallet, lifted a brow and glanced curiously at the pointe shoes, still pressed lovingly to Ophelia's heart. "No arguments about how you can't accept them? My, my. I'm intrigued."

"Would you like me to argue with you, Mr. Drake?"

"Never," he said. "And somehow, always."

She shrugged, feigning nonchalance, while her heart beat wildly in her chest. Part of her, the same part that still yearned to kiss him with utter abandon, wanted to tell him the truth. But how could she possibly explain that the satin clutched to her chest was every bit as priceless as the Drake Diamond itself? Maybe even more so.

The pointe shoes her grandmother had worn for her final performance lived in a glass case at the Hermitage in Saint Petersburg, alongside the shoes of other ballet greats like Anna Pavlova and Tamara Karsavina. Ballerinas went through hundreds of pointe shoes during the course of their career. Usually more than a hundred pairs in a single dance season. But none was ever as special as the last pair. The pair that marked the end.

Until this moment, Ophelia hadn't even known what had become of them. She remembered weeping as a nurse at the hospital removed them from her feet the night she'd fallen onstage. Then there'd been the MRIs, the blood tests, the spinal tap. And then the most devastating blow of all. The diagnosis. In all the heartbreak, her pointe shoes had been lost.

Like so much else.

Jeremy must have taken them. And now by some twist of fate, she'd found them again. Artem had bought them for her, and somehow it felt as though he'd given her back a missing part of her heart. Holding the shoes, she felt dangerously whole again.

The massive chandeliers hanging from the lobby ceiling flickered three times, indicating the start of the performance was imminent.

"Shall we?" Artem gestured toward the auditorium with one of the champagne flutes.

Ophelia took a deep breath, suddenly feeling as light and airy as one of the tiny bubbles floating to the top of the glass in his hand. "Lead the way."

They were seated on the first ring in private box seats, which shouldn't have come as a surprise, but somehow did. Ophelia had never come anywhere near such prestigious seating in the theater. When she'd been with the ballet, she always watched performances from the audience on her nights off. But like the other dancers, she'd sat in the fourth ring, at the very tip-top of the balcony. The nosebleed section. Those seats sold for twenty dollars each. She couldn't even fathom what the Drake Diamond seats must have cost. No doubt it was more money than all the dancers combined got paid in a year.

What exactly did tens of thousands of dollars get you on the first ring of the theater? For one, it got you privacy.

The box was closed in all sides, save for the glorious view of the stage. Ophelia sank into her chair with the ballet shoes still pressed to her heart, and her stomach fluttered as she looked around at the gold crown molding and thick crimson carpet. This was intimacy swathed in rich red velvet.

The lights went black as Artem handed her one of the glasses of champagne. His fingertips brushed hers, and she swallowed. Hard.

But as soon as the strains of Mozart's Piano Concerto no. 21 filled the air, Ophelia was swept away.

The music seemed filled with a delicate ache, and the dancers were exquisite. Gorgeous and bare, in their nude bodysuits. There was no hiding in a ballet like *Petite Mort*. There were no fluffy tutus or elaborate costumes. Just the beauty and grace of the human body.

Ophelia had never danced *Petite Mort*. She'd never thought she had what it took to dance such a provocative ballet. It was raw. Powerful. All-consuming. In the way perfect sex should be.

Not that Ophelia knew anything about perfect sex. Or ever would.

No wonder she'd never danced this ballet. How could she dance something called *Petite Mort* when she'd never had an orgasm? Things with Jeremy hadn't been like that. He'd been more interested in the height of her arabesque than the height of passion. She'd never been in touch with her own sensuality. She'd done too much dancing and not enough living. And now it was too late.

She watched the couple performing the pas de deux onstage turn in one another's embrace, legs and arms intertwined, and she'd never envied anyone more in her entire life. Somehow, some way…if she had the chance, she'd dance the hell out of that ballet now.

If only she could.

She felt different about her body than she had before. More appreciative. Maybe it was knowing that she'd never dance, never make love, that made her realize what gifts those things were. Or maybe it was the way the man sitting beside her made her feel…

Like a dancer.

Like a woman.

Like a lover.

Artem shifted in his chair, and his thigh pressed against hers. Just the simple brush of his tuxedo pants against her leg made her go liquid inside. She slid her gaze toward him in the dark and found him watching her rather than the dancers onstage. Had he been look-ing at her like that the entire time?

Her breath caught in her throat, and the ache between her legs grew almost too torturous to bear. What was happening to her? The feeling that she'd had in the limo was coming back—the desire, the need. Only this time, she didn't think she had the power to resist it. It was the shoes. They'd unearthed a boldness in her. Ophelia Baronova was struggling to break through, like cream rising to the top of a decadent dessert.

The shoes in her hands felt like a sign. A sign that she could have everything she wanted.

Just this once.

One last time.

Another dance. Another chance.

Intermission came too soon. Ophelia's head was still filled with Mozart and dark decadence when the lights went up. She turned to face Artem and found him watching her again.

"What do you think?" he whispered, and the atypi-cal hoarseness in his voice scraped her insides with shameless longing.

Just this once.

"I think when this is over—" she leaned closer, like a ballerina bending toward her partner "—I want to dance for you."

Chapter Seven

A better man would have stopped her.

A better man would have asked the limo driver to take her back to her apartment instead of sitting beside her in silent, provocative consent as the car sped through the snowy Manhattan streets toward the Plaza. A better man wouldn't have selected Mozart's Piano Concerto no. 21 once they'd reached the penthouse and she'd asked him to turn on some music.

But Artem wasn't a better man. And he couldn't have done things differently even if his overindulgent life had depended on it.

Instead he sat in the darkened suite watching as she slipped on the ballet shoes she'd chosen at Lincoln Center, and wound the long pink ribbons around her slender ankles. He could feel the music pulsing dead center in his chest. Or maybe that rhythmic ache was simply a physical embodiment of the anticipation that had taken hold of him since she'd leaned into him at intermission, eyes ablaze, face flushed with barely contained passion.

I want to dance for you.

Artem would hear those words in his darkest fantasies until the day he died.

"Are you ready, Mr. Drake?" Ophelia asked, settling in the center of the room with her heels together, toes pointing outward and willowy arms softly rounded.

So damned ready.

He nodded. "Proceed, Miss Rose."

The lights of Fifth Avenue drifted through the floor-to-ceiling windows, casting colorful shadows between them. When Ophelia began to move, gliding with slow, sweeping footsteps, she looked almost like she was waltzing through the rainbow facets of a brilliant cut gemstone. Outside the windows, snow swirled against the glass in a hushed assault. But a slow-burning simmer had settled in Artem's veins that the fiercest blizzard couldn't have cooled. His penthouse in the sky had never seemed so far removed from the real world. Here, now, it was only the two of them. He and Ophelia. Nothing else.

No other people. No ghosts. No rules.

I want to dance for you.

The moment Ophelia rose up on tiptoe, Artem knew that whatever was transpiring before him wasn't about ballet. This was more than dance. So much more. It was passion and heat and life. It was sex. Maybe even more than that.

The only thing Artem knew with absolute certainty was that sitting in the dark watching the adagio grace of Ophelia dancing for him was the single most erotic moment he'd ever experienced.

It was almost too much. The sultry swish of her ballerina dress, the exquisite bend of her back, the dizzying pink motion of her pointed feet—all of it. Artem had to fight against every impulse he possessed in order to stay put, to let her finish, when all he wanted was to rise out of his chair, crush his lips to hers and make love to her to the timeless strains of Mozart.

To keep himself from doing just that, he maintained a vise grip on the arms of the leather chair. Ophelia fluttered past him on tiptoe with her eyes closed and her lips softly parted, so close that the hem of her skirt brushed against his knee. Artem's erection swelled to the point of pain. Had he been standing, his arousal would have crippled him. Dragged him to his knees. For a moment, he even thought he saw stars. Then he realized the flash of light came from the diamonds around Ophelia's neck.

It didn't occur to Artem to wonder about the shoes or how she'd known they would fit. Nor did he ask himself how she could move this way. Questioning anything about this moment would have been like questioning a miracle. A gift.

Because that's what she'd given him.

Every turn of her wrist, every fluid arm movement, every step of her pink satin feet was a priceless gift. Then she stopped directly in front of him and began a dizzying sequence of elaborate turns, and he swore he could feel the force of each jackknife kick of her leg dead center in his heart. He could no longer breathe.

Artem wasn't sure how long Ophelia danced for him. Somehow it felt like both the longest moment of his life and, at the same time, the most fleeting. He only knew that when the music came to an end, she stood before him breathless and beautiful, with her breasts heaving and her porcelain skin glistening with exertion. And he knew that he'd never witnessed such beauty in his life. He doubted he ever would again.

Without breaking her gaze from his, Ophelia lowered herself into a deep curtsy. At last—at *long* last—Artem rose and closed the distance between them. As gently as he could manage while every cell in his body throbbed with desire, he took her hand in his and lifted her to her feet.

She rose up on the very tips of her toes, so that they were nearly eye level. When she smiled, it occurred to Artem that he'd never seen her so happy, so full of joy. Even her eyes danced.

He glanced down at her feet and the satiny pink ribbons that crisscrossed her ankles in a neat X.

"I used to be a dancer," she whispered, by way of explanation.

Used to be? *Used to be* was ridiculous. Artem didn't know what had happened in her past, but something clearly had. Something devastating. It didn't matter what that something was. He wasn't about to let it steal anything from her. Or make her believe she was anything else less than what she was.

"No." He took her chin in his hand. "Ophelia, you *are* a dancer."

Her eyes filled, and a single tear slipped down her lovely cheek. Artem wiped it away with the pad of this thumb.

He wished he had a bouquet of roses to place in her arms. Petals to scatter at her feet. She deserved that much. That much and more. But all he had to offer was the ovation rising in his soul. So he did what little he could. He brought her hand to his lips and pressed a tender kiss there.

"Artem." With a waver in her voice, she took a backward step, out of his reach.

For a single, agonizing moment, he thought she was going to run away again. To glide right out of the penthouse on her pink-slippered feet. He wouldn't let her. Not this time.

She didn't run, though. Nor did she say a word.

She simply reached her lithe arms behind her and unfastened the bodice of her strapless gown. Artem felt like he lived and died a thousand *petite morts* in the time it took her dress to fall away. It landed on his floor in a whispery puff of tulle, right where it belonged, as far as he was concerned.

She was gloriously naked, save for the diamonds around her neck, just as he'd imagined. Only no fantasy could have prepared him for the exquisite sight of her delicate curves, her rose-tipped breasts and all that marble-white flesh set off to perfection by the glittering jewels and the pink satin ribbons wrapped round her legs.

"Ophelia, my God." He swallowed. "You're beautiful."

* * *

Who is this woman I've become?

By putting on the shoes and dancing again, Ophelia had thought she could be her old self just for a moment. Just for a night. But this bold woman standing in front of Artem Drake and offering herself in every possible way wasn't Ophelia Baronova any more than she was Ophelia Rose. This was someone she didn't recognize. Someone she'd never had the courage to be.

Someone who actually believed Artem when he called her beautiful.

She *felt* beautiful, adorned in nothing but diamonds and pink satin shoes. Beautiful. And alive.

And aching.

She needed him to touch her. Really touch her. She needed it so much that she was on the verge of taking his hand and placing it exactly where she wanted it.

She stepped out of the pile of tulle on the floor and went to him, feeling his gaze hot on her exposed skin. Then she wrapped her arms around his neck, rose up en pointe and touched her lips ever so gently to his.

Artem let out a long, agonized groan, and to Ophelia, the sound was sweeter than Mozart. She'd never had such an effect on a man before. She'd never considered herself capable of it. And now that she knew she could—on this man, in particular—it was like a drug. She wanted to see him lose control, for once. She wanted him as raw and needy as she felt.

She got her wish.

His tongue parted her lips and he kissed her violently. Hard enough to bruise her mouth. He pulled her against him, and it seemed wholly impossible that this could be their first kiss. Their lips were made for this. For worshipping one another.

God, was it supposed to feel this way? So deliciously dirty?

She slid against him, reveling in the sensation of his wool tuxedo against her bare skin. Her eyes fluttered open as his mouth moved lower, biting and licking its way down her neck until he found her nipples. She cried out when he took her breast in his mouth, and a hot ribbon of need seemed to unspool from her nipple to between her legs. In the glossy surface of the snow-battered window, she caught a glimpse of their reflection and was stunned by what she saw—her bare body writhing against Artem, who had yet to shed a single article of clothing.

Before she could bring herself to feel an ounce of shame, he gathered her in his arms and carried her to his massive bed, that blanketed wonderland that had so intimidated her the first time she'd been here. Had it been only fourteen days ago that they'd sworn to one another they had no desire to sleep together?

She'd been lying then. Lying through her teeth. Ophelia had wanted this since the moment she'd set eyes on Artem Drake. No, not *this*. Not exactly. Because she hadn't known anything like *this* existed.

She struggled to catch her breath as Artem set her down on the impossibly soft sheets. Then he leaned over her and kissed her again, with long, slow thrusts of his tongue now, as if his body was telling her they had all the time in the world and he intended to make good use of every wanton second. As his hands found her hair and unwound her ballerina bun, she couldn't stop touching his face—his perfect cheekbones, his chiseled jaw and that secret place where his dimple flashed in those rare, unguarded moments when he smiled. The most beautiful man she'd ever seen, looking down at her as if he'd been waiting for this moment as long as she had. It hardly seemed possible.

He wound a finger in the diamonds around her neck and grinned as wickedly as the devil himself. "My grace."

Ophelia balled the sheets in her fists, for fear she might float away. Everything seemed to be happening so fast, yet somehow not quickly enough. She wasn't sure how long she could survive the heavenly warmth flowing through her. It was beginning to bear down on her. Hot and insistent. Then Artem moved his hand lower, and lower still, drawing a tremulous, invisible line down her body, until with a gentle touch he parted her and slipped his fingers inside her.

"Oh," she purred, in a voice she'd never heard come out of her mouth.

"Ophelia, open your eyes. Look at me."

She obeyed and found him watching her, his gaze filled with dark intention. His hand began moving faster. Harder, until she had to bite her lip to keep from crying out.

Before she knew what was happening, he'd begun kissing his way down her body. And were those really her breasts, arching obscenely toward his mouth?

And were those her thighs, pressed together, holding his hand in place?

Yes, yes they were. Artem's touch had made her a slave to sensation. She'd lost all ability to control her body, this body she'd once moved with such perfect precision.

Then his mouth was poised over her center, and she found she couldn't breathe for wanting.

"Please," she whimpered. *Oh, please.*

She wasn't even sure what she was begging for. Just some kind of relief from this exquisite torture.

"Shh," Artem murmured, and his breath fluttered over her, causing a fresh wave of heat to pool between her legs. It was excruciating. "I'm here, kitten."

Kitten.

Oh, God.

He pressed a tender kiss to the inside of one thigh, then the other, and the graze of his five o'clock shadow against her sensitive, secret places nearly sent her over the edge.

Then his mouth was on her, kissing, licking, tasting, and it was too much. She suddenly felt too exposed, too vulnerable. She was drowning in pleasure, and she knew that if she let it pull her under, there would be no turning back. No forgetting.

How could she return to normal life after this? How could she live the rest of her life alone, knowing what she was missing?

"Relax, kitten," Artem said in a hoarse whisper. He sounded every bit as wild and desperate as she felt. "I want to see you come. Let go."

He slipped a finger inside her again and she closed her eyes, tangled her fingers in his hair and held on for dear life. She didn't want to lose this moment to worry and fear. She wanted to stay. Here.

In this bed.

With this man.

So she did it. She let go. And the instant she stopped fighting it and let the blissful tide sweep her away, she shattered.

Stars exploded behind her eyes and she went completely and utterly liquid. She felt like she was blossoming from the very center of her being, and for the first time, the concept of *petite mort* made sense. *Little death.* Because it was like she'd died and gone someplace else. Somewhere dreamlike and enchanted. She could feel herself throbbing against Artem's hand, and it seemed as though he held her entire life force, every heartbeat she'd ever had, in the tips of his fingers.

And still he lapped and stroked, prolonging her pleasure, until it began to build again. Which seemed wholly unbelievable. She wouldn't survive it again. So soon? Was that even possible?

"Artem," she protested, even as she arched beneath him, seeking it again, that place of impossible light. Wanting him to take her there.

"Yes, kitten?" He pressed a butterfly-soft kiss to her belly and stood.

Ophelia had come completely apart, and there he was. Still fully dressed in a tuxedo, with his bow tie crooked just a fraction of an inch. He looked like he could have just walked out of a black-tie board of directors meeting…aside from the impressive erection straining the confines of his fly.

Ophelia swallowed. Hard. She needed to see him, to feel him.

Now.

She rose up on her knees and ran her hands over the expanse of his muscular chest. He cupped her breasts and pressed a kiss to her hair as she slid her palms under his lapels and pushed his jacket down his arms. It landed on the floor with a soft thud.

"Are you undressing me, Miss Rose?" he growled, and bent to take a nipple in his mouth. That crimson ribbon of need unwound inside her again, and she arched into him.

"I am." She sighed, dispensing with his shirt as quickly as she could manage. One of his cuff links flew off and bounced across the floor. Neither of them batted an eye.

She had no idea what she was doing. She'd never undressed a man in her life, but she was no longer nervous, hesitant or the slightest bit bashful. He'd unlocked something in her. Something no man had ever come close to discovering. Something wild and free.

She unzipped his fly and slid her hand inside, freeing him. He was hard—harder than she'd imagined he could possibly be—and big. Intimidatingly big. But the weight of his erection in her hands sent a thrill skittering up her spine.

She linked her gaze with Artem's and stroked him. He moaned, and his eyes went dark. Dreamy. *Bedroom eyes*, she thought. Watching him watch her as she pleasured him made her head spin. As if she'd done too many pirouettes. Ophelia's pulse pounded in the hollow of her throat, right where Princess Grace's diamonds nestled.

When she bent to take him in her mouth, Artem's hands found her hair. He wound her curls around his fingers and she could feel a shudder pass through him as surely as if it had passed through her own body. After this, after tonight, they would be tied to one another. Forever. Years from now, when her condition grew worse and she could no longer dance or even walk, she would remember this night. She would remember that she had once been cherished and adored. And when she closed her eyes and came back to this bed in her dreams, the face she would see in those stolen moments would be Artem's.

He might forget her someday. He probably would. There would be other women in his life, other mistresses. She wasn't foolish enough to believe that making love to her would change anything for him.

But it would change everything for her. It already had. *He* already had.

"Oh, kitten…" He hissed, and his fists tightened their grip on her hair.

She looked at up him. She wanted to etch this moment in memory. To somehow make it permanent.

He pulled her back up to her knees on the bed and rested his forehead against hers. "I need to be inside you," he whispered.

A knot lodged in her throat. Unable to speak, barely able to breathe, she nodded. *Yes, yes please.*

Then he was on top of her, covering her with the heat of his perfectly hard, perfectly male body. He stroked her face and kissed her closed eyelids as his arousal nudged at her center.

Ophelia had expected passion. She'd expected frenzy. And Artem had given her those things in spades. But this unexpected tenderness was more than she could bear. Then he groaned as he pushed inside, and she realized exactly how unprepared she'd been for the dangers of making love to Artem Drake.

Her pulse roared in her ears.

Remember.

Remember.

Remember.

Then with a mighty thrust, he pushed the rest of the way inside and Ophelia knew there would be no forgetting.

How could she ever forget the way the muscular planes of his beautiful body felt beneath her fingertips, or the glimmer of pleasured pain in his dark eyes, or the catch in her throat when at last he entered her? And the fullness, the exquisite fullness. She felt complete. Whole. Healed.

She knew it didn't make sense, and yet somehow it did. With Artem moving inside her, everything made sense. Because in that moment of sweet euphoria, nothing else mattered. Not her past, not her future, not even her disease. Nothing and no one else existed. Just she and Artem.

Which was the sort of thing someone in love would think.

But she wasn't in love with him. She couldn't be in love. With *anyone*. Least of all Artem Drake.

This was lust. This was desire. It wasn't love. It couldn't be. Could it?

No. Please no. No, no, no.

"Yes," Artem groaned, gazing down at her with an intensity that made her heart feel like it was ripping in half. Two pieces. Before and after.

"Yes," she whispered in return, and she felt herself nodding as she undulated beneath him, even as she told herself it wasn't true.

You don't love him. You can't.

She could feel Artem's heartbeat crashing against hers. She was free-falling again, lost in sensation and liquid pleasure. Her breath grew quicker and quicker still. She looked into his eyes, yearning, searching, and found they held the answers to all the questions she'd ever had. Somewhere behind him, snow whirled in dreamlike motion as he reached between their joined bodies to stroke her.

"Die with me, Ophelia," he whispered.

La petite mort.

Die with me.

With those final words, she perished once again and fell alongside Artem Drake into beautiful oblivion.

Chapter Eight

Artem slept like the dead.

Hours later, he woke to find Ophelia's shapely legs
entwined with his and the pink ballet shoes still on her
feet. Moonlight streamed through the windows, casting her porcelain skin in a luminescent glow. He felt
as though he had a South Sea pearl resting in his arms.

What in the world had happened? He'd done the one
thing he'd vowed he wouldn't do.

He wound a lock of Ophelia's hair around his fingers
and watched the snow cast dancing shadows over her
bare body. God, she was beautiful. Artem had seen a
lot of beauty in his life—dazzling diamonds, precious
gemstones from every corner of the earth. But nothing
he'd ever experienced compared to holding Ophelia in
his arms. She was infinitely more beautiful than the dia-

monds that still decorated her swan-like neck. Thinking about it made his chest ache in a way that would have probably worried him if he allowed himself to think about it too much.

There would be time for thinking later. Later, when he had to sit across a desk from her at Drake Diamonds and not reach for her. Later, when all eyes were on the two of them and he'd have to pretend he hadn't been inside her. Later, when he walked into his office and saw the portrait of his father.

He wasn't Geoffrey Drake. Artem may have crossed a line, but that didn't make him his father. He refused to let himself believe such a thing. Especially not now, with Ophelia's golden mane spilled over his pillow and her heart beating softly against his.

He let his gaze travel the length of her body, taking its fill. Arousal pulsed through him. Fast and hard. What had gotten into him? She'd reduced him to a randy teenager. Insatiable.

He should let her rest awhile. And should remove the pointe shoes from her feet so she could walk come morning.

He slipped out of bed, trying not to wake her, and gingerly took one of her feet in his hands. He untied the ribbon from around her ankle, and the pink satin slipped like water through his fingers. As gently as he could, he slid the shoe off her foot. She let out a soft sigh, but within seconds her beautiful breasts once again rose and fell with the gentle rhythm of sleep.

Artem cradled the pointe shoe in his hands for a moment, marveling at how something so lovely and delicate in appearance could support a woman standing on the tips of her toes. He closed his eyes and remembered Ophelia moving and turning across his living room. Poetry in motion.

He opened his eyes, set her shoe down on the bedside table and went to work removing the other one. It slipped off as quietly and easily as the first.

As he turned to place it beside its mate he caught a glimpse of something inside. Script that looked oddly like handwriting. He took a closer look, folding back the edges of pink satin to expose the shoe's inner arch.

Sure enough, someone had written something there.

Giselle, June 1. Ophelia Baronova's final performance.

Artem grew very still.

Ophelia Baronova?

Ophelia.

It couldn't be a coincidence. That he knew with the utmost certainty. It wasn't exactly a commonplace name. Besides, it explained why the shoes had fit. How she'd known she could dance in them. On some level, he'd known all along. Tonight hadn't been some strange balletic Cinderella episode. These were Ophelia's shoes. They always had been.

It explained so much, and at the same time, it raised more questions.

He studied the sublimely beautiful woman in his bed. Who was she? Who was she really?

He fixed his gaze once again on the words carefully inscribed in the shoe.

Baronova.

Why did that name ring a bell?

"I can explain." Artem looked up and found Ophelia holding the sheet over her breasts, watching him with a guarded expression. Her gaze dropped to the shoe that held her secrets. "It was my stage name. It's a family name, but my actual name is Ophelia Rose. I didn't falsify my employment application, if that's what you're thinking."

Her *employment application*? Did she think he was worried about what she'd written on a piece of paper at Drake Diamonds, while she was naked in his bed?

"I don't give a damn about your employment application, Ophelia." He hated how terrified she looked all of a sudden. Like he might fire her on the spot, which was absurd. He wasn't Dalton, for crying out loud.

"It's just—" she swallowed "—complicated."

Artem looked at her for a long moment, then positioned the shoe beside the other one on the nightstand and sat next to her on the bed. He could deal with complicated. He and complicated were lifelong friends.

He cradled her face in his hands and kissed her, slowly, reverently, until the sheets slipped away and she was bared to him.

This was how he wanted her. Exposed. Open.

He didn't need for her to tell him everything. It was enough to have this—this stolen moment, her radiant body, her passionate spirit. He didn't give a damn about her name. Of all people, Artem knew precisely how little a name really meant.

"Please," she whispered against his lips. "Don't tell anyone. Please."

"I won't," he breathed, cupping her breasts and lowering his head to take one of her nipples in a gentle, openmouthed kiss. She was so impossibly soft.

Tender and vulnerable.

As her breathing grew quicker, she wrapped her willowy legs around his waist and reached for him. "Please, Artem. I need you to…"

"I promise." He slid his hands over her back and pulled her close. Her thighs spread wider, and she began to stroke him. Slow and easy. Achingly so.

She felt delicate in his embrace. As small and fragile as a music-box dancer. But it was the desperation in her voice that was an arrow to his heart.

It nearly killed him.

Which was the only explanation for what came slipping out next. "I'm not really a Drake, Ophelia."

No sooner had the words left his mouth than he realized the gravity of what he'd done. He'd never confessed that truth to another living soul.

He should take it back. Now, before it was too late.

He didn't. Instead, he braced for her reaction, not quite realizing he was holding his breath, waiting for her to stop touching him, exploring him…until she didn't stop. She kept caressing him as her eyes implored him. "I don't understand."

"I'm a bastard," he said. "In the truest sense of the word."

"Don't." She kissed him, and there was acceptance in her kiss, in the intimate way she touched him. Acceptance that Artem hadn't even realized he needed. "Don't call yourself that."

His father had used that word often enough. Once he'd found out about Artem's existence, that is. "My real mother worked at Drake Diamonds. She was a cleaning woman. She died when I was five years old. Then I went to live in the Drake mansion."

Dalton had been eight years old, and his sister Diana had been six. Overnight, Artem had found himself in a family of strangers.

Wouldn't the tabloids have a field day with that information? It was the big, whopping family secret. And after keeping it hidden for his entire life, he'd just willingly disclosed it to a woman he'd known for a fortnight.

"Oh, Artem." Her lips brushed the corner of his mouth and her hands kept moving, kept stroking.

And there was comfort in the pleasure she offered. Comfort and release.

Artem didn't know her story. He didn't have to. Ophelia was no stranger to loss. Her pain lived in the sapphire depths of her eyes. He could see it. She understood. Maybe that was even part of what drew him toward her. Perhaps the imposter in her had recognized the imposter in him.

But he couldn't help being curious. Why the secrecy? *Slow down. Talk things through.*

But he didn't want to slow down. Couldn't.

"Kitten," he murmured, his breath growing ragged as he moved his hands up the supple arch of her spine.

She was so soft. So feminine. Like rose petals. And she felt so perfect in his arms that he didn't want to revisit the past anymore. It no longer felt real.

Ophelia was the present, and she was real. Nothing was as authentic as the way she danced. Reality was the swell of her breasts against his chest. It was her tender voice as she whispered in his ear. It was her warm, wet center.

Then there were no more words, no more confessions. She was guiding him into her, taking him fully inside. All of him. His body, his need, his truths.

His past. His present.

Everything he was and everything he'd ever been.

He didn't know what time it was when he finally heard the buzzing of his cell phone from inside the pocket of his tuxedo jacket, still in a heap on the floor. Pink opalescent light streamed through the windows, and he could hear police sirens and the rumble of taxicabs down below. The music of a Manhattan morning.

Artem wanted nothing more than to kiss his way down Ophelia's body and wake her in the manner she so deserved, but before he could move a muscle the phone buzzed again. Then again.

And yet again.

Artem sighed mightily, slid out of bed and reached for his tuxedo jacket. He fished his phone from the pocket and frowned when he caught his first glimpse of the screen. Twenty-nine missed calls.

Every last one of them was from his brother.

Bile rose to the back of his throat as he remembered the last time Dalton had blown up his phone like this. That had been two months ago, the night of their father's heart attack. By the time Artem had returned Dalton's calls, Geoffrey Drake had been dead for more than four hours.

He dialed his brother's number and strode naked across the suite, shutting himself in his small home office so he wouldn't wake Ophelia.

Dalton answered on the first ring. "Artem. Finally."

"What's wrong?" he asked, wondering why Dalton sounded as cheerful as he did. Artem wasn't sure he'd ever heard his brother this relaxed. Relaxing wasn't exactly the elder Drake's strong suit.

"Nothing is wrong. Nothing at all. In fact, everything is right." He paused. Long enough for alarm bells to start sounding in the back of Artem's consciousness. Something seemed off. "You, my brother, are a genius."

Now he was really suspicious. Dalton wasn't prone to flattery where Artem was concerned. Although he had to admit *genius* had a better ring to it than *bastard*. "What's going on, Dalton? Go ahead and tell me in plain English. I'm rather busy at the moment."

"Busy? At this hour? I doubt that." Artem could practically hear Dalton's eyes rolling. At least something was normal about this conversation. "I'm talking about the girl."

Artem's throat closed. He raked a hand through his hair and involuntarily glanced in the direction of the bed. "To whom are you referring?"

The girl.

Dalton was talking about Ophelia. Artem somehow just knew. He didn't know why, or how, but hearing Dalton refer to her so casually rubbed him the wrong way.

"Ophelia, of course. Your big discovery." Dalton let out a laugh. "She's not who we think she is, brother."

So the cat was out of the bag. How in the world had Dalton discovered her real name?

"I know." But even as he said it, he had the sickening feeling he didn't know anything. Anything at all.

"You know?" Dalton sounded only mildly surprised. "Oh. Well, that's good, I suppose. Although you could have told me about her connection to the Drake Diamond before I had to hear about it from a reporter at *Page Six*."

Artem froze.

The Drake Diamond? *Page Six?* What the hell was he talking about?

"I can't believe we've had Natalia Baronova's granddaughter working for us this entire time," Dalton said. "You did a good thing when you recommended her designs. A really good thing. Like I said, genius."

Baronova. No wonder the name had rung a bell. "You mean the ballerina who wore the Drake Diamond back in the forties? *That* Natalia Baronova?"

"Of course. Is there another famous ballerina named Natalia Baronova?" Dalton laughed again. He was starting to sound almost manic.

"Ophelia is Natalia Baronova's granddaughter," Artem said flatly, once he'd put the pieces together.

He remembered how passionately she'd spoken about the stone, the dreamy expression in her eyes when he'd spied her looking at it, and how ardently she'd tried to prevent him from selling it.

Why hadn't she told him?

I can explain.

But she hadn't explained, had she? She'd just said that Baronova had been a stage name. She'd said things were complicated. Worse, he'd let her get away with it. He'd actually thought her name didn't matter. Of course, that was before he'd known her family history was intertwined with *his* family business.

Artem had never hated Drake Diamonds so much in his life. He'd never much cared for it before and had certainly never wanted to be in charge of it. He could remember as if he'd heard them yesterday his father's words of welcome when he'd come to live in the Drake mansion.

I will take care of you. You're my responsibility and you will never want for anything, least of all money, but Drake Diamonds will never be yours. Just so we're clear, you're not really a Drake.

Artem had been five years old. He hadn't even known what the new man he called Father had even meant when he said, "Drake Diamonds." Oh, but he'd learned soon enough.

He should have tendered his resignation as CEO just like he'd planned. It had been a mistake. All of it. He'd stayed because of her. Because of Ophelia. He hadn't wanted to admit it then, but he could now. Now that he'd tasted her. Now that they'd made love.

It was bad enough that she had any connection to Drake Diamonds at all. But now to hear that she had a connection to the diamond… Worse yet, he had to hear it from his brother.

He should have pushed. He should have known

something was very wrong when she'd mentioned her employment application. He should have demanded to know exactly whom he'd taken to bed.

Instead he'd told her things she had no business knowing. Of course, she had no business in his bed, either. She was an employee. Just as his mother had been all those years ago.

Pain bloomed in Artem's temples. He'd been at the helm of Drake Diamonds for less than three months and already history had repeated itself. *Because* you *repeated it.*

"Natalia Baronova's granddaughter. I know. That's what I just said." Dalton cleared his throat. "I've set up a meeting for first thing Monday morning. You. Me. Ophelia. We've got a lot to discuss, starting with the plans for the Drake Diamond."

A meeting with Dalton and Ophelia? First thing Monday morning? Spectacular. "There's nothing to talk about. We're selling it. My mind is made up."

"Since when?" Dalton sounded decidedly less thrilled than he had five minutes ago.

"Since now." It was time to start thinking with his head. Past time. The company needed that money. It was a rock. Nothing more.

"Come on, Artem. Think things through. We could turn this story into a gold mine. We've got a collection designed by Natalia Baronova's granddaughter, the tragic ballerina who was forced to retire early. Those ballerina rings are going to fly out of our display cases."

Tragic ballerina? He glanced at the closed door that

led to the suite's open area, picturing Ophelia, naked and tangled in his sheets. Perfect and beautiful.

Then he thought about the sad stories behind her eyes and grew quiet.

"I'll crunch the numbers. It might not be necessary to sell the diamond," Dalton said. "Sleep on it."

Artem didn't need to sleep on it. What he needed was to get off the phone and back into the bedroom so he could get to the bottom of things.

Tragic ballerina...

He couldn't quite seem to shake those words from his consciousness. They overshadowed any regret he felt. "You mentioned *Page Six*. Tell me they're not doing a piece on this."

Not yet.

He needed time. Time to figure out what the hell was going on. Time to get behind the story and dictate the way it would be presented. Time to protect himself.

And yes, time to protect Ophelia, too. From what, he wasn't even sure. But given the heartache he'd seen in her eyes when she'd asked him to keep her stage name a secret, she wasn't prepared for that information to become public. Not now. Perhaps not ever.

Tragic ballerina...

He'd made her a promise. And even if her truth was infinitely more complicated than he'd imagined, he would keep that promise.

"Why on earth would you want me to tell you such a thing? The whole point of your appearance at the ballet last night was to create buzz around the new collection."

"Yes, I know. But..." Artem's voice trailed off.

But not like this.

"The story is set to run this morning. It's their featured piece. They called me last night and asked for a comment, which I gave them, since you were unreachable."

Because he'd been making love to Ophelia.

"You can thank me later. We couldn't buy this kind of publicity if we tried. It's a pity about her illness, though. Truly. I would never have guessed she was sick."

Artem's throat closed like a fist. He didn't hear another word that came out of his brother's mouth. Dalton might have said more. He probably did. Artem didn't know. And he didn't care. He'd heard the only thing that mattered.

Ophelia was sick.

Ophelia woke in a dreamy, luxurious haze, her body arching into a feline stretch on Artem's massive bed. Without thinking, she pointed her toes and slid her arms into a port de bras over the smooth surface of the bedsheets, as if she still did so every morning.

It had been months since she'd allowed her body to move like this. In the wake of her diagnosis, she'd known that she still could have attended ballet classes. Just because she could no longer dance professionally didn't mean she had to give it up entirely. She could still have taken a class every so often. Perhaps even taught children.

She'd known all this in her head. Her head, though,

wasn't the problem. The true obstacle was her battered and world-weary heart.

How could she have slid her feet into ballet shoes knowing she'd never perform again? Ballet had been her love. Her *whole* life. Not something that could be relegated to an hour or so here and there. She'd missed it, though. God, how she'd missed it. Like a severed limb. And now, only now—tangled in bedsheets and bittersweet afterglow—did she realize just how large the hole in her life had become in these past few months. But as much as she'd needed ballet, she'd need this more. *This.*

Him.

She'd needed to be touched. To be loved. She'd needed Artem.

And now...

Now it had to be over.

She squeezed her eyes closed, searching for sleep, wishing she could fall back into the velvet comfort of night. She wasn't ready. She wasn't ready for the harsh light of morning or the loss that would come with the rising sun. She wasn't ready for goodbye.

This couldn't happen again. It absolutely could not. No amount of wishing or hoping or imagining could have prepared her for the reality of Artem making love to her. Now she knew. And that knowledge was every bit as crippling as her physical ailments.

I'm not really a Drake, Ophelia.

Last night had been more than physical. So much more. She'd danced for him. She'd shown him a part of herself that was now hers and hers alone. A tender, aching secret. And in return, he'd revealed himself to her. The real Artem Drake. How many people knew that man?

Ophelia swallowed around the lump in her throat. Not very many, if anyone, really. She was certain. She'd seen the truth in the sadness of his gaze, felt it in the honesty of his touch. She hadn't expected such brutal honesty. She hadn't been prepared for it. She hadn't thought she would fall. But that's exactly what had happened, and the descent had been exquisite.

How could she bring herself to walk away when she'd already lost so much?

She blinked back the sting of tears and took a deep breath, noting the way her body felt. Sore, but in a good way. Like she'd exercised parts of herself she hadn't used in centuries. Her legs, her feet. Her heart.

It beat wildly, with the kind of breathless abandon she'd experienced only when she danced. And every cell in her body, every lost dream she carried inside, cried out, *Encore, encore!* She closed her eyes and could have sworn she felt rose petals falling against her bare shoulders.

One more day. One more night.

Just one.

With him.

She would allow herself that encore. Then when the weekend was over, everything would go back to normal. Because it had to.

She sat up, searching the suite for signs of Artem. His clothes were still pooled on the floor, as were hers. Somewhere in the distance, she heard the soothing cadence of his voice. Like music.

A melody of longing coursed through her, followed by a soft knock on the door.

"Artem," Ophelia called out, wrapping herself in the chinchilla blanket at the foot of the bed.

No answer.

"Mr. Drake," a voice called through the door. "Your breakfast, sir."

Breakfast. He must have gotten up to order room service. She slid out of bed and padded to the door, catching a glimpse of her reflection in a sleek, silver-framed mirror hanging in the entryway. She looked exactly as she felt—as though she'd been good and thoroughly ravished.

Her cheeks flared with heat as she opened the door to face the waiter, dressed impeccably in a white coat, black trousers and bow tie. If Ophelia hadn't already been conscious of the fact she was dressed in only a blanket—albeit a fur one—the sight of that bow tie would have done the trick. She'd never felt so undressed.

"Good morning." She bit her lip.

"Miss." Unfazed, the waiter greeted her with a polite nod and wheeled a cart ladened with silver-domed trays into the foyer of the suite. Clearly, he'd seen this sort of thing before.

Possibly even in this very room, although Ophelia couldn't bring herself to dwell on that. Just the idea of another woman in Artem's bed sent a hot spike of jealousy straight to her heart.

He doesn't belong to you.

He doesn't belong to you, and you don't belong to him. One more night. That's all.

She took a deep breath and pulled the chinchilla tighter around her frame as the waiter arranged everything in a perfect tableau on the dining room table. From the looks of things, Artem had ordered copious amounts of food, coffee and even mimosas. A vase of fragrant pink peonies stood in the center of the table and the morning newspapers were fanned neatly in front of them.

"Mr. Drake's standard breakfast." The young man waved at the dining area with a flourish. "May I get you anything else, miss?"

This was Artem's standard breakfast? What must it be like to live as a Drake?

Ophelia couldn't even begin to imagine. Nor did she want to. She would never survive that kind of pressure, not to mention the ongoing, continual scrutiny by the press…having your life on constant display for the entire world to see. Last night had been frightening enough, and she hadn't even been the center of attention. Not really. The press, the people…they'd been interested in the jewelry. And Artem, of course. She'd just been the woman on Artem Drake's arm. There'd been one reporter who had looked vaguely familiar, but she hadn't directed a single question at her. Ophelia had been unduly paranoid, just as she had with the bartender.

"Miss?" the waiter said. "Perhaps some hot tea?"

"No, thank you. This all looks…" Her gaze swept over the table and snagged on the cover of *Page Six*.

Was that a photo of *her*, splashed above the fold? She stared at it in confusion, trying to figure out why in the world they would crop Artem's image out of the picture. Only his arm was visible, reaching behind her waist to settle his hand on the small of her back. A wave of dread crashed over her as she searched the headline. And then everything became heart-sickeningly clear.

"Miss?" the waiter prompted again. "You were saying?"

Ophelia blinked. She was too upset to cry. Too upset to even think. "Um, oh, yes. Thank you. Everything looks wonderful."

She couldn't keep her voice from catching. She couldn't seem to think straight. She could barely even breathe.

The waiter excused himself, and Ophelia sank into one of the dining room chairs. A teardrop landed in a wet splat on her photograph. She hadn't even realized she'd begun to cry.

Everything looks wonderful.

She'd barely been able to get those words out. Nothing was wonderful. Nothing at all.

She closed her eyes and still she saw it. That awful headline. She probably always would. In an instant, the bold black typeface had been seared into her memory.

Fallen Ballet Star Ophelia Baronova Once Again Steps into the Spotlight…

Fallen ballet star. They made it sound like she'd died.

You did. You're no longer Ophelia Baronova. You're Ophelia Rose now, remember?

And now everyone would know. *Everyone.* Including Artem. Maybe he already did.

He'd promised to keep her identity a secret. Surely he

wasn't behind this. Bile rose up the back of her throat. She swallowed it down, along with the last vestiges of the careful, anonymous life she'd managed to build for herself after her diagnosis.

She felt faint. She needed to lie down. But most importantly, she needed to get out of here.

One more night.

Her chest tightened, as if the pretty pink ribbons on her ballet shoes had bound themselves around her heart. There wouldn't be another night.

Not now.

Not ever.

Chapter Nine

Beneath the conference table, Artem's hands clenched in his lap as he sat and watched Ophelia walk into the room on Monday morning. He felt like hitting something. The wall, maybe. How good would it feel to send his fist flying through a bit of Drake Diamonds drywall?

Damn good.

He couldn't remember the last time he'd been as angry as he had when he'd finally ended the call with Dalton and strode back to the bedroom, only to find his bed empty. No Ophelia. No more ballet shoes on his night table. Just a lonely, glittering strand of diamonds left behind on the pillow.

He'd been gone a matter of minutes, and she'd left. Without a word.

At first, he simply couldn't believe it. There wasn't another woman in all of Manhattan who would dare do such a thing. No other woman had even had the chance. Artem had firm rules about sleepovers. He didn't partake in them.

Until the other night.

Nothing about his involvement with Ophelia was ordinary, though, was it? Since the moment he'd first spotted her in the kitchen at Drake Diamonds, he'd found himself doing things he'd never before contemplated. Staying on as CEO. Adopting kittens. Exposing dark secrets. He scarcely recognized himself.

He sure hadn't recognized the man who'd stormed through the penthouse suite, angrily searching for something. A sign, perhaps? Some leftover trinket, a bit of pink ribbon that would ensure that he hadn't imagined the events of the night before. A reminder that it had all been real. That spellbinding dance. The intensity of their lovemaking…

Then he'd seen the newspaper lying on the dining table, and he'd known.

She'd been the cover story on *Page Six*, and the article had been less than discreet. Worse, Ophelia had clearly seen it before he'd had a chance to warn her. The newsprint had been wet with what he assumed were tears, the paper still damp as it trembled in his hands. He must have missed her getaway by a matter of seconds.

"Mr. Drake." Without quite meeting his gaze, Ophelia nodded as she entered the room.

So they were back to formalities, were they? It took

every ounce of his self-control not to remind her that the last time they'd seen one another, they'd both been naked. And gloriously sated.

Just imagining it made him go instantly hard, which did nothing to soothe his irritation.

"Miss Rose," he said, sounding colder than he'd intended. "Or should I call you Miss *Baronova*?"

She went instantly pale. "I prefer Miss Rose."

"Just checking." Artem did his best impression of a careless shrug.

He did care, actually. That was the problem. He cared far too much.

Multiple sclerosis.

My God, how had he not known she was sick? How had he looked into those haunted eyes as he'd buried himself inside her and not realized it?

Artem was ashamed to admit that although he'd donated money to the National MS Society and even attended a few of their galas, his knowledge of the condition was less than thorough. He'd spent a good portion of the weekend online familiarizing himself with its symptoms and prognosis.

The article in *Page Six* had offered little hope and predicted that Ophelia would eventually end up in a wheelchair. Artem found this conclusion wholly beyond his comprehension. The idea that she would never dance again was impossible for him to accept. And it made the gift she'd given him all the more precious.

The story alleged she hadn't danced at all since her diagnosis. Artem hadn't needed to read those words to know it was true. There'd been something undeniably sacred about the ballet she'd performed for him. He could still see her spinning and twirling on pink satin tiptoes. As he slept, as he dreamed...even while he was awake. It was all he saw. Day and night.

Dalton had stood as she entered the room. "Good morning, Ophelia," he said now.

"Good morning." She aimed a smile at his brother. A smile that on the surface seemed perfectly genuine, but Artem could see the slight tremble in her lips.

He knew those lips. He knew how they tasted, knew what it felt like to bite into their pillowy softness.

Ophelia's smile faded as she glanced at him, then quickly looked away. Being around him again clearly made her uncomfortable. Good. He'd felt distinctly uncomfortable every time he'd tried to call her since her disappearing act. He'd felt even more uncomfortable when his knocks on her apartment door had gone unanswered. He'd felt so *uncomfortable* he'd been tempted to tear the door off its hinges and demand she speak to him.

He could help her. Didn't she know that? He could hire the best doctors money could buy. He could fix her...if only she'd let him.

Dalton cleared his throat. "We have a few things to discuss this morning."

The understatement of the century perhaps. Although what could Artem actually say to Ophelia with Dalton present? Nothing. Not a damn thing.

Ophelia nodded wordlessly. As angry as he was, it killed him to see her this way. Quiet. Afraid. His arms itched to hold her, his body cried out for her, even if logically he knew it would never happen. She'd made that abundantly clear.

Artem should have been fine with that. He should have been relieved. He didn't want a *relationship*. Never had. He didn't want marriage or, God forbid, children. His own childhood had been messed up enough to turn him off the idea for life. Even if he did want a relationship, she was still his employee. And Artem was *not* his father, recent behavior notwithstanding.

But sitting an arm's length away from Ophelia right now felt like torture. He felt anything but fine.

"I'd like to propose a new marketing campaign for the ballerina collection now that certain, ah, facts have come to light." Dalton nodded.

So he was going right in for the kill, was he? Artem's fists clenched even tighter.

"A new marketing campaign?" Ophelia's eyes went wide, and the panic Artem saw in their sapphire depths took the edge off his anger and softened it a bit. Changed it to something that felt more like sorrow. Deep, soul-shaking sorrow.

"Yes. I'm thinking a print campaign. Artful black-and-white shots, perhaps even a few television commercials, featuring you, of course."

"Me?" She swallowed, and Artem traced the movement up and down the slender column of her throat.

For a moment, he was transfixed. Caught in a memory of his mouth moving down Ophelia's neck. In his mind, he heard the soft shudder of a moan. He felt the tremulous beat of her pulse beneath his tongue. He saw a sparkling flash of diamonds against porcelain skin.

Then he blinked, and he was back in the conference room, with Ophelia appraising him coolly from the opposite side of the table.

If only Dalton weren't present. Artem would tell her exactly how enraged he felt about being ghosted. Or maybe he'd simply lay her down on the smooth oak surface of the table and use his mouth on her until she shattered.

Perhaps he'd do both those things.

But Dalton was most definitely there, and he was talking again. Going on about advertisements in the *Sunday Times* and a special catalog for the holidays. "You'll wear ballet shoes, of course. And a tutu."

Finally, *finally*, Ophelia looked at Artem. Really looked at him. If he'd thought he'd caught a glimpse of brokenness in her gaze before he'd known about her MS, it would have been unmistakable now. Somewhere in the sapphire depths of her gaze, he saw a plea. Someone needed to put a stop to what was happening.

The things Dalton was proposing were out of the question. How could his brother fail to understand that dressing the part of what she could no longer be would kill Ophelia? Artem could almost hear the sound of her heart breaking.

He cleared his throat. "Dalton…"

But his brother wasn't about to be dissuaded so easily. Clearly, he'd been mulling over new marketing strategies all weekend. "You'll wear the Drake Diamond, of course. I'd like to get it reset in your tiara design as soon as possible. You'll be the face of Drake Diamonds. Your image will be on every bus and in every subway station in New York. Possibly even a billboard in Times Square. Now I know you haven't performed in a while, but if you could dance for just a bit, just long enough to tape a commercial segment, we'd be golden."

Artem couldn't believe his ears. Now Dalton was asking Ophelia to dance? No. Just no. Ballet was special to her. Far too special to be exploited, even if it meant saving Drake Diamonds. Maybe Dalton wasn't capable of understanding just what it meant to her, since he'd never seen her dance. But Artem had.

He knew. He knew what it felt like to go breathless at the sight of her arabesque. He knew how just the sight of her arched foot could cause a man to ache with longing. Artem would carry that knowledge to his grave.

And Dalton expected her to dance for him? In a television commercial, of all things?

Ophelia would never agree to it. Never. Even if she did, Artem wouldn't let her.

Over his dead fucking body.

Ophelia did her best to look at Dalton and focus on what he was saying, as ludicrous and terrifying as it was, but he was beginning to look a bit blurry around the edges.

Not now. Please not now.

She hadn't even managed to get back to her own apartment on Saturday morning before her MS symptoms began to make themselves felt. She'd taken a cab rather than the subway, afraid of being spotted in public in her ball gown from the night before. The same ball gown she was wearing on the front page of the morning newspaper. As she'd sat in the backseat of the taxi, biting her lip and staring at the snow swirling out the window while she'd tried not to cry, she'd felt a strange numbness creeping over her.

It had started with her fingertips. Just a slight tingling sensation, barely noticeable at first. She'd stared down at her hands, clutching the pointe shoes she'd almost left behind, and realized she was shaking. That's when she'd known.

She'd been unable to stop the tears when she realized she'd become symptomatic. Fate hadn't exactly been kind to her lately, but this seemed impossibly cruel. Too cruel to believe. Her lips had still been swollen from Artem's kisses, her body still warm from his bed. Why did it have to happen then? Why?

Logically, she knew the answer. Stress.

The doctors had been clear in the beginning—stress could make her condition worse. Even a perfectly healthy body responded to stress, and as Ophelia was only too aware, her body was neither perfect nor healthy. Her medical team had counseled her to build a life for herself that was as stress-free as possible, which was why she'd begun volunteering at the animal shelter. And one of the multitude of reasons why she'd never considered dating. Or even contemplated the luxury of falling in love.

She'd slipped. Once. Only once.

For a single night, she'd forgotten she was sick. She'd allowed herself to live. Really live. And now her life, her secrets, everything she held dear, was front-page news. Something to read about over morning coffee.

All of that would have been stressful enough without the added heartbreak of knowing that Artem would see those words and that he'd never look at her the same way again. Never see her with eyes brimming with desire rather than pity.

It was no wonder her fingertips had gone numb. No wonder she'd fallen down when she'd exited the cab. No wonder the tingling sensation had only gotten worse when Artem had shown up at her apartment and practically beaten down the door, while she'd curled in the fetal position on the sofa with Jewel's tiny, furry form pressed to her chest.

She'd wished then that the numbness would overtake her completely. That it would spread from her fingers and toes, up her arms and legs, until it reached her heart. She wished she could stop feeling what she felt for him.

She missed him.

She missed him with an intensity that frightened her.

So the blurry vision really should have come as no surprise as she sat across from Artem in the Drake Diamonds conference room and listened to his brother's horrifying idea for promoting her jewelry collection.

Dalton wanted her to dance. On television.

"No," Artem said. Calmly. Quietly. But the underlying lethality in his tone was impossible to ignore.

"I beg your pardon?" Dalton said, resting his hands on the conference table.

"You heard me."

Dalton cast a tense smile in Ophelia's direction. "I think the choice is Ophelia's, Artem."

Ophelia cleared her throat. She suddenly felt invisible, which should have been a relief. But there was something strangely disconcerting about the way Artem studiously avoided her gaze, even as he came to her rescue.

Why was he doing this, even after she'd refused to take his calls or see him? She didn't know, and thinking about it made her heart hurt.

"That's where you're wrong, brother. The choice isn't hers to make because there *is* no choice. We're not doing the campaign. We're not resetting the Drake Diamond. It's going up for auction three weeks from today."

Wait. *What?*

Dalton let out a ragged sigh. "Tell me the contract hasn't been signed. Tell me it's not too late to undo this."

Artem shrugged as if they were discussing something as banal as what to order for lunch rather than a priceless gem that glittered with family history. Both his and hers. "The papers are on my desk awaiting my signature, but I'm not changing my mind. Ophelia will not wear your tiara, and neither will she dance in your ad campaign."

Silence fell over the room, so thick that Ophelia could hardly breathe.

She shook her head and managed to utter a single syllable. "Don't."

"Don't?" Artem turned stormy eyes on her. "Are you telling me you actually *want* to go along with this marketing strategy?"

"That's not what I'm saying at all." She slid her gaze to Dalton. "Dalton, I'm sorry. I can't. Won't, actually."

She'd needed to say it herself. The truth of the matter was she didn't need Artem to fight her battles. She could—and *should*—be fighting them herself.

She might be on the brink of a relapse, but she could still speak for herself and make her own decisions. Besides, Artem wouldn't always be there to take her side, would he? In fact, she couldn't figure out why in the world he was trying to protect her now. Other than the obvious—he felt sorry for her. Pity was the absolute last thing she wanted from him.

Exactly what do *you want from him?*

So many things, she realized, as a lump formed in her throat. Maybe even love.

Stop.

She couldn't allow herself to think that way. Despite his wealth and power, the man had obviously had a tumultuous emotional life. Could she really expect him to take on a wife who would certainly end up a burden?

Wife? *Wife?* Since when had she allowed herself to even fantasize about marriage? She needed to have her head examined.

"I don't understand." Dalton frowned.

"There's nothing to understand. You heard Miss Rose. She isn't dancing, and the diamond is going up for auction. Case closed." Artem stood and buttoned his suit jacket, signaling the meeting was over.

How was everything happening so fast?

"Wait," Ophelia said.

She'd lost her family. And her health. And ballet.

And she'd never have Artem, the only man she'd ever wanted.

But she would *not* lose the Drake Diamond. She

knew Artem would never understand. How could he? But that diamond—that *rock*, as he so frequently called it—was her only remaining connection to her family.

She would never marry. Never have children. Once she was gone, the Baronova name would be nothing more than a memory. She could live with that. She could. But that knowledge would be so much easier to swallow if only something solid, something real, remained. A memory captured in the glittering facets of a priceless jewel. A jewel that generations of people would come to see. People would come and look at that diamond, and they would remember her family.

The Baronovas had lived. They'd lived, and they'd mattered.

"Please, Artem." Her voice broke as she said his name. She was vaguely aware of Dalton watching her with a curious expression, but she didn't care. "Don't sell the diamond. Please."

Her eyes never left Artem's, despite the fact that being this close to him and pretending the memory of their night together didn't haunt her with every breath she took was next to impossible. She'd had no idea how difficult it would be to see him in this context. To sit a chaste distance apart when she longed for his touch. To see the indifference in his gaze when she could all but still feel him moving inside her. It was probably the hardest thing she'd ever done in her life apart from hearing her diagnosis. Maybe even worse.

Because if she'd only taken his calls or answered the door when he'd pounded on it, he wouldn't be looking at her like that, would he? He wouldn't be so angry he couldn't look her in the eye.

"I'm sorry, Miss Rose." But he didn't sound sorry at all.

Then he focused on the floor, as if she was the last person in the world he wanted to see. In that heartbreaking moment, Ophelia understood that pity wasn't the worst thing she could have found in his gaze, after all.

"My mind is made up. This meeting is adjourned."

Chapter Ten

Ophelia was certain Artem would change his mind at some point in the weeks leading up to the auction. He couldn't be serious about selling the diamond. Worse, she couldn't understand why he'd made such a choice. And why didn't Dalton put up more of a fight to keep it in the family?

Granted, the decision was Artem's to make. He was the CEO. The Drake family business was under *his* leadership. Not that he took to the mantle of authority with enthusiasm. After all, he'd been set to resign on the day they'd met.

And now she thought she knew why.

I'm not really a Drake, Ophelia.

She got a lump in her throat every time she thought about the look in his eyes when he'd said those words.

Storm-swept eyes. Eyes that had known loss and long-ing. Eyes like the ones she saw every time she looked in the mirror.

She and Artem had more in common than she would ever have thought possible.

But if what was being printed in the newspapers was any indication, he had every intention of going through with the sale of the diamond. And why wouldn't he, since he clearly felt no sentimental attachment to it?

She did, though. And now Artem knew exactly how much that diamond meant to her. The fact that he ap-parently didn't care shouldn't have stung. But it did.

She hated herself for wishing things could be dif-ferent. She'd slept with Artem. She'd thrown herself at him, naked in both body and soul, knowing it was for only one night. What had she thought would happen?

Not this.

Not the persistent ache deep in the center of her chest. Not the light-headed feeling she got every time she thought about him. Not the constant reminders ev-erywhere she turned.

Artem's face was everywhere. On the television. On magazines. In the papers. Details of the auction were front-page news. Appraisers speculated about the pur-chase price. Most of them agreed the diamond would go for at least forty-five million. Probably more.

If there was a silver lining to the sale of the diamond, it was that in the excitement over the auction, *Page Six* had all but forgotten about Ophelia. Up until the press release, her photo had been in the paper every day. The paparazzi gathered outside her building and followed her to work in the morning. They followed her to the subway station. They even followed her to her volunteer shifts at the animal shelter. It was beyond unnerving. Ophelia lived in fear of losing her balance and being photographed facedown on the pavement. She knew that was what the photographers were waiting for. A disastrous stumble. A breakdown. An image that showed how far she'd fallen since her glory days as a promising ballerina. Something that would make the readers cry for her. With her.

She was determined not to give it to them. She'd lost Artem. And now she was losing the diamond. She refused to lose her dignity. It was all she had left.

But once news of the auction broke, the mob outside her door vanished. Overnight, she became yesterday's news.

She knew she should be grateful. Or at the very least, relieved. But it was difficult to feel anything but regret as days passed without so much as a word from Artem. Or even a glimpse of him.

He hadn't set foot inside Drake Diamonds since that awful Monday morning in the conference room. Three weeks of silence. Twenty-one days of absence that weighed on her heavier than a fur blanket.

Even on the lonely Friday morning when the armed guards from Sotheby's showed up to remove the Drake Diamond from its display case on the sales floor, Artem had been conspicuously absent. Ophelia couldn't bring herself to watch.

Not until the day of the auction did she finally come to accept that not only was Artem actually going through with the sale of the diamond, but he might never return to Drake Diamonds. She might never see him again. Which was for the best, really. Absolutely it was. She wasn't sure why the prospect made her feel so empty inside.

Because you're in love with him.

No.

No, she wasn't. She was in love with the way he'd made her feel. That was different, wasn't it? It had to be. Because she couldn't be in love. With anyone. Least of all, Artem Drake.

The auction was set to begin at noon sharp, and the store had set up an enormous television screen in the ground level showroom. Champagne was being served, along with platters of Drake-blue petits fours and rock candy in the shape of emerald cut diamonds. It was a goodbye party of sorts, and half of Manhattan had shown up.

Ophelia shut herself in her tiny office and tried to pretend it was a regular workday. Her desk was covered in piles of half-drawn sketches for the new collection she was designing to mirror the art deco motif of the Plaza. But losing herself in her work didn't even help, because Artem's absence was there, too. The memory of their night together lived in the glittering swirl of the pavé brooch she'd finally finished. The unbroken pattern of the diamonds mirrored the whirl of a midnight snowfall, and the inlaid amethysts were as pale pink as her ballet shoes.

Would it always be this way? Was she destined to live in the past? In the grainy black-and-white photos of her grandmother's tiara and in the jewels that told the story of the night she'd made what had probably been the biggest mistake of her life?

Her fingertips tingled and the pencil slipped out of her hand. She tore the sheet of paper from her sketchpad and crumpled it in a ball, but she couldn't even manage to do that properly. It fell to the floor.

Ophelia sat staring at it, and reality hit her. Hard and fast. This was her present. Right here. This moment. Dropping things. Feeling frustrated. Missing someone.

It would also be her future. Her future wouldn't be one of diamonds and dancing or making love while a snowstorm raged against the windows of Artem's penthouse in the sky. It wouldn't be ballet or music or the velvet hope of a darkened theater. Her future would be moments just like this one.

She should never have slept with him.

She'd done what she'd set out to do. She was a jewelry designer at the most prestigious diamond company in North America, if not the world. She'd reinvented herself.

And still, somehow, it wasn't enough.

Artem slipped out of Sotheby's once the bids exceeded twenty million dollars, the sum total of the Drake Diamonds deficit, thanks to dear old dad and his worthless Australian mine.

Ophelia's ballerina diamonds had brought in close to five million in under a month, which was remarkable. Sometimes Artem wondered if it would have been enough. If they'd only had more time.

If...

Artem had never been one to indulge in what-ifs. Since his night with Ophelia, he'd been plagued with them. What if he'd been able to warn her about the article on *Page Six* before she found it herself? What if he wasn't her boss? What if she wasn't sick?

What if he'd never agreed to sell the diamond?

But none of that mattered, did it? Because all those obstacles existed. Now he just wanted to forget. He wanted to forget Drake Diamonds. He even wanted to forget Ophelia. He would have done anything to erase the memory of the way he'd felt when he'd seen her dance. Spellbound. Captivated. And now that night haunted him.

He just wanted out. *Needed* out.

So the moment the bidding escalated and he knew that Drake Diamonds would live to see another day, he left. Walked right out the door, and no one even seemed to notice. Even the reporters gathered at the back of the room were focused so intently on the auctioneer, they didn't see him as he strode past. For the first time in weeks, he slid into the backseat of his town car without being photographed.

"Home, sir?" the driver asked, eyeing him in the rearview mirror.

Artem shook his head. "The store."

"Yes, sir."

It was time to put an end to things. For good.

As expected, the showroom was a circus. The auction was still in progress, apparently, so once again his presence went wholly undetected. Good. He'd go upstairs, leave his letter of resignation on Dalton's desk and set things right. He'd do what he should have done weeks ago, before he'd gotten so hopelessly distracted by Ophelia Baronova.

The tenth floor was a ghost town. For once, there wasn't a single pair of doe-eyed lovers in Engagements trying on rings over champagne and petits fours. Artem wasn't sure whether he found the heavy silence a relief or profoundly sad. Perhaps a little bit of both.

He wasn't sure why he glanced inside the kitchen as he walked past. Probably because that's where he'd first seen Ophelia, where everything had changed. With one look. One word. One tiny bite of cake.

His gaze flitted toward the room, and for a moment, he thought he was seeing things. There she was, in all her willowy perfection, surrounded by champagne flutes and petits fours just as she'd been all those weeks ago. As if somehow his desire had conjured her into being.

He blinked and waited for her image to shimmer and fade, as it always did. Since the night she'd spent in his bed, he'd been haunted. Tormented. She moved through the shadows of his penthouse in balletic apparitions. A ghost of a memory.

He'd intentionally stayed away from the store so he wouldn't be forced to look at her. But still he'd seen her everywhere. So he was almost surprised when she spoke to him, confirming that she was, in fact, real and not just another one of his fantasies.

She said one word. His name. "Artem."

Her voice faltered a little.

He glanced at the petit four in her hand. It trembled slightly, either from nerves or a by-product of her MS. An ache formed in the center of his chest.

He'd once enjoyed toying with Ophelia, rattling her, getting under her skin. That was before he'd seen her so boldly confident when she'd stood before him and let her dress fall to the floor. He wanted that Ophelia back. He didn't want to frighten her. He wanted her fearless and bold. He wanted her breathless. He wanted her bared.

He wanted her.

Still. He always would.

How could she possibly be sick? Time and again, he'd tried to wrap his mind around it. He'd read all the articles about her in the papers. He'd even Googled the coverage of her incident onstage—the sudden fall that had led to her diagnosis. No matter how many times he saw the words in print, he still couldn't bring himself to believe it. It just didn't seem possible that a woman who could dance the way Ophelia had danced for him could have a chronic medical condition. She'd moved with such breathless abandon. How could it be true?

That dance was all he could think about. Even now. *Especially* now, as he stood looking at her in the Drake Diamonds kitchen. Again.

This was where they'd begun. He supposed it was only fitting they should end here, as well.

He just needed to get in and get out, to at *long last* tender his resignation and never set foot in the building again. He'd done what he needed to do. He'd sold the diamond. He'd saved the company.

He wasn't needed at Drake Diamonds anymore. Dalton could take it from here. It's what his brother had always wanted, anyway, and Artem was only too happy to let him.

"We must stop meeting like this, Ophelia," he said, trying—and failing—not to look at her mouth.

"You're back." She sounded less than thrilled. Good. *Get mad, Ophelia. Feel something. Anything.*

He shook his head. "Not really."

She rolled her eyes. "Don't tell me you're quitting again."

"As a matter of fact, that's exactly why I'm here."

She lowered the petit four to the plate in her hand and set it down on the counter. "I was joking."

He shrugged. "I'm afraid I'm not."

How ridiculous that the last conversation they would ever have would be about business. It was absurd.

"You're quitting?" Her voice softened to almost a whisper, but somehow it still seemed to carry the weight of all the words they'd left unsaid. "Is this because…"

Every muscle in Artem's body tensed. "Don't say it, Ophelia." He did *not* want to discuss his illegitimacy. Not here. Not now. "I'm warning you. Don't go there."

"You're the one who should be running this company, Artem. It's your birthright, just as much as it is Dalton's." She rested her hand on his forearm. Her touch was as light as a butterfly, but it was nearly his undoing. If he stayed another minute, he would kiss her. Another five, and he'd be tempted to lay her across the kitchen table.

He shrugged her off. "We're not having this discussion."

"Fine. But you should at least talk to your brother about it before you do something ridiculous like resign."

"You're the last person who should be lecturing me about quitting," he said, knowing even as he did that he was taking things too far. He couldn't seem to make himself stop, though.

"What are you talking about? I'm not the one quitting my job." She jammed her pointer finger into his chest. "You are."

"You're right about that. I'm quitting my job." He crossed his arms. "But you, my darling, have quit everything else. You've quit life."

Her eyes glittered with indignation. "You don't understand."

"Make me, Ophelia. Make me understand." He reached for her hand, but she pulled away.

Then she threw his words right back at him. "We're not having this discussion."

"As you wish." He nodded.

This was better. Anger was better than ache. She didn't want to discuss her illness any more than he wanted to discuss his family history. They had nothing left to say to one another.

Other than goodbye.

He took a deep breath. *Just say it. Say the words. Goodbye, Ophelia.*

"Goodbye, Artem." She brushed past him with an indifference he would have envied if he'd bought it for even a second.

He turned to stop her just in time to see her stumble.

The world seemed to move in slow motion as she lost her footing and fell against the kitchen counter. Artem rushed to her side, but she gripped the counter instead of his arm. She righted herself, then refused to meet his gaze.

"Are you all right?" He regretted the words the moment they left his mouth.

Of course she wasn't all right. She was sick. Nothing about that was right.

"I'm fine," she snapped.

But she didn't look fine. Far from it. Her skin had gone ghostly pale. He had the strangest feeling that she wasn't altogether there. As if in the midst of a conversation, she might fade and disappear.

"Don't." She shook her head. "Do not ask me if I'm all right. And please don't look at me like that."

"Like what?" he prompted. He was looking at her the only way he knew how. Like he missed her.

Because by God, he did. He knew he shouldn't. But he did.

"Like you feel sorry for me. Like I'm this fragile, broken creature that needs to be fixed." She lifted her chin and finally looked him in the eye. "That's not how I want you to see me."

"Your illness is the last thing I see when I look at you, Ophelia. Surely you know that."

She blinked, but her eyes didn't seem to fully take him in.

Artem needed her to hear him. He needed her to understand that he didn't see her as a tragic waif, but as a balletic beauty. Desire personified. Nothing would ever change that. Not even the goodbye that was on the tip of his tongue.

"Artem," she whispered. "I think I…"

Her voice was the first thing to fade away, then her lovely sapphire eyes drifted shut and she fell unconscious into his arms.

Chapter Eleven

She had to be dreaming.

The heat of Artem's body, the rustle of his smooth wool suit jacket against her cheek, the sheer comfort of once again being in his arms…none of it could be real.

She had to be dreaming.

Ophelia fought the instinct to open her eyes. Railed against it. She wanted to linger here in the misty place between sleep and wakefulness, the place where she could dream and dance. The place where things hadn't gone so horribly wrong.

No matter how hard she tried, though, she couldn't seem to stop the sounds of the real world from pressing in—the ding of a bell, a familiar grinding noise and the soothing cadence of Artem's voice.

"Ophelia, wake up. Please wake up."

Her eyes fluttered open, and though things looked hazy, as if she were seeing them through a veil, the familiarity of Artem's chiseled features was unmistakable. Her heart gave a little lurch as she took in the angle of his cheekbones and the sureness of his square jaw.

He was so close she could have reached out and traced the handsome planes of his face with her fingertips, if only she could move. But her arms seemed impossibly heavy. And she couldn't feel her legs beneath her at all. She *wasn't* dreaming, but what on earth was happening?

"Ah, Sleeping Beauty. You've returned." Artem smiled down at her.

He was here. He was smiling. And, oh, God, he was *carrying* her in his strapping arms.

She managed to lift one hand and push ineffectively against his chest. His solid, swoon-worthy chest. "Put me down."

His smile faded, which did nothing to lessen the effect of his devastating good looks. If anything, he was more handsome when he was angry, which was wrong on so many levels.

"No," he growled.

"Artem, I'm serious." Why did her voice sound so slurred?

"As am I. You fainted, and now I'm taking you to the hospital."

Fainted? *Hospital?*

She heard another ringing sound and managed to tear her gaze away from Artem. She recognized the close quarters now—the neat row of numbered buttons, the dark wood paneling, the crystal chandelier overhead. They were standing in the posh elevator of Drake Diamonds. Correction—*Artem* was standing. She most definitely was not.

"Put me down. I'm not letting you carry me through the showroom and out the front door of the store." There were hundreds of people downstairs, including the media.

He glared down at her. "And have you faint on me again? No, thank you."

The fog in her head began to clear, and things started coming back into focus. She remembered sneaking off to the kitchen. It had been the first time she'd set foot in there since the day she'd met Artem. When would she learn her lesson? And just what did the universe have against her indulging in a tiny bit of cake every now and then?

But had it really been a coincidence? Or somewhere deep inside had she been hoping he would come?

"Artem, please." She fought the sob that was making its way up her throat. "The photographers."

His blue eyes softened a bit, and he lowered her gently to her feet. He kept a firm grip on her waist, though, and all but anchored her to his side. "Hold on to me while we walk to the car. My driver is meeting us at the curb."

She nodded weakly. She felt impossibly tired as the reality of what just happened came crashing down on her.

She'd fainted. At work.

She'd fainted only one other time in her life, and that

had been the day her dancing career had ended. Why was this happening again? She was relapsing. It was the only explanation. For weeks now, she'd been experiencing minor symptoms. She'd been so ready to chalk them up to stress. But this was serious. She'd passed out.

In front of Artem, of all people.

The elevator chimed as they reached the ground floor, and he pulled her closer against him. In the final moments before the elevator doors swished open, he took her hand and placed her arm around his waist, all but ensuring they looked like lovers rather than what they were.

What were they, anyway? Ophelia didn't even know.

The doors opened. She blinked against the dazzling lights of the showroom and stiffened, resisting the instinct to burrow into Artem's side.

He whispered into her hair, "Do not let go of me, Ophelia. If you try to walk out of here on your own, I'll turn you over my shoulder and carry you out caveman-style while every photographer in Manhattan snaps your photo. Understood?"

Her cheeks flared with heat. "Fine."

The man was impossible.

And no, she didn't understand. Why was he doing this? Why didn't he just call an ambulance and let the paramedics carry her away on a stretcher? Surely he wasn't planning on actually accompanying her all the way to the hospital? When she'd fainted midperformance at the ballet, not one person had ridden with her to the ER. Not even Jeremy.

She kept her gaze glued to the floor as Artem escorted her across the showroom, through the rotating doors and onto the snowy sidewalk. Beside her, he spoke politely—charmingly even—to the photographers as the shutters on their cameras whirred and clicked. At first she didn't understand why. Then she realized he was putting on a show, distracting them from what was really going on. Everyone would think they were a couple now, but at least she wouldn't look sick and vulnerable in front of the entire world.

The press peppered him with questions. At first, they didn't make sense. Then, as she looked around, she realized what had happened. While she and Artem had been arguing in the kitchen, the auction had ended.

"Mr. Drake, do you have anything to say about the auction? Are you happy with the purchase price of fifty-six million?"

"How do you feel about the Drake Diamond moving to Mexico City?"

Mexico City? The diamond wouldn't even be in the country anymore.

Ophelia's knees began to grow weak as they approached the car. Artem's driver held the door open and she slid across the bench seat of the limousine. Artem followed right behind and eyed her with concern as she exhaled a deep breath and sank into the buttery leather.

Snowflakes swirled against the car windows and her heart suddenly felt like it could beat right out of her chest. This—Artem, the snow, the unexpected intimacy of the moment—stirred up every memory she'd been fighting so hard to repress, and brought them once again into sharp focus. She couldn't be here. Not with him. Not again.

"Artem." She would tell him to leave. To just go back inside and let the driver drop her off at the hospital. She'd be fine. She'd done this before all by herself. Why should this time be any different?

"Ophelia." He reached and cupped her cheek, and despite her best intentions, she let her head fall into the warmth of his touch.

She went liquid, as liquid as the sea, powerless to fight his pull. Because Artem was as beautiful as the moon, and whatever this was between them felt an awful lot like gravity.

"Thank you," she whispered.

Artem paced back and forth in Ophelia's hospital room, unable to sit still. At least he'd managed to get her immediately moved to a private room rather than the closet-sized space where they'd originally placed her. He'd walked in, taken a look around and marched right back out.

If she suspected his influence was behind her relocation to more acceptable surroundings, she didn't mention it. Then again, she wasn't exactly in fighting form at the moment. Case in point—she hadn't tried to kick him out of her room yet, which was for the best. Artem would rather avoid a nasty scene, and he had no intention of leaving her here. Alone.

She looked as beautiful as ever, asleep on the examination table with her waves of blond hair spilled on the pillow like spun gold. She looked like Sleeping Beauty, awaiting the kiss that would bring her back to life. The comparison brought an ache to Artem's gut.

She'd scared the hell out of him when she'd fainted. His heart had all but stopped the moment she slumped into his arms. He needed to know she was okay before he even thought about walking out the door.

Or out of her life.

But she wasn't okay. MS didn't simply go away. Artem could throw all the money he had at the situation, and it wouldn't do a bit of good. He'd never felt so helpless, so out of control, in his life. It didn't sit well. He'd thought he could fix this, if only she'd let him. Now he realized how very wrong he'd been.

The door opened, and a nurse in blue scrubs walked in. "Miss Rose?"

"She's sleeping," Artem said.

"I just have a few questions." The nurse smiled.

Artem did not.

They'd already listened to her heart, taken her pulse and filled up three vials with her blood. He was ready for answers or, at the very least, a conversation with an actual doctor.

He forced himself to quit pacing and stand still. "Is that really necessary?"

"I'm afraid so, Mr, ah..." She flipped through the folder in her hand until her gaze landed on a name. "...Davis."

Artem lifted a brow. "I beg your pardon. Who?"

"Miss Rose's emergency contact. Mr. Jeremy Davis. I'm sorry. I assumed that was you." She frowned down at the papers in her hand. Clearly, the staffers in the emergency room hadn't filled her in on Artem's identity, which probably would have irritated him if he hadn't been momentarily distracted by being called by another man's name. "Shall I give Mr. Davis a call?"

"No." Ophelia, awake now, sat bolt upright on the exam table. "Absolutely not. In fact, take his name off my paperwork."

Artem crossed his arms and regarded her as she studiously avoided his gaze.

The nurse made a few notes and then looked back up as her pen hovered over the page. "Whose name would you like to write down in place of Mr. Davis?"

"Um…" Ophelia cleared her throat. "Can we just leave that space blank for now? Please?"

The nurse shook her head. "I'm afraid we must have an emergency contact. It's hospital policy."

"Oh." Ophelia stared down at her lap. "In that case, um…"

"Allow me." Artem reached for the nurse's clipboard and pen.

"Artem, don't." Ophelia struggled to her feet.

"Sit. Down." His command came out more sternly than he'd intended, but he'd already had enough of a fright without watching her faint again and hitting her head on the hospital's tile floor.

Ophelia sat and fumed in silence while Artem finished scribbling his name and number, then thrust the clipboard back at the nurse. "Done. Now when can we talk to the doctor?"

He didn't want to think about why he thought it only proper that he should be Ophelia's emergency contact.

Nor did he want to contemplate the identity of Jeremy Davis. He just wanted to make Ophelia better.

What in the world was he doing? He'd never taken care of anyone in his life. He'd certainly never been anyone's emergency contact. Not even for his siblings. The truth of the matter was he'd carefully arranged his life in a way to avoid this kind of obligation. He'd had enough of those. He'd been an obligation his entire life—the child the Drakes had accepted because they'd had to. It was easier to remain entirely self-contained.

Except Ophelia didn't feel like a chore. She felt more like a need he couldn't quite understand.

This wasn't him.

"The doctor will be by any minute. We're just waiting on some test results from the lab." The nurse turned her attention back to Ophelia. "Can you tell me more about your symptoms? Have you been experiencing any dizziness before this morning?"

Ophelia nodded. "A little."

This was the moment he should leave. Or at the very least, step into the hallway. He'd delivered Ophelia to the hospital. He'd seen to it that she would have the best care money could buy. But in reality, her health was none of his business.

He glanced at her, fully expecting to be given his marching orders. She'd certainly never minced words with him before, which made it all the more poignant when she said nothing, but instead looked back at him with eyes as big as saucers.

She was afraid.

She was afraid, and if he left her now, she'd be sitting

in this sterile room in her flimsy paper gown, waiting for bad news all alone.

Artem felt an odd stirring in his chest. He sat beside her on the examination table and took her hand in his.

The nurse pressed on with more questions. "Any other problems associated with your MS? Tingling? Numbness?"

"Yes." Beside him, Ophelia swallowed. "And yes. In my hands mostly."

Artem stared down at their interlocked fingers. He'd had no idea she'd become symptomatic. Then again, since their night together he'd seen her only once—at that awkward meeting in the conference room.

"And how long has this been going on?" the nurse asked.

"Three weeks ago last Saturday," she said, with an unmistakable note of certainty in her tone.

Three weeks ago last Saturday. The morning after. That dark winter morning when everything had spun so wildly out of control.

Shit.

Artem felt like pummeling somebody. Possibly himself. The nurse gathered more information, but he could barely concentrate on what was being said. When she'd finally filled what seemed like a ream of paper with notes, she flipped her folder closed and left the room.

Before the door even clicked shut behind her, Ophelia cleared her throat. Artem knew what was coming before she said the words.

"You don't have to stay. I mean, thank you for everything you've done. But I understand. You don't want to be here, and that's fine. I don't blame you." She let out a laugh. "I don't want to be here myself."

"Stop," he said.

"What?"

He reached for her chin, held it in place and forced her to look at him. "Stop telling me how I feel. I'll leave when I'm good and ready. Not a minute before. Understood?"

She narrowed her gaze and prepared to argue, which he'd fully expected. Things that had perplexed and frustrated him before were beginning to make more sense—her reluctance to adopt the kitten, her abrupt announcement on the first day she'd set foot in his penthouse that she didn't have relationships. Or sex. Something…or some*one*…had convinced Ophelia that having a medical condition meant she had to close herself off from the rest of the world. He could see it now, as clear and sharp as a diamond.

Of course, that made it no less frustrating.

"I—" she started.

He cut her off, ready to get to the crux of the matter. "Who is Jeremy Davis?"

She lifted an irritated brow. He'd struck a nerve. Good. An angry Ophelia was far preferable to a frightened Ophelia.

"He's the director of the ballet company," she said primly.

"*And* your emergency contact?" he prompted, noting—to his complete and utter horror—how very much he sounded like a jealous boyfriend.

"Yes." She waited a beat, then added, "And my former fiancé."

"Fiancé?" Now he didn't just sound like a jealous boyfriend. He felt like one, too. Except he didn't have any claim on Ophelia. He had no right at all to these unwelcome feelings that had taken hold of him.

He wasn't sure why people called it the green-eyed monster. While indeed monstrous, there was nothing green about it. His mood was as black as ebony. "What happened? Why didn't you marry him?"

"Isn't it obvious?" She gestured toward their sterile surroundings. "It was for the best, really. I didn't love him. I thought I did, but it wasn't love. I know that now."

If the idiot named Jeremy Davis had been standing beside them, Artem would have given the man a good reason to make use of the hospital's facilities. He didn't need to know what Ophelia's former fiancé had said or what, exactly, he'd done. He didn't need to know anything else at all, frankly. The truth was written all over Ophelia's face. It showed in the way she locked herself away from the world.

He'd hurt her.

Maybe Ophelia's biggest problem wasn't her MS. Maybe it was her past.

Yet another thing they had in common.

"I'm sorry," he whispered, and gave her hand a tender squeeze.

"For what?" The quaver in her voice nearly slayed him.

"For everything."

He meant it. Every damn thing. He was sorry for not

trying harder to reach her after the news of her medical condition became a front-page story. He was sorry he hadn't forced her to see him. He was sorry for selling the diamond, when he knew how much it meant to her. He should have found a way to keep it, to let her hold on to just one thing.

But most of all he was sorry for every bad thing that had ever happened to her. He was sorry for the past, both hers and his, and the way it seemed to overshadow everything. Never had he wanted so badly to let it all go.

The door swung open. A woman in a white coat entered and extended her hand toward Ophelia. "Miss Rose, I'm Dr. April Larson."

"Hello." She shook the doctor's hand and gestured toward Artem. "This is Artem Drake, my, ah…"

"Emergency contact," he said, and smiled.

"Wonderful. It's great to meet you both." Dr. Larson sat on the stool facing them and spread a folder open on her lap. "So, Ophelia. You had a fainting spell this morning? How are you feeling now?"

Beside him, Ophelia took a deep breath. "A little tired, actually."

Dr. Larson nodded. "That's completely normal, given your condition."

"My condition. Right." She smiled, but it didn't reach her eyes.

The doctor nodded again. "I'm afraid so. You need to get some rest, Ophelia. And I would suggest that you avoid stress as much as possible. There's not much else we can do for you."

"I see. So it's that bad, is it? The symptoms I've been

experiencing and the fainting…" She blinked back tears. "I'm no longer in remission. I'm relapsing. This is only the beginning. It's going to get worse, much worse. Just like last time. I'm on the verge of a full-blown MS attack. Is that what's happening?"

"What?" The doctor leaned forward and placed a comforting hand on her knee. "No, not at all."

Ophelia shook her head. "I don't understand."

But Artem did.

The godforsaken past was repeating itself. And this time, it was all his doing. He had no one to blame but himself. It wasn't enough to sit at his father's desk and run his father's company. How had he let this happen? How had he actually allowed himself to become the man he most despised?

The doctor smiled. *Don't say it. Do* not. "You're not relapsing, Ophelia. You're pregnant."

Chapter Twelve

*P*regnant?

Ophelia couldn't believe what she was hearing. There had been a mistake. Of course there had. She couldn't possibly be pregnant.

With *Artem's* child.

She couldn't even bring herself to look at him. He'd gone deadly silent beside her. She could feel the tension rolling off him in waves. She wished he were somewhere else. *Anyplace* else, so she could have had an opportunity to figure out how and when to tell him. Or *if* she would have told him.

But she would have. Of course she would. Having someone's child was too important to keep secret.

A child.

She couldn't have a child! "But I'm on birth control

pills. I've been on them since my diagnosis. My primary physician said there was evidence that the hormones in oral contraceptives helped delay the onset of certain MS symptoms."

She'd never imagined she'd use them for actual birth control. But still. They were called *birth control pills* for a reason, weren't they?

Dr. Larson eyed Ophelia over the top of her glasses. "Did your primary doctor also tell you that your MS medications could decrease the effectiveness of oral contraceptives?"

"No." Of course not. She would have remembered an important detail like that. Or would she? She'd decided never to have sex again. And if she'd stuck to that decision—as she so clearly should have—that detail wouldn't have been so important. It wouldn't have mattered at all.

She dropped her head in her hands. "I don't know. It's possible. I hadn't planned on—" Goodness, this was mortifying. How could she have this discussion with Artem right here, seething quietly beside her? "—meeting anyone."

"Well, the heart has its own ideas, doesn't it? Congratulations." Dr. Larson smiled and shot a wink in Artem's direction. "To you both."

Obviously, the doctor had seen past Artem's introduction as her emergency contact and detected there was something more between them. Even though there wasn't. Other than the fact that he was apparently the *father of her unborn child.*

Ophelia felt faint again, but this time she knew it was

just psychological. She'd been so sure she was relapsing. She almost wished she were. How could she possibly raise a child? And what about the physical demands of pregnancy? Could she even do this?

According to what the doctor was saying, yes. Of course she could. She was even talking about how pregnancy frequently eased MS symptoms. Women with MS had children every day. Dr. Larson was going on about how having children was a leap of faith for anyone, and there was no reason why she shouldn't have a healthy, loving family.

Except there was. Two months ago, Ophelia couldn't bring herself to adopt a kitten. And now she was supposed to have a family? She was supposed to be someone's *mother* when she was terrified that one day she wouldn't even be able to take care of herself?

She didn't hear another word the doctor said. It was too much to wrap her mind around. She felt sick to her stomach. What was she going to do? Could she raise a baby? All on her own?

A baby changed everything. How could she have been so incredibly foolish? She'd wanted one night with Artem.

Just one.

But that wasn't altogether true, was it? She wasn't sure when it had happened—maybe when he'd kissed her hand after she'd danced for him, when he'd whispered the words she so desperately needed to hear. *Ophelia, you* are *a dancer.* The exact moment no longer mattered, but sometime on that snowy night she'd begun to want more. More life. More everything. But most of all, more of *him*.

"Ophelia."

She blinked. Artem was standing now, holding all her paperwork in one hand and cupping her elbow with his other.

"Let's go, kitten." He smiled. But it was a sad smile, one that nearly tore her heart in two.

What had she done?

"I didn't do this on purpose," she said, once they were settled in the backseat of his town car. "I promise."

"I know." His tone was calm. Too calm. Too controlled, given the fact that the set of his jaw looked hard enough to cut diamonds. "I know it all too well."

She nodded. "Good."

Artem's driver glanced over his shoulder as the car pulled away from the curb. "To the Plaza, sir?"

"No." Artem shook his head. Thank goodness. Ophelia had no intention of accompanying him back to his penthouse. Or anywhere. She needed a little time and space to come to grips with her pregnancy and figure out what she was going to do. "City hall, please."

City hall?

She slid her gaze toward Artem. "Have you got a parking fine you need to take care of or something?"

"No, I do not," he said. Again, in that eerily placid tone he'd adopted since they'd left the hospital. "You're an intelligent woman. You know very well why we're stopping at city hall."

Ophelia stared at him in disbelief. Surely he didn't expect her to marry him. Here. Now. Without even so much as a discussion about it. Or a proposal, for that matter. "I'm afraid I don't."

"We're to be married, of course." He couldn't be serious. But he certainly looked it as he stared back at her, his gaze steely with determination. "Straight away."

The driver—usually the epitome of professional restraint—let out a little cough. Artem didn't seem to notice. Apparently, he was so laser focused on the idea of a wedding that other opinions didn't matter. Hers included.

A hot flush rose to her cheeks. "I'm not marrying you, Artem."

Marrying him was out of the question. He knew that. She'd told him in the beginning that she didn't have relationships. Of course, she'd also told him she didn't have sex.

But still.

Artem Drake could marry anyone he chose. He couldn't possibly want to marry her. This was about the pregnancy. *Not* her. And even if the prospect of having a baby terrified her more than she would ever admit, she wouldn't marry a man who didn't love her.

Even if that man was Artem. And even if the thought of being his wife made her heart pound hard in her chest, just like it did when she danced.

"Yes, you are," he said, as if their marriage was a foregone conclusion.

Our marriage. Something stirred inside Ophelia. Something that felt too much like love.

Stop. You cannot *consider this.*

"If you want a more formal affair, or even a church

wedding, we can do that later. Whatever and wherever you wish. Vegas, Paris, Saint Patrick's Cathedral. Your choice. We can plan it for next week, next month or even after our baby is born, if that's what you prefer." *Our baby.* Ophelia's throat grew tight. She couldn't seem to swallow. Or breathe. "But we are getting legally married at city hall. Today. Right now."

It would have been so easy to say yes, despite the fact that he'd ordered her to marry him rather than actually asking. And despite the fact that she still couldn't forget the things Jeremy had once said to her. *Burden. Too much to deal with...*

Marrying Artem would mean she would have help with the baby. She wouldn't have to face her questionable future all alone. None of that mattered, though. The only thing that did was that marrying him would mean she could pledge her heart, her soul, her life to the man she loved.

She loved him. There was no more denying it. She'd loved him since the moment he'd seen past the wall she'd constructed around her heart and forced a kitten on her. Maybe even before then.

She loved him, and that's exactly why she couldn't marry him.

"Artem, please don't." She fixed her gaze out the window on the snowy blur of the city streets. She couldn't bring herself to look at him. Why was this so hard? Why did she have to fall in love? "I can't."

"Ophelia, I will not father a child out of wedlock. That is unacceptable to me. Please understand." He reached for her hand and squeezed it. Hard. Until she finally tore her gaze from the frosted glass and looked him in the eyes, the tortured windows to his soul. "Please."

His voice had dropped to a ragged whisper. A crack in his carefully measured composure. At last… That look, coupled with that whisper, nearly broke her.

Please understand.

She did. She understood all too well. She understood that Artem didn't want his baby to grow up without a father. His desire to get married had more to do with his past than it did with her. He was offering her the world. Paris. London. He was offering her everything she wanted, with one notable exception.

Love.

He hadn't said a single word about loving her. Maybe he did. But how could she possibly know that if he didn't tell her? And this ache she felt—the longing for him that seemed to come from deep in the marrow of her bones—was so intense it was dangerous. Desperate. Could something so wholly overwhelming possibly be reciprocated?

Because if it wasn't, if this was unrequited love, and Artem wanted to marry her out of obligation to their child, or as a way of mending his past, what would happen when her MS became worse? What would happen if she was one of the unlucky ones, one of the patients who ended up severely disabled? What then? If he loved her, they could get through it. Maybe. But if he didn't…

If he didn't, she would be a burden. Just as Jeremy had predicted. Artem would grow to resent her, and the thought of that frightened her even more than trying to raise a child by herself.

It would never work.

"I'm sorry." She shook her head and tried her best to maintain eye contact, but she just couldn't. She focused on the perfect knot in his tie instead. It grew blurry as she blinked back tears. *Say it. Just say it before you break down.* "I can't marry you, Artem. I can't, and I won't."

Chapter Thirteen

Artem sat seething across the desk from Dalton, unable to force thoughts of Ophelia and their unborn child from his mind. Fourteen hours and half a bottle of Scotch hadn't helped matters. If anything, he was more agitated about the unexpected turn of events than he'd been the night before.

She'd said no.

He'd asked Ophelia to marry him, and she'd said no. Rather emphatically, if memory served.

I can't marry you, Artem. I can't, and I won't.

"What's this?" Dalton asked, staring down at the envelope Artem slid toward him.

My long overdue letter of resignation. His personal life might be in a shambles at the moment, but he was determined to end the farce of his reign as CEO of

Drake Diamonds. At least that's why he told himself he'd come into the office today. If it had been to ask Ophelia to marry him—*again*—he would have been out of luck, anyway. Her office door had remained firmly closed for the duration of the morning.

Artem nodded at the letter. "Just read it."

Why should he disclose the contents when Dalton would know what the letter said as soon as he opened it?

If he opened it.

"Whatever it is can wait," he said calmly. *No. No, it can't.* "There's a matter we need to discuss."

Dalton tossed the sealed envelope on his desk, opened the top drawer and pulled out a neatly folded newspaper. Artem sighed and closed his eyes for a moment. He knew what was coming before he even opened them and found Dalton leaning back in his chair, waiting for some sort of explanation. As if there could possibly be a plausible excuse for the photographs of him and Ophelia entwined with one another as they climbed into the car the day before.

"Well?" Dalton tapped with his pointer finger the copy of *Page Six* spread open on the desk.

Artem gave the paper a cursory glance. He didn't like looking at the picture. Seeing it reminded him of how he'd felt watching Ophelia fall, lifeless, into his arms. Powerless. Stricken.

Artem sighed. "What is your question, exactly?"

He had no desire to beat around the bush. The past twenty-four hours had been a godforsaken mess, and he was fresh out of patience.

I can't marry you, Artem. I can't, and I won't.

Why couldn't he get those words out of his head?

Dalton cleared his throat. "For starters, is the caption correct? Was this photo taking *during* the auction, when you were supposed to be at Sotheby's?"

At that moment, if Artem hadn't been the CEO, he might have begged to be fired. But alas, he couldn't be terminated. Much to his chagrin, he was untouchable.

"Yes." There wasn't a hint of apology in his voice. If anything, that simple syllable contained a thinly veiled challenge.

His mood was black enough to be ripe for a fight. At least if Dalton was his opponent, he'd have a decent chance of winning. Because Ophelia had shown no sign of surrender. After refusing to marry him, she'd asked the driver to drop her off at her apartment, and had all but ran inside in order to get away from Artem.

She wasn't going to get away with ghosting him again. Not when she was pregnant with his child. She would talk to him before the day's end. He'd seen to that already.

"I suppose it doesn't matter. The auction was successful." Dalton stared at the picture again, then lifted a brow at Artem. "But you're sleeping with Ophelia. That much is obvious. While you were away on your latest disappearing act, she started designing another collection. It's good. Brilliant, actually. The auction pulled us out of the red, but we need her."

Artem shifted in his chair. *We need her. I need her.* "It's not what you think, brother."

"Not what I think?" Dalton let out a laugh. "So you're not sleeping with her?"

"I didn't say that."

Another sigh. "Have you thought about what will happen when you get bored and still have to work with her every day?"

Bored? Not likely. Not when she had a certain knack for driving him to the brink of madness. In his bed, as well as out of it. "She's pregnant."

Why hide it? If he got his way, she'd be living under his roof within hours. Months from now, she'd be giving birth to his son or daughter. He'd never wanted to be a father, never even imagined it. But that no longer mattered. Artem had every intention of being a doting dad.

Marriage or no marriage.

The set of his jaw hardened, as it always did when he thought back on her trembling refusal. *I can't. I won't.*

"Pregnant?" Dalton paused. "With *your* child?"

Artem's mood grew exponentially blacker. "Of course the child is mine."

"Sorry, give me a minute. I'm still trying to wrap my head around this. Given our family past…" Dalton cleared his throat. Artem had to give him credit for choosing his words delicately, rather than just coming out and saying what they were both thinking. *Given the fact that you're my bastard brother…* "I'm surprised you weren't more careful."

So was Artem, to be honest. He'd never bedded a woman without wearing a condom. Never. Until Ophelia. But nothing about that night had been ordinary. The music, the ballet, the snow. The way he'd forgotten how to breathe when he'd seen her bare body for the first time.

It had been a miracle he'd remembered his own name, never mind a condom. "This was different. *She's* different."

Dalton eyed him with blatant curiosity. "How, exactly?"

Because I love her.

By God, he did. He loved her. That's why he'd insisted on signing that emergency contact form before he'd even known she was pregnant. It's why he hadn't been able to work, sleep or even think since the morning she'd disappeared from his bed. It's why he wanted so very badly to take care of her. To make love to her again. And again.

To marry her.

It wasn't just the baby. It was *her.*

Artem cleared his throat and tried to swallow the realization that he was in love. With the mother of his child. With the woman who'd made it clear she had no intention of marrying him.

"My God, you're in love with her, aren't you?" Dalton said, as if he'd somehow peered right inside Artem's head.

"I didn't say that." But it was a weak protest. Even Artem realized as much the moment the words left his mouth.

"You don't have to. It's obvious." Dalton shrugged one shoulder. "To me, anyway."

Artem narrowed his gaze. It hadn't been obvious to himself until just now. Or maybe it had, and he hadn't wanted to believe it. "How so?"

"If you didn't love her, you would have never allowed this to happen. It's simple, really."

Artem wished things were simple. He'd never wished for anything as much. "You give me far too much credit, brother. Why don't you go ahead and say what we're both thinking?"

Dalton's gaze grew sharp. Pointed. "What is it I'm thinking?"

"The truth. I've become our father." No matter how many times he'd thought it, believed it, Artem felt sick saying it aloud. Like reality was a vile, dark malady crushing his lungs, stealing his breath.

Dalton looked at him for a long, silent moment before he finally replied. "That couldn't be further from the truth, brother. In fact, it might be the biggest load of bullshit I've ever heard."

If Dalton had ever been the type to humor him, Artem would have taken his reaction with a grain of salt. But Dalton hadn't been that sort of brother. Ever. If anything, Dalton had been hard on him, with his sarcastic comments about Artem's lavish lifestyle and what Dalton considered to be his less-than-stellar work ethic. As if any normal person's work ethic could compare to his workaholic brother's.

No, Dalton didn't make a practice of mincing words, but what he was saying made no sense. "Think about it. I've done exactly what Dad did. I had a fling with an employee, and now she's pregnant."

It was a crude way of putting it, and in truth, it didn't feel at all like what had happened. But it was, wasn't it?

No. It was more. It had to be.

Dalton shook his head. "You're forgetting something. Dad was married with two kids, and you are most assuredly not."

He had a point.

Still…

"I just can't believe this has all happened right after I stepped into his place here at the office. It's like he knew something I didn't." Artem dropped his head in his hands. "It should have been you, Dalton."

Dalton wanted to run the company. Artem didn't. He never had. He hated that he'd been the one chosen. Worse, he hated thinking their father had done it on purpose. That he'd known how alike they really were.

Like father, like son.

"No," Dalton said quietly. "It should have been you. It *had* to be you. Don't you get it?"

Artem lifted his head and met his brother's gaze. "*What?* No."

"*Yes.* Dad knew he was sick, Artem. He also knew about the mine."

This was news to Artem. "You mean he knew it was worthless before he died?"

Dalton nodded. "The accountant confirmed it last week. If you'd bothered to show up at the office before now, I would have told you."

"I was trying to keep my distance from Ophelia." He'd thought he could get her out of his system. What a waste of time that had been. "He knew about the mine. What does that have to do with me?"

"*Everything.* It has everything to do with you. Dad knew the only way to save the company was to sell the diamond, and he knew I'd never do it. Hell, he couldn't even do it himself, otherwise he would have arranged for its sale as soon as he knew the mine was worthless."

Artem let this news sink in for a moment. Dalton was right. Their father never would have auctioned off the diamond. To him, it would have been like selling his family heritage. Worse, it would have been an admission that he'd failed. He'd failed the company and the long line of Drakes that had come before him.

Artem didn't give a damn about the long line of Drakes. Or the diamond. He didn't give a damn about being CEO. Ophelia was the only reason he'd stuck around as long as he had.

"You were the only one who would do it," Dalton said. "That's why he chose you, Artem. He didn't appoint you because he thought you were like him. He appointed you as CEO because you weren't like him at all."

Artem concentrated on breathing in and out while he processed what his brother was saying. He wanted to believe Dalton's theory. He wanted to believe it with everything in his soul.

"Listen to me, brother. What you did saved the company," Dalton said.

"It also helped push Ophelia away. That diamond meant something to her." He could still hear the desperation in her voice that day in the conference room. *Please, Artem. Don't sell the diamond. Please.* He hadn't listened.

He'd told himself he was doing the right thing. He'd been trying to put a stop to Dalton's ridiculous ad campaign. He'd been trying to protect her.

Maybe he had. But he'd also hurt her in the process. And now there was no going back.

"The fact remains that you saved the family business, and that makes you more of a Drake than anybody. More than me. More than Dad."

Artem wished he could take comfort in those words. There was a time when hearing Dalton say such a thing would have been a balm. Those words may have been all the healing he'd needed. Before.

Before Ophelia. Without her, they meant nothing. *He* meant nothing.

"About this." Dalton picked up the envelope containing Artem's letter of resignation. "Is this what I think it is?"

"It's my notice that I intend to step down as CEO," Artem said.

Dalton tore it neatly in half without bothering to open it. "Unaccepted."

For crying out loud. Could one thing go as planned? Just one? "Dalton…"

"Think on it for a while. Think about the things I've said. You may change your mind. The position pays awfully well."

As if Artem needed more cash. "I don't care about the money. I have plenty."

"You sure about that? After all, soon you'll have another mouth to feed." Dalton smiled, as if jumping at the chance to become a doting uncle.

A child. He and Ophelia were having a *child*. He'd been so stunned at the news, so abhorred by the idea that he'd become his father, that he hadn't realized how happy he was.

Ophelia was having his baby. That's all that mattered now. That, and convincing her to speak to him again. But he already had that covered.

"Think on it," Dalton said again. "I like having you around. It's about time we Drakes stuck together."

Ophelia blinked against the swirling snow and pulled her scarf more tightly around her neck as she stalked past the doorman of the Plaza, who was dressed, as usual, in a top hat and dark coat with shiny gold buttons. After hiding out in her office all day specifically to avoid facing Artem, she couldn't believe she was willingly setting foot in the hotel where he lived.

But he'd given her no choice, had he? He infuriated her sometimes. He had since the very beginning. But now...now he'd gone too far.

"Welcome to the Plaza." The concierge smiled at her, then before she even told him who she was, handed her a familiar-looking black key card, plus another, slimmer card. *Odd.* "The black card will give you access to the penthouse elevators and the other is the key to Mr. Drake's suite. He's expecting you."

I'll bet he is.

"Thank you." She did her best to smile politely. After all, the concierge had nothing to do with this ridiculous situation.

Or maybe he did. Who knew? Even Artem couldn't have pulled off a stunt like this without help.

And what was with the key to his suite? That had to

be a mistake. No way was she going to walk into his penthouse without knocking first. Although she supposed she was entitled, after what he'd done.

The elevator ride felt excruciatingly slow. Since arriving home from work and realizing what had happened, she hadn't stopped to think. She'd simply reacted. Which was no doubt what Artem had been counting on.

Now that she was moments away from seeing him again, she was nervous. Which was silly, really. She was having the man's baby. She should at least be able to carry on a simple conversation with him.

That was the trouble, though, wasn't it? Her feelings for Artem were anything but simple.

Yes, they are. You love him. Plain and simple.

She swallowed. That might be true, but it didn't mean she had to act on it. Or, God forbid, say it. But what *would* she say to him after refusing to marry him? And how could she see him again, so soon? She'd kept her office door closed all day for a reason. She didn't think she could take being in the same room with him without being able to touch him, to kiss him, to tell him how hard it had been to refuse him yesterday.

To pretend she didn't love him.

She'd told herself she'd done the right thing. Just because they were having a baby didn't mean they should get married. No matter how badly one of them wanted to.

She'd started to wonder, though, which one of them really wanted marriage. In her most honest moments, she realized it was her.

She didn't know what to do with these feelings. Everything had been so much easier when she'd kept to herself, when she'd gone straight home after work every day. No kitten. No nights at the ballet. No Artem.

Was it better then? Was it really?

At last the elevator reached the eighteenth floor, and Ophelia stepped into the opulent hallway. When she reached the door to penthouse number nine, she pounded on it before she had time to chicken out.

Artem opened it straightaway and greeted her with a devastating smile that told her she'd played right into his hand, just as she'd suspected. "Ophelia. Hello, kitten."

Her heart leaped straight to her throat, and to her complete and utter mortification, a ribbon of desire unfurled inside her. In an instant, her center went hot and wet.

She willed herself not to purr. "Kitten? Interesting choice of words, given the circumstances."

"Enlighten me. What would those circumstances be, exactly?" He crossed his arms and leaned casually against the door frame. Apparently, he was intent on making her go through the motions of this ludicrous charade.

"Artem, stop. You and I both know that you kidnapped my cat." She brushed past him into his suite, scanning the surroundings for a glimpse of Jewel.

Ophelia had been panicked when she'd come home from work and the little white fluffball hadn't greeted her at the door, winding around her ankles as she did every night. Then she'd seen the bouquet of white roses on the coffee table and Artem's business card propped against the lead crystal vase. No note. Just the card. *Artem Drake. Chief Executive Officer. Drake Diamonds.*

Chief Executive Ass was more like it.

Artem had broken into her apartment. He'd barged right in, and he'd stolen her cat.

"I beg your pardon. *Your* kitten?" He raised a sardonic brow. "As I recall, I'm the one who adopted her from the animal shelter when you refused to do so. That would make her *my* cat, would it not?"

No. Just…

No.

She looked over his shoulder and saw Jewel curled into a ball in the middle of his massive bed, right on top of the chinchilla blanket. The same blanket she'd wrapped around her naked self the last time she'd stood in this room. It was surreal. And possibly the most manipulative thing Artem Drake—or any other self-entitled male—had ever done.

"You can't be serious," she sputtered.

"Surely you remember how adamant you were about not adopting. I thought it best to relieve you of your cat-sitting responsibilities." He glanced at the kitten on the bed. "She rather likes it here. It's not such a bad place to be, Ophelia."

She heaved out a sigh and looked at Jewel. Memories of being in that same bed hit her, hard and fast. She envisioned herself waking up with her legs wrapped around Artem, her head nestled in the crook of his neck…

But wait, she wasn't actually considering letting him get away with this, was she? No. Of course she wasn't.

"Artem, you can't do this. I'm not marrying you, and if you think repossessing your kitten is going to change my mind, you're sorely mistaken."

"Who said anything about marriage? You don't want to marry me? Fine. I'm a big boy. I can take it." His tone went soft, sincere. The switch caught her off guard, and she felt oddly vulnerable all of a sudden. "But if you think I'm going to stand by and let you do this by yourself, you're the one who's mistaken. Let me be there for you, kitten. Let me take care of you. At least stay here."

"Stay here? With you?" She rolled her eyes.

"With me. Yes." There wasn't a hint of irritation in his tone. He'd dropped the overbearing act and was looking at her with such tenderness that her heart hurt.

Let me take care of you.

It was so close to *I love you* that it almost made her want to forgive him for breaking into her home. Seriously, who did that?

The man she was in love with. That's who.

"I shouldn't have come here." She shook her head and headed for the door.

She couldn't do this. If she stayed here for even one night, she'd end up back in his bed. And she'd never be able to leave him. Not again.

"Ophelia, stop. Please." Artem chased after her.

She shook her head. "I don't… I can't…"

He slid between her and the door, raised her chin with a gentle touch of his fingertips and forced her to look him in the eyes. "He was wrong, Ophelia. I don't know what Jeremy Davis said to you to make you believe that your MS made you unlovable, undesirable, but he was wrong. Dead wrong."

She took a few backward steps and wrapped her arms around herself in an effort to hold herself together. Because it felt like the entire world was falling to pieces around her. Not just her heart. "Artem…"

"I'm not going to force you to stay here. And I'm sure as hell not going to force myself on you. I'm leaving town for a few days, and I'd love nothing more than to find you here when I come back." He walked past her and grabbed a messenger bag from the table in the center of the room.

Ophelia couldn't believe what she was hearing. He'd taken her cat and lured her here, and now he was leaving? "You're *leaving*? Where are you going?"

"I'd rather not say. I've been called away for work, and I'll be back as soon as I can. The hotel staff has orders to provide whatever you need. You'll find them rather accommodating. Make yourself at home while I'm gone." His gaze flitted around the penthouse and paused, just for a moment, on the closed door to his home office. The room where he'd shut himself off on the morning she'd slipped away. "Take a look around."

Then he turned and walked right out the door.

Ophelia stared after him, dumbstruck. *This is insane.*

She walked to the bed and scooped Jewel into her arms, fully intending to give Artem a five-minute head start before going back downstairs and hailing a cab home.

She couldn't believe he actually expected her to stay here while he was gone. As if she could sleep in his bed, rest her head on his pillow, wake up every morning in his home and not wonder what it would be like to share it with him. Impossible. She couldn't do it.

"Come on, Jewel." She held the kitten closer to her heart. "Let's go home."

Home.

She blinked back tears. Damn Artem Drake. Damn him and his promises. *Let me take care of you.*

He was tender when she least expected it, and it messed with her head. As ridiculous as it seemed, she preferred it when he did things like break into her apartment and steal her cat.

She needed to get out of here. Now. She couldn't keep standing in his posh penthouse while the things he said kept spinning round and round in her head. She marched toward the door, but as she passed his office, her steps slowed.

Take a look around. What had that meant, anyway?

Nothing, probably.

She lingered outside the room, wanting to reach for the doorknob, even though she knew she shouldn't. She rolled her eyes. What could possibly be in there that would change her mind about anything?

Nothing. That's what.

He'd probably bought a crib. Or a bassinet. No doubt he thought she'd see it and go all mushy inside. Well, he was wrong. If he'd bought a crib—now, when she was only weeks pregnant—she'd know that the only reason he wanted to marry her was because of the baby. Giving the baby a proper, nuclear family was all he could think about. Just to prove it, if only to herself, she turned the knob and stepped inside his mysterious, secret room.

What she saw nearly made her faint again.

There was no crib. This wasn't a baby's room, and it most definitely wasn't an office. Ophelia's reflection stared back at her from all four of the mirrored walls. Beneath her feet was a smooth wood floor that smelled like freshly cut pine. A ballet barre stretched from one end of the room to the other.

Artem had built her a ballet studio, right here in his penthouse.

A lump formed in her throat. She couldn't swallow. She could barely even breathe.

Ophelia, you are *a dancer.*

He'd whispered those words before he knew about her illness, before he knew she was Natalia Baronova's granddaughter. She hadn't believed him then. Even as she'd danced across the moonlit floor of his living room, she'd doubted. She'd been performing a role, playing a part. That part had been the ballerina she'd been. The woman who could have done anything, been anything. A dancer. A mother. A wife. Once upon a time.

Ophelia, you are *a dancer.*

He'd really meant it. And now, standing in this room, she almost believed it, too.

Almost.

Chapter Fourteen

Artem was away longer than he'd planned. Three days, three nights. He'd hoped to take no more than an overnight trip, but things hadn't gone as smoothly as he'd anticipated. He hated being away and not knowing what was going on with Ophelia, but he'd been prepared to be gone as long as it took to set matters straight.

He returned to New York on the red-eye, hoping against hope he wasn't coming home to an empty penthouse. According to Dalton, Ophelia had been at work in the store on Fifth Avenue every day and seemed to be in perfectly good health. No fainting spells. No indication whatsoever that she was sick, or even pregnant. She hadn't missed a beat at work. But Artem had drawn the line at checking in with the staff at the Plaza to see whether or not she'd been staying in his suite. In truth, he hadn't been sure he wanted to know. Probably because he was almost certain she'd gone straight back to her own apartment after he'd left.

Sure enough, when he slipped inside the penthouse at 2:00 a.m.—quietly so as not to wake her, because a shred of optimism survived somewhere deep in his gut—the penthouse was empty. As was his bed.

Shit.

He let his messenger bag slide from his shoulder and land with a thud on the floor, its precious cargo forgotten. The air left his lungs in a weary rush. Until that moment, he hadn't realized he'd been all but holding his breath in anticipation as he'd flown clear across the continent.

He needed to see her. Touch her. Hold her. Three days was a damn long time.

He loosened his tie, crossed the room and collapsed on the bed. Eyes shut, surrounded by darkness, he could have sworn he caught Ophelia's sweet orchid scent on his pillow. The sheets felt sultry and warm. He must have been even more tired than he'd realized, because his empty bed didn't feel empty at all. He had to remind himself he was only being swallowed in sheets of memories.

But he could have sworn he heard the faint strains of music. Mozart's Piano Concerto no. 21. *La Petite Mort.* What was wrong with him? Clearly, he'd lost not only his Ophelia, but his mind, too.

You haven't lost her. Not yet.

There was still a ray of hope. A whisper of possibility. It was small, but he could feel it. He could see it in his mind's eye. It glittered like a gemstone.

Thud.

Out of nowhere, something landed on his chest, surprising him. He coughed and reached to push whatever it was off, and his hand made contact with something soft. And furry. And unmistakably feline.

He sat up and clicked on the light on the bedside table. Ophelia's tiny, white fluffball of a cat blinked up at him with wide, innocent eyes.

"Jewel. What are you doing here?" He gave the kitty a scratch on the side of her cheek and she leaned into it, purring furiously.

Artem had never been so happy to see an animal in his entire life. "Where's your mama, huh? Where's my Ophelia?"

My Ophelia.

There was no way she would have left the cat at his penthouse all alone. No possible way. She had to be here somewhere, but where?

He stood while Jewel settled onto his pillow, kneading her paws and purring like a freight train. At least someone was happy to see him.

The cat was in his apartment, though. That had to be a good sign.

"Ophelia?" His gaze swept the penthouse twice before he noticed a pale shaft of light coming from beneath his office door. Or what had *been* his office.

The ballet studio. Of course. He'd been so weary from the stress of the past few days that he'd almost forgotten he'd arranged a place for her to dance. Because she needed such a place, a room where she could let her body dream. If his trip had been a failure, if he could have given her only one thing, it would be the knowledge that she was perfect just as she was. Just as she'd always be. Ophelia would forever be a dancer. No illness, and certainly no man, could ever take that away from her.

He smiled to himself. The music hadn't been a product of wishful thinking, after all. Nor had it simply been a tender, aching memory. It was real, and it swelled as he approached the closed door, until the subtle strains of the violin exploded into a chorus of strings and piano notes that seemed to beat in time with the pounding of his heart.

He paused with his hand on the knob, remembering the last time he'd seen her dance to this music. He knew every moment, every movement by heart. He still dreamed about that dance every night, the whisper of her ballet shoes in the moonlight and the balletic bend of her spine when she'd arched against him as he'd entered her. Even his body remembered, perhaps more so than his mind. Because hearing that wrenching music and knowing Ophelia was right on the other side of the door, pointing her exquisite feet and arching her supple back, sent every drop of blood rushing straight to his groin. He was harder than he'd ever been in his life, hard as a diamond, and he'd yet to even set eyes on her.

With exaggerated slowness, he turned the knob and pushed the door open. The room was dark, the music loud. So loud she didn't notice his presence. She hadn't bothered to turn on the lights, and moonlight streamed through the skylights casting a luminescent glow on the smooth wood floors he'd had installed less than a week ago.

Ophelia stood at the barre with her back to him, wearing nothing more than her pink-ribboned pointe shoes and a sheer, diaphanous nightgown that ended just above her knees. In the soft light of the moon, Artem could see no more than a hint of her graceful spine and the curve of her ballerina bottom through the thin, delicate fabric. She rose up on tiptoe, reached her arm toward the center of the room, then bent toward the barre in an achingly glorious curve.

Seeing her like this, lost in her art, was like being inside a lucid dream. A lovely, forbidden fantasy. Part of him would have been happy to remain there in the doorway, a worshipful voyeur in the shadows. A sudden, fierce urge to inspect her body, with the thrill of knowing she was expecting his child, seized him. He took in the new softness of her frame, hips lush with femininity and a delicate voluptuousness that pierced his soul. But the other part of him—the demanding, lustful part that refused to be ignored—wanted to rip her gossamer gown away and bury himself inside her velvet soft warmth.

He prowled closer, footsteps swallowed by Mozart's tremulous melody. Artem didn't stop until he was close enough to feel the heat coming from her body, to see the dampness in the hair at the base of her swan-like neck. His fists clenched at his sides as he suppressed the overwhelming urge to touch her. Everywhere.

She turned on her tiptoes, and suddenly they were

face-to-face. Mouths, hearts, souls only inches apart. Artem would have given every cent he had for a sign— *any* sign—that she was happy to see him, that while he'd been gone she'd lain awake in his bed craving his hands on her body, dreaming of him bringing her to shattering climax with his mouth, his fingers, his cock.

"Artem." Her eyes were wide, her voice nothing but a breathy whisper, and for an agonizing moment, he thought she was on the verge of dancing away from him. As she'd done so many times.

But she didn't. She stayed put, breathing hard from exertion, breasts heaving with new fullness, her rose-petal nipples hardening beneath her whisper-thin gown. Pregnancy had changed her body in the most beautiful of ways, and knowing he'd been the one responsible for that divine transformation sent a surge of proprietary pride through him. The baby growing inside her was his. *She* was his, and he had every intention of showing her how profoundly that knowledge thrilled him.

She looked at him with eyes like flaming sapphires. And when the heat of her gaze dropped to his mouth with deliberate intent, it was all the invitation he needed.

"Kitten," he groaned, and pulled her to him, molding her graceful body to his.

His lips found hers in an instant, and the desperation that had been building in him in the weeks since he'd last tasted her reached its crescendo. He poured every bit of it into that kiss—all the fitful, restless nights, all the moments of the day when he'd thought of nothing but making love to her again. And again. And again.

They'd had one night together. He'd known it hadn't

been enough, but now he realized he'd never get his fill of her. If he lived a thousand years and spent every night buried in the sanctity of her precious body, he'd still want more.

Her hands found his hair and he deepened the kiss, trying to get closer to her. And closer still, until she let out a little squeak and he realized he'd pushed her up against the ballet barre.

Somehow he tore his mouth from hers long enough to gather her wisp of a nightie in his hands and lift it over her head. Then his lips found her again, this time at the base of her neck, where the erratic beat of her pulse told him how badly she'd wanted this, too. Needed it. Missed it. Missed *him.*

He cupped her breasts, lowered his head and kissed one nipple, then the other, drawing a deep moan of satisfaction from Ophelia's lips. She was so soft, so beautiful. Even more perfect than he remembered.

Time and again, he'd told himself that if he ever got to make love to her again, he'd go slow. He'd draw out each kiss, each caress, each lingering stroke as long as possible. He'd savor every heartbeat that led to their joining. But his blood boiled with need. He couldn't have slowed down if his life depended on it. And Ophelia matched his breathless hunger, sigh for sigh. She pulled at his hair, then clutched at his tie and wrapped it around her hand, holding him tightly to her as he drew her breast into his mouth, suckling. Savoring.

"Please, Artem," she begged. "Please."

"I'm here, kitten," he whispered against the soft

swell of her belly, where life—the life they'd created together—was growing inside.

He was here. And this time there would be no leaving. On either of their parts.

He unclenched her hands from his tie and placed each one on the ballet barre, curled them in place.

"I suggest you hold on," he murmured against her mouth, dipping his tongue inside and sliding it against hers for a final, searing kiss before dropping to his knees.

He slid his hands up and down the length of her gorgeous legs, parting her thighs. She had the legs of a dancer, legs that were made for moving to music and balancing on tiptoe. And for wrapping around his waist when he pushed himself inside her. But first, this. First the most intimate of kisses.

He devoured her like a starving man. And still he couldn't seem to get enough, even when she spread her ballerina thighs wider to give him fuller access. Somehow he grew only hungrier as she ground against him and her breathy little sighs grew louder and more urgent, rising with the music. He had to have her like this, wild and free and unafraid, forever.

Forever and always.

"Artem, I..." Her hands tightened in his hair with so much force that it bordered on pain, and he hummed against her parted flesh.

He wouldn't have stopped, even if she begged, even if she slid right down the wall into a puddle on the floor. Not until she found her release. Blood roared in his ears. If he hadn't been on his knees, his legs would have buckled beneath him. He was on the verge of coming himself and he'd yet to shed a single article of clothing.

Not yet.

He wanted her spent and trembling when he finally drove into her. He'd lived with the torture of wanting her for weeks, since he'd last touched her. They'd wasted so much time. Days. Weeks. Time when he'd fought his feelings for her and told himself what he'd done was wrong, when it couldn't have been more right.

Did she have any idea the kind of restraint it had taken not to act on his desire? To see her and pretend every cell in his body wasn't screaming to love her?

He needed her to know. He needed her to feel it with explosive force.

He moved his hands up the back of her quaking thighs, and the moment he dug his fingertips into the lush flesh of her bottom, she convulsed against him in rapturous release. And when she finally let herself go, the words on her lips were the ones Artem had waited a lifetime to hear.

"I love you."

Oh, my God.

Ophelia tightened her grip on the ballet barre as Artem rose to his feet and began to undress, his fiery gaze decisively linked with hers.

She was grateful for the barre, for the way it felt solid and familiar in her hands. She needed something real, something substantial to hold on to because this couldn't possibly be reality. This was too heavenly, too much like a beautifully choreographed dance—the kind that left you with a lump in your throat and tears running down your face at the end—to possibly be real.

She was naked and shivering and ravished, and she'd never felt more alive, more whole in her entire life. What had just happened? What had she just *said*?

I love you.

The words had slipped out before she could stop them, and now she'd never be able to take them back. Artem had certainly heard them—the Artem who stood in front of her, naked and hard now, more aroused than she would have thought humanly possible, plus the roomful of Artems reflected in the mirrored walls. He was everywhere. Here. Now. Surrounding her with his audacious, seductive masculinity.

She couldn't think, couldn't breathe, couldn't even figure out where to look. Her gaze flitted from the hard, chiseled planes of his abdomen to the mirror where she could see the sculpted sinews of his back and his firmly muscled backside. He was beautiful, like a god—the Apollo of Balanchine's *Orpheus*, an embodiment of poetry, music, dance and song, all the things she held most near and dear to her heart.

"Oh, kitten," he whispered, sliding a hand through her hair and resting his forehead against hers.

His erection pressed hot and wanting against her stomach, and in that perfect, precious moment he felt so big and capable that anything seemed possible. He was bigger than her fears. Bigger than her past. Bigger than her illness.

"I love you, too," he breathed, as he pushed inside her, pressing her into the barre. "I've loved you all along."

It was such ecstasy to have him filling her again, she could have wept. She'd been waiting for this since the morning she'd fled his penthouse. She just hadn't wanted to admit it. How could she have been so foolish to think she could live without this, without *him*, when the notion was impossible in every way? She rested her hands on his chest, wanting to imprint her touch there somehow, to mark him as hers, this magnificent man who refused to let her push him away.

At the moment of their joining, he groaned and she slid her hands down and around, reaching for his hips so she could anchor him in place. She wanted to hold on to this moment, this moment of coming together, while her entire body sighed in relief.

She could feel him throbbing and pulsing deep in her center, and it was almost too much. Too much pleasure. Too much sensation. She was going to come again. Soon. And he hadn't even moved.

"Do you have any idea how I've missed you?" he whispered into her hair, as he started to slide in and out. Slow at first, with languid, tender strokes as the pressure gathered and built, bearing down on her with frightening intensity.

"Yes," she whimpered. "I do... I do."

I do.

Wedding vows.

"My bride," he murmured, with aching sincerity in his voice as he thrust faster. Harder.

And she didn't fight it this time. Couldn't, even if she'd wanted to. Because since the moment she'd walked into this room, this mirrored place of hope, all her fractured pieces had somehow come together. She'd stayed at Artem's penthouse while he'd been gone. Because of this room. Every night, she found herself slipping on her ballet shoes and dancing again. Because of this room. She was healing. Because of this room.

She didn't feel like Ophelia Rose anymore—that sad, sick girl who'd given up on life. On dance. On love. Nor did she feel like Ophelia Baronova, because that Ophelia had known nothing but ballet. She'd never known how it felt to come apart in the arms of a man who loved her. She'd never lived with secret knowledge that life was growing inside her. A future. A real one.

A family.

No, she felt different now. Hopeful. Whole. The woman she felt like now was a dancer, a lover, a mother. And her name was Ophelia Drake.

"Tell me," Artem commanded, his eyes going sober, his strokes longer, deeper. She didn't think it was possible to love him more, but the deeper he pulsed inside her, the deeper she fell. "Look at me, kitten. I need to hear it. I love you with everything I have, everything I am. Tell me you'll be my wife."

"Yes," she whispered, unable to stop the tears from filling her eyes. "I will."

He kissed her with a tenderness so different from the violent climax building inside her that it felt like a dream. A beautiful, impossible dream.

"Don't be scared, baby," he murmured against her lips.

"I'm not." She clenched her inner muscles around

him, drawing a moan of pure male satisfaction from his soul. "Not anymore."

Then he was slamming into her with such delicious desperation that she could no longer keep her orgasm at bay. It tore through her and she cried out just as Artem pushed into her with a final mighty thrust. He shuddered and groaned his release as her back pressed harder against the ballet barre, and somehow she had the wherewithal to open her eyes so she could watch him climax. She wanted to see the perfection of his pleasure mirrored back at her, silvery reflections as plentiful and exquisite as the facets of a diamond.

They stayed that way, against the wall with their hearts crashing into each other, until their breathing slowed and the music went silent. Then, and only then, did Artem pull back to look at her. He brushed the hair from her eyes and covered her face with tender kisses.

I love you.

I love you.

I love you.

She wasn't sure if the words were hers or his. If they were merely thoughts or if one of them said them aloud. It had become like a heartbeat. Natural. Unstoppable.

Artem lowered his lips to her ear and whispered, "I think this occasion calls for a diamond. Don't you?"

Laugher bubbled up her throat. "Don't tell me you still have Princess Grace's necklace lying about?"

"No." He shook his head. His sensual lips were curved in a knowing grin, but the look in his eyes was pure seriousness. "Better."

She swallowed. Hard. "Better?"

Had he bought her an engagement ring? Was he about to reach into his suit pocket on the floor and retrieve one those infamous Drake-blue boxes with a white satin bow?

"Wait here," he ordered, his gaze flitting ever so briefly to her discarded nightgown pooled at her feet. "And don't even think about getting dressed."

She grinned as her heart pounded against her rib cage. "As you wish."

He blew her a kiss and strode naked out of the room, while she stared openly at his beautiful body. She could hardly believe this breathtaking man was going to be her husband. The father of her baby.

She slid her hands over her belly and marveled at the subtle, firm swell and the new heaviness in her breasts that meant Artem's child was growing inside her. It felt like a miracle. The doctor at the hospital had been right. Her breakout MS symptoms had all but gone away over the past few days. She felt healthier now, more herself, than she had since before her diagnosis. Some new mothers with MS experienced a relapse shortly after giving birth, but she wasn't worrying about that yet. She had the best doctors money could buy, and whatever happened, she could deal with it. Just like other new mothers did.

"You're beautiful, you know. More beautiful than I've ever seen you," Artem said, as he walked back into the studio holding a large black velvet box. Far too large for a simple engagement ring. "I have a mind to keep you barefoot and pregnant."

Ophelia laughed. "Are you forgetting I have a job

that I love? Besides, I'm not barefoot. There are ballet shoes on my feet."

She pointed a toe at him, and he grinned. "Even better, kitten. Be still my heart."

"What have you got there?" she asked, eyeing the velvet box. "Elizabeth Taylor's bracelet? Queen Elizabeth's tiara?"

"No," he said quietly. "Your grandmother's."

He lifted the lid of the box to reveal a glittering diamond tiara resting on a dark satin pillow. Eight delicate scrolls of tiny, inlaid diamonds curled up from the base, surrounding a stunning central stone. A yellow diamond. Just like…

"No." She started to tremble from head to toe. "This isn't…"

She couldn't even form the words. *The Drake Diamond*. It was too much to hope for. Too much to even dream.

"Yes, kitten." It is. He lifted the tiara from the box and placed it gingerly on her head. "The Drake Diamond has found its way home."

She caught a glimpse of her reflection in the mirror and nearly fainted again. The Drake Diamond was back. In New York. Reset in its original design. And she wasn't looking at it in a fancy glass case, but sitting on her very own head.

She bit her lip to keep from crying. "But I don't understand. How is this possible? I thought a buyer in Mexico City bought it at the auction."

Realization dawned slowly. Mexico City… Artem's urgent business trip. *Oh, my God.*

Artem shrugged. "I bought it back."

"Drake Diamonds bought it back? Just days after it was auctioned off?" She started to shake her head, but was afraid to move when a priceless stone was sitting atop her head.

"No." Artem's voice softened, almost as if he were imparting a secret. "*I* bought it back. Not Drake Diamonds."

"You? *Personally?*" It was too much to wrap her bejeweled head around. Did Artem have that kind of money? Did anyone?

"Yes, me. So not to worry. There won't be any more talk about resigning as CEO. It looks like I'll be working at Drake Diamonds for the rest of my life now." He let out a laugh. "With Dalton, actually. We've decided to share the role."

"I think that's perfect," she said through her tears. "But why? You didn't have to do this for me. It's too much."

She was crying in earnest now, unable to stop the flow of tears. She'd never expected this. She'd come to terms with the loss of the diamond. It had been hard, but she'd accepted it. She was pretty much an expert on loss now.

Not anymore, a tiny voice whispered inside. *Not anymore.*

Artem gathered her in his arms and pulled her against his solid chest. "Shh. Don't cry. Please don't cry. I wanted you to have it. I want you to wear that diamond tiara when you walk down the aisle to me on the day I make you my wife. You were right. It's not just a stone. It's a part of family history. Mine. Yours."

He raised her chin with a touch of his finger so her gaze met his. It seemed as if all the love in the world was shining back at her from the depths of his eyes. "And now ours."

Then he kissed away each and every one of her diamond tears.

* * * * *

THE PRINCESS PROBLEM

TERI WILSON

For my English writer friend and fellow royal
enthusiast, Rachel Brimble.

"The pearl is the queen of gems and the gem of queens."

Grace Kelly

Chapter One

It was the pearls that tipped Dalton off.

Dalton Drake knew a string of South Sea pearls when he saw one, even when those pearls were mostly hidden behind the crisp black collar of an Armani suit jacket. He stood in the doorway of his office, frowning at the back of the Armani-clad figure. The pearls in question were a luminous gold, just a shade or two darker than a glass of fizzy Veuve Clicquot. The rarest of the rare. Worth more than half the jewels in the glittering display cases of Drake Diamonds, the illustrious establishment where he currently stood. And owned. And ran, along with his brother, Artem Drake.

Dalton had grown up around pearls. They were in his blood, every bit as much as diamonds were. What he couldn't figure out was why such a priceless piece of jewelry was currently draped around the neck of a glorified errand boy. Or why that particular errand boy possessed such a tiny waist and lushly curved figure.

Dalton had paid a small fortune for a private plane to bring someone by the name of Monsieur Oliver Martel to New York all the way from the royal territory of Delamotte on the French Riviera. What the hell had gone wrong? It didn't take a genius to figure out he wasn't looking at a *monsieur*, the simple black men's suit notwithstanding. Delicate, perfectly manicured fingertips peeked from beneath the oversized sleeves. Wisps of fine blond hair escaped the fedora atop her head. She lowered herself into one of the chairs opposite his desk with a feline grace that wasn't just feminine, but regal. Far too regal for a simple employee, even an employee of a royal household.

There was an imposter in Dalton's office, and it most definitely wasn't the strand of pearls.

Dalton closed the door behind him and cleared his throat. Perhaps it was best to tread lightly until he figured out how a royal princess from a tiny principality on the French Riviera had ended up on Fifth Avenue in New York. "Monsieur Martel, I presume?"

"Non. Je suis désolé," the woman said in flawless French. Then she squared her shoulders, stood and slowly turned around. "But there's been a slight change of plans."

Dalton should have been prepared. He'd been researching the Marchand royal family's imperial jeweled eggs for months. Dalton was nothing if not meticulous. If pressed, he could draw each of the twelve imperial eggs from memory. He could also name every member of the Marchand family on sight, going back to the late 1800s, when the royal jeweler had crafted the very first gem-encrusted egg. Naturally, he'd seen enough photographs of the princess to know she was beautiful.

But when the woman in his office turned to face him, Dalton found himself in the very rare state of being caught off guard. In fact, he wasn't sure it would have been at all possible to prepare himself for the sight of Her Royal Highness Princess Aurélie Marchand in the flesh.

Photographs didn't do her beauty justice. Sure, those perfectly feminine features could be captured on film—the slightly upturned nose, the perfect bow-shaped lips, the impossibly large eyes, as green as the finest Colombian emerald. But no two-dimensional image could capture the fire in those eyes or the luminescence of her porcelain skin, as lovely as the strand of pearls around her elegant neck.

A fair bit lovelier, actually.

Dalton swallowed. Hard. He wasn't fond of surprises, and he was even less fond of the fleeting feeling that passed through him when she fixed her gaze with his. Awareness. Attraction. Those things had no place in his business life. Or the rest of his life, for that matter. Not anymore.

"A change of plans. I see that." He lifted a brow. "Your Highness."

Her eyes widened ever so slightly. "So you know who I am?"

"Indeed I do. Please have a seat, Princess Aurélie." Dalton waited for her to sit, then smoothed his tie and lowered himself into his chair. He had a feeling whatever was coming next might best be taken sitting down.

There was a large black trunk at the princess's feet, which he assumed contained precious cargo—the imperial eggs scheduled to go on display in the Drake

Diamonds showroom in a week's time. But there was no legitimate reason why Aurélie Marchand had delivered them, especially after other transport had been so painstakingly arranged.

Coupled with the fact that she was dressed in a man's suit that was at least three sizes too big, Dalton sensed trouble. A big, royal heap of it.

"Good. That makes things easier, I suppose." She sat opposite him and removed her fedora, freeing a mass of golden curls.

God, she's gorgeous.

Sitting down had definitely been a good call. A surge of arousal shot through him, as fiery and bright as a blazing red ruby. Which made no sense at all. Yes, she was beautiful. And yes, there was something undeniably enchanting about her. But she was dressed as a royal bodyguard. The only thing Dalton should be feeling right now was alarmed. He sure as hell shouldn't be turned on.

Stick to business. This is about the eggs.

Dalton inhaled a fortifying breath. He couldn't recall a time in his entire professional life when he'd had to remind himself to stick to business. "Do explain, Your Highness."

"Don't call me that. *Please.*" She smiled a dazzling smile. "Call me Aurélie."

"As you wish." Against every instinct Dalton possessed, he nodded his agreement. "Aurélie."

"Thank you." There was a slight tremble in her voice that made Dalton's chest hurt for some strange reason.

"Tell me, Aurélie, to what do I owe the pleasure of a visit from a member of the royal family?" He tried not to look at her crazy costume, but failed. Miserably.

"Yes, well…" There was that tremble in her voice

again. Nerves? Desperation? Surely not. What did a royal princess have to feel desperate about? "In accordance with the agreement between Drake Diamonds and the monarchy of Delamotte, I've delivered the collection of the Marchand imperial eggs. I understand your store will be displaying the eggs for fourteen days."

Dalton nodded. "That's correct."

"As I mentioned, there's been a slight change of plans. I'll be staying in New York for the duration of the exhibit." Her delicate features settled into a regal expression of practiced calmness.

Too calm for Dalton's taste. Something was wrong here. Actually, a lot of things were wrong. The clothes, the sudden appearance of actual royalty when he'd been dealing with palace bureaucracy for months, the notable absence of security personnel...

Was he really supposed to believe that a member of the Marchand royal family had flown halfway across the world with a trunkful of priceless family jewels without a single bodyguard in tow?

And then there was the matter of the princess's demeanor. She might be sitting across from him with a polite smile on her face, but Dalton could sense something bubbling beneath the surface. Some barely contained sense of anticipation. She had the wild-eyed look of a person ready to throw herself off the nearest cliff.

Why did he get the awful feeling that he'd be expected to catch her if something went wrong?

Whatever she was up to, he didn't want any part of it. For starters, he had more important things to worry about than babysitting a spoiled princess. Not to mention the fact that whatever was happening here was in strict violation of the agreement he'd made with the palace. And he wasn't about to risk losing the eggs. Press releases had been sent out. Invitations to the gala were in the mail. This was the biggest event the Drake Diamonds flagship store had hosted since it opened its doors on Fifth Avenue back in 1940.

"I see." He reached for the phone. "I'll just give the palace a call to confirm the new arrangements."

"I'd rather you didn't." Aurélie reached to stop him, placing a graceful hand on his wrist.

He narrowed his gaze at her. She was playing him. That much was obvious. What he didn't know was why.

He leaned back in his chair. "Aurélie, why don't you tell me exactly why you're here and then I'll decide whether or not to make that call?"

"It's simple. I want a holiday. Not as a princess, but as a normal person. I want to eat hot dogs on the street. I want to go for a walk in Central Park. I want to sit on a blanket in the grass and read a library book." Her voice grew soft, wistful, with just a hint of urgency. "I want to be a regular New Yorker for these few weeks, and I need your help doing so."

"You want to eat hot dogs," he said dryly. "With *my* help?" She couldn't be serious.

Apparently she was. Dead serious. "Exactly. That's not so strange, is it?"

Yes, actually. It was. "Aurélie…"

But he couldn't get a word in edgewise. She was going on about open-air buses and the subway and, to Dalton's utter confusion, giant soft pretzels. What was with her obsession with street food?

"Aurélie," he said again, cutting off a new monologue about pizza.

"Oh." She gave a little jump in her chair. "Yes?"

"This arrangement you're suggesting sounds a bit, ah, unorthodox." That was putting it mildly. He couldn't recall ever negotiating a business deal that involved soft pretzels.

She shrugged an elegant shoulder. "I've brought you the eggs. Every single one of them. All I ask is that you show me around a little. And let me stay without notifying the palace, or the press, obviously. That's all."

So she wanted a place to hide. And a tour guide. And his silence. *That's all.*

And face the wrath of the palace when they realized what he'd done? Have the eggs snatched away before the exhibit even opened? Absolutely not. "All the arrangements are in place. I'd have to be insane to agree to this. You realize that, don't you?"

"Not insane. Just a little adventurous." She was beginning to have that wild-eyed look again. He could see a whole secret, aching world in her emerald gaze. She leaned closer, wrapping Dalton in a heady floral aroma. Orchids, peonies, something else he couldn't quite place. Lilacs, maybe. "Live a little, Mr. Drake."

Live a little. God, she sounded like his brother. And his sister. And pretty much everyone else in his life. "That's not going to work on me, Your Highness."

She said nothing, just smiled and twirled a lock of platinum hair around one of her fingers.

Flirting wasn't going to work either.

He ignored the hair twirling as best he could and shot her a cool look. "The eggs are here, as agreed upon. Give me one legitimate reason why I shouldn't call the palace."

She was delusional or, at the very least, spoiled rotten. Did she really think he had time to drop everything

he was doing to babysit an entitled princess? He had a
company to run. A company in need of a fresh start.

He sat back in his chair, glanced at the Cartier
strapped around his wrist, and waited.

He'd give her two more minutes.

That's all.

Aurélie was beginning to think she'd made a mistake. A big one.

Granted, she hadn't exactly thought this whole adventure through. Planning had never been her strong
suit. Firing Oliver Martel and demanding that he hand
over his suit so she could take his place on the flight to
the States had been easy enough. That guy was an arrogant jerk. He needed to go, and he'd made enough
passes at her over the course of his employment at the
palace for her to have plenty of leverage over him. No
problems there.

Impersonating a royal courier had also gone swim-
mingly. It was startling how little attention the pilot had
paid her. He seemed to look right through Aurélie, as if
she were a ghost rather than a living, breathing person.
Then again, Aurélie had lived in a fishbowl her entire
life. She was accustomed to being watched every waking
moment of her existence. That's what this whole charade
was about—getting away from prying eyes while she
still could. In a few short weeks, her entire life would
change. And, if her father got his way, she'd never get
this kind of chance again.

Aurélie didn't regret walking away from her royal
duties for a moment. Placing her trust in Dalton Drake,
on the other hand, might not have been the wisest idea.
For starters, she hadn't expected the CEO of Drake Dia-

monds to be so very handsome. Or young. Or handsome. Or stern. Or handsome.

It was unsettling, really. How was she supposed to make a solid case for herself when she was busy thinking about Dalton's chiseled jaw or his mysterious gray gaze? And his voice—deep, intense and unapologetically masculine. The man could probably read a software manual aloud and have every woman in Manhattan melting at his feet.

But it was his attitude that had really thrown Aurélie off-balance. She wasn't accustomed to people challenging her, with one notable exception. Her father.

That was to be expected, though. Her father ran a small country. Dalton Drake ran a jewelry store. She'd assumed he would be easy to persuade.

She'd thought wrong, apparently. But he would come around. He had to. Because she was *not* going to spend her last twenty-one days of freedom staring at the castle walls.

She swallowed. These wouldn't be her last twenty-one days of freedom. Her father would change his mind. But she shouldn't really be thinking about that right now, should she? Not while Dalton Drake was threatening to pick up the phone and tattle on her.

Give me one legitimate reason why I shouldn't call the palace.

Aurélie's heart beat wildly in her chest as she met Dalton's gaze. "Actually, Mr. Drake, I have a very good reason why you and I should reach an agreement."

He glanced at his watch again, and she wanted to scream. "Do elaborate, Your Highness."

"It's best if I show you."

She bent to open the buttery-soft Birkin bag at her

feet, removed a dark blue velvet box from inside and placed it square in the center of Dalton Drake's desk.

He grew very still. Even the air between them seemed to stop moving. Aurélie had managed to get his attention. *Finally.*

He stared at the box for a long moment, his gaze lingering on the embossed silver *M* on its top. He knew what that *M* stood for, and so did she. Marchand. "One of the eggs, I presume?" Clearly, Mr. Drake had done his homework.

"Yes." Aurélie offered him her sweetest princess smile. "And no."

Before he could protest, she reached for the box and removed its plush velvet lid. The entire top portion of the box detached from the base, so all that was left sitting atop the desk was a shimmering, decorated egg covered in pavé diamonds. Pale pink, blush enamel and tiny seed pearls rested on a bed of white satin.

Aurélie had seen the egg on many occasions, but it still took her breath away every time she looked at it. It glittered beneath the overhead lights, an unbroken expanse of dazzling radiance. Her precious, priceless secret.

She hadn't realized how very strange this would feel to share it with someone else. How vulnerable. She felt as though she'd unlocked a treasure chest and offered this strange man her heart. How absurd.

"I don't understand," he said, shaking his head. "I've never seen this egg before."

But there was a hint of a smile dancing on his lips, and when he trained his eyes on Aurélie, she could see the glittering egg reflected in the cool gray of his eyes, and she knew. She just knew.

Dalton Drake would agree to everything she'd asked.

"No one has," she said quietly.

She didn't know how she managed to sound so calm, so composed, when she was this close to having the one thing she'd wanted for such a long time. Freedom. However temporary.

He lifted a brow. "No one?"

"No one outside the Marchand family."

"So there's a thirteenth egg? I don't believe it," he said.

"Believe it, Mr. Drake. My father gave this egg to my mother on their wedding day. Other than the palace jeweler, no one even knew it existed." A familiar, bittersweet ache stirred inside Aurélie. She'd always loved the idea of her parents sharing such an intimate secret. Their wedding, their engagement and even their courtship had been watched by the entire world. But they'd managed to save something just for themselves.

What must it be like to be loved like that? To trust someone so implicitly? She'd never know, whether her father went through with his plans or not.

Of course, her parents' fairy-tale romance hadn't been as real as she'd always believed. Fairy tales never were.

Her throat grew tight. "I inherited it when my mother died three years ago. Even I was stunned to learn of a thirteenth egg."

Many things had surprised her then, but none so much as the shocking details of her parents' marriage. Her mother was gone, and Aurélie was left with nothing but the egg, a book with gilt-edged pages and a father she realized she'd never really known. And questions. So many questions.

When had things changed between her parents? Or

had the greatest royal romance of the past fifty years always been a lie?

Her eyelashes fluttered shut and memories moved behind her eyes—her mother and father waltzing in a sweeping circle beneath glittering chandeliers, the whirring of paparazzi cameras and her mother's elegant features setting into her trademark serene expression. A smile that never quite reached her eyes. How had Aurélie never noticed?

She opened her eyes and found Dalton watching her intently from across the desk. "Why are you showing this egg to me, Aurélie?"

Aurélie. Not Princess. Not Your Highness. Just her name, spoken in that deep, delicious voice of his.

Her head spun a little. *Concentrate.* "Because, I'd like you to display it in your exhibition."

"You're certain?"

"Absolutely." She paused. "On one condition."

Dalton gave her a sideways glance. "Just one?"

"Give me my adventure, Mr. Drake. On my terms. No bodyguards, no notifying the palace, no press. That's all I ask." And it was a lot to ask. She had enough dirt on the courier to guarantee he wouldn't go running to the palace. But someone would notice she'd gone missing. She just didn't know when.

It would be a miracle if she got away with this, but she had to try. She wouldn't be able to live with herself if she didn't.

She stood and extended her hand.

Aurélie had never in her life shaken a man's hand before. Certainly not the hand of a commoner. In Delamotte, Dalton wouldn't be permitted to touch her. Under royal protocol, he'd be required to bow from a chaste three-foot distance. "Do we have a deal?"

"I believe we do."

Then Dalton Drake rose to his feet and took Aurélie's hand in his warm, solid grip.

Delamotte had never felt so far away.

Chapter Two

"So let me get this straight." Artem Drake, Dalton's younger brother, pointed at the diamond-and-pearl-encrusted Marchand egg sitting in the middle of the small conference table in the corner of his office and lifted a brow. "You're saying no one has ever seen this egg before."

Dalton nodded and glanced over his shoulder to double-check that he'd closed the door behind him when he'd entered. He didn't want anyone else on the staff knowing about the egg. Its unveiling needed to be carefully planned, and he couldn't risk the possibility of a potential leak.

Satisfied with the privacy of their surroundings, Dalton turned to face his brother again and noted the enormous empty spot on the wall above his desk. The spot where the portrait of their father had hung for the better part of the past thirty years.

He was a bit taken aback by the painting's absence, since Artem hadn't mentioned his plan to remove it. And Drake Diamonds had never been about change. It was about tradition, from the store's coveted location on Fifth Avenue to the little blue boxes they were so famous for. Drake Diamond blue. The color was synonymous with class, style and all things Drake. It was the shade of the plush carpeting beneath Dalton's feet, as well as the hue of the silk tie around his neck. If Dalton were to slit his wrists, he'd probably bleed Drake Diamond blue.

But time changed things, even in places where tradition reigned. Their father was dead. This was no longer Geoffrey Drake's office. It was Artem's, despite the fact that there'd never been any love lost between Dalton's younger brother and their father. Despite the fact that Dalton himself had been groomed for this office since the day he'd graduated from Harvard Business School.

He was relieved the portrait was gone. Now he'd no longer be forced to stop himself from hurling his glass of scotch at it on nights when he found himself alone in the store after hours. Which was often. More often than not, to be precise.

Dalton averted his gaze from the empty wall and re-focused his attention on Artem. There was no point in dwelling on the wrongness of the terms of their father's Last Will and Testament. He probably should have expected it. Geoffrey Drake hadn't been known for his sense of fairness. He certainly hadn't had a reputation as a loving family man. He'd been shrewd. Calculating. Brusque. As had all the Drake men, Dalton included, for as long as grooms had been slipping revered Drake Diamonds on their brides' fingers. Empires weren't built on kindness.

He leveled his gaze at Artem. "That's exactly what I'm saying. No one outside the Marchand family is aware of this egg's existence. Until now, of course."

Artem reached for the egg.

"Seriously?" Dalton sighed, pulled a pair of white cotton jeweler's gloves from his suit pocket and threw them at his brother. "Put these on if you insist on touching it."

Artem caught the gloves midair and shook his head. "Relax, would you? A secret Marchand imperial egg just fell into our laps. You should be doing backflips between the cases of engagement rings downstairs."

"We're on the tenth floor. Engagements is just down the hall, not downstairs," Dalton said dryly.

It was a cheap shot. Artem actually showed up to work on a regular basis now that they'd talked things through and agreed to share the position of Chief Executive Officer. The fact that Artem was now married and expecting a baby with their top jewelry designer, Ophelia Rose Drake, didn't hurt either.

Artem was a husband now, and soon he'd be a father. Dalton couldn't fathom it. Then again, he'd never actually witnessed a healthy marriage. To be honest, he wasn't sure such a thing existed.

Artem's features settled into the lazy playboy expression he'd been so famous for before he'd surprised everyone by settling down. "I know that, brother. You're missing the point. This is good. Hell, this is fantastic. You should be smiling for a change."

Dalton's frown hardened into place. "I'll smile when the unveiling of the collection goes off without a hitch. And when I'm certain I won't be facing jail time in Delamotte for kidnapping the princess."

"She came here of her own free will." With the hint

of a rueful smile, Artem shrugged. "Besides, the way I see it, you have a much bigger problem to worry about."

More problems. Marvelous. "Such as?"

"Such as the fact that you've been charged with showing a runaway princess a good time." Artem let out a chuckle. "Sorry, but surely even you can see the irony of the situation."

Dalton was all too aware he wasn't known as the fun brother. Artem typically had enough fun for both of them. In reality, his younger brother had probably had enough fun for the greater population of Manhattan. But that was before Ophelia. Artem's face might no longer be a permanent fixture on *Page Six*, but against all odds, Dalton had never seen him happier.

"Fun is overrated," Dalton deadpanned.

Fun didn't pay the mortgage on his Lenox Hill penthouse. It hadn't landed him on *Fortune*'s "40 Under 40" list for five consecutive years. And it sure as hell didn't keep hordes of shoppers flocking to Drake Diamonds every day, just to take something, anything, home in a little blue box.

Artem's smirk went into overdrive. "From what you've told me, the princess doesn't seem to share your opinion on the matter. It sounds as though Her Royal Highness is rather fond of fun."

Her Royal Highness.

There was a princess sitting in Dalton's office. And for some nonsensical reason, she was waiting for him to take her on a grand adventure involving hot dogs and public transportation. How such things fit into *anyone's* definition of a good time was beyond him.

A sharp pain took up residence in Dalton's temples. "Aurélie," he muttered.

Artem's eyebrow arched, and he stared at Dalton for a moment that stretched far too long. "Pardon?"

Dalton cleared his throat. "She's asked me to call her Aurélie."

"Really?" Artem's trademark amused expression made yet another appearance. To say it was beginning to grate on Dalton's nerves would have been a massive understatement. "This princess sounds rather interesting."

"That's one way of putting it, although I'd probably use another word."

"Like?"

Unexpected. "Impulsive." *Whimsical.* "Volatile." *Breathtaking.* "Dangerous."

"That's three words," Artem corrected. "Interesting. The princess—excuse me, *Aurélie*—must have made quite an impression in the twenty minutes you spent with her."

Twenty minutes? Impossible. It had been precisely 10 a.m. when he'd first set eyes on those golden South Sea pearls. On that straight, regal back and exquisitely elegant neck. If the severity of the tension between his shoulder blades was any indication, he'd been dealing with the stress of harboring a royal runaway for at least two hours. Possibly three.

Dalton glanced at his Cartier. It read *10:21.* He'd need to add a massage therapist to the payroll at this rate. *If he managed to keep an aneurysm at bay for the next few weeks.*

"I dare say you appear rather intrigued by her." Artem's gaze narrowed. "If I didn't know you better, I'd go so far as to say you seem smitten. But of course the Dalton I know would never mix business and pleasure."

Damn straight. Dalton preferred pleasure of the no-strings variety, and he seldom had trouble finding it. Sex belonged in the bedroom, not the boardroom. He wasn't Artem, for crying out loud. He could keep his libido in check when the situation called for it. "I assure you I'm not smitten. I have no feelings toward the princess whatsoever, aside from obligation."

"Ah yes, your bargain." Artem turned the egg in his grasp, inspecting it. Blinding light reflected off its pavé diamonds in every direction, making the egg look far more precious than a collection of carefully arranged gemstones. Dynamic. Alive. A brilliant, beating heart.

Dalton had never seen anything quite like it. The other Marchand imperial eggs paled in comparison. When it went on display in the showroom, Drake Diamonds would be packed wall-to-wall with people. People who wouldn't go home without a Drake-blue bag dangling from their arms.

If the egg went on display.

It would. The exhibition and gala would take place as scheduled. The spectacular secret egg was just what Drake Diamonds needed. When Dalton and Artem's father died, he'd left the family business on the verge of bankruptcy. They'd managed to climb their way back to solvency, but Drake Diamonds still wasn't anywhere near where it had been in its glory days.

Dalton aimed to fix that. With the egg, he could.

He would personally see to it that the palace in Delamotte had nothing to worry about. He'd keep Aurélie under lock and key. Then, in three weeks' time, she'd pack up the eggs and go straight home. Dalton would strap her into her airplane seat himself if he had to.

Artem returned the egg to its shiny satin pedestal, peeled off the jeweler's gloves and tossed them on the table. Then he crossed his arms and shot Dalton a wary glance. "Tell me, what sort of fun is the princess up to at the moment?"

Dalton shrugged. "She's in my office."

"Your office? Of course. Loads of fun, that place." Artem shot him an exaggerated eye roll.

This was going to stop. Dalton might have agreed to escort the princess on her grand adventure, but under no circumstances would he succumb to constant commentary on his personal life. "I've asked Mrs. Barnes to get her settled with a glass of champagne and a plate of the petit fours we serve in Engagements."

"So you have absolutely no interest in the woman, yet she's in your office snacking on bridal food."

Before Dalton could comment, there was a soft knock on the door.

The brothers exchanged a loaded glance, and Dalton swiftly covered the jeweled egg with the lid to its tasteful indigo box.

Once the treasure was safely ensconced in velvet, Artem said, "Come in."

The door opened, revealing Dalton's secretary balancing a plate of petit fours in one hand and a glass of champagne in the other, wearing a distinct look of alarm. "I'm sorry to interrupt…"

Dalton's gut churned. Something wasn't right. *But what could have gone wrong in the span of a few minutes?* "Yes, Mrs. Barnes?"

"Your guest is gone, Mr. Drake."

Surely she was mistaken. Aurélie wouldn't just take off and leave the eggs behind. She wouldn't think about walking around a strange city all alone, without her security detail.

Or would she?

Dalton swore under his breath. Why did he get the feeling that Aurélie would do both of those things without bothering to consider the possible disastrous consequences of her actions?

Live a little, Mr. Drake.

"Shall I take a look in the ladies' room?" Mrs. Barnes asked.

Dalton shook his head. If he thought for one second that Aurélie Marchand could be found in the ladies' room of Drake Diamonds, he'd march in there and go get her himself. "No, thank you. I'll see to her whereabouts. That will be all, Mrs. Barnes."

"Yes, sir." She nodded and disappeared in the direction of Dalton's office.

"Calm down, brother. I'm sure she hasn't gone far. She's not going to just disappear and leave the Marchand family jewels behind." Artem waved a casual hand at the velvet box in the center of the table.

Dalton sighed. "Have you forgotten that she's in a strange city? In a foreign country. All alone."

"Exactly. She's hasn't ventured any further than the Plaza. Come on, I'll help you track her down." Artem reached for the suit jacket on the back of his chair.

"No," Dalton said through gritted teeth. He pointed at the velvet box. "You stay, and see to it that the eggs are safely locked away in the vault. I'll find Miss Marchand."

And when he did, he'd lay down some ground rules for their arrangement. *After* he'd made it clear that he considered her behavior wholly unacceptable. Princess or not.

"As you wish," Artem said. "But can I give you one piece of advice?"

Dalton glared at him. "Do I have a choice?"

"Whatever you do, don't take her to bed." Artem's mouth curved into a knowing grin. "Assuming you find her, of course."

Who did Dalton Drake think he was?

She hadn't traveled halfway across the world, and risked the wrath of her father, only to stay trapped in a closed room on the tenth floor of Drake Diamonds. Not that the surroundings weren't opulent. On the contrary, the place was steeped in elegant luxury, from the pale blue plush carpet to the tasteful crown molding. It felt more like being in a palace than a jewelry store.

Which was precisely the problem.

She didn't want to be stuck inside this grand institution. It wasn't what she'd signed on for. Did he not realize the risks she'd taken to get here? She already had three missed call notifications on her cell from Delamotte. None from her father, thank goodness. It would take him days, if not weeks, to realize she was gone. The Reigning Prince had more important things to worry about than something as trivial as his only daughter fleeing the country. Oh, the irony.

But the palace staff was another story. They watched her every move and minced no words when it came to their opinions on her behavior. Or her fashion sense. Or her hair.

Or her love life. They had plenty to say about that.

How on earth was she going to pull this off? What if her father came looking for her?

She sighed. She wasn't going to think about that now. Besides, she was lost in the maze of pale blue and the sparkle of the diamond store. How would she find her way around New York when she couldn't even manage to navigate the terrain of Drake Diamonds?

Every room looked the same. Row upon row of diamonds sparkled beneath gleaming glass. Chandelier earrings. Long platinum chains with dazzling pendants shaped like antique keys. Shiny silver bracelets with heart-shaped charms.

Engagement rings.

Aurélie looked around and realized she was surrounded by couples embracing, holding hands and clinking champagne flutes together while they gazed into one another's eyes. Everywhere she turned, teary-eyed brides-to-be were slipping diamond solitaires on their fingers.

She felt oddly hollow all of a sudden. Numb. Empty. Alone.

For some silly reason she remembered the feel of Dalton's palm sliding against her own when they'd shaken on their deal. He had strong hands. The hands of a man accustomed to getting what he wanted. What he wanted right now was her secret egg, of course. She'd given it to him on a silver platter.

And now he was gone.

Her cell phone vibrated in her pocket. Again. Aurélie switched it off and removed the SIM card without bothering to look at the display. Without a SIM card, the GPS tracking on her iPhone wouldn't work. At least she thought she remembered reading that somewhere.

She really should have had a better escape plan. Or at least *a plan*.

Her gaze snagged on a silver sign hanging on the wall with discreet black lettering. *Will you? Welcome to the Drake Diamond Engagement Collection.*

She rolled her eyes, marched straight to the elevator and jabbed at the down button with far too much force.

But as she waited, something made her turn and look again, some perverse urge to torture herself. Maybe she needed a reminder of why she'd fled Delamotte. Maybe she wanted to test herself to see if she could stand there in the midst of so much romantic bliss without breaking down. Maybe she'd simply left the vestiges of dignity back in her home country.

She stared at the happy couples, unabashed in their affection, and felt as though she were disappearing. Fading into the tasteful cream-colored wallpaper.

None of this is real, she told herself. She didn't believe any of it for a minute.

She wanted to, though. Oh how she wanted to. She wanted to believe that happy endings were real, that love could last, that marriage was something more than just another transaction. A business deal.

A bargain.

But she didn't dare, because believing the fairy tale would hurt too much. Believing would mean admitting she was missing out on something she'd never have. Something worth more than deep crimson rubies, cabochon emeralds and the entire collection of imperial Marchand eggs.

Why was the elevator taking so long? She pushed the button a few more times, yet still jumped in surprise when the chime signaled the elevator's arrival. The doors swished open, and she half ran, half stumbled inside.

A hand caught her elbow. "Are you all right, miss?"

She blinked up at the elevator attendant dressed in a stylish black suit, pristine white shirt and a bowtie the same hue as the Windsor knot that had sat at the base of

Dalton Drake's muscular neck. Aurélie's gaze lingered on that soft shade of blue as she remembered how perfectly Dalton's silk tie had set off his strong jawline.

"I'm fine, thank you." The elevator closed and began its downward descent, away from all those engagement rings and the quiet solitude of Dalton's office.

The elevator attendant smiled. "Do you need help finding anything?"

Aurélie shook her head, despite the fact that she didn't know the first thing about New York. She didn't know how to hail a cab or ride the subway. She didn't even have a single American dollar in her fancy handbag. She had a wallet full of euros, yet she wasn't even familiar with the exchange rate.

But none of that mattered. She just wanted to get out of there.

Now.

Chapter Three

Right around the time he was on the verge of losing his mind, Dalton spotted Aurélie on the outskirts of Central Park. She was standing beneath a portable blue awning at the corner of Central Park South and 59th Street, directly across the street from the Plaza Hotel. She was holding a dog. Not a hot dog, but an actual dog. Which for some reason only exacerbated the pounding in Dalton's temples. The woman was impossible.

What had she been thinking? She didn't want to be discovered, yet she'd walked right out the door. Unaccompanied. Unprotected. Undisguised. It was enough to give Dalton a coronary.

At least he'd been able to find her with relative ease. All told, it had only taken about a quarter of an hour. Still, those fifteen minutes had undoubtedly been the longest of Dalton's life.

To top things off, a street musician had parked himself right outside the entrance of Drake Diamonds with his violin and his tip bucket. This marked the third time in less than a month that Dalton had ordered him to leave. Next time, he'd call the cops.

He squinted against the winter wind and shoved his bare hands into his trouser pockets. He'd been in a panic when he'd spun his way out of the store through the revolving door and onto the snowy sidewalk. Filled with dread and angry beyond all comprehension, he hadn't even bothered to grab a coat, and now, three blocks later, he was freezing.

Freezing and absolutely furious.

He dashed across the street without bothering to wait for the signal at the pedestrian crossing, enraging a few cab drivers in the process. Dalton didn't give a damn. He wasn't about to let her out of his sight until he'd returned her safely to his office. And then...

What?

He wasn't actually sure what he'd do at that point. He'd cross that bridge when he came to it. Right now he simply planned on escorting her back to his store on the corner of Fifth Avenue and 57th Street while administering a searing lecture on the dangers of disappearing without giving him any sort of notice whatsoever.

"Aurélie!" He jogged the distance from the curb to where she stood, still holding onto the damn dog.

She didn't hear him. Either that, or she was intentionally ignoring him. It was a toss-up, although Dalton would have greatly preferred the former.

"Aurélie," he said again, through gritted teeth, when he reached her side.

An older woman wearing a hooded parka and fingerless mittens stood next to her. There was a clipboard in her hands and a small playpen filled with little dogs yipping and pouncing on one another at her feet. The woman eyed Dalton, giving him a thorough once-over, and frowned.

"Oh good, you're here," Aurélie said blithely, without tearing her gaze from the trembling, bug-eyed dog in her arms.

It stared at Dalton over her shoulder. He stared back and decided it was possibly the ugliest dog he'd ever set eyes on. Its pointed ears were comically huge, which might have been endearing if not for the googly eyes that appeared to be looking in two completely different directions. And it had a wide, flat muzzle. Not to mention the god-awful snuffling sounds coming from the dog's smashed little face.

"Hello." The woman with the clipboard nodded. "Are you the boyfriend?"

Boyfriend?

Hardly.

He opened his mouth to say no—*God no*—but before he could utter a syllable, Aurélie nodded. "Yes, here he is. Finally."

Dalton didn't know what kind of game she was playing, and frankly, he didn't care. If she wanted to pose as some kind of couple in front of this random stranger who could possibly recognize her from the tabloids, then fine. Although, the idea was laughable at best.

"Yes, here I am." He turned sharp eyes on her with the vague realization that he wasn't laughing. Not even close. "*Finally.* Surely you're aware I've been looking for you, sweetheart."

At last she met his gaze. With snowflakes in her eyelashes and rosy, wind-kissed cheeks, she looked more Snow Queen than princess.

And lovelier than ever.

Nature suited her. Or maybe it was winter itself, the way the bare trees and dove-gray sky seemed to echo the lonely look in her eyes. Seeing her like this, amidst the quiet grace of a snowfall, holding onto that ugly dog like a child hugging a teddy bear, Dalton got a startling glimpse of her truth.

She was running from something. That's why she'd left Delamotte. That's why she'd shown up in men's clothes and begged him not to call the palace. She wasn't here on holiday. She was here to get lost in the crowd.

Not that her reasons had anything to do with Dalton. He was simply her means to an end, and vice versa.

"What's our address again? Silly me, I keep forgetting." She let out a laugh.

Dalton fought to keep his expression neutral. Surely she wasn't planning on moving into his apartment. That's what hotels were for. And there were approximately 250 of them in New York.

Then again, who knew what sort of trouble she could get into unsupervised.

His headache throbbed with renewed intensity. "*Our* address?"

"Of course, darling. You know, the place where we live." Quicker than a blink, her gaze flitted to the woman with the clipboard. "Together."

Struggling to absorb the word *darling*, he muttered the address of his building in the Upper East Side. The woman with the clipboard jotted it down.

Who was this person, anyway? And why did Aurélie

think she had any business knowing where they lived? *Where* I *live. Not* we. *Good God, not we.*

He leaned closer to get a look at whatever form she appeared to be filling out. The bold letters at the top of the page spelled out *Pet Adoption Agreement.*

"Wait," Dalton said, as something wet and foul-smelling slapped against the side of his face. He recoiled and realized, with no small degree of horror, that it was the googly-eyed puppy's tongue.

Marvelous. He wiped his cheek with the cuff of his suit jacket, and aimed his fiercest death glare at Aurélie. "What do you think you're doing?"

"*We* are adopting a dog, darling." Again with the *darling.*

And again with the *we.*

"I believe this is the type of thing we should discuss," he said, trying not to imagine the dreadful dog snoring like a freight train in his office while he tried to run the company.

Or, God forbid, snoring in his bed. Because if adopting homeless animals was the sort of thing she did on a whim when he wasn't looking, she'd need to stay with him. Who knew what kind of trouble she could get into if he left her all alone in a hotel room for a fortnight?

He'd been wrong when he'd described her to Artem as impulsive. *Impulsive* didn't even begin to describe Aurélie. She was full-blown crazy. Either that or the most manipulative woman he'd ever met.

"But we *did* discuss it. This morning." Her bow-shaped lips curved into a beguiling smile that hit Dalton square in his libido, despite the deafening clang of warning bells going off in his head.

She was business. She was irritating to no end. And

what's more, she was far too headstrong for his taste. He shouldn't be attracted to her in any way, shape or form. Nor should he be thinking about that troublesome mouth of hers and the myriad ways in which he'd prefer to see her use it.

She rested a hand on his bicep and gave it a firm squeeze. "Surely you remember our agreement?"

Unbelievable. She was using the secret egg to blackmail him into adopting a dog. She wasn't crazy at all. *Cunning.* Most definitely.

Dalton Drake didn't take orders. Nor did he allow himself to be manipulated in such a manner. Aurélie would learn as much soon enough. But not until he'd taken the pathetic animal home, apparently.

"Well?" The clipboard-wielding woman tilted her head. "What's it going to be? Do you want to adopt him or not?"

Aurélie nodded furiously. "Absolutely. We do. Right, darling?" She looked at him expectantly. So confident. So certain he'd acquiesce to whatever she demanded.

He had a mind to refuse and put her on the next plane back to the French Riviera, along with the dog and all of the Marchand family jewels. Yes, they had a deal. But it didn't encompass sending him on a wild goose chase. Nor did it include sharing his apartment. With her, or the dog.

He hadn't taken a woman into his home since Clarissa. But that had been a long time ago. He'd been a different man.

Think of the egg. What it could do for business.

He looked at Aurélie for a long moment, and for some ridiculous reason, Artem's warning came flooding back.

Whatever you do, don't take her to bed.

He wouldn't. Of course he wouldn't. The very fact that Artem had seen fit to mention the possibility was preposterous. Dalton wasn't the one who'd bedded half the women in Manhattan. That had been Artem's doing. Dalton's self-control was legendary.

But looking into Aurélie's aching emerald eyes did something to him. That vulnerability that she hid so well was barely noticeable, but very much there. And it made him wonder what she'd look like bare in the moonlight, dressed in nothing but pearls.

Damn you, Artem.

Then, before he could stop himself, he heard himself say, "Fine. We'll take the dog."

What kind of person didn't like animals?

The kind who was seething quietly beside Aurélie, evidently.

Dalton hadn't uttered a word since he'd paid the adoption fee and slipped the receipt into his suit pocket. He'd simply aimed a swift, emotionless glance at Aurélie, cupped her elbow in the palm of his hand and steered her back in the direction of Drake Diamonds. Now, less than a block later, he was walking so fast that she struggled to keep up with him. She had a mind to give up entirely and pop into the Plaza for afternoon tea, but looking at the tense set of Dalton's muscular shoulders as he marched in front of her, she got the distinct feeling there'd be hell to pay if she didn't fall in step behind him.

Plus she didn't have any money. Or credit cards. Which meant she was totally dependent on the very cranky Dalton Drake.

Besides, every three or four paces, he glanced over his shoulder, probably to assure himself of her obedience. It was infuriating, particularly when Aurélie recalled the archaic Delamotte law that stated royal wives must walk a minimum of two paces behind their husbands in public. No doubt a man had come up with such a ludicrous decree.

She held the trembling little dog tight against her chest and hastened her steps. She wasn't Dalton's lowly subordinate, and she refused to act like it. Even if, as they said in Delamotte, *la moutarde lui monte au nez.* The mustard was getting to his nose. In other words, he was angry.

Fine. So was she. And she wasn't spending another second scurrying to keep up with him.

"*Arrête!* Stop it." She tugged on his sleeve, sending him lurching backward.

Dalton's conservative businessman shoes slid on the snowy pavement, but he righted himself before he fell down. Pity.

He exhaled a mighty sigh, raked his disheveled hair back into place and stared down at her with thunder in his gaze. "What is it, Aurélie?"

She blinked up at him, wishing for what felt like the thousandth time, that he wasn't so handsome. His intensity would be far easier to take if it didn't come in such a beautiful package.

His gray eyes flashed, and a shiver coursed through Aurélie. As much as she would have liked to blame it on the cold, she knew the trembling in her bones had nothing to do with the weather. He got to her. Especially when he looked at her like he could see every troublesome thought tumbling in her head. "What do you want?"

What did she want?

Not this. Not the carefully controlled existence she'd lived with for so long. Not the future awaiting her on the distant shores of home.

She wasn't sure exactly what she wanted, only that she needed it as surely as she needed to breathe. She couldn't name it—this dark, aching thing inside her that had become impossible to ignore once her father had sat her down and laid out his plans for her future.

Palace life had never come easily to Aurélie. Even as a child, she'd played too hard, laughed too loudly, run too fast. Then that little girl had grown into a woman who felt things too keenly. Wanted things too much. The wrong things.

Just like her mother.

Aurélie had learned to conduct herself like royalty, though. Eventually. It had been years since she'd torn through the palace halls, since she'd danced with abandon. She'd become the model princess. Proper. Polite. Demure.

But since the awful meeting with the Reigning Prince and his advisors a month ago, her carefully constructed façade had begun to crack. She couldn't keep pretending, no matter how hard she tried.

What do I want? She couldn't say, but she'd know it when she found it.

Dalton glowered at Aurélie.

She inhaled a breath of frigid air and felt as if she might freeze from the inside out. "Are you always this cranky?"

He arched a single, accusatory brow. "Are you always this irresponsible?"

"Irresponsible?" The nerve. He didn't know a thing

about her life in Delamotte. "Did I just hear you correctly?"

People jostled past them on the sidewalk. Skyscrapers towered on either side of the street. The snow was coming down harder now, like they were inside a snow globe that had been given a good, hard shake.

"You certainly did," he said.

God, he was rude. Particularly for a man who wanted something from her. "You do realize who you're speaking to, don't you, Mr. Drake?"

He looked pointedly at the puppy in Aurélie's arms.

The little dog whimpered, and she gave him a comforting squeeze.

If she put herself in Dalton's shoes, she could understand how adopting a dog on a whim might appear a tad irresponsible. But it wasn't a whim. Not exactly. And anyway, she shouldn't have to explain herself. They had a deal.

He crossed his arms. Aurélie tried not to think about the biceps that appeared to be straining the fabric of his suit jacket. How did a man who so obviously spent most of his time at work get muscles like that? It was hardly fair. "You said you wanted a hot dog, not a French bulldog."

What was he even talking about? Oh, that's right— her grand speech. "The hot dog was a metaphor, Mr. Drake."

"And what about the pretzel? Was that a metaphor, as well?"

"No. I mean, yes. I mean…" *Merde*. Why did she get so flustered every time she tried to talk to him? "What do you have against dogs, anyway?"

"Nothing." He frowned. How anyone could frown in

the presence of a puppy was a mystery Aurélie couldn't begin to fathom. "I do, however, have a problem with your little disappearing act."

"And I have a problem with your patronizing attitude."

She needed to put an end to this ridiculous standoff and get them both inside, preferably somewhere other than Dalton's boring office. "I could very easily pack up my egg and go home, if you like."

"Fine." He shrugged, and to her utter astonishment, he began walking away.

"I beg your pardon?" she sputtered.

He turned back around. "Fine. Go back to your castle. And take the mutt with you."

A slap to the face wouldn't have been more painful. She squared her shoulders and did her best to ignore the panicked beating of her heart. "He has a name."

"Since when? Five minutes ago?"

"It's Jacques." She ran a hand over the dog's smooth little head. "In case you were wondering."

A hint of a smile passed through his gaze. "Very French. I'm sure the palace will love it."

She wasn't sure if his praise was genuine or sarcastic. Either way, it sent a pleasant thrill skittering through Aurélie. A pleasant thrill that irritated her to no end.

Why should she care what he thought about anything? Clearly he considered her spoiled. Foolish. Irresponsible. He'd said as much, right to her face. When he looked at her, he saw one thing. A princess.

She wondered what it would be like to be seen. *Really* seen. Every move she made back home was watched and reported. Not a day passed when her face wasn't on the front page of the Delamotte papers.

"Let's be serious, Mr. Drake. We both know I'm not going anywhere. You want that egg."

He took a few steps nearer, until she could feel the angry heat of his body. *Too close. Much too close.* "Yes, I do. But not as much as you wish to escape whatever it is you're running from. You're not going anywhere. I, on the other hand, won't hesitate to call the palace. Tell me, Princess, what is it that's got you so frightened?"

As if she would share any part of herself with someone like him. She hadn't crossed an ocean in an effort to get away from one overbearing man, only to throw herself into the path of another.

She leveled her gaze at him. "Nothing scares me, Mr. Drake. Least of all, your empty threats. If you're not prepared to uphold your end of our bargain, then I will, in fact, leave. Only I won't take my egg back to Delamotte. I'll take it right down the street to Harry Winston."

She pasted a sweet smile on her face. Dalton gave her a long look, and as the silence stretched between them, she feared he might actually call her bluff.

Finally, he placed a hand on the small of her back and said, "Come. Let's go home."

Chapter Four

The next morning, Dalton woke to the sensation of a warm body pressed against his. For a moment—just an aching, bittersweet instant—he allowed himself to believe he'd somehow traveled back to the past. Back to a time when there'd been more to life than work. And his office. And yet more work.

Then an unpleasant snuffling sound came from the body beside him, followed by a sneeze that sprayed his entire forearm with a hot, breathy mist. Dalton opened one eye. Sure enough, the beast he found staring back at him was most definitely not a woman. It was the damned dog.

He sighed. "What are you doing in here? I thought we agreed the bedroom was off-limits?"

The puppy's head tilted at the sound of his voice, a gesture that would have probably been adorable if the dog weren't so ridiculous-looking. And if he weren't currently situated in Dalton's bed, with his comically oversized head nestled right beside Dalton's on his pillow—eiderdown, imported from Geneva.

Dalton's gaze landed on a dark puddle of drool in the center of the pillowcase. Eiderdown or not, the pillow had just become a dog bed.

He rolled his eyes as he strode naked to the marble bathroom at the far end of the master suite and turned on the shower. Perhaps a soggy pillow was his penance for allowing a royal princess to sleep on his sofa rather than giving up his bed. Not that he hadn't tried. But at 1 a.m., she'd still been perched cross-legged on the oversized tufted ottoman in the living room, flipping through the hundreds of channels his satellite dish company offered, like a giddy child on holiday. Dalton hadn't even known he subscribed to so much programming. In fact, he couldn't remember the last time he'd turned on the television.

Sleeping in his office had become something of a habit, especially in recent years. But he couldn't very well spend the night there with Aurélie. He wasn't about to let the staff at Drake Diamonds see her hanging about his office in her pajamas. Explaining her sudden presence in his life—and the need for a duplicate key to his apartment—to the doorman of his building had been awkward enough. Until she'd slipped her arm through his and called him darling, that is.

They were masquerading as a couple. Again.

Dalton wasn't sure why he found that arrangement so vexing. She couldn't introduce herself as a princess. That was out of the question. Posing as his lover was the obvious choice.

Dalton stepped under the spray of his steam shower and let the hot water beat against the rigid muscles in his shoulders. Every inch of his body was taut with tension. He told himself it had nothing to do with the bewildered expression on the doorman's face as Aurélie had gripped his arm with her delicate fingertips and given him a knowing smile, as if they'd been on their way upstairs so he could ravish her. Was the idea of a woman in his life really so far-fetched?

Yes, he supposed it was. He didn't bring dates here. Ever. There were too many ghosts roaming the penthouse.

It isn't real. It's nothing but a temporary illusion, a necessary evil.

In just thirteen days, Dalton's existence would return to its predictable, orderly state. He'd have his life back. And that life would be significantly improved, because the display cases in the first floor showroom of Drake Diamonds would be filled with sparkling, bejeweled eggs.

He knew precisely where he would put the secret egg—in the same glass box that had once housed the revered Drake Diamond. The 130-carat wonder had held a place of honor in the family's flagship store since the day the doors opened to the public. Tourists came from all over the city just to see the stone, which had only been worn by two women in the 150 years since Dalton's great-great-great-great-great-grandfather had plucked it from a remote mine in South Africa and subsequently carved it into one of the most famous gemstones in the world.

The loss of that diamond just three months after the death of Dalton's father had been like losing a limb.

Granted, Artem had managed to buy it back for his wife, Ophelia. But it belonged to her personally now. Not the store. The Drake Diamond's display case sat empty.

Not that Dalton despised the sight of that vacant spot for sentimental reasons. The Drakes had never been an emotional bunch, and sentimentality had been the last thing on Dalton's mind once he'd learned he'd been passed over in favor of Artem for the CEO position. His pride was at stake. His position in the family business.

He didn't want to restore Drake Diamonds to its former glory. He wanted to surpass it, to make the institution into something so grand that his father wouldn't even recognize it if he rose from his grave, walked through the front door and set foot on the plush Drake-blue carpet.

Selling the Drake Diamond had been a necessity. Geoffrey Drake had plunged the family business so far into debt that there'd been no other option. And he hadn't told a soul. He'd sat in an office just down the hall from Dalton every day for years and hadn't said a word about the defunct diamond mine that had stripped the company of all its cash reserves. About the debt. About any of it.

Dalton shouldn't have been surprised. Honesty had never been his father's strong suit. Artem's very existence was a testament to their father's trustworthiness, or lack thereof. Dalton hadn't even known he had a brother until his father had brought five-year-old Artem home to the Drake mansion. Judging from the look of hurt and confusion on his mother's pale face, it had come as a surprise to her as well. Less than a year later, she was dead. To this day, Dalton's sister blamed their mother's death on a broken heart.

If there was a bright side to any of his family's sordid past or the recent sudden death of their patriarch, it was that the brothers had made peace with each other. At long last. When Artem had made the decision to sell the Drake Diamond, he'd saved the company. Dalton could admit as much.

But that didn't mean he had to like it.

He needed to be the one to transform Drake Diamonds into something more spectacular than it had ever been. It was the only way to justify his years of mindless devotion to the family business. He needed those years to mean something. He needed something to show for his life. Something other than loss.

He switched the shower faucet to the off position with more force than was necessary, and then grabbed a towel. On any other day, he would already have put in a solid hour behind his desk by now. He dressed as quickly as possible, adjusted the Windsor knot in his Drake-blue tie and resigned himself to the fact that it was time to venture into the living room and wake Aurélie. But first he needed to get the snoring beast out of his bed.

Dalton scooped the dog up and tried to wrap his mind around how something so tiny could make so much noise. Then his gaze landed on a wet spot in the center of the duvet. The little monster had peed in his bed. Perfect. Just perfect.

"Seriously?"

The animal's googly eyes peered up at Dalton. He sighed mightily.

"Aurélie!" He stormed into the living room without bothering to deal with the mess. "Your charge requires attention."

The television was blaring and the sofa was piled with

pillows and blankets, but Aurélie wasn't there. Dalton's temples began to pound. She'd run off? Again?

The puppy squirmed in his arms and let out a little yip, so Dalton lowered him to the floor. He scampered toward the kitchen, tripping over his own head a few times in the process.

"Mon petit chou!"

Dalton didn't know whether to feel relieved at the sound of Aurélie's voice or angry. Angry about the dog. About the near heart attack he'd just experienced when he'd thought she'd run off again. About every ridiculous thing she'd done since she'd breezed into his life less than twenty-four hours ago.

He settled on relief, until he followed the dog into the kitchen and caught his first glimpse of Aurélie's appearance.

She stood leaning against the counter with her mass of blond hair piled in a messy updo, wearing nothing but her luminous strand of gold pearls and a crisp men's white tuxedo shirt. His tuxedo shirt, if Dalton wasn't mistaken. But it wasn't the idea that she'd slept in his freshly pressed formal wear that got under his skin. It was the sight of her bare, willowy legs, the curve of her breasts beneath the thin white fabric of his shirt, the lush fullness of her bottom lip.

All of it.

He went hard in an instant, and the thought occurred to him that perhaps the only ghost inhabiting the apartment in the past few years had been him.

Whatever you do, don't take her to bed.

"Bonjour." Aurélie smiled. "Look at you, all dressed and ready for work. Why am I not surprised?"

Dalton shook his head. He was aroused to the point of pain. "We're not going to the office."

"Non?"

Non. Very much *non.* Suddenly, there was a more pressing matter that required attention—clothing the princess living under his roof before he did something royally stupid.

"Get ready. We're going shopping." He lifted a brow at the puppy in her arms. "As soon as you clean up after your dog."

After more cajoling than Aurélie could have possibly anticipated, Dalton finally acquiesced and agreed to take the subway rather than using his driver. He appeared distinctly uncomfortable doing so.

Aurélie couldn't help but wonder how long it had been since he'd ridden any form of public transportation. Granted, he was rich. That much was obvious. And just in case it hadn't been so glaringly apparent, the Google search Aurélie had conducted of Drake Diamonds on her phone the night before had confirmed as much.

According to *Forbes*, the flagship store on the corner of Fifth Avenue and 57th Street was the most valuable piece of real estate in the entire country. The building and its contents were worth slightly more than Fort Knox, where America's official gold reserves were held.

So yes, Dalton Drake was quite wealthy. And as he took such pleasure in pointing out over and over again, he was also busy. But this was New York. She'd assumed that everyone rode the subway, even rich workaholics like Dalton Drake.

Aurélie was also tempted to ask him how long it had been since he'd set foot in a building that didn't bear his name. She couldn't help but notice the discreet script lettering spelling out *The Drake* on the elegant black awnings of his apartment building. He seemed to spend every waking moment inside his sprawling penthouse or his jewelry store, where the name *Drake* was splashed everywhere, including across the structure's granite Art Deco exterior.

She didn't ask him either of those things, though. Instead, she soaked up every detail of riding the city's underground—the click of the silver turnstiles, the bright orange seats, the heady feeling of barreling through tunnels. The train sped from stop to stop, picking up and letting off people from all walks of life. Students with backpacks. Mommies with infants. Businessmen with briefcases.

None of those businessmen, however, were quite as formidable as the man standing beside her. No matter how much she tried to ignore him, Aurélie was overly conscious of Dalton's presence.

As fascinated as she was by the hordes of New Yorkers, the bustling subway stations, even the jostling movement of the train, she couldn't fully focus on any of it. Her gaze kept straying to Dalton's broad shoulders, his freshly shaven square jaw, his full, sensual mouth.

If only she could ignore him properly. But it proved an impossible task, no matter how hard she tried. During the frantic disembarking process at one of the stops, someone shoved Aurélie from behind and she found herself pressed right up against Dalton's formidable chest, her lips mere inches from his. She stiffened, unable to move or even breathe, and prayed he couldn't feel the frantic beating of her heart through the soft cashmere of his coat.

She'd been so overwhelmed by the sheer closeness of him that she couldn't quite seem to think, much less right herself. Until he glared down at her with that disapproving gray gaze of his. *Again.*

Right. He was a serious CEO, and she was nothing but a spoiled, irresponsible princess. Duly noted.

"We're here," he said, as the doors of the train whooshed open.

Aurélie glanced at the tile mosaic sign on the wall. *Lexington Avenue.* "Wait, this isn't…"

But Dalton's hand was already in the small of her back and he was guiding her through the station and out onto the snowy sidewalk before she could finish her thought. As usual, he was on a mission. Aurélie was just along for the ride, but at least when he noticed how enraptured she was by the opulent shop windows, he slowed his steps. When she stopped to admire a display of dresses made entirely of colorful paper flowers, she caught a glimpse of Dalton's reflection, and it looked almost as though he were smiling at her.

Then their eyes met in the glittering glass and any trace of a smile on his handsome face vanished as quickly as it had appeared.

He cleared his throat. "Shall we continue?"

That voice. Such a dark, low sound that sent a dangerous chill skittering up Aurélie's spine, for which she heartily admonished herself. She shouldn't be attracted to Dalton Drake. She couldn't. He had too much leverage over her as it was. Besides, she had enough men in her life. More than enough.

"Yes." She breezed past him as if she knew precisely where they were headed, when in fact, she hadn't a clue. "Let's."

"Aurélie," he said, with a hint of amusement in his tone. "We're going that way."

He pointed over his shoulder. This time, he most definitely smiled, and his grin was far too smug for Aurélie's taste.

Fine, she thought. No, not fine. Good. He was much easier to despise when he was being arrogant. Which, to Aurélie's great relief, was most of the time.

They walked the next few blocks in silence until they reached a sleek black marble building that appeared to take up an entire city block. Like both of Dalton's namesake buildings, it had a doorman stationed out front. And gold-plated door handles. And a glittering, grand chandelier Aurélie could see through the polished windows. She squinted up at the sign. *Bergdorf Goodman.*

Without even setting foot inside, she could tell it was elegant. Tasteful. Expensive. Everything she didn't want.

She shook her head. *"Non."*

Beside her, Dalton sighed. "I beg your pardon?"

Aurélie pretended not to notice the hint of menace in his deep voice. "No, thank you. I'd rather go someplace else."

"But we haven't even gone inside." He eyed her.

Let him be mad. Aurélie didn't care. The rest of her life would be spent in designer dresses and kitten heels. This was *her* holiday, not his. She had no intention of spending it dressed like a royal. "I don't need to go in. I can tell it's not the sort of place where I want to shop for clothes."

The doorman's gaze flitted toward them. He'd looked utterly bored as they approached, but now his expression was vaguely hopeful. She realized he probably thought she and Dalton were a couple in the midst of some sort of domestic squabble.

Dalton lowered his voice. "Aurélie, you need clothes. This building is full of them. Dresses, blouses, pants." He cast a pointed glance at her legs. "Pajamas."

Pajamas?

So that's what this oh-so-urgent shopping spree was about. Dalton had been so horrified to find her wearing his tuxedo shirt this morning that he'd felt the need to cancel all his plans for the day and drag her to this fancy, impersonal department store.

She dropped all attempts at civility. "I'm not going in there, Mr. Drake."

Aurélie might not be American, but she'd seen *Pretty Woman*. Several times, actually. She knew precisely what would happen if she followed him inside the boutique. She'd walk out an hour from now looking like a princess from head to toe.

He crossed his arms and stared at her for a moment that stretched on too long. "May I ask why not?"

Intense much?

She felt breathless all of sudden, much to her annoyance. "I have no desire to play the part of Julia Roberts to your Richard Gere."

His broad shoulders shifted. Not that Aurélie was looking at them, because she wasn't. Not intentionally anyway. "I have no idea what you're talking about."

Of course he didn't. The man had probably never watched a movie in his life. Or done anything else fun, for that matter. "I'd prefer to go somewhere else. A vintage shop, perhaps?"

"A vintage shop?" He laughed, but somehow didn't

sound the faintest bit amused. "You're royalty and you want to wear a dead person's discarded clothes?"

"Yes. I do, even though you seem to be doing your best to make it sound disgusting."

Aurélie quite liked the idea of browsing through a vintage shop. She'd never shopped at one before, never even seen one. It sounded like fun. Or it would have, if she hadn't been accompanied by the world's most surly escort. "Come now, Mr. Drake. You and I both know you have a fondness for old treasures."

Like imperial jewels.

She very nearly said it, but she didn't have to.

"Fine, but we're taking a town car this time." He stalked to the curb, lifted an arm and a sleek black sedan materialized within seconds. Naturally. Even the traffic in New York obeyed his orders.

"After you." He held the door open.

"Merci." Aurélie climbed inside. "So where are we going?"

"Williamsburg. That's in Brooklyn," he clarified in his usual stiff tone.

The driver must have overheard, because they soon began a slow crawl across Manhattan. Aurélie had never seen such crowded streets in her life. In Delamotte, the major highway wrapped around a seaside cliff. More people drove mopeds than cars. There were sea breezes and salt air. Here, there were bike messengers zipping between automobiles, musicians on street corners and people selling things in stalls on the sidewalk—newspapers, purses, winter hats and gloves.

She felt suddenly as if she were in the center of everything and the whirling snow, the people and the cars with their blaring horns were all part of some mysterious, magnificent orbit.

So much life, so much movement—it made her giddy. A person couldn't stand still in a place like this, and Aurélie had been doing just that for such a very long time. All her life, it seemed.

"It's wonderful, isn't it?" she whispered with an awestruck tremble to her voice.

Dalton regarded her closely. Curiously. "What's wonderful?"

"This." She waved a hand toward the scene outside the car windows, where dizzying snow fell on the beating heart of the city. "All of it."

Dalton looked at her for a beat too long. Long enough for her cheeks to grow warm. Without taking his eyes off her, he spoke to the driver. "Pull over, please."

The driver's gaze flitted to the rearview mirror. "Here, sir? We're only halfway to Brooklyn."

"Yes, I know," Dalton said. He knocked on the window and pointed at something outside. Aurélie wasn't sure what. There was so much to look at, so much to take in. She didn't know where to look first.

He glanced at Aurélie. "Stay here. I'll be right back."

He was *leaving*? Unbelievable.

"Wait. Where are you going?" Had he sensed a diamond emergency somewhere? Had the store run out of those little blue boxes? She placed a hand on his forearm.

He looked at her fingertips gripping the sleeve of his coat and then met her gaze. "Let go, Aurélie. And for once in your life, could you please do as I say and stay here? I'll be back momentarily."

She released his sleeve and crossed her arms. What was she doing, grabbing him like that anyway? Dalton was free to go wherever he liked. She'd actually prefer to spend the rest of the day on her own. Of course she would. "Fine."

In a flash, he climbed out of the car and shut the door behind him. A flurry of snowflakes blew inside the cab and danced in the air, as soft as feathers. Aurélie watched them drift onto the black leather seat and melt into tiny puddles. And for an odd, empty moment, she felt acutely alone.

She felt like crying all of a sudden, and she didn't even know why.

Aurélie exhaled slowly, willing the tears that had gathered in her eyes not to fall. What was wrong with her? This was what she wanted. Adventure. Independence. Freedom. All the things her mother had never experienced.

She reached for her Birkin, removed her iPhone from the interior pocket and slipped the SIM card back inside. Now seemed as good a time as any to check her messages and see who all had figured out she'd gone missing.

The phone seemed to take forever to power up and once it finally did, the display didn't show a single voice mail message. Nor any texts.

That couldn't be right, could it?

While she was staring at the little screen, the phone rang, piercing the silence of the backseat. It startled her so much that she nearly dropped it.

She took a deep breath and closed her eyes.

Maybe it was Dalton. Maybe he was calling to apologize for running off. *Not likely.* Deep down, she knew it couldn't be him. The only people who had anything to say to her were on the other side of the world.

She opened her eyes. A glimpse of the display confirmed her deepest fears. *Office of Royal Affairs.* Her private secretary.

The palace was looking for her. Aurélie's heart beat against her rib cage like a wild bird caught in a net. She peered out the window in search of Dalton, but the city had swallowed him up.

She cleared her throat, pressed the talk button and very nearly answered in English, which would have been a massive red flag. *Focus. "Allô?"*

"*Bonsoir*, Your Royal Highness." *Bonsoir. Good night.* It was already evening in Delamotte, which made it seem somehow farther away, only not quite far enough. "Do you have a moment to go over your schedule for the rest of the week?"

"My schedule?" Aurélie swallowed. What was happening? Had her own staff not even realized she was missing yet? "Of course."

"As we discussed last week, Lord Clement will be coming to the palace the day after tomorrow to take your picture. The Reigning Prince would like a new photo for the impending press release."

Aurélie's stomach churned. *Breathe. Just breathe.* Lord Clement was the official royal photographer, one of her father's oldest and dearest friends.

"The day after tomorrow isn't a good day." *Since I'm 4,000 miles away and everything.* "We need to reschedule, *s'il vous plaît.*"

"I'm afraid we can't, Your Royal Highness. The press announcement is scheduled for next Friday."

Aurélie felt like she might be sick all over the backseat. She'd thought if she left Delamotte she could slow things down somehow. She'd only been gone a day and a half, and already she felt different.

But nothing had really changed, had it? They hadn't even realized she'd gone. She might be in America, but her life in Delamotte was still proceeding as planned. With or without her.

"Your sitting with Lord Clement is scheduled for 4:00 in the afternoon in the state ballroom. The Reigning Prince would like you to wear the gold brocade dress and the Marchand family tiara." Because apparently, although Aurélie was a grown woman, she wasn't allowed even the simple freedom of choosing her own clothes.

Her throat grew tight. "I understand."

"*Trés bien.* I'll phone Lord Clement and tell him you've confirmed. *Au revoir.*"

The line went dead before Aurélie could respond. She sat staring at the darkened phone in the palm of her hand. Dread fell over her in a thick, suffocating embrace.

What have I done?

Her escape may have gone unnoticed by royal staffers thus far, but failing to show up for a sitting with Lord Clement most definitely would not. Every royal office in Delamotte would hear about it. As would her father. And possibly even the press. Her face would be on the front page of every newspaper on the French Riviera, beneath the headline *Runaway Princess*.

Her heart lurched. But it wasn't too late, was it? If she caught a plane tomorrow, she could be standing in the ballroom with the Marchand family tiara anchored to her head within forty-eight hours. Then next week, she would be headline news for a different reason altogether.

She powered down her phone and removed the SIM card again. Although she wasn't even sure why she both-

ered. She should go home. Leaving hadn't changed anything. Not really. Staying in New York wouldn't, either.
She couldn't outrun her destiny. Believing that she could
was just a naïve, reckless mistake. Her mother hadn't
been able to escape, and neither could she.

The car door opened, and suddenly Dalton was back
inside the car in a flurry of snow and frosty wind. He
slid in place beside her, holding a tissue-wrapped bundle. Aurélie tried her best to focus on him without really looking at him. She couldn't face him. Not after
the phone call.

She was confused enough as it was without having to
worry about what he'd have to say if she turned tail and
ran back home. After everything she'd put him through—
the disappearing, the dog, the constant arguing—he'd be
furious. Or quite possibly relieved. Aurélie wasn't sure
which she preferred.

"Look at me," he ordered. He cupped her face and
forced her to meet his gaze. "Aurélie, is something
wrong?"

Yes. Everything is wrong.

"No." She smiled her perfectly rehearsed princess
smile, slid her cell phone back inside her purse and concentrated all her efforts on keeping her tears at bay.

But she felt his gaze on her, hot and penetrating. She
couldn't look him the eye. She just couldn't. If she did,
the truth would come tumbling out of her mouth. All
of it. Her father's plans. The looming palace announcement. If she said the words aloud, they would feel real.
And she so desperately needed to believe they weren't.

Just a little bit longer.

She focused instead on the knot in his Drake-blue tie.
"Where have you been?"

"Getting this for you." He handed her the tissue-wrapped bundle. It warmed her hands.

Aurélie's defenses dropped, and she stared at him in disbelief. "You bought me a gift."

He frowned, which in no way diminished the potency of his chiseled good looks. "No, I didn't."

She looked at the plain white package in her lap and then back up at Dalton. He seemed nearly as surprised by this strange turn of events as she was. "Yes, you did."

He rolled his eyes. "Don't get too excited. Trust me. It's nothing."

She couldn't imagine what it could be, but something told her it meant more than Dalton was letting on. He wasn't the kind of man to waste time with frivolity.

With great care, she peeled back the tissue. When she realized what he'd done, she couldn't seem to utter a word. She blinked to make sure what she was seeing was real—a hot dog. He'd gotten her a hot dog.

"It's a metaphor." He shrugged as though he were right, as if this silly little gesture meant nothing at all, when to Aurélie, it meant everything. "With mustard."

She didn't fully understand what happened next. Maybe she wasn't thinking straight after getting the call from the palace. Maybe the thought of going back home had broken something inside her. Maybe she no longer cared what happened to her at all.

Because even though she knew it was undoubtedly the gravest mistake of her life, Her Royal Highness Aurélie Marchand tossed her hotdog aside, grabbed Dalton Drake by the lapels and kissed him as though she wasn't already engaged to another man.

Chapter Five

The engagement wasn't quite official, but the royal wedding was already scheduled to take place in just under three months at the grand cathedral in Delamotte. Top secret of course, until the palace made its big announcement in twenty days.

Not that Aurélie was keeping track of the days, exactly. On the contrary, she'd been trying rather aggressively not to think about her pending engagement at all. As it turned out, though, being married off to a man thirty years her senior, a man she'd yet to actually meet in person, was something she couldn't quite make herself forget. No matter how very hard she tried.

Kissing Dalton Drake, however, proved to be a powerful diversion. Frighteningly powerful. The moment Aurélie's lips came crashing down on his, the constant ache in her heart seemed to tear wide open. It was excruciating. And exquisite. She was aware of nothing but sensation. Sensation so sweetly agonizing that there wasn't room for a single thought in her head. How was it possible to feel so beautifully broken?

His mouth was cold from the snowstorm, his tongue like ice as it moved against hers. Deep. Devouring. Delicious. God, was this what kissing was supposed to be like? Because it wasn't close to anything Aurélie had experienced before. She couldn't seem to catch her breath. And were those whimpering noises echoing in the interior of the car actually coming from her?

She should have been embarrassed, but she didn't seem to be capable of feeling anything but longing. Longing as hard and bright as a diamond. She'd needed to be kissed like this. She'd needed it so badly.

No, she realized. She hadn't needed this. She'd needed *him*. Dalton Drake.

"Oh Aurélie," he whispered, his breath now warm and wonderful against her lips.

Then he slid his hands into her hair, cradling the back of her head, pulling her closer. Closer, until their hearts pounded against each other and she could no longer tell where hers ended and his began.

If her actions had caught Dalton off guard, he certainly didn't let it show. On the contrary, the way he went about ravishing her mouth gave her the very real sense that he'd been ready for this. Ready and waiting, for perhaps as long as Aurélie had been waiting for something like this herself. Maybe even longer.

But that couldn't be true. Dalton had made it clear he was merely tolerating her until the imperial eggs went on display. And that was okay, because she'd never be a real part of his life, and he would never be part of hers. Nothing about her time in New York was real.

The kiss sure felt real, though. More than the crown on her head or the white dress she'd slip over her head in less than a month. *This is what life is supposed to be like,* she thought. *This* was passion. Raw. Bold. Blazing hot.

And wrong. So very, very wrong.

Would her husband ever kiss her like this? Would he twirl her gold pearls around his fingertips and use them to pull her into his lap like Dalton was doing? Would she thrill at the press of his erection through their clothes as she sat astride him? Would she have to stop herself from reaching for his zipper and begging him to enter her in the backseat of a town car in full view of the driver and all of greater Manhattan?

No.

Despite her staggering level of inexperience in the bedroom, Aurélie knew how rare this connection was. She sensed it. And as surely as she sensed it, she knew that no man's lips would ever touch her like this again. No other man would kiss her like she was a gemstone, cool and shimmering. A precious object that had been buried somewhere dark and deep, waiting for a kiss of perfect heat to bring her volcanic heart to the surface. Only this man. Only this place and time.

Dalton deepened the kiss, groaned into her mouth and Aurélie's head spun with the knowledge that he wanted her. She wrapped her fingertips around the smooth blue silk of Dalton's tie, anchoring herself in the moment before it slipped away.

What would he say if he knew? What would he think when he picked up the newspaper after she went back to Delamotte and saw her photograph alongside an older man who was her fiancé? How would he feel watching her on television stepping out of a glass coach on her wedding day? He would be furious. It would confirm every notion he'd ever had that she was spoiled, reckless and irresponsible.

At least, she hoped that was how he would feel. Fury she could handle. What she couldn't bear from Dalton was pity. She'd grown quite fond of the way he looked at her as if she were some rare exotic bird instead of a grown woman living under her father's thumb. Of course, those moments were heavily punctuated with looks of complete and utter exasperation. But every so often, when he turned his gray gaze on her, she felt herself blooming from the inside out. Like a peony unfolding before the dazzling heat of the summer sun in a tremulous display of flowering fragility.

He saw *her*. That was the difference. She didn't have to hide who she was when she was with Dalton Drake. For all the secrets she was keeping from him, he saw her for who she really was. Which was more than she could say for the entire kingdom of Delamotte.

She really should have seen the engagement coming. Women in her position had been subjected to arranged marriages since the beginning of time. But she'd been so blissfully naïve about her circumstances, she'd had no idea that something so archaic and demeaning could actually touch her perfect life.

If Aurélie hadn't found her mother's diary the day after her funeral, she would have never known the truth. Sometimes she wished she'd never opened that book and flipped through its gilt-edged pages. Then she might still believe the fairy tale, when in reality, her parents had never loved each other. Her father had one mistress after another, while her mother had no one. Theirs had been a marriage of convenience, a carefully arranged bargain of politics and power.

Now Aurélie's would be, as well.

She squeezed her eyes shut tight, and with each breath, each touch of her lips, she begged Dalton to make it stop. To somehow change the course of her future so she could always be this girl, this bold woman who could write her own destiny.

Please. Please. Please.

"Please…"

Oh God, had she really just said that out loud?

"Not here, darling. Not here." Dalton's voice was little more than a sigh, but it carried just enough of a reprimand to bring her back to her senses.

She opened her eyes and found him staring at her with an intensity that left her painfully vulnerable. Exposed. Ashamed. *Not here.* She looked down at herself and couldn't believe what she saw—her thighs straddling his lap, her hands on the solid wall of his chest, her lipstick smeared all over his mouth. What was she *doing*?

She'd all but begged him to make love to her when he'd shown no interest in her whatsoever. Actually, she may have even begged.

"Oh my God." She pulled away, horrified.

Then she heard a snap, like the sound of something breaking in two. For an odd moment, she was sure it was her heart. Until she realized her pearls were still twirled around Dalton's fingertips. Not the whole strand…only half of them. The remaining pearls were falling from her neck, one by one, dripping into Dalton's lap.

Aurélie gasped and her hand flew to her throat.

Dalton cursed, slid out from beneath her and started

chasing the gold pearls around the moving car, gathering them in his hands. But they rolled everywhere, as if refusing to be captured.

Aurélie remembered reading somewhere that pearls were a symbol of sadness and that each bead of a string of pearls represented a teardrop. She'd never given much thought to the legend before, but now she couldn't quite shake the idea of her mother's tears spilling all over the car. Lost.

What a mess she'd made of things.

By Dalton's best guess, he had $50,000 worth of South Sea pearls rolling around his feet…give or take a few thousand. The fact that Aurélie's priceless broken necklace was the least of his problems at the moment spoke volumes about the magnitude of the mistake he'd just made.

What the hell was going on? Had he seriously just had a make-out session with a princess in the backseat of a hired car while a total stranger drove them across the Brooklyn Bridge? Yes. Apparently, he had. And judging by the magnitude of the erection straining his fly, he'd quite enjoyed it.

But now…

Now Aurélie was looking around with a dazed expression on her face, her eyes shiny with unshed tears. Shell-shocked. Horrified.

Meanwhile, the driver kept shooting glances in the rearview mirror while Dalton crawled all over the car trying to save the pearls. Who knew it was possible for a simple kiss to cause this much mayhem?

Who are you kidding, you idiot? There was nothing simple *about that kiss.*

He sat up and poured a handful of pearls into his pocket. "I'm sorry, Aurélie."

God, was he ever sorry.

Dalton had done the one thing he'd promised himself he wouldn't do. Granted, he hadn't slept with her. But what he'd done might have been worse. They were in a public place. Anyone could see them through car windows. Not to mention the chauffeur!

What if the driver recognized him? What if the driver recognized *her*? There were more things wrong with this scenario than there were pearls bouncing around the car.

"No, it was my fault. I shouldn't have…" Aurélie bit her pillowy bottom lip, and Dalton had to look away to stop himself from pillaging her rosy mouth all over again.

"I'm the one who's sorry." Dalton let out a strained exhale and focused on the pearls. If he met Aurélie's gaze for even a second, surely she'd see the truth written all over his face—it had taken every last shred of self-control to stop things when he did. Part of him wondered how he'd managed it.

Please. There'd been a world of promise in that sweet whisper. Promise that taunted him now, like the perfume of hyacinths left hanging in the air after a lucid fever dream. And now every heartbeat was a knife to his ribs. His hands shook so hard he couldn't manage to piece together the necklace. Pearls kept slipping through his fingers.

Please. That word would haunt him for a thousand sleepless nights to come, which in a way would be a painful relief. He'd grown altogether weary of the regret that had been his only bedtime companion since the night Clarissa died.

He hadn't been in love with Clarissa. He'd realized that in the years since her passing. Perhaps he'd known as much all along. He'd cared about her, of course. He never would have asked her to marry him if he hadn't, despite the expectations of both their families. But his feelings for Clarissa had been closer to the brotherly affection he felt for Diana than romantic love.

If he'd felt differently, he would have picked up the phone that night. He would have been home instead of sitting behind his desk. Clarissa would still be alive, and he wouldn't be situated in the back of a car with his thigh pressed against Aurélie's, wanting, *needing*, to touch her. Kiss her. Taste her.

He blamed himself. Not just for Clarissa—that was a given. But the responsibility for what had just happened with Aurélie also rested squarely on his shoulders. He wanted her. He'd wanted her since the moment he'd seen the hope that shone in her eyes. Hope like emerald fire.

That first day in his office, she'd turned her aching eyes on him as the glittering egg sat between them. And the force of her yearning had nearly knocked him out of his chair.

Desire. It had shimmered in the air like diamond dust. He hadn't known what it was she wanted so badly. He still didn't. But that ache, that need, had kindled something inside him. He'd been numb for so long that he couldn't remember what it was like to feel, to want, to need.

One look at Aurélie had been enough to conjure a memory. His life hadn't always been this way. He'd felt things once. What might it be like to feel again?

Dalton had no idea. All he knew was that he wanted to consume Aurélie, to devour her, until he figured it out. He wanted to want the things she wanted, to feel the things she felt—life, longing.

Love.

No. Not love. Anything *but love.*

He wasn't wired that way. He wasn't capable of love. Hadn't history proved as much? He had even less to offer now, after the way he'd failed Clarissa. She'd deserved better. So did Aurélie. And Dalton refused to be like his father. He wouldn't be the kind of man who did nothing but take.

Take, take, take.

He stared ahead. He couldn't bring himself to look at Aurélie quite yet. He couldn't bear to see the heat in her gaze, the light that radiated from her as if she were a brilliant-cut ruby. Not now. Not while the taste of her scarlet lips still lingered on his tongue.

If he did, there'd be no stopping this time. Not until he'd plunged himself fully inside her and felt her exquisite body shuddering beneath him.

The city whirred past them in a blur of snow, steel and melancholy gray. Dalton breathed in and out, clenching his hands into fists in his lap. He'd let himself slip. He wouldn't do so again. Aurélie was off-limits, and besides, he was comfortable with his life now. His orderly, predictable life.

But despite every effort to regain control, to slide back into a state of numbness, he couldn't seem to still the incessant pounding of his pulse. *Please. Please. Please.*

Chapter Six

Dalton was behind his desk at Drake Diamonds the next morning before the sun came up. He'd left instructions with the doorman to arrange for a driver to bring Aurélie to the store whenever she liked. Granted, leaving her alone for any length of time was a risk, given her penchant for running away. But nothing seemed as dangerous as it would have been for Dalton to play house with her all morning.

Aurélie had come home with piles of eclectic clothing from their trip to Williamsburg, but not a single pair of pajamas. After the disastrous car ride, Dalton couldn't take watching her move about his apartment in his tuxedo shirt again. He just couldn't. Another glimpse of her willowy porcelain legs stretching from beneath the bottom of his own shirt while she peered up at him with those luminous emerald eyes of hers would have been more than his suddenly overactive libido could take. He was only human.

He and Aurélie had danced carefully around each other for the remainder of the day. At the vintage shop, she'd disappeared behind dressing room curtains with one colorful outfit after another, but never came out to model anything.

Dalton told himself that was fine. For the best, really. But he hadn't realized how much he would have liked seeing her twirl in front of the shop's floor-to-ceiling mirrors until he'd found himself relegated to a purple velvet chair in the corner. Alone. And more sexually frustrated than he'd ever been in his life.

How had his life gotten so absurdly complicated in the span of just a few days?

Enough was enough. He couldn't live like this. He wouldn't. He had work to do. Loads of it. He should be busy confirming the arrangements for the upcoming gala or working on the spring advertising campaign. Instead he was flipping through a stack of tabloids, praying he wouldn't stumble on a photo of himself ravishing Aurélie in the back of a car.

There was a knock on his office door, and before Dalton could stash his pile of newspapers, Artem poked his head inside.

"Good morning, brother." His gaze dropped to the copy of *Page Six* spread open on Dalton's desk. "Interesting reading material."

God help Dalton if he and Aurélie had been caught on film. He'd never hear the end of it. "Good morning." He flipped the paper closed and waved Artem inside.

His brother clicked the door shut behind him. "I was wondering if you were going to show up today. When you didn't turn up yesterday, I assumed you were on your deathbed or something. I can't recall when you've ever missed a day of work before. You know we have Diana's horse show in the Hamptons tomorrow, don't you?"

"Of course I do." Dalton sighed.

He'd actually forgotten about his sister's event. That would mean more time away from the store, and he'd just missed nearly two full days of work because he'd been tied up with Aurélie.

He'd never been away from the office for two consecutive days before. Ever. He'd even managed to put in a solid eight hours the day of Clarissa's funeral. It had made perfect sense at the time, but now he wasn't so sure.

Nothing made much sense at the moment.

"Have a seat. I need to discuss something with you." He shoved the tabloids in a drawer so Artem wouldn't be prompted to mention them again. Dalton would have been quite happy to forget them himself.

"Sure. I'm glad you're here. I wanted to ask you…" Artem's voice trailed off.

Dalton looked up to find him staring at Jacques who was curled in a ball on the sofa in the corner of the office. "Am I seeing things, or is that a puppy?"

He rolled his eyes. "Don't ask."

"Oh, I'm asking." Artem shook his head and let out a wry laugh. "I've known you since I was five years old, and somehow I missed the part about you being an animal lover. When did you get a dog?"

Dalton aimed an exasperated glance at Jacques, who responded by panting and wagging his entire backside. The dog was obsessed with him. The pup had responded to the pet sitter Dalton had hired the day before with overwhelming nonchalance. But he worshipped Dalton. Just his luck. "I didn't."

Artem sank onto the sofa beside Jacques and rested a hand on the little dog's back. Jacques went into an ecstatic fit of snuffling sounds as he shuffled toward his lap. "Then where did this sweetheart come from?"

Dalton cleared his throat. "He belongs to Aurélie."

Jacques flopped onto his back. The minute Artem started rubbing his belly, the puppy's tongue lolled out of the side of his mouth. A long string of drool dripped onto the sofa cushions. Naturally. "And he's at work with you because…"

"He likes me. God knows why. The feeling is definitely not mutual." The puppy was a walking train wreck. And constantly underfoot. Dalton could barely walk across the room without tripping over him, but his presence at Drake Diamonds pretty much guaranteed Aurélie would eventually show up. She'd never run off without her *petit chou*. "The homely little thing has hijacked my bed and destroyed half the pillows in my apartment."

"Your apartment?" Artem lifted a brow. "Does this mean Aurélie's staying with you?"

"It does." Dalton shrugged to indicate his nonchalance, but the gesture felt disingenuous. Forced.

Artem's gaze narrowed. "Let me see if I've got the facts straight here. You haven't been at work for a day and a half, Aurélie is living with you and you're letting her puppy—whom you clearly dislike—eat your furniture and slobber all over your office."

Sounds about right. "I realize how this looks."

"Do you really? Because it sort of looks like you're

sleeping with a runaway princess while you plan on exhibiting stolen royal jewels for your personal gain."

Dalton blinked. He'd never been on the receiving end of a lecture from his younger brother before. This was quite a role reversal, and it didn't sit well. Not at all.

"That's a gross representation of what's actually happening. For starters, she didn't steal the egg. She inherited it."

Artem stood and walked toward the desk, while Jacques grunted his displeasure at being left behind. "And do you think the palace will see it that way?"

Maybe. Maybe not.

He'd considered this complication, of course. But if things went as planned, the officials in Delamotte wouldn't know the egg was missing until its unveiling at the gala. By then, Drake Diamonds would be on the front page of every newspaper in the country. Mission accomplished. Aurélie would have a lot to answer for, but that wasn't his problem. Was it?

In retrospect, that attitude seemed rather harsh. When had he become his father?

Dalton swallowed. "Also, not that it's any of your business, but I'm not sleeping with her."

Artem looked down at him for a long, loaded moment.

Dalton hadn't slept with Aurélie. That much was true. It was also true that all he seemed to think about was how very much he wanted to take her to bed. Not wanted. *Needed.* He needed to feel the soft perfection of her curves beneath his palms once again, to feel the pulse at the base of her throat thundering at the touch of his lips, to hear that breathy whimper. *Please.*

Was it so obvious?

Judging by the look on Artem's face, yes. Apparently,

it was. "Look, do what you like with Aurélie. You're right. Whether or not you sleep with her isn't my business. Although, I can't help but mention that if I were sharing my home with the princess of a foreign principality whose most precious jewels are currently in the Drake Diamond vault, you'd have a few things to say about it."

Artem lifted a sardonic brow.

Dalton couldn't argue. He was right. And even though he had no intention of admitting as much to his younger brother, a line had most definitely been crossed.

He hadn't just crossed the line. He'd leaped right over it.

The way things stood, the two brothers had practically traded places, like they were in some third-rate comedy film.

Except Artem was married now, and he had a baby on the way. He was no longer the black sheep of the family. Apparently Dalton now held that title.

What kind of alternate reality was he living in? He was appalled at himself.

"You should probably know that while you were out of the office, you got a phone call." Artem sank into the wing chair on the opposite side of Dalton's desk. His uncharacteristically serious expression gave Dalton pause. "From the palace in Delamotte."

Great. Just great.

So they'd already found out. The palace officials knew about Aurélie. They probably even knew about the secret egg. His ambition, coupled with Aurélie's naïveté, had created an even more profound disaster than he'd anticipated.

He'd been an idiot to think he could get away with something like this. "How bad is it?"

Artem shrugged. "Not very. When Mrs. Barnes couldn't reach you on your cell, she came to me. I took the call."

When Mrs. Barnes couldn't reach you on your cell...

Memory hit Dalton hard and fast. Unexpected. Bile rose to the back of his throat, and he squeezed his eyes shut. But he could still see the notification on his phone. *Clarissa Davies, 19 Missed Calls.*

It wasn't as if he hadn't known. He'd seen the calls come rolling in, but he'd ignored them. Every last one.

Artem spoke again, his voice dragging Dalton mercifully back to the present. "Relax, brother. I handled it. Look, I know how you feel about your phone, but it's not a crime to miss a call."

"Don't go there, Artem," he said as evenly as he could manage. "Not now."

Artem held up his hands in a gesture of surrender. "Sorry. I know it's a difficult subject, but it's been six years. You don't have to be tethered to your phone twenty-four seven. Honestly, when Mrs. Barnes told me you weren't picking up, I was elated. I thought you'd actually gone and gotten yourself a life."

Dalton let out a bitter laugh. He didn't deserve a life. Not anymore. He probably never had, because he was a Drake through and through.

Like every other Drake man that had ever sat behind a desk, he was good at one thing: making money. Selling diamonds didn't leave much room for relationships, or for "a life" as Artem put it. Not the way the Drake men did it.

Dalton had tried it once, hadn't he? Never again. One dead fiancée was more than enough.

"It wasn't your fault, you know. She would have eventually found another time, another way," Artem said quietly.

They'd been over this before. The discussion was closed, as far as Dalton was concerned. What good could come of revisiting the past? Nothing. It wouldn't change a godforsaken thing. "Can we just cut to the chase? Tell me about the call."

Artem sighed. "They were calling to see if the eggs had arrived safely. It seems the palace courier, Monsieur Martel, still hasn't returned to work. There was some concern that he might have absconded with the royal jewels."

Dalton should have thought about this detail. He should have quizzed Aurélie about the courier before he'd even agreed to her terms. He was off his game. He'd been off his game since she'd walked through the door of his office. The time had come to get his head on straight again.

"What did you tell them?" he asked.

"I assured them the pieces for the exhibition had arrived, and the royal jewels were safely locked away in the Drake Diamond vault." Artem cleared his throat. "I failed to mention the treasure locked away in your apartment."

Glaring at his brother, Dalton exhaled.

Artem shrugged. "In all seriousness, have you thought about what you're going to do when they realize she's missing? Surely someone will notice."

Dalton's response rolled off his tongue before he even realized what he was saying. "With any luck, they won't before tomorrow. I'm putting Aurélie on a flight back to Delamotte tonight at midnight."

He'd been toying with the idea all morning, but hadn't realized he'd reached a decision until that precise moment. He'd known, though. He'd known all along that he should send her back. He should never have agreed to her silly plan in the first place.

Now he was just waiting. Waiting for her to show up so he could break the news that he was sending her away.

Dalton's gaze flitted to Jacques sleeping on the sofa, snoring loud enough to peel the Drake-blue paint off the walls. He frowned. What was to become of the dog? Surely she wouldn't leave the mutt behind.

Forget about the dog. This isn't about a dog.

It was about business, nothing more. At least that's what he'd been busy telling himself as he'd looked up the flight schedules to the French Riviera.

Artem leveled his gaze at Dalton. "What about the secret egg?"

"She can take it back with her. It's just not worth the risk." Something hardened inside Dalton. Something dark and deep. "Not anymore."

"What changed?"

Dalton grew still as memories moved behind his eyes in an excruciatingly slow, snow-laden waltz of wounded desire. He saw his fingers tangled in the silken madness of Aurélie's hair, her eyes glittering in the dark like the rarest of diamonds, her lips, bee-stung and bruised from his kisses as she pleaded with him for sweet relief. He saw pearls falling like teardrops, spilling into cupped hands faster than he could catch them.

What changed?

Everything.

Everything had changed.

He shrugged one shoulder and did his best to affect an indolent air. "I came to my senses. That's all."

Artem looked at him, long and hard. "You sure about this? Because I'll back you up, whatever you decide. We're a team, remember?"

All his life—from the time he'd barely been old enough to walk on the Drake-blue carpeting of the Fifth Avenue store, right up until the morning he'd listened to a lawyer recite the terms of his father's Last Will and Testament—Dalton had imagined himself running Drake Diamonds someday. Alone, not alongside his brother. Just him. Dalton Drake, Chief Executive Officer.

He'd never pictured himself as part of a team. Never wanted it. In reality, it wasn't so bad. One day, he might even grow accustomed to it.

"Absolutely." He nodded and gave his brother a genuine, if sad, smile. "I've made my decision. The princess is going back home where she belongs."

Aurélie should have been relieved to wake up alone in Dalton's pristine apartment. She still wasn't sure quite how to act around him after mauling him in the car.

What had come over her? She'd acted as if this person she'd been pretending to be in New York, this impulsive life she was leading, was actually real. It wasn't. Not at all. This was a holiday, nothing more.

But the holiday was clearly messing with her head. In a really big way.

She would have loved to blame her outlandish behavior on the hot dog. Or at the very least, the bearer of the hot dog.

She'd grown so accustomed to Dalton's straight-laced

businessman persona, that his simple act of kindness had caught her completely off guard. Every so often, he was soulful when she least expected it.

In those stolen moments of tenderness, she felt like she was seeing the real Dalton. The man behind the serious gray eyes and the Drake-blue tie. A man devastatingly beautiful in his complexity.

But really, how desperate did a girl have to be to throw herself at a man over a hot dog?

Sleep provided a temporary reprieve from Aurélie's mortification, but the moment her eyes drifted open, it all came crashing back—the cold fury of Dalton's lips, his wayward hands, the way he'd made her forget she was nothing but a virgin princess being married off to a complete and total stranger.

For one dazzling moment, she'd been more than that. She'd blazed bright, filled with liquid-gold, shimmering desire.

Until it was over.

Not here.

She'd felt herself disappearing again, falling away.

Maybe none of it had really happened. Maybe it had just been a bad dream. Aurélie's hand flew to her throat, hoping against hope that she'd find the smooth string of pearls still safely clasped around her neck, as she did every morning. But it wasn't. She found only her bare, unadorned neck beneath the open collar of Dalton's tuxedo shirt.

What was she still doing sleeping in that thing? The first night it had been a matter of necessity. It wasn't anymore.

But she liked waking up in Dalton's shirt. She liked the way his masculine scent clung to the fabric. She liked the way the cuffs skimmed the very tips of her finger-tips. She liked imagining him slipping it on sometime in the distant future and remembering a princess who lived on the other side of the world.

What was wrong with her? She had no business thinking such things. She was an engaged woman. Almost, anyway.

She sat up and glanced around the spacious living room in search of Jacques, but the little bulldog was nowhere to be seen. Aurélie sighed. He'd probably snuck his way into Dalton's bedroom again. Jacques seemed to be forming quite an attachment to the man, even though the infatuation was clearly one-sided. Aurélie would have probably found it amusing if it didn't remind her of her own nonsensical attachment to Dalton's shirt.

The bedroom was empty, of course. No dog. No Dalton.

On some level, she'd known. The air was calm, still. Void of the electricity that always seemed to surround him, like an electrical storm. He'd left a note in the kitchen with the number to call when she was ready for a driver to come round and pick her up. The note didn't say where the car would be taking her. It didn't have to.

Heigh-ho, heigh-ho, it's off to work we go.

Did the man do anything else?

Judging by the looks of his apartment, no. With its sleek lines and elegant white furniture, it was the epitome of moneyed simplicity. Tasteful. Pristine. But more than a tad sterile. After living there for a few days, Aurélie still marveled at the absence of photographs. There wasn't a single picture in the place. No candid snapshots, no family memories. It left her feeling strangely hollow. And sad for Dalton, although she knew she shouldn't.

He'd never given her the slightest indication he was unhappy with his station in life. On the contrary, he exuded more confidence than anyone she'd ever met.

She needed to get out of here, out of this apartment that felt so oddly unsettling without Dalton's brooding presence. Even if the car took her straight to the glittering store on Fifth Avenue. At least in Dalton's place of business, she would be less likely to accidentally kiss the stuffing out of him again. Before she went anywhere, though, she needed to check the news to make sure she still wasn't a headline.

Dalton's laptop was situated on the dining room table. Perfect. She could take a look at the US tabloids and then access the Delamotte papers online. She made a cup of coffee, sank cross-legged onto one of the dining room chairs and flipped open the computer. Then she nearly choked on her coffee when Dalton's screensaver came into view.

It was a photograph—a picture of a woman on horseback, and she was quite beautiful.

Aurélie stared at it until a sick feeling came over her. A sick feeling that seemed an awful lot like jealousy.

Oh, no. She slammed the computer closed. *This cannot be happening.* But it was. It *was* happening. She was jealous of a silly little screensaver, jealous over Dalton Drake.

She was in over her head. Whether she liked it or not, what had happened the day before changed things. She couldn't stay here. Not anymore. It was time to pack up her egg and go home.

She opened the laptop back up, steadfastly refused to allow herself even a glimpse at the pretty equestrian smiling at her from the screen and logged onto the internet. Within minutes, she'd booked herself on a commercial flight out of New York that would allow her to get back to Delamotte in time for her portrait session with Lord Clement the next day.

With any luck, by this time tomorrow she'd be back home, and it would be as though she'd never come to New York, never walked through snowy Central Park, never shopped for vintage clothes in Brooklyn. Never kissed Dalton Drake.

Her flight left at midnight. Now all she needed to do was get her egg back…

…and break the news to Dalton.

Chapter Seven

Aurélie dragged her feet for a good long while before leaving the apartment. She made a second cup of coffee and drank it while she watched the New Yorkers milling about on the crowded streets below. Steam rose up from the manhole covers, and snow covered everything, from the neat grid of sidewalks to the elegant spire of the Chrysler building towering over the Manhattan skyline. From above, the city looked almost like an old black-and-white movie—the kind she used to watch with her mother on late nights when her father was out on official crown business. Or so she'd thought.

She'd been so naïve. Naïve and happy. Ignorance really was bliss, wasn't it?

How different would things be right now if she'd never read her mother's journal? Would she be dreading her arranged marriage so much that she'd actually flee the country? Would she even be standing right here, right now, in Dalton Drake's quiet apartment?

Maybe.

Maybe not.

She almost wished she hadn't. Almost.

Stop. What's done is done.

She turned her back on the window and got down to the business of preparing to leave. She rinsed her coffee cup, put it in the dishwasher. She stripped the sofa of the sheets and blankets she'd been using, washed and dried them, then tucked them away in the massive walk-in closet in Dalton's master suite. All the while, she gave the dining room and Dalton's laptop a wide berth.

His closet was meticulously organized, of course. Even more so than her own closet at the palace. Unlike her walk-in, which was packed with gowns of every color under the sun, Dalton's was distinctly monochromatic. The spectrum ranged from sedate dove-gray and charcoal designer business suits to sleek black tuxedos. The sole splash of color was the selection of ties hanging side-by-side on two sections of wooden spools that flanked his full-length mirror. All the highest quality silk. All the same recognizable shade of blue.

Drake blue.

Aurélie shook her head. The man's identity was so tied to his family business that he didn't even own a single tie in a different hue. He took workaholic to a whole new level.

She found a small suitcase tucked away behind the wall of Armani and used it to pack her new vintage wardrobe. If Dalton balked, she'd arrange to send him a new one after she got home. It wasn't like he might need it between now and then. She doubted he'd even miss it. She wondered when he'd last taken a vacation. Then she reminded herself that Dalton Drake's vacation schedule was none of her concern.

I'll never see him again.

She froze. Swallowed. Then forced herself to take a deep breath.

Of course you won't see him again. That's the whole point of leaving.

It was for the best. The longer she stayed, the harder it would be to walk out the door. She'd already had a nonsensical fit of jealousy after seeing his screensaver. How much worse could things get if she stayed longer?

A lot worse. No question. Besides, if she didn't get on that midnight plane, she'd miss her portrait sitting. She was doing the right thing. The *only* thing. She'd run out of options.

She folded her new dresses with meticulous care and tried not to think about the fact that she'd probably never wear most of them. They were wholly inappropriate for royal life. But she couldn't dwell on that now. If she did, she might just fall apart. Anyway, she loved her new clothes. Maybe she'd get to wear them again…someday.

Keep busy. That's what she needed to do. Just stay as busy as possible between now and the time she needed to head to the airport.

When at last she'd erased every trace of her presence from the apartment, she asked Sam to fetch the driver. With only a matter of hours left before her flight, she couldn't put off the inevitable any longer. She had to tell Dalton she was leaving and demand that he return her egg.

As unpleasant as such a confrontation sounded, at least it would take place at the glittering store on Fifth

Avenue, where she wouldn't be tempted to repeat yesterday's mistake.

Of course she'd forgotten that making her way to Dalton's office would involve walking through the Engagements section on the tenth floor. Tightness gathered in her chest as the elevator doors slid open.

"Welcome." The elevator attendant's smile was too kind. Aurélie recognized him as the same man who'd witnessed her last near-panic attack.

Super. Even the elevator attendant pitied her. "Thank you," she said, and forced herself to put one foot in front of the other.

The showroom was even more crowded than it had been last time. A man wearing a Drake-blue bowtie walked past her holding a tray of champagne flutes. Couples sat, two by two, at each and every display case. One of the shoppers even had the word *Bride* spelled out in rhinestones on her white slim-fit tee.

Aurélie's mouth grew dry. *Bride.* She had trouble breathing all of a sudden. Even remaining upright seemed challenging. She swayed a little on her feet.

How many engaged couples could there possibly be in Manhattan?

"It's a little overwhelming, isn't it?" said someone beside her.

"Excuse me?" Aurélie turned to find a woman, blonde, graceful and judging by the size of her adorable baby bump, a few months pregnant.

"You must be Aurélie." She gave her a conspiratorial wink. "I'm Ophelia Drake, and believe me, I know how you feel."

Ophelia Drake—Artem's wife, Dalton's sister-in-law and the head jewelry designer for the company. Aurélie recognized her from the photo in the Drake Diamonds brochure she'd read in Dalton's office on her first day in New York.

What she hadn't gleaned from the brochure was how warm and open Ophelia Drake seemed. But nice as she appeared, she couldn't possibly know how Aurélie felt. No one could.

Upon closer inspection, something in the depths of Ophelia's gaze told Aurélie that she was no stranger to heartache. Interesting.

"Come with me. I know the perfect cure." Ophelia wrapped an arm around her waist and steered her through the maze of wedded bliss and down the hall. In the time it took to leave Engagements behind, Aurélie decided she quite liked Ophelia. She liked her a lot.

"Here we go. Grab a seat," Ophelia said, ushering her into a small room filled with sleek silver appliances, trays of champagne and at least ten or twelve plates of tiny cakes.

Aurélie looked around. "Is this a kitchen?"

Ophelia nodded and slid a plate of petit fours onto the table in front of Aurélie. "I used to hide in here sometimes." She waved a flippant hand toward Engagements. "When it got to be a little much out there, I'd sometimes sneak in here for some cake. This is where I met my husband, actually."

"Here in the kitchen?" Aurélie picked up a petit four, a perfect replica of the small Drake-blue boxes wrapped with white ribbon that customers carried home everyday. It looked too pretty, too perfect to eat.

"Yes. In this very spot." Ophelia frowned at the tiny cake in Aurélie's hand. "Are you going to eat that or just stare at it? Because I'm eating for two and if it sits there much longer, I can't promise I won't snatch it right out of your hand."

Aurélie laughed. It felt good to laugh. Right. Easy. She hadn't laughed much since she'd kissed Dalton. The past twenty-four hours or so had been spent mired in regret.

She smiled at Ophelia and popped the petit four in her mouth. "Oh. My. God. This is delicious."

Ophelia shrugged. "Told you. It's a wonder what just a little bite of cake can do sometimes."

Aurélie licked a crumb from her fingertip and shamelessly reached for another petit four. "Can I ask you something?"

"Sure." Ophelia leaned back in her chair and rested a hand on her belly the way blissful expectant mothers had a tendency to do.

She was a lovely woman. Aurélie remembered reading in the brochure that Ophelia's first designs for Drake Diamonds had been a dance-inspired collection because she used to be a ballerina. Her training showed. Even pregnant, she carried herself with the grace and poise of a former dancer.

But it wasn't her willowy limbs that made her beautiful, nor the elegance of her movements. It was the way she glowed. Ophelia was happy. Truly happy.

Aurélie couldn't help but feel a little envious. "Isn't Artem the CEO? How is it that you first met him here instead of on the sales floor?"

Ophelia's lips curved into a smirk. "Let's just say Artem wasn't always so serious about this place. It took a while for him to adjust to the role." She tilted her head and gave Aurélie a puzzled look. "I'm surprised Dalton hasn't mentioned it to you. You're staying with him, right? Artem's work habits used to bother him to no end."

"*Oui*. I'm staying with him. But we don't really talk much." *We just argue. And kiss. Then argue some more.* "I'm not sure if you've noticed, but Dalton isn't exactly the chatty type."

"Oh, I've noticed." Ophelia grew quiet for a moment. Pensive. "I've also noticed he seems a bit different since you arrived."

Aurélie sighed. "If he's been extra cranky, I'm afraid that's my fault. We rub each other the wrong way." A bigger understatement had never been uttered.

Ophelia's brow furrowed. "Actually, I was thinking the opposite."

Aurélie opened her mouth, and for a few prolonged seconds, nothing came out of it. *The opposite?* Meaning that she and Dalton somehow rubbed each other the *right* way? Impossible. No. Just...no.

Yet her heart gave a rebellious little lurch all the same.

She cleared her throat and reminded herself that in a matter of hours she'd be on an airplane headed halfway across the world. As she should. "I have no idea what you're talking about."

Ophelia smiled. "I'm talking about the dog in his office, for one thing."

Oh yes, that.

"And his scarcity around here the past few days. Dalton doesn't take time off. Ever." She shrugged. "Unless Diana has a horse show in the area, like she does tomorrow."

Aurélie's heart stuttered to a stop. So the horsewoman had a name. Diana.

Well whoever Diana was, Aurélie pitied her. She

couldn't imagine being in a relationship with a man who was so clearly addicted to his work, was pathologically allergic to fun and hated rescue puppies.

For some reason though, the storm of emotions brewing in Aurélie's soul felt very little like pity. She swallowed around the lump that had taken up swift residence in her throat. "I…um…" *Don't ask about Diana the horse lover. Do* not.

"Diana is Artem and Dalton's younger sister," Ophelia explained. "The third Drake."

"Oh, I see." It was ludicrous how delighted she sounded. Borderline thrilled. She prayed Ophelia didn't pick up on it.

Judging by her amused expression, she did. Mercifully, Artem strode into the kitchen before Ophelia could comment. He took one look at the empty plate in the center of the table and aimed a knowing grin at his wife. "Busted. Again."

Ophelia lifted a challenging brow. "I'm eating for two, remember?"

As Aurélie watched Artem bend to give his wife a tender kiss on the cheek, she was struck by how different he appeared from Dalton, despite the fact that they had similar aristocratic good looks. Same dark hair, same chiseled features. But Aurélie had grown so accustomed to the thunder in Dalton's gaze and the underlying intensity of his movements that witnessing Artem's casual elegance was like seeing the flip side of a silver coin.

"Sweetheart," Ophelia said. "Have you met Aurélie?"

Artem straightened and shook her hand. "Not officially, although I've heard quite a bit about you. It's a pleasure to meet you."

"*Enchanté.*"

Meeting Dalton's family felt strange. She'd known Drake Diamonds was a family institution, but Dalton sure didn't seem much like a family man. Probably because he so obviously wasn't, the photograph on his laptop notwithstanding.

His sister.

Diana is Artem and Dalton's younger sister. The third Drake.

The woman's identity didn't change a thing. It didn't change the fact that she had no business kissing Dalton. And it most definitely didn't change the fact that Dalton had put an abrupt stop to her advances in the car. Or that she had a real life with real responsibilities on the other side of the world.

Which made the extent of her relief all the more alarming.

Where the hell is she?

Dalton checked the hour on his Cartier for what had to be the hundredth time. 8:45 p.m. Outside his office window, the sky had long grown dark. The store would be closing in less than fifteen minutes. Aurélie's plane was due to board in just under three hours, and he still hadn't managed to tell her she'd be on it.

He sighed mightily. According to Sam, she'd left the apartment building an hour ago. She should have breezed into his office by now, but of course, she hadn't. Dalton didn't know why he was surprised. Aurélie wasn't exactly a paragon of predictability. A rebellious spike of arousal shot through him, and he was forced to acknowledge that he found her lack of predictability one of her most intriguing qualities.

Too bad it also drove him batshit crazy.

By this time tomorrow, she'll be out of your life for good. He just had to make it through the next few hours and see that Aurélie got on the plane. Surely getting her strapped into a first-class airplane seat on time was a doable task. Of course, it would help if he knew where she was.

"What now?" Dalton groaned as he felt an all-too familiar nudge on his shin. He looked down to find Aurélie's dog staring up at him with its big, round googly eyes. Yet again. "You can't be serious."

The puppy pawed at him again and let out a pitiful whine. Dalton had already been forced to have Mrs. Barnes walk the blasted thing twice since lunchtime when he'd done the honors himself. There had also been an unfortunate accident on his office floor, evidenced by a wet spot on the Drake-blue carpet that belied the dog's small size. Tempted as Dalton was to ignore the persistent pawing on his shins, he knew better.

He buzzed his secretary's desk, but the call went unanswered. Which didn't come as much of a surprise since she'd been officially relieved of her duties at 6:00. Sometimes she stayed late in case Dalton needed any after-hours assistance, but he figured puppy-sitting didn't exactly fit into her job description.

"Fine," he muttered, scooping the tiny bulldog into the crook of his elbow. "Let's do this."

The dog buried his oversized head into Dalton's chest, made a few of the snuffling noises that Aurélie somehow found endearing and left a smear of god-knows-what in the middle of Dalton's tie.

Splendid. "Thanks for that," he muttered.

Jacques snorted in response. Dalton rolled his eyes and stalked down the hallway, intent on getting the business over with as swiftly as possible. But as he approached the kitchen, Jacques's sizeable ears pricked forward. His stout little body trembled with excitement, and when they reached the doorway, the reason for his elation came into view.

"Aurélie." Dalton stopped in his tracks.

There she was—sitting calmly at the kitchen table nibbling on petit fours like Marie Antoinette while her dog slobbered all over his Burberry suit. Why hadn't he been notified of her arrival? And why were Artem and Ophelia chatting her up like the three of them were old friends?

"You're late," he said without prelude or ceremony.

Artem cleared his throat.

"How is that possible when I don't even work here?" Aurélie popped the remaining bit of cake in her mouth, affording Dalton a glimpse of her cherry pink tongue, a view that aroused him beyond all reason.

She made no move to stand, instead remaining regally seated in her chair wearing one of the vintage dresses she'd chosen the day before—pale blue with a nipped in waist, voluminous skirt and large white polka dots. Wholly inappropriate for winter in New York, yet undeniably lovely. Dalton found himself wishing the dress were a shade or two darker. He'd like to have seen her dressed in Drake blue. His color...

His.

Mine. The word pulsed in his veins with a predatory fervor.

He needed to get her out of his store, his life and back to Delamotte where she belonged. The fact that she'd yet to so much as look at him, focusing instead on the squirming puppy in his arms, did nothing to suppress his desire. Much to his frustration.

The ways in which she vexed him were innumerable. He smiled tightly. "Apologies, Your Highness. I forget that work—or responsibility of any kind—is a foreign concept for you."

When at last she met his gaze, thinly veiled fury sparkled in the depths of her emerald eyes.

"Okay, then," Artem said with forced cheerfulness. "It's getting rather late. I need to get my pregnant wife home. We'll give you two some privacy, because don't you have something you need to discuss with Aurélie, Dalton?"

Artem shot Dalton a loaded glance.

"Is that right?" Aurélie stood, and the folds of her pale blue skirt swirled around her shapely legs. "I have something to discuss with you as well. Something important."

"Very well." Dalton nodded. "But at the moment, your dog requires attention. Shall we?"

She reached for Jacques, and the dog went into a spastic fit of delight. Dalton was all but ignored, which should have been a relief. The fact that he felt the opposite was every bit as mystifying as it was infuriating.

He smoothed down his dampened tie and waited as Aurélie gathered the puppy in her arms and walked past him, out the door. He glanced at his brother and sister-in-law, still sitting at the kitchen table, looking mildly amused. "Good night, Ophelia. Artem." He nodded.

Artem arched an expectant brow, but said nothing. He didn't need to. Dalton got the message loud and clear. The time had come to tell Aurélie she was leaving. It was now or never.

Chapter Eight

Aurélie's hands were shaking. Thank goodness she could hide them beneath the solid warmth of Jacques's trembling little form. She'd rather die than let Dalton see the effect he had on her, especially after his dig about her work ethic. Or lack thereof.

She really couldn't stand that smug look in his eye, but what she despised even more was the fact that he'd been right. She'd never worked a day in her life. Not technically. Of course she'd always considered being royal a job in and of itself. But being here in New York and seeing how many people it took to keep Drake Diamonds running day in and day out, made her painfully aware of how easy she had it, her dreaded arranged marriage notwithstanding.

Like it or not, Dalton had been right about her to some extent. She'd come to New York for a taste of real life, but holing up in a workaholic diamond heir's luxury apartment wasn't any more real than life in a palace.

It feels real, though. At the moment, nothing in the world felt as real as the forbidden heat of Dalton's palm in the small of her back as he escorted her down the hall. A tremble coursed through her, and for some ridiculous reason she felt like crying as the Engagements showroom came into view.

"Are you all right?" he asked, much to her horror.

Get it together, Aurélie. She refused to break down in front of Dalton Drake. She'd have nine uninterrupted hours to cry all she wanted on her flight back to Delamotte.

"I'm perfectly fine," she said as Jacques licked a tear from her cheek.

Dalton stared at her for a beat, and a dangerous-looking knot formed in his jaw. He looked like he could grind coal into diamonds with his teeth. Tears made him angry? It figured, seeing as he seemed allergic to the full scale of human emotions.

"You're fine. Clearly," he muttered and jabbed at the elevator's down button.

The elevator attendant, who felt almost like a friend by now, was nowhere to be seen. He must have gone home for the day. Aurélie stared straight ahead as the doors slid closed, despite the array of sparkling diamond engagement rings assaulting her vision. She didn't dare venture another glance at Dalton while they were trapped together in a small, enclosed space. Not after what she'd done the last time they were in a similar situation.

"Is it true that Gaston Drake invented the concept of

the engagement ring?" she asked, purely for something to say to pierce the sultry silence.

She wasn't even sure where she'd picked up the bit of trivia about Dalton's great-great-great-great-great-grandfather. Probably from one of the brochures she'd had time to all but memorize while Dalton left her unattended in his office.

"Been reading up on the company, have you?" His voice carried a note of surprise.

"I *can* read, you know. I have a master's degree from the Sorbonne." Granted, she'd completed most of her coursework long-distance. But Dalton didn't need to know that. "Does that surprise you, Mr. Drake?"

She couldn't help herself, and glanced up at him for the briefest second. Big mistake. Huge.

Instead of finding a superior glint in his eye, as she'd come to expect, he was appraising her with a penetrating stare. As if he could see every part of her, inside and out, and despite his penchant for mocking her, he liked what he saw.

The corner of his lips curved into a half grin. "You have a habit of surprising me on a daily basis, Princess."

Aurélie blinked, and despite every effort to maintain respectable, chaste eye contact, her gaze dropped straight to his mouth.

It was happening again. She was thinking about kissing him. She was thinking about his hands in her hair and the cold fury of his lips and the delicious ache that was beginning to stir low in her belly. Just under five minutes in the man's presence was all it had taken.

They didn't even like each other. What on earth was wrong with her?

Thank God for the squirming puppy in her arms. He

was the only thing keeping her from making a complete and utter fool of herself. Again.

Somewhere amid the fog of arousal, she was vaguely aware of a bell ringing and a whooshing sound, followed by Dalton's voice saying her name.

"Hmm?" she heard herself say.

"We're here. The ground floor." He stood beside her, holding the elevator door open, eyeing her with concern. She'd been so lost in illicit thought that she hadn't even noticed the elevator had come to a stop. "Are you quite sure you're all right?"

No. Not one bit. "Yes, of course."

She brushed past him, out of the elevator and into the gleaming lobby. She was immediately taken aback by the unexpected serenity of the showroom. There wasn't a soul in sight, not even a salesperson. As soon as she set foot on the marble foyer floor, the overhead lights flickered and dimmed.

The store was closing? Already?

She still hadn't uttered a word to Dalton about leaving. Nor had she even seen her egg since the day she'd arrived.

"You forgot your coat." Dalton paused in front of the revolving door and frowned down at her bare arms.

She sighed. Time was running out. There was no way she was going to go all the way back to the kitchen for her coat, especially if it meant another ride up and down the elevator with Dalton, filled with sexual tension.

She plopped Jacques on the floor, wrapped his leash around her wrist and crossed her arms. "I'll be fine like this. We'll hurry."

Thankfully, Dalton didn't look any more inclined than

she was to get back into the elevator. He glanced at his watch and his frown deepened.

"Don't be ridiculous." Dalton slipped out of his overcoat and placed it around her shoulders. "Here."

Despite the stormy disapproval in his gray gaze, or maybe because of it, an undeniable thrill coursed through Aurélie at the intimacy of the gesture. She turned her head as she obediently slid her arms into the sleeves of his coat, because it was just too much, this sudden closeness. His coat was impossibly soft—cashmere, obviously—and warm from the heat of his body. Dalton's face was right there, just inches away from hers as he buttoned her up, and all at once she was enveloped in him. His woodsy clean scent. His sultry warmth. All of him.

Aurélie's heart thundered against her ribs, and she prayed he couldn't hear it. She didn't trust herself to look at him, so she focused instead on the dazzling array of jewels behind him, sparkling and shimmering in their illuminated display cases. Treasures in the dark.

"There," Dalton muttered with a trace of huskiness in his voice that seemed to scrape Aurélie's insides.

She had to say something. If she didn't do it now, she might never go through with it.

The revolving doors were flanked on either side by two large banners advertising the upcoming exhibit of the Marchand imperial eggs. The first and oldest egg of the collection, known as the jeweled hen egg, was pictured on a pristine white background. This particular egg stood out from the rest as the simplest in design. On the surface, it looked almost like an actual egg. But in reality, it had been crafted from solid gold and coated in creamy white enamel. Upon close inspection, a barely discernible gold line was visible along the egg's center, where its two halves were joined. Once the hidden fitting was opened, a round gold yolk could be found nestled inside. And inside the yolk, a diamond-encrusted platinum crown. A precious, priceless secret.

Aurélie stared at the image of her family heirloom looming larger than life over Dalton's shoulder. *So many secrets.*

She was thoroughly sick of all of them.

"There's something I need to tell you," she heard herself say.

Dalton arched a single eyebrow. "So you said."

She swallowed. The words were gathering in her throat. She could taste their ripeness on the tip of her tongue and still she wasn't quite sure what form they would take.

You're right about me. I'm every bit as silly and irresponsible as you suspect.

I'm engaged to be married.

I'm leaving.

"I…" she started, but a sharp bark pierced the loaded silence. Then another, followed by a wholly impatient canine growl.

Aurélie looked down at Jacques, who'd stretched himself into a downward dog position that would have made even the most die-hard yogi green with envy. He woofed again and wagged his stump of a tail.

"Hold that thought," Dalton said. "I've already cleaned up after your little monster enough times today."

He strode toward the revolving door with Jacques nipping at his heels, and Aurélie had no choice but to follow. They made their way down the block to Central Park and back without uttering another word. There was something about the gently falling snow and the quiet city streets awash with white that forbade conversation.

A chill coursed through her, and she slipped her hands in the pockets of Dalton's overcoat. The fingertips of her right hand made contact with something buried in the silk pocket lining. Something small. Round. Familiar.

She knew without even looking at it that the object in her hand was one of her mother's pearls. A broken reminder of their kiss.

Aurélie was painfully aware of each passing second. Time seemed to be moving far more quickly than usual, in a twilight violet-hued blur. She couldn't help but wonder if Dalton felt it, too, especially when the echo of his footsteps on the bluestone slate sidewalk seemed to grow further and further apart.

They could walk as slowly as they wanted, but they'd never be able to stop time. Midnight was approaching, and if she didn't ask for her egg back now—right now— it would be too late. Even if she wanted to stay, she couldn't.

She glanced up at the amethyst sky and the billowing snow, like something out of a fairy tale, and told herself to remember this. Remember the magic of the bustling city. Remember what it felt like to be wrapped in borrowed cashmere with frost in her hair. Remember the music falling down from the stars.

Music?

She blinked. "Do you hear that?" she whispered.

"Hear what?" Dalton paused alongside her.

"Music." Aurélie slowed to a stop, and Jacques plopped into a lopsided sitting position at her feet. "Listen."

She couldn't quite grab hold of it, and for a split second she thought she must have only imagined the plaintive sounds of a violin floating above the distant blare of horns and the thrum of city's heartbeat center. But then she closed her eyes and when she did, she found it again.

"Do you hear it? Vivaldi." Her eyelashes fluttered open, and beyond the puff of her breath in the frosty air, she saw Dalton watching her with an intensity that made her cheeks go warm. She swallowed. "Where do you think it's coming from?"

He looked at her for a moment that seemed to stretch far too long, then he took her hand. "I'll show you."

She started to protest before she realized they were covering familiar territory, treading the now-familiar path back toward Drake Diamonds. They passed the entrance to the Plaza Hotel with its grand white pillars and crimson steps, and as they walked beneath the ghostly glow of gas lamplights, the music grew louder and louder. It swelled to a crescendo just as the violinist came into view.

He was situated right beside the entrance to Drake Diamonds with a tip bucket at his feet. Eyes closed, hands covered with fingerless mitts, he moved his bow furiously over the instrument. He was just a street musician, but Aurélie had never seen a violinist play with such passion, not even at Delamotte's royal symphony. He was so lost in his music that a lump formed in Aurélie's throat as she stood watching him, grinning from ear to ear.

For a perfect, precious moment, she forgot she was supposed to be saying goodbye. She forgot she shouldn't be standing in the dark, holding Dalton's hand. She forgot that when she looked up at him, she'd find the sculpted planes of his face so beautiful that she'd go breathless. He reminded her of all those diamonds glittering in their lonely display cases in the dark. Hard. Exquisite. Forever beyond her reach.

"It's lovely, isn't it?" she breathed.

At the sound of her voice, the music abruptly stopped.

"I'm sorry, Mr. Drake." The violinist bent to return his instrument to its case.

Clearly he'd been forewarned against occupying the precious sidewalk space in front of Drake Diamonds. As if Dalton owned the entire walkway where they were standing.

He probably does.

"Don't stop, it's okay. Please continue." Without tearing his gaze from Aurélie, Dalton reached into his suit pocket for his wallet, pulled out a thick wad of bills and tossed them in the musician's tip bucket. He angled his head toward her. "Anything in particular you'd like to hear, Princess?"

Princess. His voice didn't have the bite to it that she'd grown accustomed to. On the contrary, he said the word almost as if it were an endearment.

Tell him. Just say it—I'm leaving.

Maybe she could have if his gaze hadn't gone tender and if he'd looked less like a tragic literary hero all of a sudden rather than what he was—a ruthless, self-contained diamond heir. Instead, she heard herself say, "How about some Gershwin?"

His handsome face split into a rare, unguarded grin. "Gershwin? How very New York of you." He shrugged and called out to the violinist. "You heard the lady. I don't suppose you know any Gershwin?"

The familiar, sweeping strains of "Rhapsody in Blue" filled the air, and Aurélie couldn't even bring herself to look at Dalton, much less utter a goodbye. So she focused intently on the violinist instead.

"He's quite good, isn't he?" Dalton said.

She nodded and pretended not to notice the overwhelming magic of the moment. "Perfect."

The song had always been a favorite of hers, but she'd never heard it like this before. Not with the notes rising and floating over the city as snowflakes danced and spun in the glow of the streetlights. It was at once altogether beautiful yet hauntingly sad.

She turned toward Dalton. He had that look about him again, a fleeting tragic edge that drew her fingertips to her throat in search of her mother's pearls even though she knew they were no longer there.

"About earlier…in the tenth floor showroom," he said, his gaze searching.

The tenth floor showroom. Engagements. So he'd noticed her unease at being surrounded by all those wedding rings? Of course he had.

He smiled, but it didn't quite reach his eyes. "For what it's worth, Engagements isn't my favorite department, either."

She wasn't sure what she'd expected him to say, but it certainly hadn't been that. *"Non?"*

He shook his head. "I despise it, actually."

They had something in common after all. She couldn't help but wonder why he felt that way. *Despise* was an awfully strong word. But she didn't dare ask, lest he reciprocate with questions of his own.

She offered only a wry smile. "Not the marrying type?"

He didn't respond, just stared straight ahead. Whatever tenderness she'd seen in his gaze earlier had evaporated, replaced by the cool indifference she'd come to know so well over the past few days.

She rolled her eyes. "Right. Why am I surprised when you're so clearly married to your work?"

"Something like that." The coldness in his voice made her wince, and he kept his gaze fixed on the musician. Then, as if the awkward exchange had never happened, he said, "Shall we dance?"

She let out a laugh. Surely he'd meant the offer as a joke. "Isn't there a spreadsheet somewhere that needs your attention?"

His eyes flashed in the darkness. "I'm dead serious. Dance with me."

He slid one arm around her waist and took her hand with the other. He pulled her close, so close that she could feel the full length of his body pressed against hers. A tight, hard wall of muscle. She wasn't at all prepared for such sudden closeness. The confidence with which he held her and the warmth of his fingertips on her wrist was disorienting, and before she knew what was happening, they were floating over the snowy sidewalk.

The world slowed to a stop. In a city of millions, it felt as if they were the only two people on earth. Aurélie was scarcely aware of the violinist's presence, nor of Jacques's leash winding itself slowly around their legs. Tears gathered in her eyes. She had to stop herself from burying her face in his chest and pressing her lips to the side of his neck.

She wanted to cry, because how could she possibly walk away now, when this would undoubtedly be the most romantic moment of her life?

"You've gone awfully quiet all of sudden," he whispered, and his voice rumbled through her like distant thunder.

It was strange the things people remembered when they found themselves at an impasse. Aurélie's mind should have been on the pink enamel egg coated in seed pearls that was sitting inside the Drake Diamonds vault. She should have been trying to figure out a way to get herself back home. Instead, she suddenly remembered something Artem had said earlier in the kitchen.

Don't you have something you need to discuss with Aurélie, Dalton?

She'd been so nervous about announcing her early departure that she'd forgotten the way Dalton's jaw had hardened in response to Artem's question. She glanced up at him now. "Wasn't there something you wanted to tell me?"

He fixed his gaze with hers, and Aurélie saw something new in his eyes. A fleeting hesitancy. Above them, the darkness of the night sky felt heavy, swollen with so many words left unspoken between them. Everything they wouldn't, couldn't, say.

"It can wait," he said.

She nodded, and somehow she knew there would be no goodbyes. Not now. Not tonight.

Their legs became too entangled in the dog leash to keep dancing, so they slowed to a stop until they were standing still in one another's arms. The music may have gone quiet. Aurélie wasn't even sure. She'd slipped into a hazy, dreamlike state, drunk on music and sensation.

Dalton reached, wove his fingers through hers and brushed his lips against the back of her hand. "Let's go home."

Aurélie took a deep breath. If she didn't leave for the

airport right now, she'd miss her flight. She'd never get to Paris in time to catch a connection to Delamotte. She'd miss her appointment with Lord Clement.

The palace would undoubtedly come looking for her, and there would be no turning back. Not this time.

One more day. Just one more day.

Dalton released her hand and bent to untangle Jacques's leash. He walked a few steps in the direction of his apartment building with the little bulldog trotting alongside him, then turned and stopped. Waited. "Are you coming, Princess?"

"Oui. Une seconde." She reached into the pocket of Dalton's coat for the lonely gold pearl, held it tightly in her closed fist then dropped it in the violinist's tip bucket, where it swirled to an iridescent stop in the moonlight.

No turning back.

Chapter Nine

This is a mistake.

Dalton was fully aware of what would happen when he made the fatal choice to take Aurélie back to the apartment instead of to the airport. He knew what he was doing was wrong. Reckless. Probably even downright dangerous.

He'd been so prepared to tell her it would be best if she went back home. He'd waited all day for her to show up so he could break the news to her in person. Her little holiday was over. He was a busy man. He didn't have time to babysit a princess. Especially a princess who wore her heart on her sleeve the way that Aurélie did.

She wasn't anything like the other women who'd been in Dalton's life. More specifically, the women who'd been in his bed. If the problem had been as simple as sex, and sex alone, he would have broken down and succumbed to temptation by now.

But he had the distinct feeling that sex with Aurélie would be anything but simple. She got emotional over street musicians and homeless puppies and hot dogs.

To Dalton's complete and utter astonishment, he found it charming. Sexy. Altogether irresistible, if he was being honest.

Which was precisely the problem. Aurélie wasn't a woman he could just sleep with and then move on. She'd only been in his life for a few days, and in that small span of time, she'd thrown his entire existence into an uproar. She was sentimental to her core. She was also a runaway royal princess.

But he couldn't seem to resist taking her hand and leading her home. He had to stop himself from kissing her on the grand steps of the library under the watchful gaze of the stone lions, their manes laden with snow. Patience and Fortitude. Dalton had neither at the moment. But he knew if he kissed her then, beneath the moon and the stars and the ethereal lamplight glow, he'd be unable to stop.

At his building, the doorman nodded a greeting. Dalton must have said something in return, but he couldn't imagine what. He couldn't hear a thing over the roar of blood in his ears and the annoying howl of his conscience.

This is a mistake.

Dalton no longer believed in mistakes. Not tonight. Not now, when Aurélie was looking at him with eyes full of bejeweled longing. Not when it seemed as if the walls of the cool marble lobby hummed with desire and the wild percussion of their hearts.

He didn't wait for the elevator to deposit them on the penthouse floor. Couldn't. The doors slid closed with a sultry whisper, and he held Aurélie's glittering gaze until he was sure—absolutely certain—that she wanted this as badly as he did.

Then he moved toward her with a growl—a deep, primitive sound he'd never heard himself make before— and crushed his mouth to hers.

Aurélie melted into him with a slow, drawn-out inhale and slid the palms of her hands languidly up his chest. He closed his eyes and lost himself in the warm wonderland of her mouth and the quickening flutter of her breath as the kiss grew deeper.

More demanding.

The ground beneath them stirred as the elevator lifted them closer to the stars, farther and farther from the real world down below. Aurélie's delicate form felt weightless, feather-light in his arms, and he was hit with a momentary panic at the thought that she might float away.

He leaned closer, closer, until he'd pressed her against the elevator wall. His hands moved to her slender wrists and circled them loosely like bracelets. Her body softened. The dog's leash slipped from her fingers and fell to the floor. She whispered his name, and the aching hunger in her voice was so raw, so sweetly vulnerable, that it nearly brought him to his knees.

Everything went white hot. Like a diamond burning away to smoke.

Dalton was harder than he'd ever been in his life. He was seconds away from sliding his hand under her dress, up the luxurious length of her thigh, and stroking his way inside her with his fingers.

He wanted to make her come. He wanted to watch her go someplace she'd never been, knowing he was the one who'd taken her there. The only one.

He was fairly certain she was a virgin, which only

multiplied the severity of the mistake he was about to make. She was a princess, and seemed to have lived a sheltered existence. She had an air of innocent charm about her. He could still think coherently enough for that fact to register somewhere in his consciousness. But he no longer gave a damn about right and wrong. About who either of them were.

If she was a virgin, though, he needed to slow down. Be gentle. And he certainly shouldn't be on the verge of undressing her in an elevator. She deserved better than this.

"Aurélie," he groaned, pulling back to rest his forehead against hers and twirl a lock of her spun-gold hair around his fingertip.

He could see her pulse hammering in her throat, and he wanted to kiss it. To press his mouth, wet and wanting, against the life teeming beneath her porcelain skin.

"Please," she pleaded, just as she'd done in the car on the afternoon she'd kissed him, and Dalton knew he was done for.

Mistake or not, he couldn't let her down again. Perhaps a better man could, a more honorable man. But Dalton had never felt less honorable in his life.

For each and every one of his thirty-three years, he'd done exactly what was expected of him. Where had it gotten him? The empty place he currently occupied—nowhere. Nothing was as it should be.

He'd had enough. Enough of duty. Enough of restraint. Enough of denying himself what he wanted. It had been a long, long time since he'd wanted anything. Anyone. So many lost years.

And now he wanted Aurélie.

At last he remembered what it was like to want and

need and ache. But the way he felt when he looked at her, when he touched her, wasn't anything like a memory. It was better. It was intoxicating.

The elevator came to a stop. Finally. Dalton took Aurélie's hand and led her inside the apartment. Somehow, he kept his wits about him long enough to get the dog settled in his spacious laundry room with a rawhide chew and a stuffed toy that would no doubt be disemboweled by morning. Which was perfectly fine with Dalton, so long as the little troublemaker was content.

He found Aurélie waiting for him in the darkened living room. The sight of her standing there with her ruby-red lips slightly parted and swollen from his kisses, eyes bright, made him want to tell her all kinds of truths. He had to clench his jaw to keep them from spilling out.

Her back was to the window, where snow beat against the glass in a dizzying fury. The night was steeped in winter white, but Dalton had gone summer warm.

"Let me look at you," he said as he approached. "I want to see you."

Without a trace of shyness, she reached for the hem of her dress and slipped it over her head. If she was nervous, she didn't let it show. On the contrary, her knowing smile gave him the impression that she was well aware of the effect she had on him.

She knew, and she quite enjoyed it.

Her dress landed on the floor in a polka-dot whisper. With her generous waves of hair tumbling over one moonstone shoulder, she lifted her bowed head and raised her gaze to his.

Dalton had to pause for a moment and collect himself. It hurt to swallow. It hurt to breathe. Every cell in his body screamed in agony, waiting and wanting to touch her.

He stared at her too hard and too long—at the willowy length of her legs, the captivating dip between her collarbones, the generous swell of her breasts covered in pale pink lace, a prelude to her softness.

The space between them shimmered with promise.

Everything about her was heavenly. Dalton would have loved to drape her bare body in ropes of pearls, to adorn her glorious curves with the precious treasures of the South Sea. Aurélie deserved such adoration. She deserved everything.

What was it about this woman, this near stranger who filled him with such decadent thoughts and so thoroughly shattered his reserve?

She's not just a woman. She's a princess.

She was royalty. And for tonight, she was his.

Aurélie had been waiting for this moment for what felt like an eternity.

Days ago, if she'd known she would be standing in Dalton Drake's living room in nothing but her bra and panties while he, fully clothed, looked his fill, she wouldn't have believed it. The very idea would have made her blush.

She wasn't blushing now. It felt natural, right, predestined somehow, that she should be here at this exact place and time. A rare and precious moment that had somehow been lost. Forgotten. Waiting for Aurélie to step into it when time had reached its fulfillment.

Dalton's gaze was serious. Grave even, as his gray eyes glittered with intent. He wasn't just looking at her.

He was studying her, and she felt every hard stare as surely as if he'd reached out and touched her.

Why hadn't he touched her yet? How long was he going to stand there and watch her burn? The slow simmer that had begun the morning he'd first set his gaze on her from across the chaste expanse of his desk had become intolerable. Liquid heat pooled at her center, and fire skittered over skin in the wake of his gaze.

She needed his hands on her. His mouth. On her. Inside her. She thought she might die if he made her wait much longer, and she couldn't hide her desperation. Her pride had fallen away with the whisper of her dress dropping to the floor. She was too inflamed to feel any sense of embarrassment.

Eyes locked with his, she walked toward him. One purposeful step—that's all she remembered taking, because he moved toward her at the exact same time. And suddenly his hands were everywhere—in her hair, cupping her bottom, sliding beneath the wispy lace cups of her bra and skimming over her sensitive nipples with the softest of touches. Her body all but wept with relief.

He kissed her again, and this time his lips were deliberate. Knowing. She realized every other kiss had been nothing but a prelude. This time, he took her mouth, possessed it as if he were already buried deep inside her. She kissed him back, arching toward him without even realizing she'd moved.

Her arousal astounded her. Shocked her to her core. Aurélie Marchand, the dutiful princess, had vanished and been replaced by a stranger. A stranger whose body was crying out for relief. A stranger who did things like slip out of her bra, reach for Dalton's hands and place them on her bare breasts.

"So beautiful," he whispered.

She loved the way he touched her. The way his big, capable hands cradled her as if he were holding a bone china teacup. Graceful with purpose.

He lowered his mouth to her nipple and at the first touch of his warm, wet tongue, Aurélie's knees went weak. She fell against him, and he wrapped an arm around her waist, holding her in place as he devoured her.

His hands slipped inside her panties, pushing them down until she was completely naked. She wanted him to undress, too, so she could see him, touch him, feel the hard ripple of his muscles beneath her fingertips. But as her hands sought the lapels of his suit jacket, one of Dalton's hands slid between her thighs.

She opened for him, and he stared down at her without breaking his gaze as he slipped a finger inside.

Oh my God.

"Aurélie, princess, have you ever been with a man before?"

She bit her lip to keep the truth from spilling out. She could never lie to him, not when those devastating eyes of his saw straight through her the way that they did. But she was afraid to tell him the truth, to admit there'd never been another.

She wanted him to be her first. She needed this more than Dalton ever could, or ever would, know. Right now a plane was bound for Delamotte, and her seat was empty. But the palace was waiting, and it wouldn't wait forever. She would never have a chance like this again.

Still, she was terrified to actually go through with it. Because somewhere beneath her quivering need, the truth shined bright. A fire opal of awareness.

This was more than just physical. She cared for Dalton. She might even be in love with him.

No. No, I'm not. I do not love him. I can't.

She squeezed her eyes shut tight, but it was too late. The truth had settled itself in her bones, in the liquid embers flowing through her veins. She wasn't just giving her body to Dalton. She was giving him her soul, her heart, her everything. And God help her, she had no idea how she was going to walk away and take it all back.

Dalton's hand grew still, and his fingers stopped the delicious thing they were doing between her legs. She could feel him waiting, willing her to answer him. "Tell me, princess. I need to know."

There's never been anyone else. Only you. Always you.

"No." She reached between them and slid her hand over his, holding it in place as she ground against him, crushing her breasts against his chest until he released an agonizing moan. What had come over her? *Don't stop. Please don't stop. Please.* "I haven't, but…"

"Shh. It's okay." His voice was a tortured whisper, his breath hot against the curve of her neck. "We'll go slow."

She nodded, unable to form words. Unable to do anything but feel. Feel and sigh her surrender.

She was a virgin, but she wasn't completely naïve. She knew what went on between a man and a woman.

She'd thought she did, anyway.

She realized now that she knew nothing. How could she have possibly anticipated how overwhelming this would be? How utterly sublime?

Because this is special. This is love.

"No."

Dalton tilted his head. "No?"

Had she actually said that out loud? She swallowed and with trembling fingertips, unfastened the Windsor knot in his Drake-blue tie. "I don't want it slow. I want you inside me. Now."

In a single, unhesitating movement, he tossed the tie aside and shed his jacket. The desire in his eyes hardened, grew sharp, until it was a blazing, furious thing. Aurélie's breath caught in her throat, and the first traces of nerves fluttered low in her belly.

This was the end, the dying embers of the moment in between. They were going someplace else now. Someplace new. A place with no means of return. He swept an arm beneath her legs, scooped her against his chest and carried her there.

Behind a lacy veil of snow, moonlight streamed in through the bedroom windows. Dalton deposited her in the center of his massive bed, and before her eyes were fully adjusted to the cool blue shadows of the semidarkness, he'd pulled his shirt over his head and unfastened his belt.

She rose to her knees, reaching for him. She was afraid—not of what was about to happen, but about how it would end.

He was so beautiful. Beautiful and male and daunting in his intensity. She craved this intimacy far more than she feared its consequences, what it would do to her when the time had come to leave. She lifted her mouth to his, hungry and desperate, and he groaned into it as her hand slid inside his trousers, finding his steely length.

He was far bigger than she'd imagined. Big and diamond hard. She didn't know how in the world she could accommodate his size, couldn't even fathom how it would work, but she didn't care.

His breath had gone ragged, his eyelids heavy, and it thrilled her to know she could make him feel this way. That just by touching him the right way, she could make him let go of even a little bit of his steadfast control.

"Darling," he whispered, pushing her back on the bed, covering her body with his.

At last they were skin to skin, limbs intertwined, hands exploring. The weight of him on top of her was exquisite, and his erection pressed hot and wanting between her legs. Then he was pushing inside, past the bittersweet whisper of pain, and she was rising up to meet him. Wanting, wanting, wanting, until at long last, she was full.

He paused, giving her time to adjust, and finally he began to move. Thrusting, gently at first, with slow, measured strokes.

"More," she heard herself say, and she wrapped her legs around him, pulling him closer. And closer still. She wanted it all. Everything he could give. Even the parts of him he wouldn't.

He groaned, pumped faster, and something hot and wild gathered at Aurélie's center. Stars glittered behind her eyes, and she rested a palm on Dalton's chest, searching for something solid. Steady. A pulse to keep her grounded.

But she was too far gone, lost to sensation. She could only breathe and give herself up to the wondrous free fall of the climax bearing down on her. Beneath her fingertips, Dalton's heart pounded a constant beat.

Mine.

Mine.

Mine.

A rebellious tear slid down Aurélie's cheek. The snow spun its gentle dance and Dalton gazed down at her with a look so tender that she was certain she felt her heart rip in two even as she found her shuddering, shimmering release.

Chapter Ten

It couldn't happen again. Of that, Aurélie was absolutely certain.

She was certain of it in the middle of the night when she found herself tangled in the bed sheets with Dalton's head between her thighs. She was certain of it when she cried his name again and again to the diamond-studded sky. And she was *especially* certain of it when she woke in the morning reaching for him, tears welling in her eyes.

He wasn't there. The bed was still warm where he'd been. His heady, masculine scent still clung to his pillow. Aurélie closed her eyes, inhaled and lifted her arms over her head, stretching languidly. A cat who'd gotten the cream.

But the cat had no business tasting the cream. The cream was off-limits. And now that the cat had indulged, she wouldn't be satisfied with just a bland drop of milk. Ever.

Aurélie's eyes flew open, and she sat up, panicked. She began to tremble deep inside, as if her bones were trying to shake off the mistake she'd just made.

What had she done?

This was bad. She'd given herself to Dalton in every possible way. She'd meant to offer him her body, but somewhere along the way, she'd accidently given him her heart. And now she was rolling around in his bed like she belonged there when she clearly did not.

From the spacious master bath, she could hear the shower running. The rich scent of espresso hung in the air. She leaped out of the bed, determined not to let Dalton find her here when he returned. *If* he returned.

Would he come looking for her before he left for work? Would he cradle her face and claim her mouth as he'd done the night before? Over and over again, until her lips felt bruised. Taken.

A ribbon of liquid longing wound its way through her at the mere thought of his wicked mouth, his capable hands. Of his lean, hard muscles and the way her head fit perfectly in the space between his neck and shoulder.

Her body was deliciously sore from their lovemaking. It was almost as if she could still feel him inside her. And that phantom sensation made her want him all over again. Just thinking about it made her go all tingly inside.

Her heart gave a little lurch.

What was she going to do?

She couldn't bear to leave. Not now. But the longer she waited, the harder it would become. She should have never slow-danced with Dalton. She should have never made love with him. Because that was what it had been. Not sex—making love. At least that was what it had been for her. She wholeheartedly doubted Dalton felt the same way.

Even if he did, what difference would it make?

She glanced down at her bare ring finger and tried to imagine what it would look like adorned with a diamond engagement ring. Her vision grew blurry behind a veil of tears and she clenched her fist until nails dug into her palm.

Breathe. Just breathe.

Her lungs burned, and her throat felt scratchy. She climbed out of bed, looked around and found her lingerie in a lacy, decadent trail leading to the living room. The pretty new polka dot dress was pooled on the floor by the window. Scattered shoes, coats and Dalton's discarded tie painted such a vivid picture of what had gone on the night before that a lump formed in her throat as she gathered them all up.

She could straighten as much as she wanted. She could put the room back together again, even toss the clothes in the garbage, but it wouldn't change anything. There was no way to undo what she'd done. She couldn't take it back.

Even if she could, she wouldn't. Not in a million years.

Which was precisely why it wouldn't, *couldn't*, happen again.

Fresh from a cold shower, yet still inexplicably aroused beyond all reason, Dalton strolled naked toward the bedroom.

His appetite for Aurélie was insatiable. He couldn't quite understand it. Didn't want to. He'd think about it later. Much later, after he'd taken her to bed once more.

Just one more time.

Then he'd end things before they got too complicated.

Right. They'd passed *complicated* ages ago. He thought of the pink enameled egg. Their bargain. Artem's warning.

In all seriousness, have you thought about what you're going to do when they realize she's missing? Surely someone will notice.

How had he allowed things to get so far out of hand?

He needed to end it. Now. For Aurélie's sake as much as for the sake of Drake Diamonds. Because she didn't know what Dalton knew all too well—leaving New York and returning to Delamotte was the best possible thing she could do. A blessing, really. If she stayed, he'd hurt her. He didn't want to, but he would.

He'd done it before, and he couldn't risk doing it again. Not to Aurélie.

The mere thought of it caused a familiar darkness to gather inside him. Like a terrible smoke. A black, suffocating fog that threatened to swallow him up.

With each step Dalton took to the bedroom, though, it lifted. Because when he was with Aurélie, when he was buried deep inside her, he could almost forget the things he'd done. The mistakes he'd made.

He could breathe again.

Almost.

The darkness descended again when he found his bed empty. Not just empty, but completely made.

Dalton glowered at the crisp white duvet, pulled so neatly over the king-size mattress that there wasn't a wrinkle in sight. His gaze drifted toward the headboard. He couldn't believe what he was seeing. Where had Aurélie learned the art of hospital corners? He would have bet money she'd never even made a bed before. He probably would have found such a surprise amusing if it hadn't rubbed him so entirely the wrong way.

He was profoundly irritated, and the very fact that he felt this way irritated him further. Because it forced him to admit the truth he'd been trying so hard to avoid—his control was beginning to slip.

The cold shower…the coffee…neither had done a damn thing to snap him back into reality. Sunlight streamed through the bedroom windows. At his feet, the city was waking up beneath a fresh blanket of snow. Morning sparkled like an upturned sugar bowl.

But Dalton wasn't ready. Not even close. He was still lost in the opulent darkness of the night before.

This wasn't as he'd planned. He'd allowed himself one night, and one night only. One night to get Aurélie out of his system so he could get back to business.

Of course the fact that she'd indeed been a virgin gave him pause. He should have stopped things the moment she'd confirmed his suspicions in that regard. He couldn't have, though. Not if his life had depended on it.

What had he done?

An aching tightness formed in his chest. He took a deep breath, but the feeling didn't go away. It lingered, much like the memory of Aurélie's touch, her taste. The sweetness of her voice in his ear.

I don't want it slow. I want you inside me. Now.

He stared down at the neatly made bed, wondering what it meant. Nothing probably. He was overthinking things, as he'd always been prone to do.

It was getting late, anyway. The driver was scheduled to pick them up in less than half an hour. Dalton dressed quickly, then strode into the living room in search of Aurélie. He found her perched on one of his kitchen barstools reading yesterday's *New York Times* with Jacques sitting regally in her lap. The fact that she was fully dressed wasn't lost on him. He hadn't realized how badly he'd hoped to find her in a state of undress until now. Seeing her again, now that he'd been inside her, now that he knew what it was like to have those lithe legs wrapped around him, was like getting punched hard in the solar plexus. He swayed a little and gripped the edge of the countertop before he lost his head and gave in to the impulse to kiss her.

He thought of his neatly made bed and its damned hospital corners, but still his gaze found its way to Aurélie's mouth. Her pillowy lips were darker than usual, as red as the deep crimson center of a ruby. Swollen from his lavish attention.

His cock throbbed to life. Again. "Good morning," he said coolly.

"Good morning," she said, barely looking up from the newspaper.

The dog, on the other hand, stared straight at him. Dalton could have sworn he saw a trace of mockery in the French bulldog's big round eyes.

Dalton suppressed a sigh.

Jealous of the damned dog? Yet again? Pathetic.

He was losing it. But he'd be damned if he was going to stand there and pretend nothing had happened between them.

"Shall we talk about last night?" He crossed his arms, leaned against the counter and waited.

Jacques sighed and dropped his chin on the countertop as if the sheer weight of his head was more than he could handle. Which wouldn't have surprised Dalton in the least.

Aurélie rested one of her elegant hands between the dog's ears. There was a telltale tremble in her fingertips.

She devoted too much care to folding her newspaper into a tidy square, took a beat too long to meet his gaze. "If you'd like."

She was pretending.

Dalton wasn't sure why, but she obviously wanted to act like nothing had changed. When in fact everything had.

"I enjoyed it." *Don't touch her. Do not.* He shoved his hands in his trouser pockets. "Very much."

He could hear the catch in her breath, could see the pink flush rise to her cheeks.

She kept up her charade, clearing her throat. "As did I, but…"

He lifted his brows. "But?" he repeated, sounding harsher than he intended.

The dog rolled its eyes, or maybe that was just Dalton's imagination.

Aurélie lifted her chin. "But I don't think it should happen again."

He looked at her, long and hard, as the darkness gathered in him again. Thick and suffocating. And for the first time, he realized it had a name. Regret.

"I understand." But he didn't understand. Not at all.

He had no business feeling as frustrated as he did. This was for the best. It was precisely what he'd wanted, wasn't it?

Yes. Yes, it is.

He was far from relieved, however. On the contrary, he was furious.

Aurélie's gaze flitted to the digital clock display on the microwave. "I suppose you're off to work now."

He would have liked nothing more than to escape to the quiet solitude of his office on the tenth floor of Drake Diamonds. But today of all days, he couldn't.

Perfect. Just perfect.

He shook his head. "No, actually."

Aurélie blinked. "No?"

"No." Dalton's cell phone buzzed with an incoming text message. He glanced down at it and cleared the display. "In fact, that's our ride."

"*Our* ride," she repeated with a telltale wobble in her voice.

Dalton nodded, stalked past her and reached for his jacket in the coat closet. He was half tempted to leave her behind. But something told him if he walked out the door, she might not be here when he returned.

Sure enough, as he pulled his Burberry wool coat from its hanger, he spotted a suitcase tucked away at the back of the closet. *His* suitcase, he noted wryly.

He looked pointedly at the bag and then at Aurélie, waiting for her to say something. If she wanted to go, he certainly wouldn't stop her.

That's right. Run away, Aurélie. Run away from me, just like you ran from whatever it is you're trying to escape in Delamotte.

He didn't know why he hadn't seen it coming. Of course she wouldn't stick around to honor their agreement.

Wasn't it just yesterday you wanted to send her away?

Dalton's jaw hardened. His hand twitched. He should pick up the suitcase and hand it to her. Along with a plane ticket.

He wasn't sure why he didn't.

If she left, he'd have the Marchand eggs to contend with. Articles about the exhibit were in every newspaper in New York. Banners were up in every showroom in the store. The Marchand eggs could be returned after the exhibit, as planned.

But what of the secret egg? What of their bargain?

A day ago he'd been prepared to let it go, to forget he'd ever set eyes on Aurélie and her glittering treasure. Now he refused to make that concession. Not when it wasn't his call, his choice. He controlled what went on at Drake Diamonds, not an impulsive princess who'd never worked a day in her life.

Aurélie's gaze flitted anywhere and everywhere *except* at the suitcase. She swallowed, and her hand fluttered to her throat.

Dalton did his best to ignore the flash of heat that rioted through him at the memory of his mouth upon her neck, the wild beat of her pulse beneath his lips.

"Where are we off to, then?" she asked, like they were a couple about to leave on holiday. Like the suitcase meant something that had no basis in reality.

Dalton shut the closet door. Out of sight, out of mind.

"We're going to the Hamptons."

Chapter Eleven

If Aurélie wasn't mistaken, Artem did a double take when she entered the Winter Hamptons Equestrian Classic's massive white tent on Dalton's arm.

"Aurélie, what a surprise." Charming as ever, Artem smiled. Astonishment aside, he seemed genuinely happy to see her. "How nice of you to join our family gathering. Dalton neglected to tell us you were coming along."

"Thank you so much for having me." The words left a bittersweet taste in her mouth.

Her voice felt raw, rusty. Probably because she and Dalton had only exchanged a handful of words during the tense ride to the Hamptons from the City. She'd sat beside him in the backseat of the town car while he pounded away on his laptop, and she felt it had been the longest three hours of her life.

She'd been so relieved when they'd pulled up to the

show grounds. She couldn't breathe with Dalton so close, not when every cell in her body was mourning the loss of his touch. She'd needed air. She'd needed space.

What she most definitely did *not* need was to be treated like a card-carrying member of the Drake fold.

Ophelia threw her arms around Aurélie and gave her a tight squeeze. "I'm so glad you're here. Wait until you see Diana ride. She's amazing."

Tears gathered behind Aurélie's eyes. She hadn't realized Artem and Ophelia would be there. Of course they were, though. It was a family event.

What am I doing here?

"I can't wait," she said, pulling away from Ophelia's embrace, aware of Dalton's gaze on her. Too aware.

This was almost worse than the car ride.

She glanced around, trying to get her bearings. Being inside the heated tent was like stepping into another world. If a fine layer of snow flurries hadn't still dusted Dalton's imposing shoulders, Aurélie might have forgotten they'd just come in from the cold.

The ground was covered in rich red dirt, a striking contrast to the snow piled outside. A course had been arranged in the large oval in the center of the tent with sets of rails painted stripes of red and white, flanked on either side by lush greenery and bright white flowers. Magnolias. Their sultry perfume hung heavy in the air, an unexpected luxury in the dead of winter.

Riders in breeches and glossy black boots walked around the outskirts of the arena, weaving between waiters holding silver trays of champagne flutes. An enormous gray horse strutted by, with its mane tightly woven in a braid snaking down its thickly muscled neck, and hooves so shiny Aurélie could see her reflection in them.

So this is the Hamptons.

Aurélie had never seen anything quite like it. Not even in Delamotte.

"It's something, isn't it?" Artem said, turning his back on all the opulence. A look Aurélie couldn't quite decipher passed between him and Dalton. "Diana is an Olympic hopeful, but I'm guessing my brother probably told you all about it."

Actually, no. We're not exactly speaking at the moment.

She forced her lips into a smile. "I'd love to hear more."

Aurélie wasn't about to admit that the man she'd slept with the night before—the man she thought she might be in love with—hadn't shared a single personal thing about himself in the entire time she'd known him. She didn't even want to admit such a thing to herself.

Fortunately, she'd been a princess all her life. Faking a smile was one of the job requirements.

That quality should come in handy when you're married three months from now.

Her gaze strayed rebelliously to Dalton. It hurt to look at him, to see the anger in his stormy eyes. It hurt even worse when she realized it wasn't only anger looking back at her, but disappointment as well.

She couldn't blame him. Not this time.

"Here she is now." Artem waved at a petite young woman making her way toward them.

She wore immaculate white breeches, a midnight-blue fitted riding jacket and a pair of neat white gloves. An elegant black horse pranced alongside her at the end of a blue lead rope. Drake blue.

She was definitely the woman from the screensaver

on Dalton's laptop. Same rich auburn hair twisted into a tight chignon. Same perfectly proportioned figure. Same confident smile. Dalton's sister.

Aurélie turned toward Dalton.

He lifted a brow. "Yes?"

"Are you going to tell your sister who I am?" she whispered.

Dalton frowned and muttered under his breath, "No. The fewer people who know, the better. Artem and Ophelia are involved with the business, so it makes sense for them to know. Let's leave Diana out of it."

"Good. I agree." They agreed on something. Miracles never ceased. "How are you going to explain my presence?"

"I'll introduce you as my friend, Aurélie." His *friend*. He looked down at her, and she saw too much on his face then—the fury and the heat still simmering between them. "She won't have any idea who you are. I doubt she's picked up a tabloid in years. Diana's life revolves around horses twenty-four seven."

"I see. So you typically bring dates to her horse shows, then?" Her face went hot with the effort it took not to sound like a jealous mistress, even though that was precisely what she was at the moment.

Pull yourself together.

Dalton's gaze strayed to her lips and lingered there. Long enough for Aurélie to grow breathless before he looked away without answering her question.

Diana greeted Artem with a warm embrace, gave Ophelia's tiny baby bump a gentle pat, then turned her attention to Dalton.

"Hi there, big brother. Thanks for tearing yourself away from the office to come see me jump." She threw her arms around him, all the while glancing curiously at Aurélie.

"Diana, this is Aurélie." Dalton's arm slid around Aurélie's waist, and she was immediately too aware of his palm resting against the curve of her hip. She fought the overwhelming impulse to melt into him.

Pathetic.

Dalton, on the other hand, seemed perfectly at ease. Impassive even. But when he looked down at her, she saw a spark of triumph in his gaze. He knew. He *knew.* He was all too aware he could drive her mad with the simplest touch, and he intended to use it to his full advantage.

"Aurélie, this is my sister, Diana Drake." His hand moved lower, his fingertips sweeping ever so lightly against her bottom.

"I'm delighted to meet you, Diana." She extended a hand and did her best to ignore her thumping heart and the way her skin suddenly felt too tight, like it could barely contain the riot of sensations skittering through her.

She wanted to strangle him.

Right after she kissed him again.

"The pleasure is all mine, I assure you." Diana ignored Aurélie's outstretched hand and pulled her into an enthusiastic embrace instead. The horse stood beside her, perfectly still other than the flicking of its glossy black tail.

"Diana," Dalton said, his voice tinged with warning.

"Ignore him," Diana whispered in Aurélie's ear. "He's all bark and no bite, in case you haven't noticed. Besides, I've been waiting for this for a long time. I haven't met one of Dalton's girlfriends since…"

"Okay, that's enough." Dalton pried the two of them apart.

Artem and Ophelia stood by, watching with amused interest.

Since when? Since whom?

Aurélie glanced at the suddenly firm set of Dalton's jaw and the flat, humorless line of his mouth. He steadfastly refused to look at her. Maybe she was just imagining the tension in the lines around his eyes. Then again, maybe not.

"We should take our seats. Surely you have last-minute things to attend to," he said, sounding more detached and robotic than Aurélie had ever heard him before.

Nope. Definitely not imagining things.

"Actually, Diamond and I are just about ready." Diana rested a hand on the horse's broad back.

Diamond's hide twitched and he stamped one hoof in greeting. His mane was braided into a graceful plait, and he'd been brushed and groomed to such an extent that he looked like a darkly elegant mirror.

"Your horse's name is Diamond? That certainly seems appropriate," Aurélie said.

"He's perfect. In showjumping a rider is only as good as her horse." Diana grinned. "Dalton bought him for me, actually. He had Diamond shipped over for me all the way from Europe."

"Did he?" She didn't quite know what to make of this news. The man was full of surprises.

"We can discuss something else now." The mysterious man in question cleared his throat.

Diana shot Aurélie a wink. "Excellent. Aurélie, why don't you tell me how you met my brother?"

Artem let out a hearty laugh.

"That wasn't what I had in mind," Dalton said flatly.

"Fine. Keep me guessing. I should probably get Diamond warmed up, anyway." Diana reached for Aurélie again and gave her another tight hug. "Thank you for coming. It was really a treat to meet you."

Aurélie wasn't accustomed to being embraced like that, especially since her mom had died. It caught her off guard.

And most of all, it made her realize what all she'd be leaving behind when she finally forced herself to leave New York. Not only Dalton, but a family. *His* family.

She'd miss seeing him like this.

She'd miss *him*.

"Good luck," she said, her breath growing shallower by the minute.

Then Diana was gone, and Artem was saying something. Aurélie wasn't sure what. A distant ringing had begun in her ears, and she had trouble hearing anything else.

What had she done?

She glanced at Dalton, at the planes of his handsome face and the dark layer of stubble on his jaw. But it was impossible for her to look at him without touching him, without wishing he would touch her in return. And she'd made it abundantly clear to him that was something she no longer wanted.

Now he would barely even look at her.

This is your doing. You did this.

She swallowed around the lump in her throat. How had she messed things up so badly? She'd been acting out of self-preservation, but suddenly she wanted to tell Dalton the truth. All of it.

She wanted to explain that she'd packed the suitcase the day before, not this morning. She wanted to confess why she'd left Delamotte. She wanted to tell him what she'd learned about her parents' marriage and about the fate that awaited her when she returned to the palace.

She wanted to tell him how she felt about him.

She wouldn't, of course. Couldn't. Not here. Not now. "I can't."

Dalton swiveled his gaze toward her. Finally.

Artem's brow furrowed. "Pardon?"

Oh God. Had she said that out loud?

Dalton slid his hand around her waist, and to her utter mortification, the tenderness in his touch nearly made her weep. "Why don't we go sit down?"

"Wait." Artem held out a hand. "Can I have a word with you, brother?"

Dalton gave a terse shake of his head. "There's no time. The show is about to start."

"Diana's class doesn't compete for another half hour. Why don't we go fetch drinks for the ladies and discuss a little business as well?" Artem's mouth curved into one of his charming smiles, but his eyes went dark.

Dalton sighed under his breath. "Very well. If it absolutely can't wait…"

"It can't." Artem reached for Ophelia's hand, gave it a squeeze. "Darling, why don't you show Aurélie around for few minutes?"

Ophelia slipped a willowy arm through Aurélie's. "I'd be happy to. Artem's right. The show doesn't technically start until ten o'clock. It's only 9:30."

9:30.

If it was 9:30 in New York right now, that meant it

was 3:30 in Delamotte. Her portrait sitting with Lord Clement was scheduled in less than an hour.

She swallowed.

Across the world, her gold dress was no doubt hanging in her dressing room with her glittering silver Jimmy Choos set out beside it. The Marchand family tiara would have been removed from its vault. Her old life was ready and waiting for her to slip back into it.

Like a dress that no longer fit.

Once they were out of earshot, Dalton didn't bother waiting for Artem to speak. He knew what was coming.

"Again, this isn't how it looks," he muttered under his breath as they fell in line at the bar.

"So you've mentioned," Artem said drily.

Clearly, Artem didn't believe him. Maybe because this time things were *exactly* how they looked.

Dalton's jaw clenched. A dull throb started up in his temples. He shouldn't have brought Aurélie here. It had been a mistake. Obviously.

Dalton didn't make mistakes. Not when it came to business. Rather, he hadn't until the past twelve hours or so.

Now he couldn't seem to stop.

And he'd tried. By God, he'd tried to get a handle on himself.

He'd intentionally spent the better part of the three-hour ride to the Hamptons on his laptop rather than interacting with Aurélie. He was woefully behind on plans for the Drake Diamonds gala. Mrs. Barnes had emailed him three menu options for review, along with photographs of floral arrangements in various sizes and shades of Drake blue, and she'd been pressing him for a response for days. He hadn't even given the guest list a cursory glance since the invitations had been mailed out. And of course the most important detail still required his attention—the arrangement of the Marchand eggs.

As much as he'd told himself he was simply doing his job, Dalton knew better. He'd wanted the distraction. Needed it. Because having Aurélie situated right beside him in the backseat of the town car, wearing another one of her quirky vintage getups, was killing him.

There was the faintest hint of lace peeking out from the hem of her dress today, and her legs were covered in opaque tights. Or perhaps they were stockings… Dalton had spent far too much time pondering the possibility of a garter belt beneath the swish of her full skirts. There wasn't a big enough distraction in the world to rid himself of his curiosity regarding that particular matter. It had consumed the majority of his thoughts during the entire stretch of I-495.

And then there'd been the matter of the email.

Less than an hour away from Manhattan, Dalton's tablet had dinged, indicating he'd gotten a new email. He'd glanced at the notification and his gut had tied itself in knots.

From: The Office of His Majesty,
The Reigning Prince, Delamotte
Re: Her Royal Highness, Aurélie Marchand

He'd switched the tablet off before Aurélie could see it. There was no reason to alarm her until he'd had a chance to read the message. It didn't necessarily mean they'd figured out where she'd gone.

But things didn't look promising. His fists clenched

at his sides and he cursed himself—yet again—for not sending her home last night. Last night…before things had gotten so carried away. Before he'd danced with her in the street. Before she'd undressed for him in that shaft of immaculate moonlight.

He'd remember how it felt to look at her beautiful body for the first time until the day he died. Like time had somehow reversed itself. He'd felt young again. Alive. Whole.

Artem stared at him long and hard, turning his back on the course where the riders and horses were warming up, preparing for competition. He shook his head and sighed. "When are you going to admit what's going on, brother?"

Dalton shrugged. "There's nothing to admit."

It was a half truth, at best. At worst, a full-fledged lie. Dalton had so much to confess where Aurélie was concerned that he'd lost track. But he didn't care to discuss it. Especially not with Artem, whom Dalton had so often chastised for failing to control his libido. The day his brother had slipped a diamond on Ophelia's hand, he'd become a different person.

Maybe you can become a different man, too.

"Who is it you're trying to fool?" Artem said. "Me? Or yourself?"

"The exhibit is going forward as scheduled. I have things under control." But that wasn't even the whole truth, was it? He still had no idea what was in the email from the palace. Even now, the cell phone in his pocket vibrated against his leg.

He reached for it and checked the screen. Incoming call: Drake Diamonds. Whatever was happening at the store could wait. For now.

He powered down the phone and slid it back in his pocket. He was having enough trouble concentrating on what was happening around him today as it was.

He took a deep breath and refocused his attention on Artem, who was still standing there. Watching. Waiting. Apparently, he wasn't going to let the Aurélie thing go.

Dalton cleared his throat. "Look, I appreciate your concern, brother. But I don't need a heart-to-heart about my sex life."

He wouldn't be taking Aurélie to bed again, anyway. His feelings on the subject no longer mattered.

Except they did matter. The fact that he couldn't stop thinking about that damned suitcase told him his feelings mattered a whole hell of a lot.

Aurélie should have been back in Delamotte by now. He'd lain awake half the night trying to figure out why he hadn't put her on the plane when he'd had every intention of doing so, and he'd been unable to come up with anything remotely resembling a logical explanation. Then again, the decadent sight of Aurélie naked in his bed might have had something to do with his inability to think.

It had taken every shred of self-control in his arsenal not to kiss her, to touch her—right here, right now—when every time he closed his eyes he saw her sitting astride him, heavy-lidded with desire.

"I'm not talking about sex," Artem said. "You have feelings for Aurélie."

Dalton couldn't believe what he was hearing. "Don't be ridiculous."

Artem rolled his eyes. "I'm not the one being ridiculous here. You're in love with her. Ophelia sees it. I see it. Why can't you?"

"Listen, I'm happy for the two of you, happy about the baby. Thrilled. Delighted. But just because you've suddenly become a family man doesn't mean I'm one."

"But you are. You always have been." Artem threw his hands up. "Look around, for crying out loud. You're at a horse show."

Dalton didn't need to look around. He knew perfectly well where he was. The Winter Hamptons Equestrian Classic was an off-season event, although most serious jumpers like Diana competed year-round. Diana participated twelve months a year, and since both their parents were now deceased, Dalton tried to attend every show within driving distance of Manhattan.

Not that their father had ever displayed much interest in his only daughter before his fatal heart attack. Geoffrey Drake had been writing checks since Diana began taking riding lessons at the age of four, but that had been the extent of his support for her career. He'd never attended a single horse show.

As far as Dalton knew, his sister hadn't considered this at all strange. The Drakes had always expressed affection via their checkbooks, after all.

Family man. Right. Dalton didn't even know what a family man looked like.

Dalton himself had never seen Diana ride until after Clarissa died. To this day, he wasn't sure why he'd turned up in the grandstand at that first show he'd attended. Maybe he'd been looking for an escape. Maybe he'd simply needed a place to go on Sunday morning before the store opened in those early days when he couldn't bear the stark white interior of his apartment.

He wasn't sure. All he knew was that it had made him feel better knowing that at least one Drake had managed to build a life that didn't revolve around the family business. He would have gladly flung himself on Diamond's back and galloped far away if he could.

If it hadn't been too late.

If he hadn't already devoted his entire existence to Drake Diamonds.

"You deserve to be happy, Dalton. Whatever is happening between you and Aurélie has nothing to do with the past." Artem's gaze shifted to the packed dirt floor. "It's got nothing to do with Clarissa."

Dalton glared at his brother. "You're out of line. And for what it's worth, categorically wrong."

You're in love with her.

In love?

Impossible.

He wanted Aurélie. He didn't love her. There was a difference. A big one.

Falling in love with Aurélie Marchand would make him the biggest idiot on the island of Manhattan. Possibly even the entire continent.

Although if he was being honest with himself, he *had* been acting rather idiotic lately.

"I'm wrong, am I?" Artem glanced at the box where Ophelia and Aurélie were chatting with each other like two old friends. Like sisters. "Then why haven't you sent the princess packing?"

Dalton wished he knew why. Oh, how he wished that.

Chapter Twelve

Aurélie did her best to make conversation with Ophelia as they sat in the Drake Diamonds private box in the front row. She listened patiently to Ophelia's explanation of the rules of showjumping, nodding in all the right places and making note of which riders were serious contenders for the Winter Hamptons Equestrian Classic Grand Prix title.

Diana was one of them. Dalton's sister rode with a passionate confidence that took Aurélie's breath away, as if she and the horse were one.

But as she followed their movements around the ring during the warm-up and Ophelia kept up her merry chit-chatting, Aurélie couldn't shake the knowledge of what was going on 4,000 miles away.

Her time was up.

Palace officials may have discovered her absence earlier this morning. In all likelihood, they had. Perhaps even yesterday. But so long as Aurélie didn't know for certain, she could hold onto the hope that she was still flying under the radar. She could choose to believe that no one would come looking for her. But once Lord Clement arrived at the palace, there would be no denying the truth. In just a few short minutes, she'd no longer be able to lie to herself.

No matter how badly she wanted to.

She couldn't stop glancing at the digital time display beside the judge's table, couldn't stop herself from counting down each minute, each precious second of freedom. Yet, she felt oddly calm. The minutes ticked by, and her pulse remained steady. There were no nervous butter-flies, no panicked heartbeats. On the contrary, a detached serenity seemed to come over her.

She was dangerously calm. Numb. So much so that it frightened her.

"I wonder what's taking Artem and Dalton so long. The show is about to start, and Diana and Diamond are the first team up." Ophelia glanced around the crowded tent. "Do you see them anywhere?"

Aurélie scanned the area by the bar, and spotted them on the way to the box. Both of them carried a champagne glass in each hand, and both of them wore grim expressions. Although Dalton's was significantly grimmer than Artem's.

"Here they come," she said.

The closer they came, the clearer she could discern the barely contained fury in Dalton's posture. She wondered if something terrible had happened back at the store. A robbery perhaps.

Or maybe…

No. She shook her head, unwilling to even consider the possibility that the palace had somehow already found out where she was. *Not that. Please not that.*

She still had a few minutes left until the palace realized she was missing. At least she thought she did.

Artem's expression softened the moment he set eyes on his wife again. He handed a glass to Ophelia and winked. "It's just water, darling. But I had them put it in a fancy glass for you."

"Thank you." They exchanged a kiss that lasted just long enough to make Aurélie clear her throat and look away.

Dalton took the seat beside her. "Your champagne."

Bubbles rose from the pale gold liquid in the glass that Dalton handed her—a saucer-style glass with a delicate stem. A *Marie Antoinette glass,* as it was known in Delamotte.

Stop. Just stop.

She vowed to quit thinking about Delamotte and what might be going on back at the palace, yet still found herself lapsing into French. *"Merci beaucoup."*

Dalton barely looked at her. He kept his gaze glued straight ahead, yet didn't seem to follow the gallop of Diamond's hooves as the horse swept a wide loop around the course. His jaw hardened into a firm line.

Something was definitely wrong.

She glanced at the clock again. 9:58.

Two more minutes.

She took a large gulp from her champagne glass and slid her gaze toward Dalton. "Is everything okay?"

"Fine," he said under his breath.

"Clearly." She took another sip of champagne and watched Diana trot into the ring on Diamond's back.

The buzzer rang, signaling the start of her run, and Diamond shot forward in a cloud of red dust. His glossy black tail streamed straight out behind him. The ground shook as he thundered past the Drake box.

Horse and rider soared over the first jump, clearing the rails by such a large height that it looked like they were flying. Diana rose out of the saddle and leaned forward. Aurélie could see the dazzling smile on her face clear across the ring.

What must it feel like to be that fearless? She wished she knew. "Wow."

Her heart leaped to her throat as they approached the second obstacle, which was a water jump. Diamond soared over the partition and then seemed to hang suspended over the glistening pool. Without thinking, Aurélie gripped Dalton's arm and held her breath until the horse touched down gracefully on the other side.

She let out a relieved exhale. Then she realized she was still holding onto Dalton's sleeve.

Her face went hot. "Sorry." She let go. "You don't get nervous watching Diana ride?"

"No. She's an excellent competitor," he said stiffly.

Okay then.

Diana and Diamond galloped past the box again. Artem, Ophelia and Aurélie all cheered while Dalton remained silent.

Aurélie stared at him. "Are you sure everything is okay?" *Other than the fact that we slept together last night and today has been awkward on every possible level.* "Because you seem awfully cranky all of a sudden. Even for you, I mean."

"Quite sure. Artem can be a real pain in my ass sometimes. That's all," he said.

Then he turned and looked at her. *Really* looked at her for the first time since he'd sat down. Possibly even for the first time since she'd so bluntly informed him that she wouldn't be sleeping with him again.

His gaze softened, and his mouth curved into a smile. But it was a sad smile. Bittersweet. All at once, memories from the night before came flooding back—the reverent expression on his face as her dress fell to the floor, the tenderness of his lips on her breasts, the exquisite fullness as he'd entered her. Tears gathered behind Aurélie's eyes, and he said, "Then again, every once in a while my brother is right about some things."

She bit her lip to keep from crying, blinked furiously and did her best to keep her attention on the ring where Diamond was gathering his front legs beneath him to soar over another set of rails. But Dalton's gaze was a palpable force.

She turned to him again.

"Dalton." Her voice was a broken whisper.

He cupped her cheek. "Princess."

And for the briefest of seconds, she felt it again—the tenuous connection they'd shared the night before, as precious as a diaphanous dream.

It was real. This is real.

A hush fell over her heart, and in that sliver of a moment, everything slipped softly into place. There was no faraway palace, no royal wedding. Just him. Just her.

Just us.

Then a tinny clang pierced the quiet and it all fell apart. Like pearls slipping from a string.

Dalton seemed to realize something was wrong before he saw it. His smile faded, lips compressed. In the final moment their eyes were still locked, Aurélie saw fear in his gaze. Raw, primal fear that made her blood run cold.

Her throat went dry, and she realized the sound she'd heard had been Diamond's front hooves hitting the rail.

Diana.

The world seemed to move in slow motion as Aurélie's head swiveled in the direction of the course. Already Dalton was scrambling to his feet, climbing out of the box, as the horse's back feet sent the rails flying and the big, graceful animal crashed into the dirt with a sickening thud. He hit the ground with such force that Aurélie's chair pitched forward and she had to grab onto the railing in front of her to keep herself from falling.

Diamond's leg twisted into a horrific angle, and a terrible sound came out of him. A sound that would haunt Aurélie's dreams for weeks to come. She wanted to close her eyes, to block it all out. But she couldn't. Not until she found Dalton's sister in the wreckage.

The horse tried to scramble to his feet, and when he did, Diana's petite form rolled out of the way.

She's okay. She's all right.

But Diamond couldn't support himself on his broken leg and fell sideways, his big, beautiful head smacking down squarely on top of Diana's helmet.

Her body went limp. A gasp went up from the crowd. Time sped up again and somewhere in the periphery, Aurélie was vaguely aware of the clock flashing 10:00.

"Oh, my god." Ophelia's hand flew to her throat.

"Let's go," Artem said, helping Ophelia up.

Aurélie wasn't sure if she should follow or stay put, but Ophelia grabbed her hand and held on tight as she walked past. So she followed the two of them out of the box and to the entrance to the ring, where Dalton stood as pale as a ghost.

"I'm so sorry, Dalton. She'll be okay. She will," Aurélie said, knowing full well it might be a lie.

But sometimes people needed to believe in lies, didn't they? Sometimes a lie was the only thing that kept a person going. At least that was what Aurélie's mother had written in her diary.

She swallowed, not quite sure what to believe anymore.

Diana was already surrounded by EMTs, since qualified medical personnel were required to be on hand at all equestrian events that included showjumping. A siren wailed in the distance, and Artem was talking in terse tones to the show chairman, worried that the ambulance would have trouble reaching the tent through the maze of horse trailers and cars parked outside in the snow.

Through the chaos, Dalton remained stoic. He didn't move, didn't say a word. He scarcely seemed to breathe.

When at last Diana had been lifted into the back of an ambulance—strapped onto a gurney with her head still in its riding helmet—Dalton seemed surprised to find Aurélie standing beside him. It was as if he'd been in a trance and forgotten she was there.

"Come with me." He placed his hand in the small of her back and escorted her out of the tent, to the edge of the parking lot where two sleek black cars sat idling, waiting to follow the ambulance to the hospital.

The sky had turned an ominous gray, heavy with snow. The cold air hit Aurélie's face like a slap. She ducked her head against the wind.

"We'll meet you there," Artem called, nodding solemnly as he and Ophelia climbed into the back of a sedan.

Dalton nodded and held the door open to the town car. Aurélie slid inside and scooted across the seat to make room for him. But he didn't get in right away. Instead he leaned into the opened window and murmured something to the driver.

"Yes, sir," the chauffeur said and shifted the car into Drive.

What was happening?

"Wait!" Aurélie scrambled to open the door.

"*Miss*," the driver said in a firm tone. "Mr. Drake has given me instructions…"

She didn't wait for him to finish. She pushed her way out of the car and ran to catch up with Dalton, who'd already begun walking away.

"Where are you going?" She could hear the panic in her own voice, but she didn't care how desperate it sounded. Didn't care how desperate she looked, slipping and sliding on the icy pavement. Because she knew what he was going to say before he even turned around.

"Aurélie." He gripped her shoulders and held her at arm's length. "Get back in the car."

She shook her head and opened her mouth to object, but no words would come out. They stuck in her throat. She couldn't seem to make a sound.

Dalton's expression hardened, and she was hit with the realization that it didn't matter what she said. Or what she didn't. There were no words that could make him change his mind.

"I want you to go, Aurélie," he said, and she wished with her whole heart that he would call her princess again. Just one more time. "Go home."

Home.

The word hung in the space between them, ominous with meaning.

He wasn't talking about his apartment back in Manhattan. He didn't mean *his* home. He meant *hers*. Delamotte.

"I can't go, Dalton. Not now." How could he expect her to walk away at a time like this?

"I'm not asking you, Aurélie. I'm telling you." He paused, took a deep breath. He suddenly didn't look so stoic anymore. Or angry, either. Just tired. So very tired.

"I want you to go. It's time."

Chapter Thirteen

Dalton hadn't set foot in a hospital since the day Clarissa died.

He'd managed to avoid the beeping machines, the drawn curtains, the memories steeped in antiseptic perfume for six long years. Even in the wake of his father's heart attack, he'd stayed away. At the time, it had been alarmingly easy to explain his absence as a necessity. While Diana sat vigil at their father's bedside and Artem had gone MIA doing God knows what, no one had actually expected Dalton to show up.

They'd expected him to be sitting at his desk. Just like always. It was what their father would have wanted, after all. This expectation had of course been partially instrumental in the events causing Dalton to despise hospitals to begin with.

Oh, the irony.

Dalton had been at the office until 2 a.m. the night Clarissa slit her wrists. What no one knew, either then or now, was that he'd put away his spreadsheets and emails sometime around 10 p.m. After scrolling through all the notifications of Clarissa's missed calls on his cell, he'd opted to sleep on the sofa in his office rather than going home.

He hadn't been in the mood for another argument about his work schedule. Or his inattentiveness. Or anything, really. Whatever feelings he'd had for Clarissa had long since faded. He'd been going through the motions for months. A year perhaps. He just hadn't gotten around to officially breaking things off, in part because he'd had too much on his plate at Drake Diamonds. But mainly because Geoffrey Drake would have been livid when he found out Dalton was calling off his engagement. It had been his father's plan all along to have Clarissa join the Drake dynasty with the diamond empire her grandfather ran.

And like the obedient son that he'd always been, Dalton had fallen into step.

Until he couldn't.

He didn't love her. He was quite sure she didn't love him, either. They'd been thrown together like two animals in a cage, and each in their own way, they'd begun fighting for a way out.

With hindsight had come the benefit of clarity. Dalton could see the arguments, the tantrums, even the suicide, for what they were. Clarissa had wanted to escape. And she'd done just that.

Nevertheless, knowing why she'd done it hadn't lifted the mantle of regret. Dalton should have seen what was happening. He'd always prided himself on his attention to detail, his keen sense of accountability. Whether they'd loved each other or not, Clarissa had been his fiancée. His responsibility. He should have gotten her the help that she needed.

He should have picked up the godforsaken phone.

Instead, he'd woken up sometime in the middle of the night and finally headed home. But only after checking his phone first and seeing that the calls had stopped. He'd assumed Clarissa had finally given up and gone to bed. He wished to hell and back that he'd been right. He wished so many things.

"Mr. Drake, your sister's room is right this way." A nurse wearing mint-green scrubs and holding a clipboard led him down a corridor on the third floor of Southampton Hospital.

Dalton fell in step behind her.

A sign on the wall announced he was in the Head Trauma unit. Just up ahead, Dalton saw a young man in a wheelchair with his skull immobilized in a halo brace, eyes staring blankly into space. He couldn't have been more than sixteen or seventeen years old. Dalton dropped his gaze to the nurse's feet in front of him and her soft-soled white shoes padding silently down the hospital corridor.

"Here we are." She stopped in front of a closed door. Room 367.

She extended a hand to push the door open, and Dalton stopped her. "Wait. Before we go in…"

"Yes?" She smiled politely at him, her kind eyes full of concern. She was being so nice. Everyone was. The paramedics. The ambulance driver. Even the damn Uber driver who'd come to pick him up at the horse show.

It made Dalton want to scream.

"How bad is it?" he asked, hating himself for sounding so desperate.

Clarissa's death should have prepared him for this. What good was the cement wall he'd so carefully constructed around his soul if it didn't protect him from falling apart in the face of tragedy?

"We're still waiting on the results of the CT scan, so I'm afraid I can't really say. She's conscious, and that's a great sign. Her head hurts, though, so she's drifting in and out. The doctor should be in to speak with you shortly. In the meantime, Diana is resting comfortably. Her monitors will alert us if her vital signs change. But if you need anything—anything at all—we're right down the hall, Mr. Drake." She smiled again. Too big. Too nauseatingly nice.

"Very well. I understand." He nodded, and pushed the door open himself, needing to feel as in control of the situation as he could.

As if such an idea were remotely possible.

The nurse checked the beeping machine by Diana's bed and made a few notations on her clipboard while Dalton shifted his weight uncomfortably from one foot to the other. The room was huge. Private. What good was all that time spent at the office if the Drake money couldn't be put to good use? The sheer size of it, along with the huge bay window overlooking the beachfront of Southampton, made the mechanical hospital bed in the center of the room seem absurdly tiny. Resting in a hospital gown and sterile white sheets with her eyes shut tight, Diana looked pale and dainty.

Dainty was a word Dalton had never associated with his sister before. *Strong*, yes. *Fearless*, most definitely. *Dainty* had never been part of the equation.

Even now, it didn't seem right. Dalton frowned, struggling for the right adjective. It was a relief to have something to concentrate on. Something concrete and logical. Until he realized the word he was looking for was *broken*.

His chest seized, and he let out a cough.

The nurse rested a comforting hand on his shoulder. "Give us a shout if you or your sister need anything."

Her voice was a soothing whisper. Dalton nodded, wondering when he'd sunk into the overstuffed leather recliner at Diana's bedside. He had no memory of it. Nor of taking his sister's hand in his own. He wondered if he might be in shock, medically speaking. Not that it mattered. Only one thing mattered right now, and it most definitely wasn't him.

Wake up.

He'd feel a lot better about her prognosis if she'd simply open her eyes. He didn't say it aloud, though. He didn't dare, lest it come out as harshly as it sounded in his head.

Wake the hell up.

Dalton didn't want to be that guy—the angry one screaming orders at an unconscious young woman. Even though deep down, he knew that was exactly who he was. The moment Diana's horse went down, the second his hooves hit the rail and his slender ebony legs buckled beneath him, something had come unwound inside Dalton. Something dark and ugly.

Anger.

Six years of bloody, blinding anger that he'd buried in numbers and sales figures and marketing strategies. But like a diamond buried in a mine, his fury hadn't crumbled during its time in the darkness. It had grown exponentially sharper. Stronger. Dazzling in its intensity.

She wasn't in a coma. She'd been alert when they'd taken her away in the ambulance. She needed rest. He knew that.

But once she'd closed her eyes, Dalton worried they wouldn't open again. After all, that's what had happened last time he sat beside a hospital bed.

His fists clenched in his lap. He was furious. Furious at the horse. Furious at Diana and whatever terrible impulse drove her to hurl herself in harm's way over and over and over again. He was even furious at poor Clarissa.

And his father. Always.

Was there anyone he wasn't angry at?

Unbidden, Aurélie's lovely face came to mind. The pull of the memory was irresistible, dragging him under. He closed his eyes and let himself drown. Just for a moment. Just long enough to summon her generous lips and the elegant curve of her neck. Regal. Classic. A neck made for ropes and ropes of pearls.

But then he remembered her expression when she'd climbed out of the car and come running after him—the bewildered hurt in her emerald eyes, coupled with the painful knowledge that such damage had been his doing.

He opened his eyes and pushed the memory back into place.

I want you to go, Aurélie. It's time.

It had been past time for her to return to Delamotte, gala or no gala. He'd done the right thing.

For both of them.

Then why does it feel so wrong?

"Dalton?"

His heart crashed to a stop. He blinked in relief at the sight of Diana's opened eyes, wide and searching.

He forced himself to smile. "You're awake."

"I am." She nodded, winced and closed her eyes again. "My head hurts. I keep drifting off."

"It's okay. I'm here." He gave her hand a reassuring squeeze.

There was a smudge of red clay on one of Diana's cheeks. Dirt from the riding arena. He wiped it away with a brush of his thumb and pondered the fact that they hadn't cleaned her up. Yet there was a startling lack of blood, given the seriousness of her condition. She didn't have so much as a bruise.

Relief flooded through Dalton's veins and he swallowed. Hard. He could taste the rusty fragrance of blood in his mouth, a sensory memory of the last time he'd sat at a bedside like this one.

With Clarissa, there'd been so much blood. Red everywhere. Afterward, he'd had the apartment painted top to bottom and all the furniture replaced with nothing but white.

Again, his thoughts drifted to Aurélie. Aurélie, with her porcelain skin and windswept hair. Aurélie, swaying to Gershwin in his arms. Aurélie, adopting a dog on a whim. The ugliest one of the bunch.

He shouldn't be thinking of her at a time like this. He shouldn't be thinking of her at all. She didn't have anything to do with his family or his life. She was business. She was temporary. She was royal, for God's sake.

Yet when Diamond's hooves hit the rail with a sickening clang, when he'd watched his sister's head slam into the ground, Aurélie had been the one he'd wanted at his side. Not wanted. Needed. Needed with a ferocity that terrified him.

He didn't want to need anyone, least of all a princess.

You're in love with her. Ophelia sees it. I see it. Why can't you?

Dalton half believed Artem had been joking. Maybe. Maybe not. But his words had touched a nerve.

Out of the question.

He couldn't have feelings for Aurélie. Absolutely not. Not before Diana's accident, and most definitely not now. Not when he'd been reminded so vividly of all the reasons why he was better off on his own.

He wasn't made for this. He never had been. He was his father's son, through and through.

The door swung open again. Dalton turned, hoping with every fiber of his being to find a doctor standing in the doorway. A shining beacon of hope. Instead, he took in the tear-stained face of his sister-in-law, followed closely by his brother.

He dropped Diana's hand and stood. "Artem. Ophelia."

"Dalton?" Ophelia's brow furrowed. "How on earth did you get here so fast?"

"I gave the driver an incentive to get me here in a hurry." Again, the Drake money had come in handy.

"Marvelous." Artem rolled his eyes. "Don't you think we've had enough accidents for one day?"

"I got here in one piece, didn't I?"

"Stop. Both of you." Ophelia's voice wobbled a little. Great. He'd reduced a pregnant woman to tears. That might be a new low, even for Dalton. "This isn't the time for bickering. Diana needs us. All of us."

Diana needs us.

Dalton sank back into the chair and dropped his head in his hands. He wanted to tear his hair out by the roots. The door opened again, and it took superhuman effort for him to look up.

A man wearing green scrubs entered the room and extended his hand. "Hello, I'm Dr. Chris Larson."

Dalton shot to his feet. "Doctor."

Artem and Ophelia introduced themselves, then Dr. Larson cut to the chase. "I have the results from your sister's tests. As you know, she took a nasty spill. Fortunately, she was wearing a helmet. A good one, by all appearances."

This came as a relief, but not as a surprise, to Dalton. As fearless as Diana was, she'd always played by the rules. She had ambition, not a death wish.

The doctor nodded. "It looks like the safety precaution did its job."

Dalton frowned. "Are you sure? She's lying in a hospital bed and can barely keep her eyes open."

"Diana is suffering from a concussion, which is to be expected after taking a hit the way she did. But she's going to be fine. I'm sure she's got a monster of a headache, but now that we know there's no permanent damage, we can start administering something stronger than Tylenol. Still, we'll want to keep an eye on her at least overnight. We'll take her vitals every hour and make sure she's doing well. But those should be precautions. Barring any unforeseen complications, I expect your sister to make a full recovery."

"Thank goodness," Ophelia said. Artem wrapped his arm around her and pulled her close.

"A full recovery?" Dalton tried to focus on the doctor's face, but he couldn't seem to tear his gaze from his sister. "You're sure?"

The doctor nodded. "The scans show no structural damage to the brain tissue. She needs time to rest, but soon she'll be able to do all the things she loves to do. Including showjumping."

"That might be a tough call," Artem said under his breath. "Her horse had to be put down today."

Dalton's gut clenched. He hadn't known what happened to the horse. He'd been so worried about Diana that he hadn't even asked about the animal.

Diamond was dead. *Shit.*

His sister would be devastated. Dalton sighed and wished he could go one day, just one, without thinking about loss. Then again, he had, hadn't he? While Aurélie had been there, he'd been able to let go. Just a little bit.

He'd lived.

And now she's gone, too.

"So what happens next?" Artem asked.

The doctor assured them the hospital staff was doing everything it could to make Diana's stay comfortable. He'd given instructions for the night nurse to call him if anything changed.

Diana woke up briefly. Just long enough to register Artem and Ophelia's presence and to answer a few questions for Dr. Larson.

When her eyes fluttered closed again, he gave her arm a pat. "You're a lucky girl, Miss Drake."

Dalton knew the doctor was right. Diana had been lucky indeed, but he doubted she'd see it that way when she found out Diamond was dead. Part of him wondered if she'd avoided asking about her horse because deep down she knew.

They all knew.

No matter how things looked on the outside, the Drakes had never had luck on their side.

Aurélie sat in the backseat, still trying to absorb Dalton's words as the snowy stretch of Long Island flew past the car windows in a melancholy blur.

I'm not asking you, Aurélie. I'm telling you. I want you to go. It's time.

How could she leave without knowing if Diana was going to be okay? And the horse?

And Dalton.

He didn't mean it. He couldn't.

He'd sure sounded like he meant it, though. Everything about his tone, his stance and the glittering determination in his gaze had been resolute. He'd made up his mind. He wanted her gone.

She had to leave, obviously. She couldn't stay. Not now.

Even if she did, what could she possibly do to help? Her presence would only do more harm than good.

Aurélie had never felt so useless in her entire life, which struck her as profoundly ironic considering she was a princess. She should have been accustomed to not being particularly useful by now, especially in view of the fact that the last time she'd had any communication with the palace, they hadn't even noticed she'd fled the country.

Surely they've noticed now.

It was nearly 6 p.m. in Delamotte. Lord Clement had no doubt come and gone in a royal huff. Everyone would be looking for her, including the Crown Prince.

Any temptation to put the SIM card back in her cell

phone and check her messages had died the moment Diana's horse went down. Aurélie couldn't think about the palace right now. Or her impending engagement. Or even her father. All those people, all those worries, seemed so inconsequential compared to what she'd just witnessed. How could she possibly be thinking about something as silly as a press release after seeing Dalton's sister fall headfirst to the ground?

She couldn't.

Aurélie squeezed her eyes closed and leaned her head against the backseat of the town car. The fall kept running through her mind in an endless loop of catastrophic images and terrible sounds. The thunder of hooves. The thud of Diamond's elegant legs crashing into the rails. Those same slender bones buckling and twisting into unnatural angles. Diana's helmet bouncing on the packed red clay.

But worse than the fall itself had been the look on Dalton's face when his sister failed to get up. In a shadow of a moment, Aurélie had seen a lifetime of pain etched in the lines around his eyes. Stories he'd never told her, never would. Something had happened to Dalton Drake. Something terrible.

Diana had to be okay. She *had* to.

Aurélie would have given everything she had to be at the hospital with the Drakes, but Dalton had made his wishes clear when he put her in the town car.

He doesn't want you there.

He doesn't want you. Period.

It stung. Aurélie knew it shouldn't. She wasn't one of them. She and Dalton weren't a couple. They were two people who'd been thrown together for a few days. Nothing more.

And now she had no idea what was going on, what had become of his sister or even the injured horse. Not knowing was torture. She thought about asking the driver if she could borrow his phone, but decided against it. If Dalton wanted to get in touch with her, he would.

Aurélie spent the entire ride back to the city in agonizing silence. At last the steely skyscrapers of Manhattan came into view. "Can you drop me at Drake Diamonds before we go back to the apartment?"

She no longer wanted the secret egg. Dalton could keep it for all she cared. She hated it now, hated what it stood for—the cheating, the lies. The egg had served its purpose. It had gotten her a few days of freedom. It was her bargaining chip, and now the bargain was over.

But her mother's pearls were at the store. Dalton had given them to Ophelia to be restrung. The last time Aurélie had seen them, they'd been lined up on a velvet tray on Ophelia's desk.

She prayed they were still there.

"Very well." The car rolled past the horse carriages lined up on the curb by Central Park and turned onto Fifth Avenue.

They passed the elegant entrance to the Plaza Hotel and too soon, the imposing façade of Drake Diamonds came into view.

"Thank you." Aurélie climbed out and paused in front of the store, blinking against the snow flurries drifting from the dove-gray sky.

Just walk inside, get your pearls back and then you can go home and put all of this behind you.

Her feet refused to move. It felt strange being here without Dalton. Wrong, somehow.

This had been a mistake. She would just ring Mrs.

Barnes when she got back to Delamotte and ask her to return the pearls by post.

She turned to get back in the car, but it had already been swallowed up in the steady stream of yellow cabs snaking their way through upper Manhattan. That's right. Even Dalton's driver couldn't just park by the curb indefinitely.

She considered staying put and waiting for him to make a loop around the block and return. It could take mere minutes. Or, given the erratic nature of New York traffic, she could be stuck standing here for half an hour.

Okay then. She took a deep breath, turned and pushed through the revolving doors.

"Oh, thank goodness." Mrs. Barnes pounced on Aurélie the moment her kitten heels hit the showroom floor. "Where's Mr. Drake?"

Aurélie blinked. "Dalton?"

"Yes." Mrs. Barnes, whom Aurélie had never seen with even a single hair out of place, looked borderline frantic. She shook her head and tossed her hands up in the air. "Or Artem. Or Ophelia. Any of the Drakes, for that matter. I've been calling all three of them for hours and can't reach anyone."

Aurélie wasn't sure how much she should divulge. It didn't appear as though Dalton's assistant knew about Diana's accident. Or maybe she did, and was hoping for more information about Diana's condition. "They're… um…unreachable at the moment."

"Yes, I know. They're in the Hamptons. But I need to speak to Mr. Drake. Now." Barnes's gaze narrowed. "I'd assumed he was with you."

"No." She shook her head. Clearly Mrs. Barnes didn't

know what was going on, and it wasn't Aurélie's place to tell her. "Is there a problem?"

"You could say that, yes. A multitude of problems, actually. We were so busy that we had lunch brought in for the staff this afternoon, and now half of them have fallen ill with food poisoning. The store has never been this shortstaffed."

"Oh, no. That's terrible."

"I've been working the sales floor all afternoon." She waved a hand around the showroom, which upon closer inspection, had a rather frantic air about it. "I've tied over 400 white bows since two o'clock."

"What can I do to help?" Aurélie knew nothing about selling diamonds. Or anything else about working at a jewelry store. But she could learn. And she was pretty sure she could tie a bow.

Mrs. Barnes eyed her with no small amount of skepticism.

"Seriously, I want to help." *Please, let me.* It was a chance to be useful for once in her life. At a time when she needed it most of all.

Mrs. Barnes's apology was swift. "No, no, no. You're Mr. Drake's guest. That's not necessary."

"From what you said, it sounds very necessary." Even an ocean away from Delamotte, people still didn't think she was capable of doing anything useful. It made Aurélie want to scream. "Please. *Please.* I'll do anything."

Dalton's secretary bit her lip and looked Aurélie up and down. "Anything?"

"Yes." Aurélie nodded furiously. "You name it."

"Okay. I hope I don't get fired for this, but they're absolutely desperate for help upstairs. Anything you could do up there would be appreciated."

Aurélie swallowed. "Upstairs?" A trickle of dread snaked its way up her spine.

Mrs. Barnes flicked a hand toward the ceiling. "In Engagements."

Not that. Anything but Engagements.

She'd rather clean the toilets than spend the rest of the day neck-deep in diamond engagement rings.

But what could she possibly say? She'd begged to help. Refusing would mean everyone was right about her. Her father. Dalton. And as much as she hated to admit it, even herself. How could she fight her destiny if she couldn't even make herself get off the elevator on the tenth floor?

"I think every bride and groom in the city decided to shop for rings today," Mrs. Barnes said. *Oh joy.* "They need champagne. And petit fours. And gift wrapping. Find the floor manager, and he'll put you to work."

"Right." Aurélie nodded.

She could do this. Couldn't she?

"I'll be up to check on you in a bit."

Aurélie watched as Mrs. Barnes crossed the showroom floor with purpose in her stride. It would have been so easy to turn around and walk back out the revolving door. So easy to get back in the car, collect Jacques from the pet sitter at Dalton's apartment and head straight to the airport.

Too easy.

She'd had enough of taking the easy way out. She squared her shoulders, marched straight toward the elevator and stepped inside.

"Tenth floor, *s'il vous plait*," she told the elevator attendant.

He eyed her warily. Not that she could blame him. "Yes, ma'am."

The elevator doors swished closed. When they opened again, she exited as swiftly as possible. Maybe she could simply outrun her panic.

Then again, maybe not. As soon as she found herself surrounded by the glass cases of sparkling diamond solitaires, the familiar tightness gathered in her chest. Her knees went wobbly, and she had trouble catching her breath. Aurélie squeezed her eyes shut, and when she did, she no longer saw herself in a white gown walking down the aisle of the grand cathedral in Delamotte. Her recurrent nightmare had been replaced. Instead, she saw Diamond barreling toward the double-rail jump. She saw him stumble and fall. She saw Diana slamming into the ground headfirst.

Aurélie's eyes flew open. This was absurd. Diana was lying in a hospital bed, possibly even fighting for her life. Surely Aurélie could tolerate a few giddy brides and grooms.

There were more than a few. There were dozens. Under the direction of the acting floor manager, Aurélie brought them flutes of champagne. She served them cake. She oohed and ahed as they tried on rings. She offered her congratulations, wrapped more rings than she could count in little Drake-blue boxes and tied white bows.

And it wasn't altogether terrible.

Granted, she got a little misty eyed if she paid too much attention to the way the grooms looked at their brides-to-be. So much unabashed adoration was a little much to take, especially when she almost allowed herself to believe Dalton had looked at her in the same way during the quiet moments before Diana's accident.

But that was just crazy. Wishful thinking, at best.

Delusional, at worst. She didn't want to fool herself into believing Dalton cared about her, maybe even loved her, when he so clearly didn't.

Dealing with the grooms got easier when she focused her gaze on their foreheads rather than their lovey-dovey expressions. Before long, the smile she'd plastered on her face began to feel almost genuine. She'd just wrapped a satiny white ribbon around a Drake-blue box containing a cushion-cut diamond solitaire in a platinum setting when the overhead lights flickered and dimmed.

"What's happening?" she asked the salesman as she handed him the box.

"It's closing time." He sighed. "Finally. It's been a day, hasn't it? Thanks for all your help, by the way. What's your name, again?"

Her Royal Highness Princess Aurélie Marchand. "Aurélie."

He nodded. "Thanks again, Aurélie. Good work."

Good work.

No one had ever uttered those words to her before. It gave her a little thrill to be praised for something other than showing up at an event with a tiara on her head. "No problem. Can I do anything else?"

He shrugged. "I've got to close out the registers and get the place cleaned up, then we can all go home."

Home.

Aurélie's throat grew tight. She'd managed to stay so busy for a few hours that she'd forgotten she was supposed to be on a plane right now.

She let out a shaky breath. "I'll help you. I'm not in any hurry."

"Suit yourself," he said and handed her a bottle of Windex and a roll of paper towels.

One by one, the customers left. It was strange being in Drake Diamonds all alone after hours, peaceful in a way that caught Aurélie off guard. After so much noisy activity, there was a grace to the sudden silence. The gemstones almost looked like holy relics glowing in the semi-darkness, the sapphires, rubies and emeralds like precious stained glass.

It was soothing, therapeutic. Almost hypnotic. Aurélie didn't realize how lost she'd become in the simple act of dusting until she heard the salesman's footsteps again.

She gave a start as he walked up behind her. "Sorry. I'm afraid I'm a bit startled."

"As am I."

She froze, unable to move. She could barely even breathe.

That voice.

She knew the particular timbre of that voice. It didn't belong to the salesman. It belonged to the person she wanted to see more than anyone else on earth.

Heart beating wildly in her chest, she turned around. "Dalton."

Chapter Fourteen

Dalton thought he might be hallucinating at first.

He was bone-weary. Diana's accident and its aftermath had exhausted him on every possible level—physically, mentally, emotionally. When he passed through the darkened corridor of Drake Diamonds and glanced toward the Engagements showroom, he didn't think for a second that what he was looking at could possibly be real.

Aurélie was supposed to be on a plane. She couldn't be standing in his store after closing time. Even if she'd ignored his request and stayed in New York, she definitely wouldn't be milling about in Engagements, of all places. When his gaze landed on the dust rag in her right hand, he was sure he was seeing things.

He was wrong of course. But what surprised him even more than Aurélie's presence was the wave of relief that washed over him when she turned around and said his name.

Dalton had never needed anyone before, and that was no accident. He'd arranged his life so that he was self-reliant in every way. He always had been. He didn't want to need anyone or anything.

But right now, he needed *her*. Aurélie. He needed her so badly it terrified him to his core.

He didn't know why she was here. Or how. All he knew was that he felt like falling to his knees in gratitude that she'd ignored him when he'd sent her away.

He shoved his hands in his pockets to stop himself from reaching for her. He couldn't be trusted. Not in the state he was in. If he touched her now, he wouldn't be able to stop. "What are you doing here?"

"I could ask you the same thing." She fiddled with the rag in her hands, nervously wadding it into a ball.

What on earth was going on? It was like he'd stepped into some weird reverse Cinderella scenario.

"I own this building," he said. "I have every right to be here."

"I suppose you do." Her gaze darted toward the empty hallway.

"You can stop looking around. I've sent everyone home already." Almost everyone.

"Oh." She swallowed, and Dalton traced the movement up and down the length of her regal neck. His willpower was crumbling by the second. "How's Diana? Is she going to be okay?"

He nodded. "Yes, thank God. She's awake. Mostly anyway. According to the doctor, she didn't suffer any permanent damage."

He dropped his gaze to the display case and the diamond rings shimmering in the darkness, like ice on fire. "Her horse had to be put down. She didn't know. I told her about an hour ago, and she didn't take it well."

His voice broke, and something inside him seemed to break right along with it. Giving Diana the news about Diamond had been the most difficult conversation he'd ever had in his life. Even more difficult than telling Clarissa's parents about her suicide.

He was just so sick of loss. Of death and dying. He couldn't carry it with him anymore. Not another damned minute.

His gaze slid back to Aurélie, standing in front of him looking so beautiful. So alive. So real.

It was enough to make him lose his head.

"I was engaged once," he said, nodding at the neat row of rings beneath the glass.

What was he doing? He hadn't planned on telling Aurélie about Clarissa. He hadn't even considered it. But once it slipped out, he felt instantly lighter. Just a little bit. Just enough that he could breathe again.

"She died," he continued. "By her own hand, but I was to blame."

He took a deep inhale and paused. He wasn't sure why. Maybe he was waiting for her to respond in horror. Maybe he'd held onto the words for so long that his voice was rebelling. But he forced them out. If he didn't say them now, he knew he never would. To anyone. He'd carry his horrible secrets to his grave, and he couldn't bear the weight of them any longer.

"She called me for help, but I didn't answer. If I had, she might still be alive today." He covered his face with his hands. It hurt to be this open, this vulnerable.

"I should have been there for her, but I wasn't. I was here. Right where I always am." He forced himself to look at Aurélie. As much as he feared seeing a look of disappointment on her face—or worse, pity—he needed to gaze into those glittering green eyes.

The compassion he saw in their emerald depths kept him going. And once he began, he couldn't get the words out fast enough. His tongue tripped over them, and he told her the entire story. He even told her little details he'd thought he'd forgotten, like the shooting star he'd seen on the way home that night and the way he'd felt like the world's biggest fraud when the mourners at Clarissa's funeral offered their condolences. He talked until there was nothing left to say.

Then he finished, breathless, and waited for her to say something. He hoped to God she didn't try and tell him it wasn't his fault. He'd been having that argument with himself for six years. He didn't want to have it with her, too.

She didn't tell him he was blameless, though. She didn't try to make him feel better, nor did she look at him like he was some kind of monster. She said the only thing he was willing to hear. The right thing. The perfect thing.

"Dalton, I'm so sorry." She placed a gentle hand on his forearm.

His name was like a prayer on her lips, her touch like a balm. The tenderness of the moment ripped him open, crushed what was left of his defenses. Without the shelter of his secrets, he was no longer capable of hiding his desperation.

He a*ched* for her.

Keeping his distance from her had been torture. The only thing stopping him from kissing her right here, right now, were those six words he'd been trying to forget since the moment she'd uttered them just hours after he'd taken her to bed.

I don't think it should happen again.

Dalton had never once come close to forcing himself on a woman. He thought men who did that were despicable. He couldn't...wouldn't...kiss her without her consent. But by God, if he stood much longer in that room, drowning in engagement rings, he was liable to do something he'd come to regret. He may already have.

"Princess," he whispered as he reached to cup her face, drawing the pad of his thumb across her lovely lower lip.

She didn't say a word, didn't even breathe as far as he could tell, just gazed at him with her sparkling emerald eyes.

Dalton remembered a story his grandfather had told him when he was a little boy. He'd said that in ancient Rome, the Emperor Nero watched gladiator battles through a large emerald stone because he found the color soothing. Since the very first emerald had been dug out of the ground, people believed healing could be found in their glittering green depths. They were once called the Jewel of Kings.

It was a fitting thing to remember in the presence of royalty.

Dalton could have been Nero in that moment. Soothed and whole. Everything he wanted, everything he needed was right there in those eyes. Acceptance. Life. Passion.

He wanted her. He wanted her again. And again and again.

Walk away.

Walk away while you still can.

"Kiss me." She turned her head just slightly, just

enough for his thumb to make contact with the wet warmth of her mouth. "Please."

Please.

Dalton went rock-hard even before his lips crashed down on hers. Had it only been a day since he'd been inside her? Impossible. It felt like years since he'd buried himself between her thighs and felt her lithe body shuddering beneath him. Too long. Much too long.

He circled an arm around her, pulling her against him as her lips opened for him and he licked his way inside her mouth with teasing strokes of his tongue. He kissed her with all the dark intensity that made him who he was. A shock of pure, primal pleasure shot through him when she whimpered and melted into him.

This, he thought.

This right here was what he wanted. What he'd missed.

She tasted like promise and hunger and hope, things Dalton had given up on long ago. And the way she responded to his touch was enough to bring him back to life.

He pinned her against one of the taller display cases and kissed her until she began to tremble violently. Until the diamonds behind her shook on their glass shelves. He liked it. He liked it far too much.

He wasn't going to rush things this time. Not even if she urged him to hurry. Not even if she begged. Hell, he *wanted* her to beg. He wanted her wet, helpless and desperate for him by the time he pushed inside her. He wanted this to mean something, so when daylight came, it would be impossible for her to look him in the eye and call this a mistake.

"Dalton," she whispered against his mouth. Her hand

moved from his chest to his fly, finding him through his clothes. Exploring. Caressing. Stroking with just the right amount of pressure.

His vision blurred. He groaned. For a moment he thought he saw stars, but then he realized it was the light from the diamonds shimmering softly behind her.

"I want you," she murmured. The next sound he heard was the slide of his zipper, then her delicate hand was around his shaft, pumping slowly. He closed his eyes, lost to the pure, hot bliss of her touch. Only for a moment. Only long enough for his desire to take on an edge of desperation.

He opened his eyes.

"Not now, princess. Not yet." *Not even close.*

He dropped his lips to the curve of her neck and worked his way down, down to the hollow of her throat, casually unbuttoning her dress as he went.

"Turn around," he said in as even a tone as he could manage.

She released her hold on his cock and obeyed, turning slowly, peering at him coyly over her shoulder. But there was heat glimmering in her emerald gaze. Molten desire.

"Put your hands over your head," he told her, his voice raw with need.

Again she did as he said without a moment's hesitation, and that alone was nearly enough to make him lose control. His hands shook as he gathered the soft folds of her dress and lifted it carefully over her head. He tossed it aside, and waves of golden curls spilled over her shoulders and down her supple back.

So gorgeous.

He drank in the sight of her exquisite curves, surrounded by the luminous diamond glow and clothed in nothing but tiny wisps of lace. She was the most beautiful woman Dalton had ever set eyes on. Always would be. He couldn't say how, or why, but he knew with absolute certainty that there would never be another woman in his life like Aurélie. Whatever this was between them came around only once in a lifetime. If that.

"Be still," he said. "Be very still."

Her hair rippled gently beneath his breath. He twirled a long, lovely lock of it around his fingertips before trailing his hand ever so softly down the length of her spine. His touch left goose bumps in its wake.

She shivered.

He leaned in, pressed a tender kiss between her shoulder blades, and a slow smile of satisfaction came to his lips when she arched her back.

So needy.

Now we're getting somewhere.

What was he doing to her?

This wasn't like before. This was something different entirely. Something far more intense.

He'd been holding back last night. She realized that now. She'd asked him not to be gentle, not to go slow. And he hadn't. But tonight, Dalton was the one in control. He was setting the pace. And the deliberate slowness of his movements seemed designed to send her into sensual distress.

Aurélie could barely keep herself upright. Her legs were on the verge of buckling, and Dalton had barely touched her. There'd been just a few brushes of his fingertips and one or two lingering kisses, but it was the wicked edge to his voice that was reducing her to a quivering mass of need. He sounded so serious. So imposing.

It shouldn't have aroused her. It absolutely shouldn't have, but it did. It inflamed her in a way she didn't understand. Couldn't, even if she'd been capable of trying. Which she wasn't. Not by a long shot.

She couldn't think. She couldn't speak. When he ran his hands down her sides, grabbed hold of her hips and gently turned her around so she was facing him again, she could barely even look at him.

She peered up at him through the thick fringe of her lashes and her face went hot. His lips curved into a knowing grin as she struggled to catch her breath. She glanced down. Her breasts were straining the lacy cups of her bra, arching toward him. Her thighs were pressed together in an effort to quell the tingling at her center. This was too much. Too much heat. Too much sensation. It didn't matter that she couldn't speak. She didn't need to say a word. Her body was pleading with him, begging him to touch her. Take her. Fill her.

She would have been mortified if she hadn't been so violently aroused.

He raised a single, dark eyebrow and pushed the hair back from her eyes. Her pulse rocketed out of control, and his gaze dropped to her throat. He knew. Dalton Drake knew perfectly well what he was doing to her.

She licked her lips and willed herself not to beg. *Please, Dalton. Touch me.*

Love me.

Love me.

At last he moved closer, unhooked her bra and slid its satiny straps down her arms. Before it even fell to the floor, his mouth was on her breasts, licking, sucking, biting. Then he pressed a languid, openmouthed kiss to her belly. She was vaguely conscious of her panties

sliding down her legs. Everything had gone so seduc-
tively fuzzy around the edges. She looked around, and
she saw Dalton's image reflected in the cool facets of
the diamonds twinkling under the shimmering lights.
Everywhere. Like a starry winter's night.

Her legs trembled as he parted her thighs, his mouth
moving lower, lower still.

The scrape of his five o'clock shadow along the soft
flesh of her inner thigh was nearly enough to send her
over the edge. What was happening? This was too intimate. Too intense. There would be no coming back from
this. She'd never be able to pretend this didn't matter.
Not to herself. Not to him.

He'd told her his deepest, darkest secret. And now he
was uncovering hers, exposing her desire for the wanton, yearning thing that it was. She couldn't be this vulnerable to him. Not when she would eventually have to
walk away.

She'd stolen another day. But this wouldn't last forever. It couldn't. She'd be lucky if it lasted until the gala.

The impossibility of the situation bore down on her.
She looked at Dalton settled between her thighs, pleasur-
ing her with his skillful mouth and she felt like crying.
But instead she heard herself crying out in pleasure, saying his name as though she had a right to it. As though
it belonged to her.

He's not yours.

He's not yours, and he never will be.

"Dalton," she murmured. She had to tell him. He'd
been so honest with her. So real. And he still didn't know
why she'd been so desperate to leave home.

"Let go." There it was again—that unflinchingly au-
thoritative tone. Her favorite sound. "Just feel, princess."

Surrender was her only choice. It was too late for anything else. She clung tightly to him, her hands moving through his hair as she writhed against him.

Just feel, princess.

Her head fell back as she fully, finally gave herself up to him. She couldn't fight it anymore. It was no use. He slipped a finger inside her, moving it in time with his mouth. She gasped, blinking in shock at the astonishing pleasure. Her mind had caught up with her body, stripped bare and open. Everything around her shimmered. Her eyes fluttered shut, and the row of dazzling engagement rings in the case beside her was the last thing she saw before her climax slammed into her and she came apart.

Dalton caught her as she slipped toward the floor. He tucked an arm beneath her legs and carried her out of the room, down the hall to his office. She tried to wrap her arms around his neck, but they'd gone impossibly heavy. Instead she nestled her head in the warm space between his neck and shoulder.

He set her down gingerly on the sofa and undressed while she watched, memorizing every detail of his sculpted body and the way it glistened like fine marble in the moonlight streaming through the window. She wanted to hold onto what she was feeling right then— the heady thrill she felt when he looked at her bare body.

He sees me.

He always has.

He stretched out next to her, and she moved to sit astride him. She gazed down at him, this man who'd found her when she hadn't even realized how lost she'd been. He rose up to kiss her, his mouth gentle and seeking. It was a reverent kiss. Worshipful, almost. The tenderness of it caught her off guard. A wistful ache squeezed her heart.

She reached for him and guided him to her entrance. She needed him to fill her again. Now, before whatever was happening between them slipped through their fingers like her mother's golden pearls.

With an excruciatingly sweet ache, he pushed inside her. Slowly, slowly, and she arched to take him in. He curled his strong hands around her hips, thrust harder. And harder. Until the sweetness gave way to blazing heat, and fire bloomed between them once again.

Diamond bright.

Chapter Fifteen

Dalton slept like the dead.

With Aurélie's head on his chest and his fingers buried in her hair, he slept the peaceful, dreamless slumber of a man who'd managed to outrun his demons. His eyes didn't open a fraction until he heard voices. Familiar voices.

"Good morning."

"I understand. There's been a family emergency, but the moment I'm able to reach Mr. Drake, I'll let him know you're here."

Was that Mrs. Barnes? What was his secretary doing in his apartment?

He pressed his eyes closed, determined not to care. He wasn't waking up. Not yet. He wanted to stay right where he was, wrapped in Aurélie's graceful limbs as long as he could. He turned, slid behind her and burrowed into her soft orchid scent. Memories from the night before came flooding back. Tastes. Sounds. The glorious sight of her sitting on top of him with her hair tumbling over her shoulders and moonlight caressing her beautiful breasts. He ran his hands over the soft swell of her hips, pulled her close to grind against her bottom and was rewarded with a sultry moan.

"Good morning, love," he whispered, already hard, already wanting her. God, what was happening to him? He was insatiable.

"I understand the urgency of the situation, but it's really not best that you come here, Your Highness."

Somewhere beneath the liquid heat of his arousal, a prickle of unease snaked its way into Dalton's consciousness.

His eyes drifted open, and he took in his surroundings. His desk. His chair. The Drake-blue walls.

Shit. They weren't in his apartment. They were in his office.

"Aurélie, wake up. We've overslept." Sunlight and the crystal reflection of snowfall streamed through his office windows.

What time was it? He never slept past 6 a.m. From the looks of things, it was far later than that. And if Mrs. Barnes was already here…

He cursed and jerked upright. The store was about to open for business. The hallways were teeming with his employees. And he was naked in his office.

With Aurélie.

She blinked, then as the reality of the present circumstances dawned, her eyes went wide with panic. "Dalton. Oh my God."

"Don't worry." He glanced at the halfway open door,

leaped off the sofa and slammed it closed. "Everything will be okay."

Her gaze darted around the room. "But my clothes…"

Shit. Shit. Shit. Her dress was still pooled on the floor of Engagements, right next to her lingerie. Not to mention the fact that there were cameras all over that room. He needed to get his hands on the store's surveillance videos. Immediately, before anyone saw them. But first he needed to get her dressed.

He laid his hands on her shoulders and pressed a kiss to the top of her head. *Don't panic.* "It will be fine. I promise. I'll go get your clothes."

She nodded, looking every bit as dazed as he felt.

How had he let this happen? He'd had sex in the store. Even Artem had never done something this outrageous. That Dalton knew of.

He shook his head. If this wasn't the first time a Drake had been in this situation, he really didn't want to know.

He grabbed his pants from the floor and pulled them on. They were wrinkled as hell. Everyone in the building would be able to recognize his stroll through the store as a walk of shame. Marvelous.

At least he had a selection of pressed shirts from the dry cleaners in one of his desk drawers. He reached for the one on top of the stack and pulled it on, fumbling with the buttons.

"Let me," Aurélie said, unfolding her legs from beneath her and walking toward him.

He allowed himself a brief glance of her bare body, even though he knew good and well it would only make him forget why he was in such a hurry to leave the room. Sure enough, one look, one glimpse of her porcelain skin, her perfect breasts and their rosebud nipples, was all it took for him to forget about everything on the other side of the door.

"Stop looking at me like that, or we'll never get out of here." She rolled her eyes and smoothed down his collar.

He felt himself grinning. "Would that be so bad?"

"You tell me, Mr. CEO."

"It might be a tad inappropriate." His hands found her waist and slid lower until they cupped the decadent softness of her bottom. "Not that I care much at the moment."

She smiled up at him and something came unloose in his chest. "But you will. Eventually."

He was beginning to doubt it.

"There. You're all buttoned up."

A pity. "How do I look?"

"Like you've been ravaging women on the sales floor." She lifted an amused brow.

"*Woman,* not *women.*" He slid his arms around her, not quite willing to tear himself away despite the absurdity of the situation. "Only the one."

The one.

The One.

"Good to know, Mr. Drake." She rose up on tiptoe and kissed the corner of his mouth, and for a moment his feet stayed rooted to the floor. He couldn't have budged for all the diamonds in Africa.

The intercom on his office phone buzzed, piercing the intimate silence. "Dalton, it's Artem. If you're in there, we need to talk. It's urgent."

He took his hands off Aurélie. Came to his senses.

"I'll be right back," he said.

Artem was waiting for him directly on the other side

of the door, holding Aurélie's clothes and wearing a grim expression.

Perfect. Just perfect.

"Whatever you're going to say, I really don't want to hear it right now. Can we talk later?"

Artem thrust Aurélie's things at him. "No, it can't."

"Fine. Lecture me all you want." God knows, he deserved it.

Artem lowered his voice. "Brother, I'm not here to lecture you. Believe me. We've got a situation on our hands."

"It's not Diana, is it?" That couldn't be it, though, could it? Otherwise, Artem wouldn't be here.

"No, she's fine. I just spoke to her doctor this morning." He sighed. "It's the palace. They've been calling. And calling. Mrs. Barnes is in a panic. Have you checked your messages?"

Dalton's gut churned. After Diana's fall, he'd forgotten all about the unread email. He hadn't even turned his phone back on.

He shook his head. "Is this as bad as it seems?"

"It's not good." Artem raked a hand through his hair. He seemed to be doing everything in his power to remain calm. "Get her dressed, and we'll deal with it. Together. Sound good?"

He nodded. "Thanks."

"That's what family's for." But there was a gravity in his expression that Dalton couldn't ignore.

"Wait. What aren't you telling me?"

Artem shook his head. His gaze dropped to the floor, and Dalton suddenly didn't want to know. He just wanted to rewind the clock to the night before and stay in that dazzling place forever.

"She's engaged." Artem sighed. "Aurélie. She's getting married. It's on the front page of every newspaper in the world."

Dalton shook his head.

There had to be some kind of mistake. He was talking about some other princess. Not her. Not Aurélie.

The one.

The One.

He swallowed hard. "No." Just…no.

She would have said something. She would have told him, wouldn't she?

A dark fury began to gather in his chest, like a rising storm. So thick, so black he choked it on it. He cleared his throat, swallowed it down, as he remembered how lost she'd been when she first arrived in New York, how she'd pushed him away after the first time they'd made love…how she'd hated even setting foot in Engagements. She *had* told him, hadn't she? Not in so many words, but he'd known. On some level, he'd known. She'd been telling him all along.

Artem reached into the inside pocket of his suit jacket and pulled out a neatly folded square of newsprint. "Here. Read it for yourself."

He didn't want to look. He really didn't. But he forced himself to unfold the paper, because he'd been blind enough for the past few days. It was time to wake up to reality.

Her Royal Highness Princess Aurélie Marchand of Delamotte to Marry Duke Lawrence Bouvier on April 20 in Lavish Royal Wedding

* * *

Aurélie knew something was horribly wrong as soon as Dalton crossed the threshold.

There was a sudden seriousness in the firm set of his jaw, and he seemed to look right through her when he handed her the folded pile of clothes. Suddenly acutely aware of her nakedness, she wanted to hide. If anything, to shield herself from the coolness in his gaze.

"Thank you," she said and slipped into her dress as quickly as she could.

He said nothing, just stood there waiting with a large Drake-blue shopping bag in his hands while she pulled on her panties.

What was going on? What had happened in the handful of minutes since she'd seen him last?

She swallowed and smoothed down the front of her dress. She knew, even without the benefit of a mirror, that she looked like a mess. A complete and utter disaster. "Dalton, what's wrong?"

"Nothing's wrong." He shrugged with a casual air of nonchalance, but the impassivity of his gaze shifted into something darker. More dangerous. "I should probably offer my congratulations, though."

For a moment, she was confused. She couldn't imagine what he was talking about.

Then she realized…

Somehow he'd found out about the wedding. He *knew*.

No. He couldn't. That wasn't feasible. How could he possibly know when it wasn't even official?

"I'm not sure I know what you mean." But her words sounded disingenuous, even to her own ears.

She hated herself.

"Save it, Princess," he snapped.

With exaggerated calmness, he pulled a newspaper from the top of the shopping bag and handed it to her.

She was afraid to take it, but she didn't dare refuse him. Not when she'd already given him every reason in the world to despise her.

Her stomach plummeted when she read the headline. The palace had made an announcement. Without even consulting her. Without her knowledge. She supposed it didn't matter after all that she'd been a no-show for the sitting with Lord Clement. They'd simply used an older picture.

She stared at herself, smiling like an idiot below the awful headline, and realized that her absence *had* mattered. It mattered so much that the palace had gone ahead and released the news. They'd played the ultimate trump card. She had no choice but to go home now. She'd never be able to move about New York, or anyplace else now, without being recognized. Not after this.

She folded the newspaper and dropped it on Dalton's desk. She couldn't stand to look at it another minute. If she did, she might vomit.

"Dalton, please. Let me explain. I wasn't engaged when I came here. I'm not…"

But she was.

She knew it. And so did he. So did everyone. She was getting married, and it was front-page news.

Someone knocked on the door, and Aurélie wished with everything in her that Dalton would tell whomever it was to go away. She needed to talk to him. She needed to fix things. She didn't know how it was possible, but she had to try. She'd never be able to live with herself if she didn't.

"Come in," he said.

The door opened, and in walked Mrs. Barnes, followed by an older gentleman wearing a dark suit and a grim expression. Aurélie's father.

Her legs gave way, and she sank onto the sofa. Her father had come all this way, just to drag her home. It was over—her holiday, Dalton, their bargain.

All of it.

"I'm sorry, Mr. Drake." Mrs. Barnes was wringing her hands, and fluttering about between Dalton and her father. "I apologize, but Mr. Marchand insisted on seeing you. I know he doesn't have an appointment…"

Dalton held up a hand. "It's okay. He doesn't need one."

Of course he didn't. The Crown Prince of Delamotte always got his way.

Bile rose to the back of Aurélie's throat.

"Father," she said.

"Aurélie." He looked her up and down, from the messy hair atop her head to the tips of her barefoot toes. Her face burned with shame. Her father didn't say a word about the meaning of her disheveled appearance. He didn't have to. He swiveled his gaze toward Dalton. "Mr. Drake, I presume?"

"Yes." Dalton nodded. The fact that he refused to bow was a major breach of royal etiquette. Aurélie suspected he knew this. She also suspected he didn't give a damn.

"My office has been trying to reach you, Mr. Drake. Aurélie failed to show up for an important engagement yesterday, so we tracked her cell phone." His lips straightened into a flat line. "Imagine my surprise when it was brought to my attention that she's been here in New York. For days, it seems."

They must have tracked her phone before she'd taken out the SIM card. They'd known where she was all along.

The air in the room went so thick that Aurélie couldn't seem to catch her breath. Her father was giving Dalton a warning. He didn't care if Dalton was her lover. He was nothing to the Crown Prince of Delamotte. No one.

Dalton shrugged. "Forgive me, Your Highness, but your daughter is a grown woman. I believe she can make her own decisions."

He glanced at her, but she couldn't even look at him. This was so much worse than anything she'd ever imagined taking place. What had she done?

"Aurélie," Dalton prompted.

If ever there was a time to stand up to her father, it was now.

She took a deep breath and met his gaze, but when she did, she didn't see the man who'd bounced her on his knee when she was a little girl. She saw her sovereign. She saw the crown. She saw everything her mother had written on the gilt-edged pages of her diary about the tragedy of fate.

"I don't want to go, and I can't marry the duke." The words came out far weaker than she'd intended.

"Nonsense. You can, and you will. I won't allow you to embarrass me, Aurélie. Nor the throne." Her father glanced at his watch. "Come along. We can discuss this when we get home. We have a plane to catch."

She shook her head. "But my things…" Her dog. Her mother's pearls. *Her heart.*

If Dalton hadn't stepped forward and handed her the shopping bag, she may have found the strength to stay. She liked to believe that she would have been able to make that choice, that she would have been strong enough to stand up for what she wanted. Love. Life. Freedom. But when she looked down and saw what Dalton was offering her, she lost her resolve.

At the bottom of the bag sat a black velvet box, embossed with the Marchand royal crest. She knew what was inside without opening it. It was the secret egg. He was giving it back to her. He wanted her gone, no matter the cost.

"I've made arrangements for Sam to deliver Jacques and the rest of your things to the airport," Dalton said coolly. He nodded at the bag.

Take it from him. Just take it.

She dug deep and summoned her pride. If he didn't want her, she wouldn't stay. He'd already sent her away once. Twice was more than she could take.

She lifted her chin and reached for the bag. Only then did she notice the small glass box on top of the velvet egg carrier. Inside were her mother's gold pearls, restrung and perfect.

Just as perfect as she was expected to be from now on.

Chapter Sixteen

Dalton operated on autopilot until the night of the gala. Those seven days were the longest of his life. He spent all day, every day at the office, preparing for the party. He talked to the caterer, the florist, the baker and the linen rental company. He gave press interviews. More press interviews than he'd ever conducted before. He didn't particularly enjoy talking about the Marchand family over and over again. But he was determined not to let it show.

He spent his evenings at the hospital, sitting at Diana's bedside, until she was discharged. After Dr. Larson released her, Dalton insisted she come stay at his apartment so he could keep an eye on her. He worried about her. He didn't like the thought of her grieving for Diamond alone, in her tiny Brooklyn walk-up. At least that was what he'd told Diana. And the rest of the Drakes.

And himself.

The truth of the matter was that he was the one who couldn't handle the solitude of an empty apartment. Everywhere he turned, he saw reminders of Aurélie: Central Park, the New York Public Library, the sidewalk outside of Bergdorf Goodman. His office. His apartment. His bed.

God, how he missed her.

He missed her quirky clothes. He missed the way she never once allowed him to tell her what to do. He even missed her snoring, silly-looking dog. The enormity of her absence may not have fully hit him until one afternoon when he and Diana were walking through the park and he stopped beneath the blue awning at the pet adoption stand.

"Um, what are you doing?" Diana asked, crossing her arms and gaping at him in disbelief as he scooped a scrawny Chihuahua from one of the pens.

Was he going crazy, or had those been his exact words to Aurélie when he'd found her standing in the same spot on the day she'd first arrived?

We're adopting a dog, darling.

"I remember you." The animal shelter volunteer narrowed her gaze at him. She was the same woman from before, wielding her clipboard in the same annoying manner. "You're the one who adopted the little French bulldog."

"The *what?*" Diana let out an astonished laugh. "You have a dog? Where is it?"

The pet adoption counselor stared daggers at him. "You've re-homed the dog? You can't do that, sir. You signed an agreement."

"I didn't re-home the dog. Look, this is all just a misunderstanding. I assure you."

But even the Chihuahua seemed to be giving him the evil eye.

Marvelous.

He set the little dog back down in its tiny playpen and moved on before he got arrested for dognapping or something equally ridiculous.

He and Diana walked the length of the park in silence. They passed the zoo, and the roar of the lions sounded strangely lonely in the snowfall. Then they made their way down the Literary Walk, and when they had to dodge out of the way to avoid a dog walker and her tangle of half a dozen leashes, Diana finally said something.

"Are you going to tell me about the missing dog? Because the suspense is killing me." She stopped in front of the statue of William Shakespeare.

The Bard peered at Dalton over her shoulder, looking every bit as serious and judgmental as the pet adoption counselor. *Or maybe I really am losing my mind.*

He sighed. "There's nothing to tell. The dog didn't belong to me. Aurélie adopted him, and she took him with her when she left. End of story. Can we keep walking now? The gala is tonight, and I've got things to do."

"No, we can't just keep walking and pretend nothing is going on." She shook her head and brushed back a loose strand of hair that had escaped from her hat.

She looked good. Healthy. But she still had a definite air of sadness about her. Dalton wished she'd start riding again, but he supposed getting back on a horse would just take time.

She crossed her arms. "You're in love with her, aren't you? You *love* her, and you miss her. That's why you wanted me to move into your apartment. That's why you were just mooning over a Chihuahua, isn't it?"

Yes. Yes, God help me. That's exactly why. "No. Don't be ridiculous. You gave us all a scare. I'm your brother, and I want to keep an eye on you. And the dog has nothing to do with Aurélie. Who wouldn't fall for that tiny little face?"

She rolled her eyes. "You're not fooling me, brother dear. You hate dogs."

Used to. He used to hate dogs. It seemed he'd developed a soft spot for them lately. But that was beside the point, especially since it looked as though the animal rescue community had probably blackballed him now.

"Anyway, don't try to change the subject. This isn't about the dog. It's about you." Diana jabbed her pointer finger into Dalton's chest. "And Aurélie."

It hurt to hear her name almost as much as it hurt to say it. "Drop it, Diana. There's nothing to discuss. She's getting married, remember?"

"But she's not." Diana shook her head.

"Yes, she is. On April 20. To a duke or a king or something like that. She'll be wearing a crown on her head, and she'll probably arrive in a damned glass coach."

"Stop yelling."

"I'm not yelling." A passerby pushing a baby carriage gave him an odd look.

Maybe he was yelling. Just a little bit.

"Calm down and listen to me for two seconds, would you? She's not getting married. I read it in the paper this morning."

"How many times have I told you that you can't believe everything you read in *Page Six*?" Artem had only actually participated in half the debauchery he'd been accused of in that rag. At least that was what he'd insisted at the time.

"Sheesh, give me some credit. I didn't read it in *Page*

Six. It was on the front page of the Books section of the *New York Times*."

He paused for a second and glanced at William Shakespeare while he tried to absorb what his sister was saying. He thought of star-crossed lovers and fate and destiny. Then he remembered how that particular story ended.

"You're mistaken," he said flatly. The one thing he wanted less than pity was false hope. "Why would news about a royal wedding appear in the Books section?"

She lifted a knowing brow. "You know what? I'm not going to tell you. You're going to have to read it for yourself."

"Diana." He meant it as a warning, but despite himself, the faintest glimmer of hope stirred in his chest.

Stop. It's over. She's not even in the country anymore.

"This is what you get for only looking at the Business section of the *Times*, by the way. There's a whole world out there that you know nothing about."

"Thank you for the sisterly advice," he said wryly.

"You're welcome, my dear brother." She rubbed her mitten-covered hands together and looped an arm through his. "Shall we walk home now? It's freezing out, and like you said, we need to get ready for your big gala."

Clearly she wasn't going to tell him anything else. And suddenly the gala seemed like the furthest thing from Dalton's mind. "Fine."

"There's a newsstand on the corner of Central Park South and 50th Street, you know. We'll pass right by it on the way home."

"Indeed. I know." He'd already made a mental note of that very fact. It was the same newsstand where he picked up his paper nearly every morning. Not that his nosy sister needed to know any more about his personal life.

He managed to grab a copy of the *Times*, pay for it and walk the rest of the way home without tearing it open and poring over the Books section. He wanted to do so in private, even though the cat was already apparently out of the bag and Diana knew how much Aurélie meant to him. Now that the possibility that she might not be going through with the wedding had been dangled in front of him, he was consumed by the idea.

He didn't see how it was possible, yet with everything in him, he wanted to believe. He wanted to believe so badly that when he'd finally closed himself off in the privacy of his bedroom, he was almost afraid to spread the newspaper open on his bed.

He tossed it down beside his Armani tuxedo and Drake-blue bowtie and told himself if Diana had been wrong, or if she'd simply been playing some cruel joke on him, nothing would change. He didn't need Aurélie in his life. He hadn't crumbled to pieces after she'd left. He was a Drake. He was perfectly content.

Liar.

He poured himself a glass of scotch, took a generous gulp and finally sat down on the edge of the bed. His hands were shaking, and the paper rattled as he tossed aside the front page and the Business section. Then there it was, emblazoned across the header of the Books section.

Her Royal Highness Aurélie Marchand of Delamotte Calls Off Wedding Following Announcement of New Book Deal

Oh my God.

Diana was right.

He read the headline three times to make sure he wasn't seeing things. Then he dove into the article, which said that Aurélie had sold the publishing rights to her mother's diary. Due to overwhelming public interest in the book, the publication of the diary had been fast-tracked. It was due to hit shelves on April 20, what would have been Aurélie's wedding day.

Dalton sat very still and tried to absorb the implications of what he'd just read. There was much the article didn't say. Was Aurélie staying in Delamotte? How had her father reacted to this extreme act of defiance? Would she be stripped of her crown?

Does she still love me?

Did she ever?

He told himself what he'd just read had no bearing on his life whatsoever. It was about Aurélie taking control of *her* life.

Not about him.

Not about them.

But damned if it didn't feel like a second chance.

Dalton folded the newspaper and slowly sipped the rest of his scotch. He dressed for the gala with the utmost care, slipping into his waistcoat and fastening his Drake Diamond cufflinks. He caught a glimpse of himself in his bedroom mirror as he reached for his tie and paused, marveling at how composed he appeared on the outside when he couldn't seem to stop the violent pounding of his heart.

He stared down at the Drake-blue tie in his hand and realized he couldn't put it on. *This is where the charade stops,* he thought. *This is where it ends.*

If Aurélie could choose, then so could he.

Thirty minutes later, he barged into Artem's office without bothering to knock. "I need to talk to you."

He'd walked straight through the first floor showroom without even a cursory glance at the display cases that housed the Marchand eggs. He should be overseeing the arrangement of the collection. The Drake Diamonds staff had strict instructions that Dalton was to have final approval before the doors opened for the gala. But he and Diana had only just arrived and what he had to say to Artem couldn't wait.

"Perfect. Because there's something I need to tell you before the gala begins." Artem glanced at his watch. "Which is in just fifteen minutes, so I may as well come out and say it."

Dalton shook his head. If he didn't do this now, he might never actually get the words out. "I'd really rather go first."

Artem raked a hand through his hair and sighed. "But…"

"I quit," Dalton blurted at the exact same moment that Artem leveled his gaze and said, "You're fired."

The brothers stared at each other for a beat, shocked into silence.

Finally, Artem cleared his throat. "Well this works out rather nicely, don't you think?"

"Wait a minute." Dalton sank into the leather chair opposite Artem. "You can't fire me. You don't have the authority. We're co-CEOs, remember?"

He didn't even know why he was arguing about it when the bottom line was the same—he was finished at Drake Diamonds. He'd had enough. If Aurélie could be brave enough to take hold of her future and change it, then so could he.

Except that he'd never been fired from a job in his life. And he also owned one third of the family business.

"Yes and no." Artem shrugged. "We agreed to share the position, but never drew up paperwork to make the change official."

"It was a gentleman's agreement." How could Dalton have anticipated the need for paperwork? Artem had always been the one constantly threatening to turn in his resignation.

My, how things change.

"Exactly." Artem shrugged and brushed an invisible speck of lint from the shoulder of his tuxedo jacket. When had he gotten so casually adept at running the company? Dalton had nothing to worry about. Drake Diamonds would be in safe hands. "As far as the paperwork goes, I'm the sole CEO of Drake Diamonds, which means…"

"You can fire me." Dalton smiled. Who smiled as he was being fired? By his own brother, no less?

I do, apparently.

"Right." Artem tilted his head and slid his hands into his pocket as he examined Dalton. "And might I say, you're taking it awfully well."

It was Dalton's turn to shrug. "That's because I quit, effective the moment this gala is over."

"You're still fired. Don't take it personally, but you can't be trusted to stay away. You've done an excellent job here. You've poured everything you have into Drake Diamonds, but it's time for you to get an actual life." He had the decency to wince, but only for a second. "No offense, of course."

"None taken." Dalton rolled his eyes.

"Come on, you know I'm right. If Diana's accident taught us anything, it's that life is precious."

Exactly.

Except Dalton should have learned that lesson years ago. Six years ago, to be exact.

How had he allowed himself to waste so much time? So much life? Aside from Diana's accident, the handful of days he'd spent with Aurélie had been the best he'd ever experienced. But he hadn't fully appreciated them, had he? Save for the times they'd made love, he'd held her at arm's length. It was time to hold her close. Now and forever.

If she'd still let him.

"Yes, you're right. That's why I'm leaving for Delamotte first thing in the morning. Or tonight, if I can arrange a flight." He had no idea how he'd even get an audience with a royal princess. But he'd figure it out. He'd kick down the palace doors if necessary.

"I'd hoped Her Royal Highness might have something to do with your decision." Artem's face split into a huge grin. "Let me be the first to congratulate you."

Dalton shook his head. "Not so fast. I don't even know if she's still speaking to me."

He'd sent her packing. Twice. That was a lot to atone for.

"I see." Artem nodded and glanced at his watch. "As much as I'd like to give you a brotherly pep talk right about now, there's no time. You should probably go take a look at the eggs and make sure everything is in order, no?"

"Will do." Dalton rose to his feet, buttoned the jacket of his tux and turned to go.

He was nearly out the door when he heard Artem say, "Nice tie, by the way."

Dalton just shook his head, laughed and headed for the elevator.

The first floor was abuzz with activity. Every member of the Drake Diamonds staff was on hand. Through the glass revolving door, he could see photographers and other members of the press lined up on the snowy sidewalk, waiting for the official start of the unveiling.

Excellent. After the many professional mistakes he'd made over the course of the past month, it was comforting to know he was leaving on a successful note.

Except as he approached the exhibit and spotted the Marchand jeweled hen egg in the first glass case, he sighed. Something wasn't right. The hen egg was the oldest piece in the collection. It had been the egg featured on all the banners and advertisements. Dalton had left instructions for it to be placed in the center of the room, in the illuminated glass case that had once housed the revered Drake Diamond.

Someone had screwed up.

He really didn't need this now. Not when the gala was set to begin in less than five minutes, and not when he had far more important things on his mind. Like how to woo a princess.

"Excuse me." He beckoned the closest employee he could find. "Who arranged the eggs this way?"

"Your brother did, sir." The salesman gestured overhead, toward the upper floors of the building. "We followed the exhibit map you'd drawn up, but Mr. Drake came down about half an hour ago and changed everything."

Dalton's fists clenched at his sides. What the hell was

going on with Artem? Firing him after he quit was one thing. Completely usurping him before he was even gone was another matter entirely.

The salesman shifted uneasily from one foot to the other. Clearly he wasn't thrilled to be the bearer of such news. Not that Dalton could blame him. "He said you might be upset, and he indicated if you wanted to discuss it, you should go upstairs to Engagements."

"Engagements?" Had his brother had an aneurysm or something? They weren't even opening Engagements up to customers tonight. Everyone was to stay on the first floor.

The salesman cleared his throat. "But first he said you should take a look at the exhibit's centerpiece, Mr. Drake."

The centerpiece.

He'd been so thrown by the obviously incorrect placement of the jeweled hen egg that he hadn't even ventured a glance at the big case in the center. Who knew what Artem had stuck in there?

He turned, and what he saw stole the breath from his lungs.

On a pedestal in the center of the room, in the very heart of Drake Diamonds, sat a pink-enameled egg, covered in shimmering pavé diamonds and tiny seed pearls.

The Marchand secret egg had found its way back to New York.

Is this a mistake?

The question had followed Aurélie all the way across the Atlantic Ocean. It nagged at her for the duration of the twelve-hour flight, as she sat sleepless in First Class, clutching the black velvet egg box like a security blanket while Jacques snored in his carrier.

Would Dalton be happy to see her? Had he thought about her at all over the past seven days?

God, she hoped so.

She'd thought of little else but him. At night when she closed her eyes, she dreamt of his sighs of pleasure as he'd touched her, kissed her…loved her. When she woke in the morning, his name was the first word on her lips, the memory of him the first tug in her heart.

She'd prayed for it to stop. She'd pleaded with God to make the memories fade.

They hadn't.

If anything, her feelings for Dalton had only grown stronger. No matter what happened now, though, she was grateful for the persistence of memory. She knew that now. Knowing Dalton had changed her. Permanently. Profoundly. If she'd never met him, never fallen in love, she would have never had the courage to stand up to her father. She would have never done what she had to do in order to take control of her own destiny.

She'd paved the way for her own future. All because of him. Because of Dalton Drake.

So even if coming back to New York turned out to be a mistake, even if he took one look at her and told her to go back home, she wouldn't regret a thing.

But she hoped it wasn't a mistake. She hoped he loved her even a tiny fraction as much as she loved him.

The elevator dinged, and her knees grew weak. Jacques yipped in her arms.

This is it.

The doors swished open, and there he was. Aurélie had to bite her lip to keep herself from crying with relief at the sight of him. He looked so handsome. Even more handsome than she remembered. His exquisitely tailored tuxedo showed off his broad shoulders to perfection. Formal wear suited him.

There was just a hint of stubble on his jawline, and his eyes were even steelier than she remembered. They glittered like black diamonds as his gaze swept over her.

Aurélie's breath caught in her throat. She felt like she might faint. Jacques squirmed with such enthusiasm at the sight of Dalton that she had to set him down on the floor. The little dog bounded toward Dalton as if he hadn't seen him in a century. Aurélie wished she could do the same, but she couldn't bring herself to go to him.

Why was this so difficult? She hadn't even been this nervous when she'd finally confronted her father and told him she'd sent her mother's diary to the biggest publisher in Europe. Sad, yes. But nervous, no. Handing over her mother's diary had been bittersweet. She hated to hurt her father, but after the way he'd treated her in New York, he'd left her no choice. It was the only way she could buy her freedom.

It was what her mother would have wanted.

She leaned against one of the glass cases of diamond rings and willed herself to stay upright. But as Dalton scooped Jacques into his arms and moved toward her in the darkness, she noticed something that gave her a tiny glimmer of hope.

Is that...

No, it can't be.

Her gaze locked on the bowtie around Dalton's neck. She couldn't believe what she was seeing. The tie was red. Not Drake-blue, but *red*. Brilliant, blazing red. She couldn't seem to stop staring at it as he made his way toward her.

"Do my eyes deceive me, or is there a princess standing in front of me?" He stood about a foot and a half away. Just out of arm's reach, but close enough to see a hint of the dimple in his left cheek that only seemed to make an appearance on the rare occasions when he laughed.

Aurélie lifted an amused brow. "Is that a red tie, or am I hallucinating?"

"Touché." A smile tugged at his lips, and swarms of butterflies took flight in Aurélie's tummy. Then as quickly as the smile appeared, it was gone. In its place was an ardent expression she couldn't quite decipher. "You brought the egg back."

"You noticed."

"Indeed." He set Jacques down and took a step closer. Aurélie felt herself leaning toward Dalton, as if even gravity couldn't keep them apart. "You didn't need to do that, you know."

"But I did. We had a bargain, remember?" She needed to touch him. She needed to feel him again. It felt like a century had passed since he'd devoured her in this very room.

But her body remembered. She felt divinely liquid just standing in front of him, steeped in memories and decadent sensation. He'd loved her in this room, between these hallowed walls. He'd shared his deepest secrets. He'd done things to her that made the diamonds blush.

"You don't owe me a thing. Our bargain fell apart." He swallowed, and a rather fascinating knot flexed in his chiseled jaw. "That was my fault, Aurélie. I'm sorry."

"Don't. Please." She shook her head and realized too late that she'd started to cry.

She didn't want tears. Not now. She just wanted to throw herself into his arms and end the aching torture of being so close to him without feeling the warmth of his skin beneath her fingertips. She just wanted to kiss him again. And again.

"I…"

But he didn't let her finish. Before she could say a word about ending her engagement, his hands were in her hair, tipping her head back so that his lips were angled perfectly over hers.

"My perfect, precious pearl," he whispered. "Don't cry."

At last he kissed her, gently at first. Then as a tumultuous heat gathered in her center, the kiss grew deeper until she trembled with need. *Please. Please.* He groaned in response to her silent plea and pulled her closer. She could feel every inch of him through the lilac chiffon of her evening gown.

He pulled back slightly, his gaze fixed on her with a new intensity. "Tell me it's true. Tell me you're not marrying him."

"It's true." She nodded, dizzy with desire. Drunk with it. It was frightening how much she wanted him, needed him. She was finished with trying to protect her heart from getting hurt. She'd tried it already and had made a spectacular mess of things. She was all in now. No fear. No regrets.

"The thought of you with another man nearly killed me, princess. Have you come back to stay?" he asked, his voice rough. Questions shone in his diamond eyes.

It was time for answers. Past time.

Her heart pounded wildly. *Do it. Do it now. Say what you came here to say.* "I can't stay. I'm just here for the gala."

Dalton nodded, and the light in his eyes dimmed. "I understand."

For a fraction of a second, the silence between them expanded, threatening to choke them both. Jacques whimpered at their feet.

"My father is abdicating." She blurted it out without preamble. *So much for finesse.*

"What?"

"He wouldn't agree to end the engagement. I tried to reason with him, but he wouldn't back down. You met him. You saw what he's like."

"I did. He reminded me of my own father." Dalton rolled his eyes. "More than you know."

"Publishing my mother's diary was my only option. He knows once her words go public, the people of Delamotte will turn on him in a flash. He wants to step down before that can happen." Her father's pride came before anything. It had come before her mother. And in the end, it had been his downfall. He'd made the choice. Not her.

She'd done the only thing she could do. Letting go of the diary was her only option for getting her life back.

"Does this mean what I think it means?"

Aurélie nodded. "I'll be the Crown Princess. I'm going to rule Delamotte."

She took a deep inhale, did her best to ignore the hummingbird beat of her heart and said what she'd traveled 4,000 miles to tell him. "And I want you there with me. You and Jacques, of course."

Dalton Drake shot a glance at the dog and smiled the biggest smile she'd ever seen him display. "As luck would have it, I was already planning to visit your principality."

Is this truly happening? Is this real? "If you come…if you stay…it will mean leaving Drake Diamonds."

"Again, your timing is impeccable. I happen to be unemployed at the moment." He hauled her hard against him and brought his mouth down on hers in a powerful kiss that robbed her legs of strength.

Would she ever grow accustomed to this, she wondered. *Never.* There was magic in his touch. She was powerless against it. And she wouldn't have had it any other way.

She'd waited a lifetime for this kiss. She'd crisscrossed the globe and nearly toppled a kingdom.

It had been worth it. *He'd* been worth it.

"Excellent," she whispered against the wicked wonderland of his mouth. "Because I think you'd make a perfect Prince Consort."

"Are you asking me to marry you, Your Highness?" His eyes were shining. They seemed lighter than when she'd first met him. Soft pearl gray. "Right here in the Engagements showroom of Drake Diamonds?"

She nodded. "I am. And I just happen to know the cathedral is available three months from now."

He slid his hands down her arms, wove his fingers through hers and guided her gently backward, until she felt the cold press of a glass case against her bare back. He couldn't be serious. Half the city was downstairs. They didn't matter, though. No one did. Not now. Only them.

"No, princess." He reached behind her and slowly unzipped the bodice of her strapless gown. "Three months is far too long to wait to marry the woman I love. I want to make you my wife as soon as possible. Any chance we could get the cathedral sooner?"

Her dress slid down her body in a whisper of lilac, and she found herself naked once again in this glittering room, dressed in nothing but the cascade of gold pearls around her neck. "I think I can pull some strings."

"That's my princess."

My princess.

His princess.

His.

Dalton reached for her necklace, twirled the pearls slowly around his finger and used them to reel her in for a kiss. This time, the priceless string held tight, binding them together.

Forever unbroken.

* * * * *

IT STARTED WITH
A DIAMOND

TERI WILSON

For Brant Schafer, because naming a polo pony after me will guarantee you a book dedication.

And for Roe Valentine, my dear writing friend and other half of the Sisterhood of the Traveling Veuve Clicquot.

Chapter One

"It's hard to be a diamond in a rhinestone world."
—Dolly Parton

Diana Drake wasn't sure about much in her life at the moment, but one thing was crystal clear—she wanted to strangle her brother.

Not her older brother, Dalton. She couldn't really muster up any indignation as far as her elder sibling went, despite the fact that she was convinced he was at least partially responsible for her current predicament.

But Dalton got a free pass. For now.

She owed him.

For one thing, she'd been living rent free in his swanky Lenox Hill apartment for the past several months. For another, he was a prince now. A literal Prince Charming. As such, he wasn't even in New York anymore. He was somewhere on the French Riviera polishing his crown or sitting on a throne or doing whatever it was princes did all day long.

Dalton's absence meant that Diana's younger brother, Artem, was the only Drake around to take the full brunt of her frustration. Which was a tad problematic since he was her boss now.

Technically.

Sort of.

But Diana would just have to overlook that minor point. She'd held her tongue for as long as humanly possible.

"I can't do it anymore," she blurted as she marched into his massive office on the tenth floor of Drake Diamonds, the legendary jewelry store situated on the corner of 5th Avenue and 57th Street, right in the glittering center of Manhattan. The family business.

Diana might not have spent every waking hour of her life surrounded by diamonds and fancy blue boxes tied with white satin bows, as Dalton had. And she might not be the chief executive officer, like Artem. But the last time she checked, she was still a member of the family. She was a Drake, just like the rest of them.

So was it really necessary to suffer the humiliation of working as a salesperson in the most dreaded section of the store?

"Engagements? *Really?*" She crossed her arms and glared at Artem. It was still weird seeing him sitting behind what used to be their father's desk. Gaston Drake had been dead for a nearly a year, yet his presence loomed large.

Too large. It was almost suffocating.

"Good morning to you, too, Diana." Artem smoothed down his tie, which was the exact same hue as the store's trademark blue boxes. *Drake* blue.

Could he have the decency to look at least a little bit bothered by her outburst?

Apparently not.

She sighed. "I can't do it, Artem. I'll work anywhere in this building, except *there*." She waved a hand in the direction of the Engagements showroom down the hall.

He stared blithely at her, then made a big show of looking at his watch. "I see your point. It's been all of three hours. However have you lasted this long?"

"Three *torturous* hours." She let out another massive sigh. "Have you ever set foot in that place?"

"I'm the CEO, so, yes, I venture over there from time to time."

Right. Of course he had.

Still, she doubted he'd actually helped any engaged couples choose their wedding rings. At least, she hoped he hadn't, mainly because she wouldn't have wished such a fate on her worst enemy.

This morning she'd actually witnessed a grown man and woman speaking baby talk to each other. Her stomach churned just thinking about it now. Adults had no business speaking baby talk, not even to actual babies.

Her gaze shifted briefly to the bassinet in the corner of her brother's office. She still couldn't quite believe Artem was a dad now. A husband. It was kind of mind-boggling when she thought about it, especially considering what an abysmally poor role model their father had been in the family department.

Keep it professional.

She wouldn't get anywhere approaching Artem as a sibling. This conversation was about business, plain and simple. Removing herself from Engagements was the best thing Diana could do, not just for herself, but also for Drake Diamonds.

Only half an hour ago, she'd had to bite her tongue when a man asked for advice about choosing an engagement ring and she'd very nearly told him to spend his money on something more sensible than a huge diamond when the chances that he and his girlfriend would live happily ever after were slim to none. *If* she accepted his proposal, they only had about an eighty percent chance of making it down the aisle. Beyond that, their odds of staying married were about fifty-fifty. Even if they remained husband and wife until death did them part, could they reasonably expect to be happy? Was *anyone* happily married?

Diana's own mother had stuck faithfully by her husband's side after she found out he'd fathered a child with their housekeeper, even when she ended up raising the boy herself. Surely that didn't count as a happy marriage.

That boy was now a man and currently seated across the desk from Diana. She'd grown up alongside Artem and couldn't possibly love him more. He was her brother. Case closed.

Diana's problem wasn't with Artem. It was with her father and the concept of marriage as a whole. She didn't like what relationships did to people…

Especially what one had done to her mother.

Even if she'd grown up in a picture-perfect model family, Diana doubted she'd ever see spending three months' salary on an engagement ring as anything but utter foolishness.

It was a matter of logic, pure and simple. Of statistics. And statistics said that plunking down $40,000 for a two-carat Drake Diamonds solitaire was like throwing a giant wad of cash right into the Hudson River.

But she had no business saying such things out loud since she worked in Engagements, now, did she? She had no business saying such things, period. Drake Diamonds had supported her for her entire life.

So she'd bitten her tongue. Hard.

"I'm simply saying that my talents would be best put to use someplace else." *Anyplace* else.

"Would they now?" Artem narrowed his gaze at her. A hint of a smile tugged at the corner of his mouth, and she knew what was coming. "And what talents would those be, exactly?"

And there it was.

"Don't start." She had no desire to talk about her accident again. Or ever, for that matter. She'd moved on.

Artem held up his hands in a gesture of faux surrender. "I didn't say a word about your training. I'm simply pointing out that you have no work experience. Or college education, for that matter. I hate to say it, sis, but your options are limited."

She'd considered enrolling in classes at NYU, but didn't bother mentioning it. Her degree wasn't going to materialize overnight. *Unfortunately.* College had always been on her radar, but between training and competing, she hadn't found the time. Now she was a twenty-six-year-old without a single day of higher education under her belt.

If only she'd spent a little less time on the back of a horse for the past ten years and a few more hours in the classroom…

She cleared her throat. "Do I need to remind you that I own a third of this business? You and Dalton aren't the only Drakes around here, you know."

"No, but we're the only ones who've actually worked here before today." He glanced at his watch again, stood and buttoned his suit jacket. "Look, just stick it out for a while. Once you've learned the ropes, we'll try and find another role for you. Okay?"

Awhile.

Just how long was that, she wondered. A week? A month? A year? She desperately wanted to ask, but she didn't dare. She hated sounding whiny, and she *really* hated relying on the dreadful Drake name. But it just so happened that name was the only thing she had going for her at the moment.

Oh, how the mighty had fallen. Literally.

"Come on." Artem brushed past her. "We've got a photo shoot scheduled this afternoon in Engagements. I think you might find it rather interesting."

She was glad to be walking behind him so he couldn't see her massive eyeroll. "Please tell me it doesn't involve a wedding dress."

"Relax, sister dear. We're shooting cuff links. The photographer only wanted to use the Engagements show-room because it has the best view of Manhattan in the building."

It did have a lovely view, especially now that spring had arrived in New York in all its fragrant splendor. The air was filled with cherry blossoms, swirling like pink snow flurries. Diana had lost herself a time or two star-ing out at the verdant landscape of Central Park.

But those few blissful moments had come to a crash-ing end the moment she'd turned away from the show-room's floor-to-ceiling windows and remembered she was surrounded by diamonds. Wedding diamonds.

And here I am again.

She blinked against the dazzling assault of countless engagement rings sparkling beneath the sales floor lights and followed Artem to the corner of the room where the photographer was busy setting up a pair of tall light stands. A row of camera lenses in different sizes sat on top of one of glass jewelry cases.

Diana slid a velvet jeweler's pad beneath the lenses to protect the glass and busied herself rearranging things. Maybe if she somehow inserted herself into this whole photo-shoot process, she could avoid being a part of anyone's betrothal for an hour or two.

A girl can dream.

"Is our model here?" the photographer asked. "Because I'm ready, and we've only got about an hour left until sundown. I'd like to capture some of this nice view before it's too late."

Diana glanced out the window. The sky was already tinged pale violet, and the evening wind had picked up, scattering pink petals up and down 5th Avenue. The sun was just beginning to dip below the skyscrapers. It would be a gorgeous backdrop…

…if the model showed up.

Artem checked his watch again and frowned in the direction of the door. Diana took her time polishing the half-dozen pairs of Drake cuff links he'd pulled for the shoot. Anything to stretch out the minutes.

Just as she reached for the last pair, Artem let out a sigh of relief. "Ah, he's here."

Diana glanced up, took one look at the man stalking toward them and froze. Was she hallucinating? Had the blow to the head she'd taken months ago done more damage than the doctors had thought?

Nothing is wrong with you. You're fine. Everything *is fine.*

Everything didn't feel fine, though. Diana's whole world had come apart, and months later she still hadn't managed to put it back together. She was beginning to think she never would.

Because, deep down, she knew she wouldn't. She couldn't pick up the pieces, even if she tried. No one could.

Which was precisely why she was cutting her losses and starting over again. She'd simply build a new life for herself. A normal life. Quiet. Safe. It would take some getting used to, but she could do it.

People started over all the time, didn't they?

At least she had a job. An apartment. A family. There were worse things in the world than being a Drake.

She was making a fresh start. She was a jeweler now. Her past was ancient history.

Except for the nagging fact that a certain man from her past was walking toward her. Here, now, in the very real present.

Franco Andrade.

Not him. Just...no.

She needed to leave. Maybe she could just slink over to one of the sales counters and get back to her champagne-sipping brides and grooms to be. Selling engagement rings had never seemed as appealing as it did right this second.

She laid her polishing cloth on the counter, but before she could place the cuff links back inside their neat blue box, one of them slipped right through her fingers. She watched in horror as it bounced off the tip of Artem's shoe and rolled across the plush Drake-blue carpet, straight toward Franco's approaching form.

Diana sighed. This is what she got for complaining to Artem. Just because she was an heiress didn't mean she had to act like one. Being entitled wasn't an admirable quality. Besides, karma was a raging bitch. One who didn't waste any time, apparently.

Diana dropped to her knees and scrambled after the

runaway cuff link, wishing the floor would somehow open up and swallow her whole. Evidently, there were indeed fates worse than helping men choose engagement rings.

"Mr. Andrade, we meet at last." Artem deftly side-stepped her and extended a hand toward Franco.

Mr. Andrade.

So it *was* him. She'd still been holding out the tiniest bit of hope for a hallucination. Or possibly a doppelganger. But that was an absurd notion. Men as handsome as Franco Andrade didn't roam the Earth in pairs. His kind of chiseled bone structure was a rarity, something that only came around once in a blue moon. Like a unicorn. Or a fiery asteroid hurtling toward Earth, promising mass destruction on impact.

One of those two things. The second, if the rumors of his conquests were to be believed.

Who was she kidding? She didn't need to rely on rumors. She knew firsthand what kind of man Franco Andrade was. It was etched in her memory with excruciating clarity. What she didn't know was what he was doing here.

Was he the model for the new campaign? Impossible.

It had to be some kind of joke. Or possibly Artem's wholly inappropriate attempt to manipulate her back into her old life.

Either way, for the second time in a matter of hours, she wanted to strangle her brother. He was the one who'd invited Franco here, after all. Perhaps joining the family business hadn't been her most stellar idea.

As if she had any other options.

She pushed Artem's reminders of her inadequate education and employment record out of her head and concentrated on the mortifying matter at hand. Where was that darn cuff link, anyway?

"Gotcha," she whispered under her breath as she caught sight of a silver flash out of the corner of her eye.

But just as she reached for it, Franco Andrade's ridiculously masculine form crouched into view. "Allow me."

His words sent a tingle skittering through her. Had his voice always been so deliciously low? The man could recite the alphabet and bring women to their knees. Which would have made the fact that she was already in just such a position convenient, had it not been so utterly humiliating.

"Here." He held out his hand. The cuff link sat nestled in the center of his palm. He had large hands, rough with calluses, a stark contrast to the finely tailored fit of his custom tuxedo.

Of course that tuxedo happened to be missing a tie, and his shirt cuffs weren't even fastened. He looked as if he'd just rolled out of someone's bed and tossed on his discarded Armani from the night before.

Then again, he most likely had.

"Thank you," she mumbled, steadfastly refusing to meet his gaze.

"Wait." He balled his fist around the cuff link and stooped lower to peer at her. "Do we know each other?"

"Nope." She shook her head so hard she could practically hear her brain rattle. "No, I'm afraid we don't."

"I think we might," he countered, stubbornly refusing to hand over the cuff link.

Fine. Let him keep it. She had better things to do, like help lovebirds snap selfies while trying on rings. Anything to extricate herself from the current situation.

She flew to her feet. "Everything seems in order here. I'll just be going…"

"Diana, wait." Artem was using his CEO voice. Marvelous.

She obediently stayed put, lest he rethink his promise and banish her to an eternity of working in Engagements.

Franco took his time unfolding himself to a standing position, as if everyone was happy to wait for him, the Manhattan sunset included.

"Mr. Andrade, I'm Artem Drake, CEO of Drake Diamonds." Artem gestured toward Diana. "And this is my sister, Diana Drake."

"It's a pleasure to meet you," she said tightly and crossed her arms.

Artem shot her a reproachful glare. With no small amount of reluctance, she pasted on a smile and offered her hand for a shake.

Franco's gaze dropped to her outstretched fingertips. He waited a beat until her cheeks flared with heat, then dropped the cuff link into her palm without touching her.

"El gusto es mio," he said with just a hint of an Argentine accent.

The pleasure is mine.

A rebellious shiver ran down Diana's spine.

That shiver didn't mean anything. Of course it didn't. He was a beautiful man, that was all. It was only natural for her body to respond to that kind of physical perfection, even though her head knew better than to pay any attention to his broad shoulders and dark, glittering eyes.

She swallowed. Overwhelming character flaws aside, Franco Andrade had always been devastatingly handsome... emphasis on *devastating.*

It was hardly fair. But life wasn't always fair, was it? No, it most definitely wasn't. Lately, it had been downright cruel.

Diana's throat grew thick. She had difficulty swallowing all of a sudden. Then, somewhere amid the sudden fog in her head, she became aware of Artem clearing his throat.

"Shall we get started? I believe we're chasing the light." He introduced Franco to the photographer, who practically swooned on the spot when he turned his gaze on her.

Diana suppressed a gag and did her best to blend into the Drake-blue walls.

Apparently, any and all attempts at disappearing proved futile. As she tried to make an escape, Artem motioned her back. "Diana, join us please."

She forced her lips into something resembling a smile and strode toward the window where the photographer was getting Franco into position with a wholly unnecessary amount of hands-on attention. The woman with the camera had clearly forgiven him for his tardiness. It figured.

Diana turned her back on the nauseating scene and raised an eyebrow at Artem, who was tapping away on his iPhone. "You needed me?"

He looked up from his cell. "Yes. Can you get Mr. Andrade fitted with some cuff links?"

She stared blankly at him. "Um, me?"

"Yes, you." He shrugged. "What's with the attitude? I thought you'd be pleased. I'm talking to the same person who just stormed into my office demanding a different job than working in Engagements, right?"

She swallowed. "Yes. Yes, of course."

She longed to return to her dreadful post, but if she did, Artem would never take her seriously. Not after everything she'd said earlier.

"Cuff links." She nodded. "I'm on it."

She could do this. She absolutely could. She was Diana

Drake, for crying out loud. She had a reputation all over the world for being fearless.

At least, that's what people used to say about her. Not so much anymore.

Just do it and get it over with. You'll never see him again after today. Those days are over.

She squared her shoulders, grabbed a pair of cuff links and marched toward the corner of the room that had been roped off for the photo shoot, all the while fantasizing about the day when she'd be the one in charge of this place. Or at least not at the very bottom of the food chain.

Franco leaned languidly against the window while the photographer tousled his dark hair, ostensibly for styling purposes.

"Excuse me." Diana held up the cuff links—18-carat white-gold knots covered in black pavé diamonds worth more than half the engagement rings in the room. "I've got the jewels."

"Excellent," the photographer chirped. "I'll grab the camera and we'll be good to go."

She ran her hand through Franco's hair one final time before sauntering away.

If Franco noticed the sudden, exaggerated swing in her hips, he didn't let it show. He fixed his gaze point-edly at Diana. "You've come to dress me?"

"No." Her face went instantly hot. Again. "I mean, yes. Sort of."

The corner of his mouth tugged into a provocative grin and he offered her his wrists.

She reached for one of his shirt cuffs, and her mortifi-cation reached new heights when she realized her hands were shaking.

Will this day ever end?

"Be still, *mi cielo*," he whispered, barely loud enough for her to hear.

Mi cielo.

She knew the meaning of those words because he'd whispered them to her before. Back then, she'd clung to them as if they'd meant something.

Mi cielo. My heaven.

They hadn't, though. They'd meant nothing to him.

Neither had she.

"I'm not yours, Mr. Andrade. Never have been, never will be." She glared at him, jammed the second cuff link into his shirt with a little too much force and dropped his wrist. "We're finished here."

Why did she have the sinking feeling that she might be lying?

Chapter Two

Diana Drake didn't remember him. Or possibly she did, and she despised him. Franco wasn't altogether sure which prospect was more tolerable.

The idea of being so easily forgotten didn't sit well. Then again, being memorable hadn't exactly done him any favors lately, had it?

No, he thought wryly. *Not so much.* But it had been a hell of a lot of fun. At least, while it had lasted.

Fun wasn't part of his vocabulary anymore. Those days had ended. He was starting over with a clean slate, a new chapter and whatever other metaphors applied.

Not that he'd had much of a choice in the matter.

He'd been fired. Let go. Dumped from the Kingsmen Polo Team. Jack Ellis, the owner of the Kingsmen, had finally made good on all the ultimatums he'd issued over the years. It probably shouldn't have come as a surprise.

Franco knew he'd pushed the limits of Ellis's tolerance. More than once. More than a few times, to be honest.

But he'd never let his extracurricular activities affect his performance on the field. Franco had been the Kingsmen's record holder for most goals scored for four years running. His season total was always double the number of the next closest player on the list.

Which made his dismissal all the more frustrating, particularly considering he hadn't actually broken any rules. This time, Franco had been innocent. For probably the first time in his adult life, he'd done nothing untoward.

The situation dripped with so much irony that Franco was practically swimming in it. He would have found the entire turn of events amusing if it hadn't been so utterly frustrating.

"Mr. Andrade, could you lift your right forearm a few inches?" the photographer asked. "Like this."

She demonstrated for him, and Franco dragged his gaze away from Diana Drake with more reluctance than he cared to consider. He hadn't been watching her intentionally. His attention just kept straying in her direction. Again and again, for some strange reason.

She wasn't the most beautiful woman he'd ever seen. Then again, beautiful women were a dime a dozen in his world. There was something far more intriguing about Diana Drake than her appearance.

Although it didn't hurt to look at her. On the contrary, Franco rather enjoyed the experience.

She stood at one of the jewelry counters arranging and rearranging her tiny row of cuff links. He wondered if she realized her posture gave him a rather spectacular view of her backside. Judging by the way she seemed intent on ignoring him, he doubted it. She wasn't posing for his benefit, like, say, the photographer seemed to be doing. Franco could tell when a woman was trying to get his attention, and this one wasn't.

He couldn't quite put his finger on what it was about her that captivated him until she stole a glance at him from across the room.

The memory hit him like a blow to the chest.

Those eyes…

Until he'd met Diana, Franco had never seen eyes that color before—deep violet. They glittered like amethysts. Framed by thick ebony lashes, they were in such startling contrast with her alabaster complexion that he couldn't quite bring himself to look away. Even now.

And that was a problem. A big one.

"Mr. Andrade," the photographer repeated. "Your wrist."

He adjusted his posture and shot her an apologetic wink. The photographer's cheeks went pink, and he knew he'd been forgiven. Franco glanced at Diana again, just in time to see her violet eyes rolling in disgust.

A problem. Most definitely.

He had no business noticing *any* woman right now, particularly one who bore the last name Drake. He was on the path to redemption, and the Drakes were instrumental figures on that path. As such, Diana Drake was strictly off-limits.

So it was a good thing she clearly didn't want to give him the time of day. What a relief.

Right.

Franco averted his gaze from Diana Drake's glittering violet eyes and stared into the camera.

"Perfect," the photographer cooed. "Just perfect."

Beside her, Artem Drake nodded. "Yes, this is excellent. But maybe we should mix it up a little before we lose the light."

The photographer lowered her camera and glanced around the showroom, filled with engagement rings. You couldn't swing a polo mallet in the place without hitting a dozen diamond solitaires. "What were you thinking? Something romantic, maybe?"

"We've done romantic." Artem shrugged. "Lots of times. I was hoping for something a little more eye-catching."

The photographer frowned. "Let me think for a minute."

A generous amount of furtive murmuring followed, and Franco sighed. He'd known modeling wouldn't be as exciting as playing polo. He wasn't an idiot. But he'd been on the job for less than an hour and he was already bored out of his mind.

He sighed. Again.

His eyes drifted shut, and he imagined he was someplace else. Someplace that smelled of hay and horses and churned-up earth. Someplace where the ground shook with the thunder of hooves. Someplace where he never felt restless or boxed in.

The pounding that had begun in his temples subsided ever so slightly. When he opened his eyes, Diana Drake was standing mere inches away.

Franco smiled. "We meet again."

Diana's only response was a visible tensing of her shoulders as the photographer gave her a push and shoved her even closer toward him.

"Okay, now turn around. Quickly before the sun sets," the photographer barked. She turned her attention toward Franco. "Now put your arms around her. Pull her close, right up against your body. Yes, like that. Perfect!"

Diana obediently situated herself flush against him, with her lush bottom fully pressed against his groin. At last things were getting interesting.

Maybe he didn't hate modeling so much, after all.

Franco cleared his throat. "Well, this is awkward," he whispered, sending a ripple through Diana's thick dark hair.

He tried his best not to think about how soft that hair felt against his cheek or how much her heady floral scent reminded him of buttery-yellow orchids growing wild on the vine in Argentina.

"Awkward?" Diana shot him a glare over her shoulder. "From what I hear, you're used to this kind of thing."

He tightened his grip on her tiny waist. "And here I thought you didn't remember me."

"You're impossible," Diana said under her breath, wiggling uncomfortably in his arms.

"That's not what you said the last time we were in this position."

"Oh, my God, you did *not* just say that." This was the Diana Drake he remembered. Fiery. Bold.

"Nice." Artem strode toward them, nodding. "I like it. Against the sunset, you two look gorgeous. Edgy. Intimate."

Diana shook her head. "Artem, you're not serious."

"Actually, I am. Here." He lifted his hand. A sparkling diamond and sapphire necklace dangled from it with a center stone nearly as large as a polo ball. "Put this around your neck, Diana."

Diana crossed her arms. "Really, I'm not sure I should be part of this."

"It's just one picture out of hundreds. We probably won't even use it. The campaign is for cuff links, remember? Humor me, sis. Put it on." He arched a brow. "Besides, I thought you were interested in exploring other career opportunities around here."

She snatched the jewels out of his hands. "Fine."

Career opportunities?

"You're not working here, are you?" Franco murmured, barely loud enough for her to hear.

Granted, her last name was Drake. But why on earth would she give up a grand prix riding career to peddle diamonds?

"As a matter of fact, I am," she said primly.

"Why? If memory serves, you belong on a medal stand. Not here."

"Why do you care?" she asked through clenched teeth as the photographer snapped away.

Good question. "I don't."

"Fine."

But it wasn't fine. He *did* care, damn it. He shouldn't, but he did.

He would have given his left arm to be on horseback right now, and Diana Drake was working as a salesgirl when she could have been riding her way to the Olympics. What was she thinking? "It just seems like a phenomenal waste of talent. Be honest. You miss it, don't you?"

Her fingertips trembled and she nearly dropped the necklace down her blouse.

Franco covered her hands with his. "Here, let me help."

"I can do it," she snapped.

Franco sighed. "Look, the faster we get this picture taken, the faster all this will be over."

He bowed his head to get a closer look at the catch on the necklace, and his lips brushed perilously close to the elegant curve of her neck. She glanced at him over her shoulder, and for a sliver of a moment, her gaze dropped to his mouth. She let out a tremulous breath, and Franco could have sworn he heard a kittenish noise escape her lips.

Her reaction aroused him more than it should have, which he blamed on his newfound celibacy.

This lifestyle was going to prove more challenging than he'd anticipated.

But that was okay. Franco had never been the kind of man who backed down from a challenge. On the contrary, he relished it. He'd always played his best polo when facing his toughest opponents. Adversity brought out the best in Franco. He'd learned that lesson the hard way.

A long time ago.

Another time, another place.

"You two are breathtaking," the photographer said. "Diana, open the collar of your blouse just a bit so we can get a better view of the sapphire."

She obeyed, and Franco found himself momentarily spellbound by the graceful contours of her collarbones. Her skin was lovely. Luminous and pale beside the brilliant blue of the sapphire around her neck.

"Okay, I think we've got it." The photographer lowered her camera.

"We're finished?" Diana asked.

"Yes, all done."

"Excellent." She started walking away without so much as a backward glance.

"Aren't you forgetting something, *mi cielo*?" he said.

She spun back around, face flushed. He'd seen her wear that same heated expression during competition. "What?"

He held up his wrists. "Your cuff links."

"Oh. Um. Yes, thank you." She unfastened them and

gathered them in her closed fist. "Goodbye, Mr. Andrade."

She squared her shoulders and slipped past him. All
business.

But Franco wasn't fooled. He'd seen the tremble in
her fingertips as she'd loosened the cuffs of his shirt.
She'd been shaking like a leaf, which struck him as profoundly odd.

Diana may have pretended to forget him, but he remembered her all too well. There wasn't a timid bone in
her body, which had made her beyond memorable. She
was confidence personified. It was one of the qualities
that made her such an excellent rider.

If Diana Drake was anything, it was fearless. In the
best possible way. She possessed the kind of tenacity that
couldn't be taught. It was natural. Inborn. Like a person's
height. Or the tone of her voice.

Or eyes the color of violets.

But people changed, didn't they? It happened all the
time.

It had to. Franco was counting on it.

Chapter Three

Diana was running late for work.

Since the day of the mortifying photo shoot, she'd begun to dread the tenth-floor showroom with more fervor than ever before. Every time she looked up from one of the jewelry cases, she half expected to see Franco Andrade strolling toward her with a knowing look in his eyes and a smug grin on his handsome face. It was a ridiculous thing to worry about, of course. He had no reason to return to the store. The photo shoot was over. Finished.

Thank goodness.

Besides, if history had proven anything, it was that Franco wasn't fond of follow-through.

Still, she couldn't quite seem to shake the memory of how it had felt when he fastened that sapphire pendant around her neck…the graze of his fingertips on her collarbone, the tantalizing warmth of his breath on her skin.

It had been a long time since Diana had been touched in such an intimate way. A very long time. She knew getting her photo taken with Franco hadn't been real. They'd been posing, that's all. Pretending. She wasn't delusional, for heaven's sake.

But her body clearly hadn't been on the same page as her head. Physically, she'd been ready to believe the beautiful lie. She'd bought it, hook, line and sinker.

Just as she'd done the night she'd slept with him.

It was humiliating to think about the way she'd reacted to seeing him again after so long. She'd practically melted into a puddle at the man's feet. And not just any man. Franco Andrade was the king of the one night stand.

Even worse, she was fairly sure he'd known. He'd noticed the hitch in her breath, the flutter of her heart, the way she'd burned. He'd noticed, and he'd enjoyed it. Every mortifying second.

Don't think about it. It's over and done. Besides, it wasn't even a thing. It was nothing.

Except the fact that she kept thinking about it made it feel like something. A very big, very annoying something.

Enough. She had more important things to worry about than embarrassing herself in front of that polo-playing lothario. It hadn't been the first time, after all. She'd made an idiot out of herself in his presence before and lived to tell about it. At least this time she'd managed to keep her clothes on.

She tightened her grip on the silver overhead bar as the subway car came to a halt. The morning train was as crowded as ever, and when the doors slid open she wiggled her way toward the exit through a crush of commuters.

She didn't realize she'd gotten off at the wrong stop until it was too late.

Perfect. Just perfect. She was already running late, and now she'd been so preoccupied by Franco Andrade that she'd somehow gotten off the subway at the most crowded spot in New York. Times Square.

She slipped her messenger bag over her shoulder and climbed the stairs to street level. The trains had been running slow all morning, and she'd never be on time now. She might as well walk the rest of the way. A walk would do her good. Maybe the spring air would help clear her head and banish all thoughts of Franco once and for all.

It was worth a shot, anyway.

Diana took a deep inhale and allowed herself to remember how much she'd always loved to ride during this time of year. No more biting wind in her face. No more frost on the ground. In springtime, the sun glistened off her horse's ebony coat until it sparkled like black diamonds.

Diana's chest grew tight. She swallowed around the lump in her throat and fought the memories, pushed them back to the farthest corner of her mind where they belonged. *Don't cry. Don't do it.* If she did, she might not be able to stop.

After everything that had happened, she didn't want to be the pitiful-looking woman weeping openly on the sidewalk.

She focused, instead, on the people around her. Whenever the memory of the accident became too much, she tried her best to focus outward rather than on what was going on inside. Once, at Drake Diamonds, she'd stared at a vintage-inspired engagement ring for ten full minutes until the panic had subsided. She'd counted every tiny diamond in its art deco pavé setting, traced each slender line of platinum surrounding the central stone.

When she'd been in the hospital, her doctor had told her she might not remember everything that had led up to her fall. Most of the time, people with head injuries suffered memory loss around the time of impact. They didn't remember what had happened right before they'd been hurt.

They were the lucky ones.

Diana remembered everything. She would have given anything to forget.

Breathe in, breathe out. Look around you.

The streets were crowded with pedestrians, and as Diana wove her way through the crush of people, she thought she caught a few of them looking at her. They nodded and smiled in apparent recognition.

What was going on?

She was accustomed to being recognized at horse shows. On the riding circuit she'd been a force to be reckoned with. But this wasn't the Hamptons or Connecticut. This was Manhattan. She should blend in here. That was one of the things she liked best about the city—a person could just disappear right in the middle of a crowd. She didn't have to perform here. She could be anyone.

At least that's how she'd felt until Franco Andrade had walked into Drake Diamonds. The moment she'd set eyes on him, the dividing line between her old life and her new one had begun to blur.

She didn't like it. Not one bit. Before he'd shown up, she'd been doing a pretty good job of keeping things compartmentalized. She'd started a new job. She'd spent her evening hours in Dalton's apartment watching television until she fell asleep. She'd managed to live every day without giving much thought to what she was missing.

But the moment Franco had touched her she'd known the truth. She wasn't okay. The accident had affected her more than she could admit, even to herself.

There'd been an awareness in the graze of his fingertips, a strange intimacy in the way he'd looked at her. As if she were keeping a secret that only he was privy to. She'd felt exposed. Vulnerable. Seen.

She'd always felt that way around Franco, which is why she'd been stupid enough to end up in his bed. The way she felt when he looked at her had been intoxicating back then. Impossible to ignore.

But she didn't want to be seen now. Not anymore. She just wanted to be invisible for a while.

Maybe she wouldn't have been so rattled if it had been someone else. But it had been *him*. And she was most definitely still shaken up.

She needed to get a grip. So she'd posed for a few pictures with a handsome man she used to know. That's all. Case closed. End of story. No big deal.

She squared her shoulders and marched down the street with renewed purpose. This was getting ridiculous. She would *not* let a few minutes with Franco ruin her new beginning. He meant nothing to her. She was only imagining things, anyway. He probably looked at every woman he met with that same knowing gleam in his eye. That's why they were always falling at his feet everywhere he went.

It was nauseating.

She wouldn't waste another second thinking about the man. She sighed and realized she was standing right in front of the Times Square Starbucks. Perfect. Coffee was just what she needed.

As soon as she took her place in line, a man across the room did a double take in her direction. His face broke into a wide smile. Diana glanced over her shoulder, convinced he was looking at someone behind her. His wife, maybe. Or a friend.

No one was there.

She turned back around. The man winked and raised his cardboard cup as if he were toasting her. Then he turned and walked out the door.

Diana frowned. People were weird. It was probably just some strange coincidence. Or the man was confused, that was all.

Except he didn't look confused. He looked perfectly friendly and sane.

"Can I help you?" The barista, a young man with wire-rimmed glasses and a close-cropped beard, jabbed at the cash register.

"Yes, please," Diana said. "I'd like a…"

The barista looked up, grinned and cut her off before she could place her order. "Oh, hey, you're that girl."

That girl?

Diana's gaze narrowed. She shook her head. "Um, I don't think I am."

What was she even arguing about? She didn't actually know. But she knew for certain that this barista shouldn't have any idea who she was.

Unless her accident had somehow ended up on YouTube or something.

Not that. Please not that.

Anything but that.

"Yeah, you are." The barista turned to the person in line behind her. "You know who she is too, right?"

Diana ventured a sideways glance at the woman, who didn't look the least bit familiar. Diana was sure she'd never seen her before.

"Of course." The woman looked Diana up and down. "You're her. Most definitely."

For a split second, relief washed over her. She wasn't losing it, after all. People on the sidewalk really had been staring at her. The triumphant feeling was short-lived when she realized she still had no idea why.

"Will one of you please tell me what's going on? What girl?"

The woman and the barista exchanged a glance.

"The girl from the billboard," the woman said.

Diana blinked.

The girl from the billboard.

This couldn't be about the photos she'd taken with Franco. It just couldn't. Artem was her brother. He wouldn't slap a picture of her on a Drake Diamonds billboard without her permission. Of course he wouldn't.

Would he?

Diana looked back and forth between the woman and the barista. "What billboard?"

She hated how shaky and weak her voice sounded, so she repeated herself. This time she practically screamed. *"What billboard?"*

The woman flinched, and Diana immediately felt horrible. Her new life apparently included having her face on billboards and yelling at random strangers in coffee shops. It wasn't exactly the fresh start she'd imagined for herself.

"It's right outside. Take two steps out the front door and look up. You can't miss it." The barista lifted a brow. "Are you going to order something or what? You're holding up the line."

"No, thank you." She couldn't stomach a latte right now. Simply putting one foot in front of the other seemed like a monumental task.

She scooted out of line and made her way to the door. She paused for a moment before opening it, hoping for one final, naive second that this was all some big mistake. Maybe Artem hadn't used the photo of her and Franco for the new campaign. Maybe the billboard they'd seen wasn't even a Drake Diamonds advertisement. Maybe it was an ad for some other company with a model who just happened to look like Diana.

That was possible, wasn't it?

But deep down she knew it wasn't, and she had no one to blame but herself.

She'd stormed into Artem's office and demanded that he find a role for her in the company that didn't involve Engagements. She'd practically gotten down on her knees and begged. He'd given her exactly what she wanted. She just hadn't realized that being on a billboard alongside Franco Andrade in the middle of Times Square was part of the equation.

She took a deep breath.

It was just a photograph. She and Franco weren't a couple or anything. They were simply on a billboard together. A million people would probably walk right past it and never notice. By tomorrow it would be old news. She was getting all worked up over nothing.

How bad could it be?

She walked outside, looked up and got her answer.

It was bad. Really, really bad.

Emblazoned across the top of the Times Tower was a photo of herself being embraced from behind by Franco. The sapphire necklace dangled from his fingertips, but rather than looking like he was helping her put it on, the photo gave the distinct impression he was removing it.

Franco's missing tie and the unbuttoned collar of his

tuxedo shirt didn't help matters. Neither did her flushed cheeks and slightly parted lips.

This wasn't an advertisement for cuff links. It looked more like an ad for sex. If she hadn't known better, Diana would have thought the couple in the photograph was just a heartbeat away from falling into bed together.

And she and Franco Andrade were that couple.

What have I done?

Franco was trying his level best not pummel Artem Drake.

But it was hard. Really hard.

"I didn't sign up for this." He wadded the flimsy newsprint of *Page Six* in his hands and threw it at Artem, who was seated across from Franco in the confines of his Drake-blue office. "Selling cuff links, yes. Selling sex, no."

Artem had the decency to flinch at the mention of sex, but Franco was guessing that was mostly out of a brotherly sense of propriety. After all, his sister was the one who looked as though Franco was seducing her on the cover of every tabloid in the western hemisphere.

From what Franco had heard, there was even a billboard smack in the middle of Times Square. His phone had been blowing up with texts and calls all morning. Regrettably, not a single one of those texts or calls had included an offer to return to the Kingsmen.

"Mr. Andrade, please calm down." Artem waved a hand at the generous stack of newspapers fanned across the surface of his desk. "The new campaign was unveiled just hours ago, and it's already a huge success. I've made you famous. You're a household name. People who've never seen a polo match in their lives know who you are. This is what you wanted, is it not?"

Yes…

And no.

He'd wanted to get Jack Ellis's attention. To force his hand. Just not like this.

But he couldn't explain the details of his reinvention to Artem Drake. His new "employer" didn't even know he'd been cut from the team. To Franco's knowledge, no one did. And if he had anything to say about it, no one would. Because he'd be back in his jersey before the first game of the season in Bridgehampton.

That was the plan, anyway.

He stared at the pile of tabloids on Artem's desk. Weeks of clean living and celibacy had just been flushed straight down the drain. More importantly, so had his one shot at getting his life back.

He glared at Artem. "Surely you can't be happy about the fact that everyone in the city thinks I'm sleeping with your sister."

A subtle tension in the set of Artem's jaw was the only crack in his composure. "She's a grown woman, not a child."

"So I've noticed." It was impossible not to.

A lot could happen in three years. She'd been young when she'd shared Franco's bed. Naive. Blissfully so. If he'd realized how innocent she was, he never would have touched her.

But all that was water under the bridge.

Just like Franco's career.

"Besides, this—" Artem gestured toward the pile of newspapers "—isn't real. It's an illusion. One that's advantageous to both of us."

This guy was unbelievable. And he was clearly unaware that Franco and Diana shared a past. Which was probably for the best, given the circumstances.

Franco couldn't help but be intrigued by what he was saying, though. *Advantageous to both of us...*

"Do explain."

Artem shrugged. *Yep, clueless.* "I'm no stranger to the tabloids. Believe me, I understand where you're coming from. But there's a way to use this kind of exposure and make the most out of it. We've managed to get the attention of the world. Our next step is keeping it."

He already didn't like the sound of this. "What exactly are you proposing?"

"A press tour. Take the cuff links out for a spin. You make the rounds of the local philanthropy scene—black-tie parties, charity events, that sort of thing—and smile for the cameras." His gaze flitted to the photo of Franco and Diana. "Alongside my sister, of course."

"Let me get this straight. You want to pay me to publically date Diana." No way in hell. He was an athlete, not a gigolo.

"Absolutely not. I want to pay you to make appearances while wearing Drake gemstones. If people happen to assume you and Diana are a couple, so be it."

Franco narrowed his gaze. "You know they will."

Artem shrugged. "Let them. Look, I didn't plan any of this. But we'd all be fools not to take advantage of the buzz. From what I hear, appearing to be in a monogamous relationship could only help your reputation."

Ah, so the cat was out of the bag, after all.

Franco cursed under his breath. "How long do you expect me to keep up this farce?"

He wasn't sure why he was asking. It was a completely ludicrous proposition.

Although he supposed there were worse fates than spending time with Diana Drake.

Don't go there. Not again.

"Twenty-one days," Artem said.

Franco knew the date by heart already. "The day before the American polo season starts in Bridgehampton. The Kingsmen go on tour right after the season starts."

"Precisely. And you'll be going with them. Assuming you're back on the team by then, obviously." Artem shrugged. "That's what you want, isn't it?"

Franco wondered how Artem had heard about his predicament. He hadn't thought the news of his termination had spread beyond the polo community. Somehow the fact that it had made it seem more real. Permanent.

And that was unacceptable.

"It's absolutely what I want," he said.

"Good. Let us help you fix your reputation." Artem shrugged as if doing so was just that simple.

Maybe it is. "I don't understand. What would you be getting out of this proposed arrangement? Are you really this desperate to move your cuff links?"

"Hardly. This is about more than cuff links." Artem rummaged around the stack of gossip rags on his desk until he found a neatly folded copy of the *New York Times.* "Much more."

He slid the paper across the smooth surface of the desk. It didn't take long for Franco to spot the headline of interest: Jewelry House to be Chosen for World's Largest Uncut Diamond.

Franco looked up and met Artem's gaze. "Let me guess. Drake Diamonds wants to cut this diamond."

"Of course we do. The stone is over one thousand carats. It's the size of a baseball. Every jewelry house in Manhattan wants to get its hands on it. Once it's been cut and placed in a setting, the diamond will be unveiled at a gala at the Metropolitan Museum of Art. Followed by a featured exhibition open to the public, naturally."

Franco's eyes narrowed. "Would the date for this gala possibly be twenty-one days from now?"

"Bingo." Artem leaned forward in his chair. "It's the perfect arrangement. You and Diana will keep Drake Diamonds on the front page of every newspaper in New York. The owners of the diamond will see the Drake name everywhere they turn, and they'll have no choice but to pick us as their partners."

"I see." It actually made sense. In a twisted sort of way.

Artem continued, "By the time you and Diana attend the Met's diamond gala together, you'll have been in a high-profile relationship for nearly a month. Monogamous. Respectable. You're certain to get back in the good graces of your team."

Maybe. Then again, maybe not.

"Plus you'll be great for the team's ticket sales. The more famous you are, the more people will line up to see you play. The Kingsmen will be bound to forgive and forget whatever transgression got you fired." Artem lifted a brow. "What exactly did you do, anyway? You're the best player on the circuit, so it couldn't have been related to your performance on the field."

Franco shrugged. "I didn't do anything, actually."

He'd been cut through no fault of his own. Even worse, he'd been unable to defend himself. Telling the lie had been his choice, though. His call. He'd done what he'd needed to do.

It had been a matter of honor. Even if he'd been able to go back in time and erase the past thirty days, he'd still do it all over again.

Make the same choice. Say the same things.

Artem regarded him through narrowed eyes. "Fine.

You don't need to tell me. From now on, you're a re-formed man, anyway. Nothing else matters."

"Got it." Franco nodded.

He wasn't seriously considering this arrangement. It was borderline demeaning, wasn't it? To both himself and Diana.

Diana Drake.

He could practically hear her breathy, judgmental voice in his ear. *From what I hear, you're used to this kind of thing.*

She'd never go along with this charade. She had too much pride. Then again, what did he know about Diana Drake these days?

He cleared his throat. "What happens afterward?"

"Afterward?"

Franco nodded. "Yes, after the gala."

Artem smiled. "I'm assuming you'll ride off into the sunset with your team and score a massive amount of goals. You'll continue to behave professionally and even-tually you and Diana will announce a discreet breakup."

They'd never get away with it. Diana hadn't even set eyes on Franco or deigned to speak a word to him in the past three years until just a few days ago. No one would seriously believe they were a couple.

He stared down at the heap of newspapers on Ar-tem's desk.

People already believed it.

"You'll be compensated for each appearance at the rate we agreed upon under the terms of your modeling contract. You can start tonight."

"Tonight?"

Artem gave a firm nod. "The Manhattan Pet Rescue animal shelter is holding its annual Fur Ball at the Wal-dorf Astoria. You and Diana can dress up and cuddle with a few adorable puppies and kittens. Every photographer in town will be there."

The Fur Ball. It certainly sounded wholesome. Nauseatingly, mind-numbingly adorable.

"I'm assuming we have a deal." Artem stood.

Franco rose from his seat, but ignored Artem's outstretched hand. They couldn't shake on things. Not yet. "You're forgetting something."

"What's that?"

Not what. Who. "Diana. She'll never agree to this."

Artem's gaze grew sharp. Narrow. "What makes you say so?"

Franco had a sudden memory of her exquisite violet eyes, shiny with unshed tears as she slapped him hard across the face. "Trust me. She won't."

"Just be ready for the driver to pick you up at eight. I'll handle Diana." Artem offered his hand again.

This time, Franco took it.

But even as they shook on the deal, he knew it would never happen. Diana wasn't the sort of person who could be handled. By anyone. Artem Drake had no idea what he was up against. Franco almost felt sorry for him. Almost, but not quite.

Some things could only be learned the hard way.

Like a slap in the face.

Chapter Four

Diana called Artem repeatedly on her walk to Drake Diamonds, but his secretary refused to put her through. She kept insisting that he was in an important business meeting and had left instructions not to be disturbed, which only made Diana angrier. If such a thing was even possible.

A billboard. In Times Square.

She wanted to die.

Calm down. Just breathe. People will forget all about it in a day or two. In the grand scheme of life, it's not that big a deal.

But there was no deluding herself. It was, quite literally, a big deal. A huge one. A whopping 25,000-square-foot Technicolor enormous deal.

Artem would have to take it down. That's all there was to it. She hadn't signed any kind of modeling release. Drake might be her last name, but that didn't mean the family business owned the rights to her likeness.

Or did it? She wasn't even sure. Drake Diamonds had been her sponsor on the equestrian circuit. Maybe the business did, in fact, own her.

God, why hadn't she gone to college? She was in no way prepared for this.

She pushed her way through the revolving door of Drake Diamonds with a tad too much force. Urgent meeting or not, Artem was going to talk to her. She'd break down the door of his Drake-blue office if that's what it took.

"Whoa, there." The door spun too quickly and hurled her toward some poor, unsuspecting shopper in the lobby who caught her by the shoulders before she crashed into him. "Slow down, Wildfire."

"Sorry. I just…" She straightened, blinked and found herself face-to-face with the poster boy himself. Franco. "Oh, it's you."

What was he doing here? *Again?* And why were his hands on her shoulders? And why was he calling her that ridiculous name?

Wildfire.

She'd loved that song when she was a little girl. So, so much.

Well, she didn't love it anymore. In fact, Franco had just turned her off it for life.

"Good morning to you too, Diana." He winked. He was probably the only man on planet Earth who could make such a cheesy gesture seem charming.

Ugh.

She wiggled out of his grasp. "Why are you here? Wait, don't tell me. You're snapping selfies for the Drake Diamonds Instagram."

He was wearing a suit. Not a tuxedo this time, but a finely tailored suit, nonetheless. It was weird seeing him dressed this way. Shouldn't he be wearing riding clothes? He adjusted his shirt cuffs. "It bothers you that I'm the new face of Drake Diamonds?"

"No, it doesn't actually. I couldn't care less what you do. It bothers me that *I'm* the new face of Drake Diamonds." A few shoppers with little blue bags dangling from their wrists turned and stared.

Franco angled his head closer to hers. "You might want to keep your voice down."

"I don't care who hears me." She was being ridiculous. But she couldn't quite help it, and she certainly wasn't going to let Franco tell her how to behave.

"Your brother will care," he said.

"What are you talking about?" Then she put two and two together. Finally. "Wait a minute…were you just upstairs with Artem?"

He nodded. Diana must have been imagining things, because he almost looked apologetic.

"So you're the reason his secretary wouldn't put my calls through?" Unbelievable.

"I suppose so, yes." Again, something about his expression was almost contrite.

She glared at him. He could be as nice as he wanted, but as far as Diana was concerned, it was too little, too late. "What was this urgent tête-à-tête about?"

Why was she asking him questions? She didn't care what he and Artem had to say to each other…

Except something about Franco's expression told her she should.

He leveled his gaze at her and arched a single seductive brow. Because, yes, even the man's eyebrows were sexy. "I think you should talk to Artem."

She swallowed. Something was going on here. Something big. And she had the distinct feeling she wasn't going to like it. "Fine. But just so we're clear, I'm talking to him because I want to. And because he's my brother and sort of my boss. Not because you're telling me I should."

"Duly noted." He seemed to be struggling not to smile.

She lifted her chin in defiance. "Goodbye, Franco."

But for some reason, her feet didn't move. She just kept standing there, gazing up at his despicably handsome face.

"See you tonight, Wildfire." He shot her a knowing half grin before turning for the door.

She stood frozen, gaping after him.

Tonight?

She definitely needed to talk to Artem. Immediately.

She skipped the elevator and took the stairs two at a time until she reached the tenth floor, where she found him sitting at his desk as if it was any ordinary day. A day when Franco Andrade wasn't wandering the streets of Manhattan wearing Tom Ford and planning on seeing her tonight.

"Hello, sis." Artem looked up and frowned as he took in her appearance. "Why do you look like you just ran a marathon?"

"Because I just walked a few miles, then sprinted up the stairs." She was breathless. Her legs burned, which was just wrong. She shouldn't be winded from a little exercise. She was an elite athlete.

Used to be an elite athlete.

He gestured toward the wingback chair opposite him. "Take a load off. I need to talk to you, anyway."

"So I've heard." She didn't want to sit down. She wanted to stand and scream at him, but that wasn't going to get her anywhere. Besides, she felt drained all of a sudden. Being around Franco, even for a few minutes, was exhausting. "Speaking of which, what was Franco Andrade doing here just now?"

"About that…" He calmly folded his hands in front of him, drawing Diana's attention first to the smooth surface of his desk and then to the oddly huge stack of newspapers on top of it.

She blinked and cut him off midsentence. "Is that my picture on the front page of the *New York Daily News*?"

She hadn't thought it possible for the day to get any worse, but it just had. So much worse.

And the hits kept on coming. As she sifted through the stack of tabloids—all of which claimed she was having a torrid affair with "the drop-dead gorgeous bad boy of polo"—Artem outlined his preposterous idea for a public relations campaign. Although it sounded more like an episode of *The Bachelor* than any kind of legitimate business plan.

"No, thank you." Diana flipped the copy of *Page Six* facedown so she wouldn't have to look at the photo of herself and Franco on the cover. If she never saw that picture again, it would be too soon.

Artem's brow furrowed. "No, thank you? What does that mean?"

"It means no. As in, I'll pass." What about her answer wasn't he understanding? She couldn't be more clear. "No. N.O."

"Perhaps you don't understand. We're talking about the largest uncut diamond in the world. Do you have any idea what this could mean for Drake Diamonds?" There was Artem's CEO voice again.

She wasn't about to let it intimidate her this time. "Yes. I realize it's very important, but we'll simply have to come up with another plan." *Preferably one that doesn't involve Franco Andrade in any way, shape or form.*

"Let's hear your suggestions, then." He leaned back in his chair and crossed his arms. "I'm all ears."

He wanted her to come up with a plan *now*?

Diana cleared her throat. "I'll have to give it some thought, obviously. But I'm sure I can come up with something."

"Go ahead. I'll wait."

"Artem, come on. We can take the owners of the diamond out to dinner or something. Wine and dine them."

"You realize every other jeweler in Manhattan is doing that exact same thing," he said.

Admittedly, that was probably true. "There's got to be a better way to catch their attention than letting everyone believe I'm having a scandalous affair with Franco."

Please let there be another way.

"Not scandalous. Just high profile. Romantic. Glamorous." Artem gave her a thoughtful look. "He told me you'd refuse, by the way. What, exactly, is the problem between you two?"

Diana swallowed. Maybe she should simply tell Artem what happened three years ago. Surely then he'd forget about parading her all over Park Avenue on Franco's arm just for the sake of a diamond. Even the biggest diamond in the known universe.

But she couldn't. She didn't even want to think about that humiliating episode, much less talk about it.

Especially to her brother, of all people.

"He's a complete and total man whore. You know that, right?" Wasn't that reason enough to turn down the opportunity to pretend date him for twenty-one days? "Aren't you at all concerned about my virtue?"

"The last time I checked, you were more than capable of taking care of yourself, Diana. In fact, you're one of the strongest women I know. I seriously doubt I need to worry about your virtue." He shrugged. "But I could have a word with Franco…do the whole brother thing and threaten him with bodily harm if he lays a finger on you. Would that make you feel better?"

"God, no." She honestly couldn't fathom anything more mortifying.

"It's your call." Artem shrugged. "He's rehabilitating his image, anyway. Franco Andrade's man-whore days are behind him."

Diana laughed. Loud and hard. "He told you that? And you believed him?"

"When did you become such a cynic, sis?"

Three years ago. Right around the time I lost my virginity. "It seems dubious. That's all I'm saying. Why would he change after all this time, unless he's already had his way with every woman on the eastern seaboard?"

It was a distinct possibility.

"People change, Diana." His expression softened and he cast a meaningful glance at the bassinet in the corner of his office. A pink mobile hung over the cradle, decorated with tiny teddy bears wearing ballet shoes. "I did."

Diana smiled at the thought of her adorable baby niece.

He had a point. Less than a year ago, Artem had been the one on the cover of *Page Six*. He'd been photographed with a different woman every night. Now he was a candidate for father of the year.

Moreover, Diana had never seen a couple more in love than Artem and Ophelia. It was almost enough to restore her faith in marriage.

But not quite.

It would take more than her two brothers finding marital bliss to erase the memory of their father's numerous indiscretions.

It wasn't just the affairs. It was the way he'd made no

effort whatsoever to hide them from their mother. He'd expected her to accept it. To smile and look away. And she had.

Right up until the day she died.

She'd been just forty years old when Diana found her lifeless body on the living room floor. Still young, still beautiful. The doctors had been baffled. They'd been unable to find a reason for her sudden heart attack. But to Diana, the reason was obvious.

Her mother had died of a broken heart.

Was it any wonder she thought marriage was a joke? She was beyond screwed up when it came to relationships. How damaged must she have been to intentionally throw herself at a man who was famous for treating women as if they were disposable?

Diana squeezed her eyes shut.

Why did Franco have to come strutting back into her life *now*, while she was her most vulnerable? Before her accident, she could have handled him. She could have handled anything.

She opened her eyes. "Please, Artem. I just really, really don't want to do this."

He nodded. "I see. You'd rather spend all day, every day, slaving away in Engagements than attend a few parties with Franco. Understood. Sorry I brought it up."

He waved a hand toward the dreaded Engagements showroom down the hall. "Go ahead and get to work."

Diana didn't move a muscle. "Wait. Are you saying that if I play the part of Franco's fake girlfriend by night, I won't have to peddle engagement rings by day?"

She'd assumed her position in Engagements was still part of the plan. This changed things.

She swallowed. She still couldn't do it. She'd never

last a single evening in Franco's company, much less twenty-one of them.

Could she?

"Of course you wouldn't have to do both." Artem gestured toward the newspapers spread across his desk. "This would be a job, just like any other in the company."

She narrowed her gaze and steadfastly refused to look at the picture again. "What kind of job involves going to black-tie parties every night?"

"Vice president of public relations. I did it for years. The job is yours now, if you want it." He smiled. "You asked me to find something else for you to do, remember? Moving from the sales floor to a VP position is a meteoric rise."

When he put it that way, it didn't sound so bad. Vice president of public relations sounded pretty darn good, actually.

Finally. This was the kind of opportunity she'd been waiting for. She just never dreamed that Franco Andrade would be part of the package.

"I want a pay increase," she blurted.

What was she doing?

"Done." Artem's grin spread wide.

She wasn't seriously considering accepting the job though, was she? No. She couldn't. Wouldn't. No amount of money was worth her dignity.

But there was one thing that might make participating in the farce worthwhile…

"And if it works, I want to be promoted." She pasted on her sweetest smile. "Again."

Artem's brows rose. "You're going to have to be more specific. Besides, vice president is pretty high on the food chain around here."

"I'm aware. But this diamond gala is really important. You said so yourself."

Artem's smile faded. Just a bit. "That's right."

"If I do my part and Drake Diamonds is chosen as the jewelry house to cut the giant diamond and if everything goes off with a hitch at the Met's diamond gala, I think I deserve to take Dalton's place." She cleared her throat. "I want to be named co-CEO."

Artem didn't utter a word at first. He just sat and stared at her as if she'd sprouted another head.

Great. She'd pushed too far.

VP was a massive career leap. She should have jumped at the opportunity to put all the love-struck brides and grooms in the rearview mirror and left it at that.

"That's a bold request for someone with no business experience," he finally said.

"Correct me if I'm wrong, but wasn't vice president of public relations the only position you held at Drake Diamonds before our father died and appointed you his successor as CEO?" Did Artem really think she'd been so busy at horse shows that she had no clue what had gone on between these Drake-blue walls the past few years?

Still, what was she saying? He'd never buy into this.

He let out an appreciative laugh. "You're certainly shrewd enough for the job."

She grinned. "I'll take that as a compliment."

"As you should." He sighed, looked at her for a long, loaded moment and nodded. "Okay. It works for me."

She waited for some indication that he was joking, but it never came.

Her heart hammered hard in her chest. "Don't tease me, Artem. It's been kind of a rough day."

And it was about to get rougher.

If she and Artem had actually come to an agreement,

that meant she was going out with Franco Andrade tonight. By choice.

She needed to have her head examined.

"I'm not teasing. You made a valid point. I didn't know anything about being a CEO when I stepped into the position. I learned. You will, too." He held up a finger. A warning. "But only if you deliver. Drake Diamonds must be chosen to cut the stone and cosponsor the Met Diamond gala."

"No problem." She beamed at him.

For the first time since she'd fallen off her horse, she felt whole. Happy. She was building a new future for herself.

In less than a month, she'd be co-CEO. No more passing out petit fours. No more engagement rings. She'd never have to look at another copy of *Bride* magazine for as long as she lived!

Better yet, she wouldn't have to answer any more questions about when she was going to start riding again. Every time she turned around, it seemed someone was asking her about her riding career. Had she gotten a new horse? Was she ready to start showing again?

Diana wasn't anywhere close to being ready. She wasn't sure she'd *ever* be ready.

Co-CEO was a big job. A huge responsibility—huge enough that it just might make people forget she'd once dreamed of going to the Olympics. If she was running the company alongside Artem, no one would expect her to compete anymore. It was the perfect solution.

She just had to get through the next twenty-one days first.

"Go home." Artem nodded toward his office door. "Rest up and get ready for tonight."

Tonight. A fancy party. The Waldorf Astoria. Franco.

She swallowed. "Everything will be fine."

Artem lifted a brow.

Had she really said that out loud?

"I know it will, because it's your job to make sure everything is fine," Artem said. "And for the record, there's not a doubt in my mind that your virtue is safe. You can hold your own, Diana. You just talked your way into a co-CEO job. From where I'm standing, if there's anyone who has reason to be afraid, it's Mr. Andrade."

He was right. She'd done that, hadn't she?

She could handle a few hours in Franco's company.

"I think you're right."

God, she hoped so.

Chapter Five

Franco leaned inside the Drake limo and did a double take when he saw Diana staring at him impassively from its dark interior.

"Buenas noches."

He'd expected the car to pick him up first and then take him to Diana's apartment so he could collect her. Like a proper date. But technically this wasn't a date, even though it already felt like one.

He couldn't remember the last time he'd dressed in a tuxedo and escorted a woman to a party. Despite his numerous exploits, Franco didn't often date. He arrived at events solo, and when the night was over he left with a woman on his arm. Sometimes several. Hours later, he typically went home alone. He rarely shared a bed with the same woman more than once, and he never spent the night. Ever.

In fact, the last woman who'd woken up beside him had been Diana Drake.

"Good evening, yourself," she said, without bothering to give him more than a cursory glance.

That would have to change once they arrived at the gala. Lovers looked at each other. They touched each other. Hell, if Diana was his lover, Franco wouldn't be able to keep his hands off her.

This isn't real.

He slid onto the smooth leather seat beside her.

It wasn't real, but it felt real. It even looked real.

Diana was dressed in a strapless chiffon gown, midnight blue, with a dangerously low, plunging neckline. A glittering stone rested between her breasts. A sapphire. *The* sapphire necklace from the photo shoot.

"Please stop staring." She turned and met his gaze. At last.

Franco's body hardened the instant his eyes fixed on hers. As exquisite as the sapphire around her neck was, it didn't hold a candle to the luminescent violet depths of those eyes. "You're lovely."

She stared at him coldly. "Save it for the cameras, would you? There's no one here. You can drop the act."

"It's not an act. You look beautiful." He swallowed. Hard. "That's quite a dress."

He was used to seeing her in riding clothes, not like this. He couldn't seem to look away.

What are you, a teenager? Grow up, Andrade.

"Seriously, stop." The car sped through a tunnel, plunging them into darkness. But the shadows couldn't hide the slight tremor in her voice. "Just stop it, would you? I know we're supposed to be madly in love with each other in public. But in private, can we keep things professional? Please?"

Something about the way she said *please* grabbed Franco by the throat and refused to let go.

Had he really been so awful to her all those years ago?

Yes. He had.

Still, she'd been better off once he'd pushed her away, whether she'd realized it or not. She was an heiress. The real deal. And Franco wasn't the type of man she'd bring home.

Never had been, never would be.

"Professional. Got it," he said to the back of her head. It felt more like he was talking to himself than to Diana.

She'd turned away again, keeping her gaze fixed on the scenery outside the car window. The lights of the city rushed past, framing her silhouette in a dizzying halo of varying hues of gold.

They sat in stony silence down the lavish length of Park Avenue. The air in the limo felt so thick he was practically choking on it. Franco refrained from pointing out that refusing to either look at him or speak to him in something other than monosyllables was hardly professional.

Why the hell had she agreed to this arrangement, anyway? Neither one of them should be sitting in the back of a limo on the way to some boring gala. They both belonged on horseback. Franco knew why he wasn't training right now, but for the life of him, he couldn't figure out what Diana was doing working for her family business.

He was almost grateful when his phone chimed with an incoming text message, giving him something to focus on. Not looking at Diana was becoming more impossible by the second. She was stunning, even in her fury.

He slid his cell out of the inside pocket of his tuxedo jacket and looked at the screen.

A message from Luc. Again.

Ellis still isn't budging.

Franco's jaw clenched. That information wasn't exactly breaking news. If he'd held out any hope of the team owner changing his mind before the end of the day, he wouldn't be sitting beside the diamond ice princess right now.

Still, he didn't particularly enjoy dwelling on the dismal state of his career.

He moved to slip the phone back inside his pocket, but it chimed again.

This has gone on long enough.

And again.

I can't let you do this. I'm telling him the truth.

Damn it all to hell.
Franco tapped out a response…

Let it go. What's done is done. I have everything under control.

Beside him, Diana cleared her throat. "Lining up your date for the evening?"

Franco looked up and found her regarding him through narrowed eyes. She shot a meaningful glance at his phone.

So, she didn't like the thought of him texting other women? Interesting.

"You're my date for the evening, remember?" He wasn't texting another woman, obviously. But she didn't need to know that. He hardly owed her an explanation.

She rolled her eyes. "Don't even pretend you're going home alone after this."

He powered his phone down and glanced back up at Diana. "As a matter of fact, I am. Didn't Artem tell you? You and I are monogamous."

She arched a brow. "Did he explain what that meant, or did you have to look it up in the dictionary?"

"You're adorable when you're jealous. I like it." He was goading her, and he knew it. But at least they were speaking.

"If you think I'm jealous, you're even more full of yourself than I thought you were." In the darkened limousine, he could see two pink spots glowing on her cheeks. "Also, you're completely delusional."

He shrugged. "I disagree. Do you know why?"

"I can't begin to imagine what's going on inside your head. Nor would I want to." She exhaled a breath of resignation. "Why?"

"Because nothing about this conversation—which *you* initiated—is professional in nature." He deliberately let his gaze drop to the sapphire sparkling against her alabaster skin, then took a long, appreciative look at the swell of her breasts.

"You're insatiable," she said with a definite note of disgust.

He smiled. "Most women like that about me."

"I'm not most women."

"We'll see about that, won't we?"

The car slowed to a stop in front of the gilded entrance to the Waldorf Astoria. A red carpet covered the walkway from the curb to the gold-trimmed doors, flanked on either side by a mob of paparazzi too numerous to count.

"Miss Drake and Mr. Andrade, we've arrived," the driver said.

"Thank God. I need to get out of this car." Diana reached for the door handle, but her violet eyes grew wide. "Oh, wait. I almost forgot."

She opened her tiny, beaded clutch, removed a Drake-blue box and popped it open. The black diamond cuff links from the photo shoot glittered in the velvety darkness.

She handed them to Franco as the driver climbed out of the car. "Put these on. Quickly."

He slid one into place on his shirt cuff, but left the other in the palm of his hand.

"What are you doing? Hurry." Diana was borderline panicking. The back door clicked open, and the driver extended his hand toward her and waited.

"Go ahead, it's showtime." Franco loosened his tie and winked. "Trust me, Wildfire."

She stretched one foot out of the car, aimed a dazzling smile at the waiting photographers and muttered under her breath, "You realize that's asking the impossible."

Franco gathered the soft chiffon hem of her gown and helped her out of the limo. They stepped from the quiet confines of the car into a frenzy of clicking camera shutters and blinding light.

He dropped a kiss on Diana's bare shoulder and made a show of fastening the second cuff link in place. A collective gasp rose from the assembled crowd of spectators.

He lowered his lips to Diana's ear. "I have everything under control."

I have everything under control.

Maybe if he repeated it enough times, it would be true.

The man is an evil genius.

Diana hadn't been sure what Franco had up his sleeve until she felt his lips brush against her shoulder.

The kiss caught her distinctly off guard, and as her head whipped around to look at him, she saw him fastening his cuff link. He curved his arm around her waist, murmured in her ear and she finally understood. He'd purposely delayed sliding the diamonds into position on his shirt cuff so it looked as though he was only just getting dressed, no doubt because their arrival at the gala had caught them in flagrante delicto.

The press ate it up.

Evil genius. Most definitely.

"Diana, how long have you and Franco been dating?"

"Diana, who are you wearing?"

"Look over here, Diana! Smile for the camera."

Photographers shouted things from every direction.

She didn't know where to look, so she bowed her head as Franco steered her deftly through the frenzied crowd with his hand planted protectively on the small of her back.

"What's the diamond heiress like in bed, Franco?" a paparazzo yelled.

Diana's head snapped up.

"Don't let them get to you," Franco whispered.

"I'm fine," she lied. The whole scene was madness. "But if you answer that question, I will murder you."

"A gentleman doesn't kiss and tell."

Their eyes met briefly in the chaos, and if Diana hadn't known better, she would have believed he was being serious.

Suddenly, the thought of doing this for twenty-one straight days seemed absurd. Absurd and wholly impossible.

"Good evening, Miss Drake, Mr. Andrade." The doorman nodded and swept the door open for them. "Welcome to the Waldorf Astoria."

"*Gracias*," Franco said. *Thank you.* He gave her waist a gentle squeeze. "Shall we, love?"

His voice rumbled through her, deliciously deep.

She swallowed. *It's all pretend. Don't fall for it. Don't fall.*

She'd told herself the same thing three years ago. A fat lot of good that had done her.

Everything was moving too fast. Even after they finally made it inside the grand black-and-white marble lobby, Diana felt as if she'd been caught up in a whirlwind. A glittering blur where everything was too big and too bright, from the mosaic floor to the grand chandelier to the beautiful man standing beside her.

"Miss Drake and Mr. Andrade, I'm Beth Ross, director of Manhattan Pet Rescue. We're so pleased you could make it to our little gathering this evening."

"Ah, Beth, we wouldn't have missed it for the world," Franco said smoothly, following up his greeting with a kiss on the cheek.

Beth practically swooned.

He was so good at this it was almost frightening. If Artem had really known what he was doing, he would have made Franco the new vice president of public relations.

Say something. You're not the arm candy. He is.

"Thank you for having us. We're so pleased to be here." Diana smiled.

From the corner of her eye, she spotted someone holding up a cell phone and pointing toward her and Franco. He must have seen it too, because he deftly wrapped his arm around her waist and rested his palm languidly on her hip. Without even realizing it, she burrowed into him.

Beth sighed. "You two are every bit as beautiful

as your advertising campaign. It's all anyone can talk about."

"So we've heard." Diana forced a smile.

"Our party is located upstairs in the Starlight Ballroom. I've come to escort you up there, and if you don't mind, we'd love to snap a few pictures of you with some of the animals we have up for adoption later this evening."

Diana stiffened. "Um…"

Franco gave her hipbone a subtle squeeze. "We'd be happy to. We're big animal lovers, obviously."

We're big animal lovers.

We.

Diana blinked. Franco seemed to be staring at her, waiting for her to say something. "Oh, yes. Huge animal lovers."

They moved from the glitzy, gold lobby into a darkly intimate corridor walled in burgundy velvet. Beth pushed a button to summon an elevator.

"That doesn't surprise me a bit," she said. "I just knew you must be animal lovers. Drake Diamonds has always been one of our biggest supporters. And, of course, both of you are legendary in the horse world."

The elevator doors swished open, and the three of them stepped inside.

"Diana has a beautiful black Hanoverian. Tell Beth about Diamond, love." Franco looked at her expectantly.

Diana felt as though she'd been slapped.

She opened her mouth to say something, anything, but she couldn't seem capable of making a sound.

"Are you all right, dear? You've gone awfully pale." Beth eyed her with concern.

"I just… I…" It was no use. She couldn't talk about Diamond. Not now.

For six months, she'd managed to avoid discussing her beloved horse's death with anyone. Not even her brothers. She knew she probably should, but she couldn't. It just hurt too much. And after so much silence, the words wouldn't come.

"She's a bit claustrophobic," Franco said.

Another lie. Diana was beginning to lose track of them all.

"Oh, I'm so sorry." Beth's hand fluttered to her throat. "I didn't realize. We should have taken the stairs."

"It's fine." Franco's voice was like syrup. Soothing. "We're almost there, darling."

The elevator doors slid open.

Diana burrowed into Franco as he half carried her to the entrance to the ballroom. She couldn't remember leaning against him in the first place.

Breathe in, breathe out. You're fine.

She took a deep inhale and straightened her spine, smiled. "So sorry. I'm okay. Really."

Her heart pounded against her rib cage. She desperately wished she were back at Dalton's apartment, watching bad reality television and curled up under a blanket on the sofa.

Don't think about Diamond. Don't blow this. Say something.

She glanced up at the stained-glass ceiling strung with twinkling lights. "Look how beautiful everything is."

Beth nodded her agreement and launched into a description of all the work that had gone into putting together the gala, a large part of which had been funded by Drake Diamonds. Diana smiled and nodded, as did Franco, although at times she could see him watching her with what felt like too much interest.

She was dying to tell him he was laying it on a little

thick. They were supposed to be dating, not engaged, for crying out loud. Besides, she'd shaken off the worst of her panic.

She was fine. She just hadn't expected him to mention Diamond. That's all. She'd assumed that Franco had known about her accident. Apparently, he hadn't. Otherwise, he never would have brought up Diamond.

She'd been shocked, and probably a little upset. But it had passed.

He didn't need to be worried about her, and he definitely didn't need to be watching her like that. But an hour into the gala they were still shaking hands and chatting with the other animal shelter donors. She and Franco hadn't had a moment alone together.

Not that Diana was complaining.

The limousine ride had provided plenty of one-on-one time, thank you very much.

"If we could just ask you to do one last thing…" Beth guided them toward the far corner of the ballroom where guests had been taking turns posing for pictures. "Could we get those photos I mentioned before you leave?"

Diana nodded. "Absolutely."

Franco's hand made its way to the small of her back again. She was getting somewhat used to it and couldn't quite figure out if that was a bad thing or a good one.

It's nearly over. Just a few more minutes.

One night down, twenty to go. Almost.

She allowed herself a subtle, premature sigh of relief. Then she noticed a playpen filled with adorable, squirming puppies beside the photographer's tripod, and any sense of triumph she felt about her performance thus far disintegrated. She couldn't handle being around animals again. Not yet.

"Well, well. What do we have here?" Franco reached

into the playpen and gathered a tiny black puppy with a tightly curled tail into his arms.

The puppy craned its neck, stuck out its miniscule pink tongue and licked the side of Franco's face. He threw his head back and laughed, which only seemed to encourage the sweet little dog. It scrambled up Franco's chest and showered his ear with puppy kisses.

Beth motioned for the photographer to capture the adoration on film. "Doesn't she just love you, Mr. Andrade?"

The puppy was a girl. Because of course.

Franco's charm appealed to females of all species, apparently.

Why am I not surprised?

"Come here, love." Franco reached for Diana's hand and pulled her toward him. "You've got to meet this little girl. She's a sweetheart."

"No, it's okay. You keep her." She tried to wave him off, but it was impossible. Before she knew what was happening, she had a puppy in her arms and flashbulbs were going off again.

"That's Lulu. She's a little pug mix."

"Franco's right. She's definitely a sweetheart." Diana gazed down at the squirming dog.

Before her brother Dalton got married and moved to Delamotte, he'd tried talking her into getting a dog on multiple occasions. At first she'd thought he was joking. Dalton didn't even like dogs. Or so she'd thought. Apparently that had changed when he met the princess. Then he'd practically become some sort of animal matchmaker and kept encouraging Diana to adopt a pet.

What had gotten into her brothers? Both of them had turned into different people over the course of the past year. Sometimes it felt like the entire world was moving forward, full speed ahead, while Diana stood completely still.

Everything was changing. Everything and everyone.

It didn't use to be this way. From the first day she'd climbed onto the back of horse, Diana had been riding as fast as she could. She'd always thought if she rode hard enough, she'd escape the legacy Gaston Drake had built. Escape everything that it meant to be part of her family. The lies, the deceit. She'd thought she could outrun it.

Now she was back in the family fold, and she realized she hadn't outrun a thing.

She swallowed hard. How could she even consider saving a dog when she wasn't even convinced she could save herself?

"Here. You take her." She tried to hand the puppy back to Franco, but he wrapped his arms around her and kept posing for the camera.

"You three make a lovely family," Beth gushed.

That was Diana's breaking point.

The touching…the endearments…the puppy. Those things she could handle. Mostly. But the idea of being a family? She'd rather die.

"It's getting late. We should probably go."

But no one seemed to have a heard a word she said, because at the exact time that she tried to make her getaway, Franco made an announcement. "We'll take her."

Beth squealed. A few people applauded. Diana just stood there, trying to absorb what he'd said.

She searched his features, but he was still wearing that boyfriend-of-the-year expression that gave her butterflies, even though she knew without a doubt it wasn't real. "What are you talking about?"

"The puppy." He gave the tiny pup a rub behind her ears with the tip of his pointer finger.

"Franco, we can't adopt a dog together," she muttered through her smile, which was definitely beginning to fade.

"Of course we can, darling." His eyes narrowed the slightest bit.

No one else noticed because they were too busy fawning all over him.

"Franco, *sweetheart*." She shot daggers at him with her eyes.

This wasn't part of the deal. She'd agreed to pretend to date him, not coparent an animal.

Besides, she didn't want to adopt a dog. Correction: she *couldn't* adopt a dog.

A dog's lifespan was even shorter than a horse's. Much shorter. She wouldn't survive that kind of heartache. Not again. *Never* again.

Franco bowed his head to nuzzle the puppy and paused to whisper in her ear. "They're eating it up. What is your problem?"

It was the worst possible time for something to snap inside Diana, but something did. All the feelings she'd been working so hard to suppress for the past few months—the anger, the fear, the grief—came spilling out at once. She gazed up at Franco through a veil of tears as the whole world watched.

"Diamond is dead. That's my problem."

Chapter Six

A *Page Six* Exclusive Report

The rumors are true! Diamond heiress Diana Drake and polo's prince charming, Franco Andrade, are indeed a couple. Tongues have been wagging all over New York since their sultry billboard went up in Times Square. The heat between these two is too hot to be anything but genuine!

Drake and Andrade stepped out last night at Manhattan's Annual Fur Ball, where witnesses say they arrived on the heels of what was obviously a romantic tryst in the Drake Diamonds limousine. During the party, Andrade was heard calling Drake by the pet name Wildfire and couldn't keep his hands off the stunning equestrian beauty.

At the end of the evening, Drake was moved to tears when Andrade gifted her with a nine-week-old pug puppy.

Chapter Seven

Franco shifted his Jaguar into Park and swiveled his gaze to the passenger seat. "I don't suppose I can trust you to stay here and let me do the talking."

Lulu let out a piercing yip, then resumed chewing on the trim of the Jag's leather seats.

"Okay, then. Since you've made no attempt at all to hide your deviousness, you're coming with me." He scooped the tiny dog into the crook of his elbow and climbed out of the car.

"Try to refrain from gnawing on my suit if you can help it."

Lulu peered up at him with her shiny, oversize eyes as she clamped her little teeth around one of the buttons on his sleeve.

Marvelous.

Franco didn't bother reprimanding her. If the past week had taught him anything, it was that Lulu had a mind of her own. Not unlike the other headstrong female in his life…

Diana hadn't been kidding when she said she didn't want anything to do with the puppy. As far as pet parenting went, Franco was a single dad. Which would have been fine, had he not known how badly she needed the dog.

She was reeling from the loss of her horse. That much was obvious. If anyone could understand that kind of grief, Franco could.

He'd had no idea that Diamond had died. But now that he knew, things were beginning to make more sense. Diana hadn't given up riding because she had a burning desire to peddle diamonds. She was merely hiding out at the family store. She was heartbroken and afraid.

But she couldn't give up riding forever.

Could she?

"Franco." Ben Santos, the coach of the Kingsmen, strolled out of the barn and positioned himself between Franco and the practice field. "What are you doing here?"

Not exactly the greeting he was hoping for.

Franco squared his shoulders and kept on walking. Enough was enough. He needed to stop worrying so much about his fake girlfriend and focus on resurrecting his career.

"Nice to see you too, coach." He paused by the barn and waited for an invitation onto the field.

None was forthcoming.

Ben squinted into the sun and sighed. "You know you're not supposed to be here, son."

Franco's jaw clenched. He'd never liked Ben's habit of calling his players *son*. Probably because the last man who'd called Franco that had been a worthless son of a bitch.

But he'd put up with it from Ben out of respect. He wasn't in the mood to do so now, though.

Seven nights of wining and dining Diana Drake at every charity ball in Manhattan had gotten him absolutely nowhere. He had nothing to show for his efforts, other than a naughty puppy and a nagging sense that Diana was on the verge of coming apart at the seams.

Not your problem.

"I was hoping we could talk. Man to man," Franco said. Or more accurately, man to man holding tiny dog.

Lulu squirmed in his grasp, and the furrow between Ben's brows faded.

"Nice pup," he said. "This must be the one I've been reading about in all the papers."

Thus far, Lulu's puppyhood had been meticulously chronicled by every gossip rag and website Franco had ever heard of, along with a few he hadn't. Just this morning, Franco had been photographed poop-scooping outside his Tribeca apartment. He supposed he had that lovely image to look forward to in tomorrow's newspapers. Oh, joy.

He cleared his throat. "So you've been keeping up with me."

Excellent. Maybe the love charade was actually working.

"It's been kind of hard not to." Ben reached a hand toward Lulu, who promptly began nibbling on his fingers.

"The publicity should come in handy when the season starts, don't you think?" Franco's gaze drifted over the coach's shoulder to where he could see a groom going over one of the Kingsmen polo ponies with a curry comb. The horse's coat glistened like a shiny copper penny in the shadows of the barn.

Diamond is dead. That's my problem.

"Except you're not on the team, so, no." Ben shook his head.

"This has gone on long enough, don't you think? You need me. The team needs me. How long is Ellis planning on making me sweat this out?"

"You were fired. And I don't think Ellis is going to change his mind. He's furious. Frankly, I can't blame him." Ben removed his Kingsmen baseball cap and raked a hand through his hair. He sighed. "You went too far this time, son. You slept with the man's wife."

Franco pretended he hadn't heard the last sentence. If he thought about it too much, he might be tempted to tell the truth and he couldn't do that. Luc had his faults—bedding the boss's wife chief among them—but he was Franco's friend. Luc had been there for him when he needed someone most.

Franco owed Luc, and it was time to pay up.

"That's over." Franco swallowed. "I'm in love."

He waited for a lightning bolt to appear out of the sky and strike him dead.

Nothing happened. Franco just kept standing there, holding the squirming puppy and watching the horses being led toward the practice field.

He missed this. He missed spending so much time with his horses. He'd been exercising them as often as possible, but it couldn't compare with team practice, day in and day out.

Diana had to miss it, too. He knew she did.

Diamond is dead. That's my problem.

Franco felt sick every time he remembered the lost look in Diana's eyes when she'd said those words.

Her vulnerability had caught him off guard. It affected him far more than her disdain ever could. He didn't mind being hated. He deserved it, frankly. But he *did* mind seeing Diana in pain. He minded it very much.

Again, not his problem. He was here to get himself, not Diana, back in the saddle.

"In love," Ben repeated. His gaze dropped to the rich soil beneath their feet. "I'm happy to hear it. I am. But I'm afraid it's going to take more than a few pictures in the paper to convince Ellis."

Franco's jaw clenched. "What are you saying?"

But the coach didn't need to elaborate, because the field was filling up with Franco's team members. They were clearly preparing for a scrimmage because, instead of being dressed in casual practice attire, they were wearing uniforms. Franco spotted Luc, climbing on top of a sleek ebony mount. But the sight that gave Franco pause was another player. One he'd never seen before, wearing a shirt with a number situated just below his right shoulder—the number 1.

Franco's number.

"Perhaps Ellis would feel differently if you were married. Or even engaged. Something permanent, you know. But right now, it looks like a fling. To him, anyway." Ben shrugged. "Surely you understand. Try to put yourself in his shoes, son. Imagine how you'd feel if another man, a man whom you knew and trusted, hopped into bed and ravished Miss Drake."

Franco's gaze finally moved away from the player wearing his number. He stared at the coach, and a nonsensical rage swelled in his chest. A thick, black rage, which he could only attribute to the fact that he'd been replaced. "Don't talk about her that way."

Ben held up his hands. "I'm not suggesting it will happen. I'm simply urging you to try and understand where Ellis is coming from."

"This isn't about Diana." Franco took a calming inhale and reminded himself that losing his cool wasn't going to do him any favors. "It's not even about Ellis and his wife. It's about the team."

The coach gestured toward the bright-green rectangle of grass just west of the barn. "Look, son. I need to get going. We've got back-to-back scrimmages this afternoon."

Franco jerked his chin in the direction of the practice field. "Who's your new number 1?"

Ben sighed. "Don't, Franco."

"Just tell me who's wearing my jersey, and I'll leave."

"Gustavo Anca."

"You can't be serious." Franco knew Gustavo. He was a nice enough guy, but an average player at best. Ellis was playing it safe. Too safe. "You know he won't bring in the wins."

"Yes, but he won't sleep with the owner's wife, either." The older man gave him a tight smile.

Franco's gaze flitted ever so briefly to Luc sitting atop his horse, doing a series of twisting stretches. He turned in Franco's direction, and their eyes met.

Franco looked away.

"Listen. Can I give you a piece of advice?"

Whatever he had to say, Franco didn't want to hear it.

"Move on. Let the other teams know you're available. Someone is bound to snap you up."

He shook his head. "Out of the question."

The Kingsmen were the best. And when Franco had worn the Kingsmen jersey, he'd been the best of the best. He'd earned his place there, and he wanted it back. His horses were there. His teammates. His heart.

Also, if the Kingsmen were already scrimmaging, it could only mean the rosters had been set for the coming season in Bridgehampton. If Franco wanted to play anywhere before autumn, he'd have to go Santa Barbara. Or even as far as Sotogrande, in Spain.

He couldn't leave. He'd made a promise to the Drakes. And for the time being, his position as the face of Drake Diamonds was the only thing paying his bills.

His hesitancy didn't have a thing to do with Diana. At least, that's what he wanted to believe.

"Think about it. Make a few calls. If another team needs a reference, have them contact me." Ben shifted from one foot to the other. "But I can only vouch for your playing. Nothing else."

"Of course." The tangle of fury inside Franco grew into something dark and terrible. He clamped his mouth shut.

"It was good to see you, but please understand. The situation isn't temporary." His coach gave him a sad smile. "It's permanent."

"Miss Drake, you have a visitor." The doorman's voice crackled through the intercom of Diana's borrowed apartment. "Mr. Andrade is on his way up."

Diana's hand flew to the Talk button. "Wait. What? *Why?*"

Franco was here? Now?

There had to be some sort of mistake. They weren't scheduled to arrive at the Harry Winston party for another hour and a half. She wasn't even dressed yet. Besides, she'd given the driver strict instructions to pick her up first. She didn't need Franco anywhere near her apartment. Their lives were already far more intertwined than she'd ever anticipated.

She'd even talked to him about Diamond. Briefly, but still. It had been the closest she'd come to admitting to anyone that she was having trouble moving past her accident. It had also been the first time she'd said Diamond's name out loud since her fall.

She'd spent the intervening days since the Fur Ball carefully shoring up the wall around her heart again. She went through the motions with Franco, speaking to him as little possible. He was the last person she should be confiding in. His casual reference to Diamond had caught her off guard. She'd had a moment of weakness.

It wouldn't happen again.

Even if the sight of him with that adorable puppy in his arms made her weak in the knees…she was only human, after all.

The doorman's voice crackled through the intercom. "I assumed it was acceptable, given the nature of your relationship, that I could go ahead and send Mr. Andrade up."

The nature of their relationship. Hysterical laughter bubbled up Diana's throat.

She swallowed it down. "It's fine. Thank you."

She took a deep breath and told herself to get a grip. She couldn't reprimand the doorman for sending the purported love of her life up to see her, could she?

The building that housed Dalton's apartment was one of the most exclusive addresses in Lenox Hill. She wholeheartedly doubted the doorman would be indiscreet. But the press was always looking for a scoop. The last thing she and Franco needed was a headline claiming she'd turned him away from her door.

Diana shook her head. Not she and Franco. She and Artem. The Drakes were the ones who were on the same team. Franco was just an accessory.

A dashing, dangerous accessory.

Three solid knocks pounded on the door and echoed

through the apartment. Diana tightened the belt of her satin bathrobe and opened the door.

"Franco, what a pleasant surprise," she said with forced enthusiasm.

"Diana," he said flatly.

That was it. No loving endearment. No scandalous quip about her state of near undress. Just her name.

She motioned for him to come inside and shut the door.

Her smile faded as she turned to face him. There was no reason for pretense when they were alone together. Although, now that she thought about it, this was the first time since embarking on their charade that they'd been alone. *Truly* alone. Everywhere they went, they were surrounded by drivers, photographers, doormen.

A nonsensical shiver passed through her as she looked up at him. His eyes seemed darker than usual, his expression grim.

"What are you doing here?"

Had something happened? Had word gotten out that they'd been faking their love affair? Surely not. Artem would have said something. She'd talked to him on the phone only moments ago, and everything had seemed fine.

"We have a date this evening, do we not?" His words were clipped. Formal.

Diana never thought she'd miss his sexually charged smile and smug attitude, but she kind of did. At least that version of Franco was somewhat predictable. This new persona seemed quite the opposite.

"We do." She nodded and waited for him to ogle her. She was wearing a white satin minibathrobe, for crying out loud.

He just stood there in his impeccably cut tuxedo with

his arms crossed. "Where are we going tonight, any-way?"

"To a party at Harry Winston."

"The jewelry store?" He frowned. "Isn't Harry Winston a direct competitor of Drake Diamonds?"

"Yes, but the Lambertis are going to be there."

"Who?" he asked blithely.

Seriously? They'd been over this about a million times. "Carla and Don Lamberti. They own the diamond, remember? *The* diamond."

"Right." His gaze strayed to her creamy satin bathrobe. Finally. "Shouldn't you be getting dressed?"

"I *was*. Until you knocked on my door." This wasn't the night for Franco to go rogue. Absolutely not. "What's with you tonight? Is something wrong? Why are you even here?"

His eyes flashed. Something most definitely wasn't right. "You're my girlfriend." He used exaggerated air quotes around the word *girlfriend*. "Why shouldn't I be here?"

"Because the car was supposed to pick me up first, and then we were going to collect you in Tribeca. That's why."

He eyed her with an intensity that made her feel warm and delicious, like she'd been sipping red wine. "I'm tired of following orders, Diana. Surely I'm not expecting too much if I want to make my own decision regarding transportation to a party."

"Um…"

"A real couple wouldn't be picked up at two separate locations. Real lovers would be in bed until the moment it was time to leave. Real lovers would, at the very least, be in the same godforsaken apartment." An angry muscle twitched in his jaw. Diana couldn't seem to look away from it. "We need this to look real. *I* need it to look real."

She'd never seen Franco this serious before. It shouldn't have been nearly as arousing as it was. Especially on a night as important as this one.

Diana nodded and licked her lips. "Of course."

She hadn't realized he'd cared so much about either the company or the diamond. Wasn't this whole lovey-dovey act just a paycheck for him? A way to get a little publicity for the Kingsmen?

Why *did* he care so much?

She realized she didn't actually know why he'd agreed to participate in their grand charade. Artem had said something about Franco changing his image, but she hadn't pressed for details. She just wanted to get through their twenty-one days together as quickly and painlessly as possible.

Franco prowled through her living room with the dangerous grace of a panther. "Where's your liquor cabinet? I need something to pass the time while you're getting ready."

Clearly this wasn't the moment for a heart-to-heart.

She crossed the living room, strode into the kitchen and pulled a bottle of the Scotch that Dalton favored from one of the cabinets. She set it on the counter along with a Waterford highball glass. "Will this do?"

Franco arched a brow. "It'll work."

"Good. Help yourself." She watched as he poured a generous amount and then downed it in a single swallow.

He eyed her as he picked up the bottle again. "Is there a problem, or are you going to finish getting dressed?"

Alarm bells were going off in every corner of her mind. Franco was definitely upset about something. She should call Artem and cancel before Franco polished off the rest of Dalton's Scotch.

But that wasn't an option. Not tonight, when they were

finally going to come face-to-face with the Lambertis. Their 1,100-carat diamond was the sole reason she was in this farce of a relationship.

She took a deep inhale and pasted on a smile. "No problem at all."

Not yet, anyway.

Chapter Eight

Diana held her breath as they climbed into the Drake limousine, hoping against hope that Franco's strange, dark mood would go unnoticed by everyone at the gala.

She kept waiting for him to slip back into his ordinary, devil-may-care persona, but somehow it never happened. They made the short trip to Harry Winston in tense silence, and for the first time, the strained, quiet ride seemed to be Franco's choice rather than hers.

She kept trying to make conversation and loosen him up, but nothing worked. She was beginning to realize how badly she'd behaved toward him over the course of the past week. *This must be how he feels every night.*

She shouldn't feel guilty. She absolutely shouldn't. This wasn't a real date. Not one of the past seven nights had been real. It had been business. All of it.

It needs to look real. I need it to look real.

As the car pulled up to the glittering Harry Winston

storefront at the corner of 5th Avenue and 57th Street—
just a stone's throw from Drake Diamonds—she turned
toward Franco.

"Are you sure you're ready for this?" she asked.

He met her gaze. The slight darkening of his irises was
the only outward sign of the numerous shots of Scotch
he'd consumed back at her apartment. Last week she
wouldn't have known him well enough to notice such a
subtle change.

"Yes. Are you?"

She felt his voice in the pit of her stomach. "Yes."

*There's still time to back out. Artem will be inside. Let
him charm the socks off the Lambertis.*

But making sure the owners of the diamond chose
to work with Drake Diamonds was her responsibility.
Not her brother's. And considering it was pretty much
her *only* responsibility, she shouldn't be passing it off
to Artem.

She'd already survived a week as Franco's faux love
interest. Surely they could pull this off for another fourteen days. Franco would get himself together once they
were in public. He'd be his usual, charming self.

He had to.

But even walking past the mob of paparazzi gathered
in front of the arched entrance and gold-trimmed gate
at Harry Winston's storefront felt different. Franco felt
stiff beside her.

Diana missed the warmth of his hand on the small of
her back. She missed his playful innuendo. God, what
was happening to her? She hadn't actually enjoyed spending time with him.

Because that just wasn't possible.

The moment they crossed the threshold, Artem and
Ophelia strode straight toward them. When her brother

first told her they were coming, Diana had been filled with relief. Tonight was important. She could use all the reinforcements she could get. Now she wished he wasn't here to witness what suddenly felt like a huge disaster in the making.

"Diana." Artem kissed her on the cheek, then turned to shake Franco's hand. "Franco, good to see you."

The two men exchanged pleasantries while Diana greeted Ophelia. Dressed in a floor-length tulle gown, her sister-in-law looked every inch like the ballerina she'd been before taking the helm of the design department of Drake Diamonds. The diamond tiara Artem had given her as an engagement present was intricately interwoven into her upswept hair.

"You look stunning," Diana whispered as she embraced the other woman.

"Thank you, but my God. Look at yourself. You're glowing." Ophelia grinned. "That sapphire suits you."

Diana touched the deep blue stone hanging from the diamond and platinum garland around her neck. She'd worn it every night she'd been out with Franco as an homage to their billboard. "Well, don't get used to it. I doubt my brother is going to let me keep it once this is all over."

"He won't have to, remember? He won't be your boss anymore." Ophelia winked and whispered, "Girl power!"

Diana's stomach did a nervous flip. *Powerful* was the last thing she felt at the moment.

Franco bowed his head and murmured in her ear, "I'm going to fetch some champagne. I'll be right back." He was gone before she could say a word.

Artem frowned after him. "What's wrong with your boyfriend?"

Diana cast him a meaningful glance. *He's not my boyfriend.*

"Sis, I'm being serious. What's wrong with Franco?" Artem murmured.

So much for Franco's somber mood going unnoticed.

"He's fine, Artem. He's doing a wonderful job, as usual." Since when did she jump to Franco Andrade's defense?

"Really? Because he seems a little tense. You're sure he's all right?"

Ophelia looped her arm through her husband's. "Artem, leave Diana alone. She's perfectly capable of doing her job."

Thank God for sisters-in-law.

"I never insinuated she wasn't." Artem gave Diana's shoulder an affection little bump with his own. "My concern is about Andrade. He's letting this whole mess with the Kingsmen get to him."

Diana blinked. "What mess with the Kingsmen?"

"The fact that he's been dropped from the team. I'm guessing by his mood that he hasn't been reinstated yet. But I'm sure you know more about it than I do." Artem shrugged.

Franco had been *fired*?

So that's why he'd signed on with Drake Diamonds. He had as much to gain from their pretend courtship as she did.

But he was one of the best polo players in the world. Why would the Kingsmen let him go? It didn't make sense. She stared at him across the room and wondered what other secrets he was keeping.

Whatever the case, she wasn't about to tell Artem that she didn't have a clue Franco had been cut. This seemed like the sort of thing his girlfriend should know. Even a fake girlfriend.

"He's fine." She forced a smile. Doing so was becoming alarmingly easy. She probably shouldn't be so good at lying. "Really."

"How is it we're here, anyway? I feel like we've breached enemy territory," Ophelia whispered.

Diana looked around at the opulent surroundings—pale gray walls, black-and-white art deco tile floor, cut crystal vases overflowing with white hydrangeas—and tried not to be too impressed. She'd never set foot in Harry Winston before. As far as she knew, no Drake ever had. Their father was probably rolling in his grave.

"We were invited. All the high-end jewelers in the city are here. It's a power move on Harry Winston's part. I think it's their strategy to show the Lambertis that Harry Winston is the obvious choice to cut the diamond. It's bold to invite all your competitors. Confident. You have to admire it."

"Well, I don't." Diana rolled her eyes. "When you put things that way, the invitation is insulting. How dare they insinuate Drake Diamonds isn't good enough? We're the best in the world."

Artem winked at her. "My sister, a CEO in the making."

Franco returned to their group carrying two champagne flutes and offered them to Diana and Ophelia. "Ladies."

"Thank you," Ophelia said.

Diana reached for a glass and took a fortifying sip of bubbly. It was time to make her move.

She wasn't about to let the Lambertis be swayed by Harry Winston. If the egotistical power players behind this party thought she was intimidated, they were sorely mistaken. Drake Diamonds was about to totally steal the show.

We need this to look real.

She stole a glance at Franco and took another gulp of liquid courage. Someone needed to make it look real, and clearly it wasn't going to be him for once.

She moved closer to him, slipped her hand languidly around his waist and let her fingertips rest on his hip.

His champagne flute paused halfway to his lips. He glanced at her, and she let her hand drift lower until she was caressing his backside right there in Harry Winston in front of all of New York's diamond elite.

Franco cleared his throat and took a healthy gulp of champagne.

Another couple joined their small group. Artem introduced them, but their names didn't register with Diana. Her heart had begun to pound hard against her rib cage. All her concentration was centered on the feel of Franco's muscular frame beneath the palm of her hand.

"What are you doing?" he whispered.

"I'm doing exactly what you wanted. I'm making it look real." Her gaze drifted to his mouth.

He stared down at her, and the thunder in his gaze unnerved her. "This is a dangerous game you're playing, Diana. And in case you haven't noticed, I'm not in the mood for games."

She handed off her champagne flute to a waiter passing by with a silver tray. "Come with me."

"We're in the middle of a conversation." He shot a meaningful glance at Artem, Ophelia and the others.

"They won't even miss us, babe." She slid her arm through his and tugged him away.

They ended up in a darkened showroom just around the corner from the party. The only light in the room came from illuminated display cases full of gemstones and platinum. Diamonds sparkled around them like stars against the night sky.

"*Babe?* Really?" Franco arched a brow. "Why don't you just call me *honey bun*? Or *boo*?"

He could make fun of her all he wanted. At least she was trying. "You're blowing it out there. You realize that, don't you?"

A muscle flexed in his jaw. He looked as lethal as she'd ever seen him. "You're exaggerating. It's fine."

"Fine isn't good enough. Not tonight. You said so yourself." She couldn't let his icy composure get to her. Not now. "Talk to me, Franco. What has gotten into you? Did you have a bad day on the polo field or something? Did your polo pony trip over your massive ego?"

She crossed her arms and waited for him to admit the truth.

He raked a hand through his hair, and when he met her gaze, his dark eyes went soulful all of a sudden. If Diana had been looking at anyone else, she would have described his expression as broken. But that word was so wholly at odds with everything she knew about Franco, she was having trouble wrapping her head around it.

"I didn't ride today," he said quietly. "Nor have I ridden for the past month. So, no. My pony did not, in fact, trip over my massive ego."

"I know. Artem just told me." Her voice was colder than she'd intended.

She wasn't sure why she was so angry all of a sudden. She'd been the one to insist they keep things professional. And now was definitely not the time or place to discuss the fact that he was no longer playing polo.

But she couldn't seem to stop herself. The emotions she'd been grappling with since Artem so casually mentioned Franco was no longer playing with the Kingsmen felt too much like betrayal. Which didn't even make sense. Not that it mattered, though, because words were coming out of her mouth faster than she could think.

"Why didn't you say something? Why didn't you tell me?" The last thing she wanted was for him to know she cared, but the tremor in her voice was a dead giveaway.

He looked at her, long and hard, until her breath went shallow. He was so beautiful. A dark and elegant mystery.

Sometimes when she let her guard down and caught a glimpse of him standing beside her, she understood why she'd chosen him all those years ago. And despite the humiliation that had followed, she would have chosen him all over again.

"You didn't ask," he finally said.

She gave her head a tiny shake. "But…"

"But what?" he prompted.

He was going to make her say it, wasn't he? He was forcing her to go there. Again.

She inhaled a shaky breath. "But I told you about Diamond."

Their eyes met and held.

Tears blurred Diana's vision, until the diamonds around them shimmered like rain. Something moved in the periphery. She wiped a tear from her eye, and realized someone was coming.

Her breath caught in her throat.

Carla and Don Lamberti were walking straight toward them. Diana could see them directly over Franco's shoulder. Panic welled up in her chest.

The Lambertis couldn't find them like this. They most definitely couldn't see her crying. She was supposed to be in love.

In love.

For once, the thought didn't make her physically ill.

"Kiss me," she whispered.

Franco's eyes glittered fiercely in the shadows, drawing her in, pulling her toward something she couldn't quite identify. Something dark and familiar. "Diana…"

There was an ache in the way he said her name. It caught her off guard, scraped her insides.

A strange yearning wound its way through her as she reached for the smooth satin lapels of his tuxedo and balled them in her fists.

What was she doing?

"I said kiss me." She swallowed. Hard. "Now."

Franco's gaze dropped to her lips, and suddenly his chiseled face was far too close to hers. Her heart felt like it would pound right out of her chest, and she realized she was touching him, sliding her fingers through his dark hair.

She heard a noise that couldn't possibly have come from her own mouth, except somehow it had. A tremulous whimper of anticipation.

You'll regret this.

Just like last time.

Franco took her jaw in his hand and ran the pad of his thumb over her bottom lip as his eyes burned into her. His other hand slid languidly up her bare back until his fingertips found their way into her hair. He gave a gentle yet insistent tug at the base of her chignon, until her head tipped back and his mouth was perfectly poised over hers.

She felt dizzy. Disoriented. The air seemed too thick, the diamonds around them too bright. As her eyes drifted shut, she tried to remind herself of why this was happening. This wasn't fate or destiny or some misguided romantic notion.

She'd chosen it. She was in control.

It doesn't mean anything.

It doesn't.

Franco's mouth came down on hers, hot and wanting. Every bone in her body went liquid. Warmth coursed through her and, with it, remembrance.

Then there was no more thinking. No more denial. No more lying.

Not even to herself.

This kiss was different than their last.

Franco thought he'd been prepared for it. After all, this wasn't the first time his lips had touched Diana Drake's. They'd been down this road before. He remembered the taste of her, the feel of her, the soft, kittenish noise she made right when she was on the verge of surrender. These were the memories that tormented him as he'd lain awake the past seven nights until, at last, he'd fallen asleep and dreamed of a hot summer night long gone by.

But now that the past had been resurrected, he realized how wrong he'd been. A lifetime wouldn't have prepared him for a kiss like this one.

Where there'd once been a girlish innocence, Franco found womanly desire. Kissing Diana was like trying to capture light in his hands. He was wonderstruck, and rather than finding satisfaction in the warm, wet heat of her mouth, he felt an ache for her that grew sharper. More insistent. Just...

More.

He actually groaned the word aloud against the impossible softness of lips and before he knew what he was doing, he found himself pressing her against the cold glass of a nearby jewelry display case as his fingertips slid to her wrists and circled them like bracelets.

What the hell was happening?

This wasn't just different than the last time he'd kissed

Diana. It was different from any kiss Franco had experienced before.

Ever.

He pulled back for a blazing, breathless moment to look at her. He searched her face for some kind of indication he wasn't alone in this. He wanted her to feel it too—this bewildering connection that grabbed him by the throat and refused to let go. Needed her to feel it.

She gazed back at him through eyes darkened by desire. Her irises were the color of deep Russian amethysts. Rich and rare. And he knew he wasn't imagining things.

"Franco," she whispered in a voice he'd never heard her use before. One that nearly brought him to his knees. "I…"

Somewhere behind him, he heard the clearing of a throat followed by an apology. "Pardon us. We didn't realize anyone was here."

Not now.

Franco closed his eyes, desperate not to break whatever strange spell had swallowed them up. But as his pulse roared in his ears, he was agonizingly aware of Diana's wrists slipping from his grasp. And in the moment that followed, there was nothing but deep blue silence.

He opened his eyes and focused on the glittering sapphire around her neck rather than turning around. He needed a moment to collect himself as the truth came into focus.

"Mr. and Mrs. Lamberti." Diana moved away from him in a swish of tulle and pretense. "We apologize. Stay, please."

It had been an act. All of it. The caresses. The tears. The kiss.

He took a steadying inhale and adjusted his bow tie as he slowly turned around.

"Mr. Andrade, we'd know your face anywhere." A woman—Mrs. Lamberti, he presumed—offered her hand.

He gave it a polite shake, but he couldn't seem to make himself focus on her face. He couldn't tear his gaze away from Diana, speaking and moving about as if she'd orchestrated the entire episode.

Probably because she had.

"Franco, darling. The Lambertis are the owners of the diamond I've been telling you about." Diana turned toward him, but didn't quite meet his gaze.

Look at me, damn it.

"It's a pleasure to meet you both," he said.

"The pleasure is ours. Everywhere we turn, we see photos of the two of you. And now here you are, as real as can be." Mr. Lamberti laughed.

"Real. That's us. Isn't it darling?" Franco reached for Diana's hand, turned it over and pressed a tender kiss to the inside of her wrist.

Her pulse thundered against his lips, but it brought him little satisfaction. He no longer knew what to believe.

How had he let himself be fool enough to fall for any of this charade?

"It's nice to see a couple so in love." Mrs. Lamberti brought her hand to her throat. "Romance is a rarity these days, I'm afraid."

"I couldn't agree more." Franco gave Diana's waist a tiny squeeze.

Diana let out a tiny laugh. He'd been around her long enough now to know it was forced, but the Lambertis didn't appear to notice.

They continued making small talk about their diamond as Diana's gaze flitted toward his. At last. Franco saw an unmistakable hint of yearning in the violet depths of her eyes. He knew better than to believe in it, but it made his chest ache all the same.

"Wait until you see it." Mr. Lamberti shook his head. "It's a sight to behold."

"I hope I do get to see it someday," Diana said. "Sooner rather than later."

Good girl.

She was going in for the kill, as she should. That baseball-sized rock was the reason they were here, after all. Another polo player was wearing Franco's jersey, and the prospect of keeping up the charade alongside Diana suddenly seemed tortuous at best.

But he'd be damned if it was all for nothing.

"We'll be making an announcement about the diamond tomorrow, and I think you'll be pleased." Mrs. Lamberti reached to give Diana's arm a pat. "Off the record, of course."

Diana beamed. "My lips are sealed."

Mr. Lamberti winked. "In the meantime, we should be getting back to the party."

"It was lovely to meet you both," Diana said.

Franco murmured his agreement and bid the couple farewell.

The moment they were gone, he stepped away from Diana. He needed distance between them. Space for all the lies they'd both been spinning.

"Did you hear that?" she whispered, eyes ablaze. "They're making an announcement tomorrow. They're going to pick us, aren't they?"

Us.

He nodded. "I believe they are."

"We did it, Franco. We did it." She launched herself at him and threw her arms around his neck.

Franco allowed himself a bittersweet moment to savor

the feel of her body pressed against his, the soft swell of her breasts against his chest, the orchid scent of her hair as it tickled his nose.

He closed his eyes and took a deep inhale.

So intoxicating. So deceptively sweet.

He reached for her wrists and gently peeled her away.

"Franco?" She stood looking at him with her arms hanging awkwardly at her sides.

He shoved his hands in his pockets to prevent himself from touching her. "Aren't you forgetting something? We're alone now. There's no reason to touch me. No one is here to see it."

She flinched, and as she stared up at him, the look of triumph in her eyes slowly morphed into one of hurt. Her bottom lip trembled ever so slightly.

Nice touch.

"But I…"

He held up a hand to stop her. There was nothing to say. He certainly didn't need an apology. They were both adults. From the beginning, they'd both known what they were getting into.

Franco had simply forgotten for a moment. He'd fallen for the lie.

He wouldn't be making that mistake again.

"It's fine. More than fine." He shrugged one shoulder and let his gaze sweep her from top to bottom one last time before he walked away. "Smile, darling. You're getting everything you wanted."

Chapter Nine

A *Page Six* Exclusive Report

New York's own Drake Diamonds has been chosen by the Lamberti Mining Company as the jeweler to cut the world's largest diamond. The massive rock was recently unearthed from a mine in Botswana and weighs in at 1,100 carats. Rumor has it Ophelia Drake herself will design the setting for the record-sized diamond, which will go on display later this month at the Metropolitan Museum of Art.

No word yet on the exact plans for the stone, but we can't help but wonder if an engagement ring might be in the works. Diamond heiress Diana Drake stepped out again last night with her current flame, polo-playing hottie Franco Andrade, at a private party at Harry Winston. Cell phone photos snapped by guests show the couple engaged in some scorching hot PDA. Caution: viewing these pictures will have you clutching your Drake Diamonds pearls.

Chapter Ten

*P*op!

The store hadn't even opened yet, and already the staff of Drake Diamonds was on its third bottle of champagne. The table in the center of the Drake-blue kitchen was piled with empty Waterford glasses and stacks upon stacks of newspapers.

Drake Diamonds and the Lamberti diamond were front-page news.

"Congratulations, Diana." Ophelia clinked her glass against Diana's and took a dainty sip of her Veuve Clicquot. "Well done."

"Thank you." Diana grinned. It felt good to succeed at something again. Although it probably should have felt better than it actually did.

Stop. You earned this. You have nothing to feel guilty about.

She swallowed and concentrated her attention on Ophelia. "Congratulations right back at you. Have you started sketching designs for the stone yet?"

Ophelia laughed. "Our involvement has only been official for about an hour, remember?"

Diana lifted a dubious brow. "So until now you've given the Lamberti diamond no thought whatsoever?"

Ophelia's expression turned sheepish. "Okay, so maybe I've been working on a few preliminary designs… just in case."

Diana laughed. "It never hurts to be prepared."

Artem's voice boomed over the chatter in the crowded room. "Okay, everyone. The doors open in five minutes. Party time's over."

Ophelia set her glass down on the table. "I'm off, then. Duty calls."

"Something tells me your job won't be in jeopardy if you hang out a little while longer," Diana said in a mock whisper.

"I know, but I seriously can't wait to get to work on the design now that I know I'm actually going to get my hands on that diamond. I almost can't believe it's happening. It hasn't quite sunk in yet." Her eyes shone with wonder. "This is real, isn't it?"

Diana took a deep breath.

This is real, isn't it?

The memory of Franco's touch hit her hard and fast… the dance of his fingertips moving down her spine…the way his hands had circled her wrists, holding her still as he kissed her…

She was beginning to lose track of what was genuine and what wasn't.

"Believe it. It's real." She swallowed around the lump in her throat and gave Ophelia one last smile before she found herself alone in the kitchen with Artem.

Diana reached for one of the tiny cakes they kept on hand decorated to look like Drake-blue boxes and bit into it. Ah, comfort food. She could use a sugary dose of comfort right now, although she wasn't quite sure why.

You're getting everything you wanted.

Why had she felt like crying when Franco uttered those words the night before?

"Can we talk for a moment, sis?" Artem sank into one of the kitchen chairs.

"Sure." Diana sat down beside him. She was in no hurry to get back to Dalton's empty apartment. She'd rather be here, where things were celebratory.

When she'd first read the news that the Lambertis had, indeed, chosen Drake Diamonds, she'd been propped up in bed sipping her morning coffee and reading her iPad. Seeing the official press announcement hadn't given her the thrill she'd been anticipating.

If she was being honest, it almost felt like a letdown. She didn't want to examine the reasons why, and she most definitely didn't want to be alone with her thoughts. Because those thoughts kept circling back to last night.

Kissing Franco. The feel of his mouth on hers, wet and wanting. The look on his face when he spotted the Lambertis.

"You okay?" Artem looked at her, and the smile that had been plastered on his face all morning began to fade.

Diana leaned over and gave him an affectionate shoulder bump. "Of course. I'm more than okay."

But she couldn't quite bring herself to meet his gaze, so she focused instead on the table in front of them and its giant pile of newspapers. The corner of *Page Six* poked out from beneath the *New York Times*, and she caught a glimpse of the now-familiar grainy image of herself and Franco kissing.

Her throat grew tight.

She squeezed her eyes closed.

"I hope that's true, sis. I do. Because I have some concerns," Artem said.

Diana's eyes flew open. "Concerns. About what?"

He paused and seemed to be choosing his words with great care.

"You and Franco," he said at last.

She blinked. "Me and Franco?"

Artem's gaze flitted to *Page Six*. "I'm starting to wonder if this charade has gone too far."

"You can't be serious. The whole plan was your idea." She waved a hand at the empty bottles of Veuve Clicquot littering the kitchen. "And it worked. We did it, Artem."

"Yes. So far it's been a remarkable success." He nodded thoughtfully. "For the company. But some things are more important than business."

Who was his guy and what had he done with her brother? Everything they'd done for the past few weeks had been for the sake of Drake Diamonds. "What are you getting at, Artem?"

But she didn't have to ask. Deep down, she knew.

"This." He pulled the copy of *Page Six* out from beneath the *Times* and tossed it on top of the pile.

She didn't want to look at it. It hurt too much to see herself like that.

"It was just a kiss, Artem." Her brother was watching her closely, waiting for her to crack, so she forced herself to look at the photograph.

It was worse than the enormous billboard in Times Square. So much worse. Probably because this time she hadn't been acting. This time, she'd wanted Franco to take her to bed.

Her self-control was beginning to slip. Along with her

common sense. The kiss had pushed her right over the edge. It had made her forget all the reasons she despised him. Even now, she was still struggling to remember his numerous bad qualities. It was like she was suffering from some kind of hormone-induced amnesia.

Artem lifted a brow. Thank God he couldn't see inside her head. "That looks like more than *just a kiss* to me."

"As it should." She crossed her arms, leaned back in her chair and glared at him. He was pulling the overprotective brother act on her now? *Seriously?* "The whole point of our courtship is to make people believe it's real. Remember?"

"Of course I remember. And yes, I'm quite aware it was my idea. But I never said anything about kissing." He shot her a meaningful glance. "Or making out in dark corners. Where was this picture taken? Because this looks much more like a private moment than a public relations party stunt."

It took every ounce of will power Diana possessed to refrain from wadding up the paper and throwing it at him. "I can't believe what I'm hearing. For your information, the only reason I kissed him was because the Lambertis were walking straight toward us. I had to do something. I didn't want them to think Franco and I were arguing."

"Were you?" Artem raised his brows. "Arguing?"

She sighed. "No. Yes. Well, sort of."

"If there's nothing actually going on between you and Franco, what do you have to argue about?"

Diana shifted in her chair. Maybe Artem *could* see inside her head.

Of course he couldn't. Still, she should have had a dozen answers at the ready. People who weren't lovers argued all the time, didn't they?

But she couldn't seem capable of coming up with a

single viable excuse. She just sat there praying for him to stop asking questions.

Finally, Artem put her out of her long, silent misery. "Is there something you should tell me, Diana?"

"There's nothing going on between Franco and me. I promise." Why did that sound like a lie when it was the truth?

Worse, why did the truth feel so painful?

You do not *have feelings for Franco Andrade. Not again.*

"You're a grown-up. I get that. It's just that you're my sister. And as you so vehemently pointed out less than two weeks ago, Franco is a man whore." Artem looked pointedly at the photo splashed across *Page Six*. "I'm starting to think this whole farce was a really bad idea."

"Look, I appreciate the concern. But I can handle myself around Franco. The kiss was my idea, and it meant nothing." It wasn't supposed to, anyway. "End of story."

She stood and began clearing away the dirty champagne flutes and tossing the empty Veuve Clicquot bottles into the recycling bin. She couldn't just sit there and talk about this anymore.

"Got it." To Diana's great relief, Artem rose from his chair and headed toward the hallway.

But he lingered in the doorway for a last word on the subject. "You know, we can stop this right now. You've proven your point. You have a lot to offer Drake Diamonds. I was wrong to put you in this position."

"What?" She turned to face him.

Surely she hadn't heard him right.

He nodded and gave her a bittersweet smile. "I was wrong. And I'm sorry. Say the word, and your fake relationship with Franco can end in a spectacular or not-so-spectacular fake breakup. Your choice."

Her choice.

But she didn't have a choice. Not really.

A week ago, she would have given anything to get Franco out of her life. Now it didn't seem right. Not when she'd gotten what she needed out of the deal and Franco apparently hadn't.

Smile, darling, you're getting everything you wanted.

He'd played his part, and she owed it to him to play hers. Like or not, they were stuck together until the gala.

"You know that's not possible, Artem. We haven't even finalized things with the Lambertis. They could take their diamond and hightail it over to Harry Winston."

"I know they could. I'm beginning to wonder if it would really be so awful if they did." Artem sighed, and she could tell just by the look on his face that he was thinking about the photo again. *Page Six.* The kiss. "Is it really worth all of this? Is anything?"

"Absolutely." She nodded, but a tiny part of her wondered if he might be right. "You're making a big deal out of nothing. I promise."

It was too late for doubts. She'd made her bed, and now she had to lie in it. Preferably alone.

Liar.

Artem nodded and looked slightly relieved, which was still a good deal more relieved than Diana actually felt. "I suppose I should know better than to believe everything I read in the papers, right?"

She picked up the copy of *Page Six*, intent on burying it at the bottom of the recycling bin. It trembled in her hand.

She tossed it back onto the surface of the table and crossed her arms. "Exactly."

How was she going to survive until the gala? She

dreaded seeing Franco later. Now that he seemed intent on not kissing her again, it was all she could think about.

Even worse, how could she look herself in the mirror when she could barely look her brother in the eye?

Franco gave the white ball a brutal whack with his mallet and watched it soar through the grass right between the goal posts at the far end of the practice field on his Hamptons property.

Another meaningless score.

His efforts didn't count when he was the only player on the field. But he needed to be here, as much for his ponies as for himself. They needed to stay in shape. They needed to be ready, even if it was beginning to look less and less like they'd be returning to the Kingsmen.

Last night had been a reality check in more ways than one. He wasn't sure what had enraged him more—seeing his number on another player's chest or realizing Diana had asked him to kiss her purely for show.

He knew his fury was in no way rational, particularly where Diana was concerned. Their entire arrangement was based on deception. He just hadn't realized he would be the one being deceived.

But even that shouldn't have mattered. He shouldn't have cared one way or another whether Diana really wanted his mouth on hers.

And yet…he did care.

He cared far more than he ever thought he would.

I'm not yours, Mr. Andrade. Never have been, never will be.

Franco wiped sweat from his brow with his forearm, rested his mallet over his shoulder and slowed his horse to an easy canter. As he watched the mare's thick muscles move beneath the velvety surface of her coat, he thought of Diamond.

He thought about Diana's dead horse every time he rode now. He thought about the way she could barely seem to make herself say Diamond's name. He thought about her reluctance to even hold Lulu. She was afraid of getting attached to another animal. That much was obvious. Only one thing would fix that.

She needed to ride again.

Of course, getting Diana back in the saddle was the last thing he should be concerned about when he couldn't even manage to get himself back on his team.

That hadn't stopped him from dropping Lulu off at Drake Diamonds before he'd headed to the Hamptons. Artem's secretary, Mrs. Barnes, had looked at him like he was crazy when he'd handed her the puppy and asked her to give it to Diana. Maybe he *had* gone crazy. But if he'd forced the dog on Diana himself, she would have simply refused.

She needed the dog. Franco had never in his life met anyone who'd needed another living creature so much. Other than himself when he'd been a boy...

Maybe that's why he cared so much about helping Diana. Despite their vastly different upbringings, he understood her. Whether she wanted to admit it or not.

Let it go. You have enough problems of your own without adding Diana Drake's to the mix.

She didn't want his help, anyway, and that was fine. He was finished with her. As soon as the gala was over and once he had his job back, they'd never see each other again. He was practically counting the minutes.

"Andrade," someone called from the direction of the stalls where Franco's other horses were resting and munching on hay in the shade.

Franco squinted into the setting sun. As he headed off the field, he spotted a familiar figure walking toward him across the emerald-green grass.

Luc.

Franco slid out of his saddle and passed the horse's reins to one of his grooms. *"Gracias."*

It wasn't until he'd closed the distance between himself and his friend that he recognized a faint stirring in his chest. Hope. Which only emphasized how pathetic his situation was at the moment. If the Kingsmen wanted him back, the coach wouldn't send Luc. Santos would be here. Maybe even Ellis himself.

He removed his helmet and raked a hand through his dampened hair. "Luc."

"Hola, mano." Luc nodded toward the goal, where the white ball still sat in the grass. "Looking good out there."

"Thanks, man." An awkward silence settled between them. Franco cleared his throat. "How was the scrimmage yesterday?"

Luc's gaze met his. Held. "It was complete and utter shit."

"I wish I could say I was surprised. Gustavo Anca. Really? He's a six-goal player." Not that a handicap of six was bad. Plenty of world-class players were ranked as such. But Franco's handicap was eight. On an average day, Gustavo Anca wouldn't even be able to give him a run for his money. On a good day, Franco would have wiped the ground with him.

Luc nodded. "Well, it showed."

Franco said nothing. If Luc was hoping for company in his commiseration, he'd just have to be disappointed.

"Look, Franco. I came here to tell you I can't let this go on. Not anymore." Franco shook his head, but before he could audibly protest, Luc held up a hand. "I don't want to hear it. We've waited long enough. The Kingsmen are going to lose every damn game this season if we don't get you back. I'm going to Jack Ellis first thing in the morning, and I'm going to tell him the truth."

"No, you're not," Franco said through gritted teeth.

He'd made a promise, and he intended to keep it. Even if that promise had sent his life into a tailspin.

"It's not up for discussion. I don't know why I let you talk me into this in the first place." Luc shook his head and dropped his gaze to the ground.

He knew why. They both did.

"It's too late to come clean." Would Ellis even believe them if they told the truth this late in the game? Would anyone? Franco doubted it, especially in Diana's case. She'd made up her mind about him a long time ago.

But why should her opinion matter? She had nothing to do with this. Their lives had simply become so intertwined that Franco could no longer keep track of where his ended and hers began.

"I don't believe that. It's not too late. I love you like a brother. You know I do. You don't owe me a thing, Franco. You never did, and you certainly don't owe me this." Luc looked up again with red-rimmed eyes.

Why was he making this so difficult? "What's done is done. Besides, what's the point? If you tell the truth, you know what will happen."

"Yeah, I do. You'll be in, and I'll be out, which is precisely the way it should be." Luc blew out a ragged exhale. "This is bigger than the two of us, Franco. It's about the team now."

He was hitting Franco where it hurt, and he knew it. The team had always come first for Franco. Before the women, before the partying, before everything.

Until now.

Some things were bigger. Luc was family. Without Luc, Franco would never have played for the Kingsmen to begin with. He would have never even left Buenos Aires. He'd probably still be sleeping in a barn at night, or worse. He might have gone back to where he'd come from. Barrio de la Boca.

He liked to think that horses had saved him. But, in reality, it had been Luc.

He exhaled a weary sigh. "What's the point anymore? The Kingsmen can't lose you, either. If you do this, the team will suffer just as much as it already has."

"No. It won't." A horse whinnied in the distance. Luc smiled. "You're better than I am. You always were."

Franco's chest grew tight, and he had the distinct feeling they weren't talking about polo anymore.

"I came here as a courtesy, so you'd be prepared when Ellis calls you tomorrow. This is happening. Get ready." Luc turned to go.

Franco glared at the back of his head. "And if things change between now and tomorrow?"

Luc turned around. Threw his hands in the air. "What could possibly change?"

Everything.

Everything could change.

And Franco knew just how to make certain it would.

Chapter Eleven

Diana was running out of ball gowns, but that wasn't her most pressing problem at the moment. That notable distinction belonged to the problem that had four legs and a tail and had peed on her carpet three times in the past two hours.

As if Franco hadn't already made her life miserable enough, now he'd forced the puppy upon her. After Diana's awkward encounter with Artem in the Drake Diamonds kitchen, Mrs. Barnes had waltzed in and thrust the little black pug at her. She'd had no choice but to take the dog home. Now here they sat, waiting for Ophelia to show up with a new crop of evening wear.

Diana had never needed so many gowns, considering thus far she'd spent the better part of her life in riding clothes. But she'd worn nearly every fancy dress she owned over the course of her faux love affair with Franco, and she wanted to make an impression tonight. More than ever before.

The Manhattan Ballet's annual gala at Lincoln Center was one of the most important social events on the Drake Diamonds calendar. Ophelia had once been a prima ballerina at the company. Since coming to Drake Diamonds, she'd designed an entire ballet-themed jewelry collection. Naturally, the store and the Manhattan Ballet worked closely with each other.

Which meant Artem and Ophelia would be at the gala. So would the press, obviously. Coming right on the heels of the Lamberti diamond announcement, the gala would be a big deal. Huge.

It would also be the first time Diana had seen Franco since The Kiss.

But of course that had nothing to do with the fact that she wanted to look extra spectacular. Then again, maybe it did. A little.

Okay, a lot.

She wanted to torture him. First he'd had the nerve to get upset that she'd asked him to kiss her, and now he'd dropped a puppy in her lap. Who behaved like that?

Lulu let out a little yip and spun in circles, chasing her curlicue tail. The dog was cute. No doubt about it. And Diana didn't completely hate her tiny, velvet-soft ears and round little belly. If she'd had any interest in adopting a puppy, this one would definitely have been a contender.

But she wasn't ready to sign on for another heartbreak in the making. Wasn't her heart in enough jeopardy as it was?

Damn you, Franco.

"Don't get too comfortable," she said.

Lulu cocked her head, increasing her adorable quotient at least tenfold.

Ugh. "I mean it. You're not staying."

One night. That was it. Two, tops.

The doorbell rang, and Lulu scrambled toward the door in a frenzy of high-pitched barks and snorting noises. Somehow, her cuteness remained intact despite the commotion.

"Calm down, you nut." Diana scooped her up with one hand, and the puppy licked her chin.

Three nights...maybe. Then she was absolutely going back to Franco's bachelor pad.

"A puppy!" Ophelia grinned from ear to ear when Diana opened the door. "This must the one I read about in the paper."

Diana sighed. She'd almost forgotten that every detail of her life was now splashed across *Page Six*. Puppy included. "The one and only."

"She's seriously adorable. Franco has good taste in dogs. He can't be all bad." Ophelia floated through the front door of Diana's apartment with a garment bag slung over her shoulder. She might not be a professional ballerina anymore, but she still moved liked one, even with a baby strapped to her chest.

Diana rolled her eyes and returned Lulu to the floor, where she resumed chewing on a rawhide bone that was three times bigger than her own head. "I'm pretty sure even the devil himself can appreciate a cute puppy."

"The last time I checked, the devil wasn't into rescuing homeless animals." Point taken.

Ophelia tossed the garment bags across the arm of the sofa. "Enough about your charming puppy and equally charming faux boyfriend. I've come with fashion reinforcements, as you requested."

"And you brought my niece." Diana eyed the baby.

There was no denying she was precious. She had Artem's eyes and Ophelia's delicate features. Perfect in every way.

Diana just wasn't one of those women who swooned every time she saw a baby. Probably because she'd never pictured herself as a mother. Not after the nightmare of a marriage her own mother had endured.

"Here, hold her." Ophelia lifted little Emma out of the baby sling and handed her to Diana.

"Um, okay." She'd never really held Emma before. She'd oohed and aahed over her. Plenty of times. But other than the occasional, affectionate pat on the head, she hadn't actually touched her.

She was lighter than Diana had expected. Soft. Warm.

"Wow," she said as Emma took Diana's hand in her tiny grip.

"She growing like a weed, isn't she?" Ophelia beamed at her baby.

Diana studied the tender expression on her face. It wasn't altogether different from the one she usually wore when she looked at Artem. "You're completely in love with this baby, aren't you?"

"It shows?"

"You couldn't hide it if you tried." Diana rocked Emma gently from side to side until the baby's eyes drifted closed.

"It's crazy. I never pictured myself as a mother." Ophelia shrugged one of her elegant shoulders.

Diana gaped at her. "You're kidding."

"Nope. I never expected to get married, either. Your brother actually had to talk me into it." She grinned. "He can be very persuasive."

"I had no idea. You and Artem are like a dream couple."

"Things aren't always how they appear on the outside. But I don't need to tell you that." Ophelia gave her a knowing look.

Diana swallowed. "I should probably be an expert on the subject by now."

"I love your brother, and I adore Emma. I've never been so happy." And it showed. Bliss radiated from her sister-in-law's pores. "This life just isn't one I ever imagined for myself."

Maybe that's how it always worked. Maybe one day Diana would wake up and magically be ready to slip one of those legendary Drake diamonds onto her ring finger.

Doubtful, considering she was terrified of keeping the puppy currently making herself at home in Diana's borrowed apartment. "Can I ask you a question?"

"Sure. That's what sisters are for," Ophelia said.

"What changed? I mean, I know that sounds like a difficult question..."

Ophelia interrupted her with a shake of her head. "No. It's not difficult at all. It's simple, really. Love changed me."

"Love," Diana echoed, as the front-page image of herself being kissed within an inch of her life flashed before her eyes.

Please. That wasn't love. It wasn't even lust. It was pretend.

Keep telling yourself that.

"I fell in love, and that changed everything." Ophelia regarded her for a moment. "I may be way off base here, but do these questions have anything to do with Franco?"

"Hardly." Diana laughed. A little too loudly.

She couldn't ignore the truth anymore...she had a serious case of lust for the man. Everyone in New York knew she did. It was literally front-page news.

But she would have to be insane to fall in love with him. She didn't even like him. When she'd had her accident, she hadn't hit her head so hard that she lost her memory.

The day after she'd lost her virginity to Franco had been the most humiliating of her life. She'd known what she'd been getting into when she slept with him. Or thought she had, anyway.

She'd been all too aware of his reputation. Franco Andrade was a player. Not just a polo player...a *player* player. In truth, that was why she'd chosen him. His ridiculous good looks and devastating charm hadn't hurt, obviously. But mainly she'd wanted to experience sex without any looming expectation of a relationship.

She'd been twenty-two, which was more than old enough to sleep with a man. It hadn't been the sex that frightened her. It had been the idea of belonging to someone. Someone who would cheat, as her father had done for as long she could remember.

Franco had been the perfect candidate.

She'd expected hot, dirty sex. And she'd gotten it. But he'd also been tender. Unexpectedly sweet. Still, it was her own stupid fault she'd fallen for the fantasy.

She'd rather die than make that mistake again.

"Nothing at all? If you say so. There just seems to be a spark between you two," Ophelia said. "I'm pretty sure it's visible from outer space."

Diana handed the baby back to her sister-in-law. "Honestly, you sound like Artem. Did he put you up to this?"

Ophelia held Emma against her chest and rubbed her hand in soothing circles on the back of the baby's pastel pink onesie. Her brow furrowed. "No, actually. We haven't even discussed it."

Diana narrowed her gaze. "Then why are you asking me about Franco?"

"I told you. There's something special when you're together." She grinned. "Magic."

Like the kind of magic that made people believe in relationships? Marriage? *Family?* "You're seeing things. Seriously, Ophelia. You're looking at the world through love-colored glasses."

Ophelia laughed. "I don't think those are a thing."

"Trust me. They are. And you're wearing them." Diana slid closer to the garment bag and pulled it onto her lap. "A big, giant pair."

Ophelia shook her head, smiled and made cooing noises at the baby. Which pretty much proved Diana's point.

"By the way, there's only one dress in there." Ophelia nodded at the garment bag. "It's perfect for tonight. You'll look amazing in it. I was afraid if I brought more options, you wouldn't have the guts to wear this one. And you really must."

"Why am I afraid to look at it now?" Diana unzipped the bag and gasped when she got a glimpse of silver lamé fabric so luxurious that it looked like liquid platinum.

"Gorgeous, isn't it? It belonged to my grandmother. She wore it to a ballet gala herself, back in the 1940s."

Diana shook her head. "I can't borrow this. It's too special."

"Don't be silly. Of course you can. That's why I brought it." Ophelia bit her lip. "Franco is going to die when he sees you in it."

First Artem. Now Ophelia. When had everyone started believing the hype?

"Not if I kill him first," she said flatly.

The more she thought about his reaction last night, the angrier she got. How dare he call her out for doing exactly the same thing he'd been doing every night for a week?

Did he think the nicknames, the lingering glances and the way he touched her all the time didn't get to her? Newsflash: they did.

Sometimes she went home from their evenings together and her body felt so tingly, so alive that she had trouble sleeping. Last night, he'd even shown up in her dreams.

Her head spun a little just thinking about it. "I have no interest in him whatsoever."

"Yeah, you mentioned that." Ophelia smirked.

A telltale warmth crept into Diana's cheeks. "I'm serious. I'm not interested in marriage or babies, either. Certainly not with him."

"I believe you." Ophelia nodded in mock solemnity.

Even the puppy stopped chewing on her bone to stare at Diana with her buggy little eyes.

"Stop looking at me like that. Both of you. I assure you, it will be a long time before you see an engagement ring on my finger. And *if* that ever happens, the ring won't be from Franco Andrade."

He was about as far from being husband material as she was from being wife material. Diana should know…

She'd spent an embarrassing amount of time thinking it through.

Dios mío.

A little under twenty-four hours had hardly been enough time to rid Franco of the memory of kissing Diana. But the moment he set eyes on her in her liquid silver dress, everything came flooding back. The taste of her. The feel of her. The sound of her—the catch of her breath in the moment their lips came together, the tremble in her voice when she'd asked him to kiss her.

No amount of willful forgetting would erase those

memories. Certainly not while Diana was standing beside him in the lobby of Lincoln Center looking like she'd been dipped in diamonds.

A strand of emerald-cut stones had been interwoven through the satin neckline of her gown and arranged into a glittering bow just off-center from the massive sapphire draped around her neck. She looked almost too perfect to touch.

Which made Franco want to touch her all the more.

"You're staring," she said, without a trace of emotion in her voice. But the corner of her lush mouth curved into a grin that smacked of self-satisfaction.

Franco had a mind to kiss her right there on the spot.

He smiled tightly, instead. She hadn't said a word yet about the puppy stunt, which he found particularly interesting. But she was angry with him. For what, exactly, he wasn't quite sure. He was beginning to lose track of all the wrongs he'd committed, and tomorrow would be far worse. She just didn't know it yet.

He cleared his throat. "I can't seem to look away. Forgive me."

She shrugged an elegant shoulder. The row of diamonds woven through the bodice of her dress glittered under the chandelier overhead. "You're forgiven."

Forgiven.

The word and its myriad of implications hung between them.

He raised a brow. "Am I?"

He knew better than to believe it.

"It's a figure of speech. Don't read too much into it." She shifted her gaze away from him, toward the crowd assembled in the grand opera-house lobby.

Franco slipped an arm around her and led her down the red-carpeted stairs toward the party. He'd been dreading the Manhattan Ballet gala since the moment he'd woken up this morning. He'd lost his head at the Harry Winston party. He couldn't make a mistake like that again. Not now. Not when there was so much riding on his fake relationship. The Drakes may have gotten what they wanted, but Franco hadn't.

He would, though.

By tomorrow morning, everything would change.

"Diana, nice to see you. You look beautiful." Artem greeted his sister with a smile and a kiss on the cheek. When he turned toward Franco, his smile faded. "Franco."

No handshake. No small talk. Just a sharp look that felt oddly like a warning glare.

"Artem." Franco reached to shake his hand.

Something felt off, but Franco couldn't imagine why. Artem Drake should be the happiest man in Manhattan right now. His family business was front-page news. Everywhere Franco turned, people were talking about the Lamberti diamond. A few news outlets had even rechristened it the Lamberti-Drake diamond.

Would the Lambertis have even chosen Drake Diamonds if not for the pretend love affair? Franco wholeheartedly doubted it. The Lambertis had looked awfully comfortable at Harry Winston.

Until the kiss.

The kiss had been the deciding factor. Or so it seemed.

The way Franco saw things, Artem Drake should be high-fiving him right now.

Maybe he was just imagining things. After all, last night had been frustrating on every possible level. Most notably, sexually. Franco still couldn't think straight. Especially when Diana's silvery image was reflected back at him from all four walls of the mirrored room. There was simply no escaping it.

"Nice to see you again, Franco," Ophelia said warmly.

"Thank you. It's a pleasure to be here." He moved to give Ophelia a one-armed hug. Artem's gaze narrowed, and he tossed back the remainder of the champagne in his glass.

"I'm sure it is," Artem muttered under his breath.

Franco cast a questioning glance at Diana. He definitely wasn't imagining things.

"Shall we go get a drink, darling?" she said.

"Yes, let's." A drink was definitely in order. Possibly many drinks.

Once they'd taken their place in line at the bar, Franco bent to whisper in Diana's ear, doing his best not to let his gaze wander to her cleavage, barely covered by a wisp of pale gray chiffon fabric. It would have been a tall order for any man. "Are you planning on telling me what's troubling your brother? Or do I have to remain in the dark since I'm just a pretend boyfriend?"

Diana's bottom lip slipped between her teeth, a nervous habit he'd spent far too much time thinking about in recent days. After a pause, she shrugged. "I don't know what you're talking about."

"Do you really think I can't tell when you're lying?" He leaned closer, until his lips grazed the soft place just below her ear. "Because I can. I know you better than you think, Diana. Your body betrays you."

Her cheeks flared pink. "I'm going to pretend you didn't just say that."

"I'm sure you will." He looked pointedly at her mouth. "We both know how good you are at pretending."

"May I help you?" the bartender asked.

"Two glasses of Dom Pérignon, please," Franco said without taking his eyes off Diana.

"You're impossible," she said through gritted teeth.

"So you've told me." He handed her one of the two saucer-style glasses of champagne the bartender had given him. "Multiple times."

Her eyes flashed like amethysts on fire. "You've had your hands all over me for weeks, and I'm not allowed to be affected by it. But I kiss you once, and you completely lose it. You're acting like the world's biggest hypocrite."

The accusation should have angered him. At the very least, he should have been bothered by the fact that she was one hundred percent right. He was definitely acting like a hypocrite, but he couldn't seem to stop.

He'd thought the kiss was real. He'd *wanted* it to be real. He wanted that more than he'd wanted anything in a long, long time.

But he was so shocked by Diana's startling admission that he couldn't bring himself to be anything but satisfied at the moment. Satisfied and, admittedly, a little aroused.

"You like it when I touch you," he stated. It was a fact. She'd said so herself.

"No." She let out a forced laugh. "Hardly."

Yes.

Definitely.

"It's nothing to be ashamed of," he said, reaching for her with his free hand and cupping her cheek. "Would you like it if I touched you now?"

He lowered his gaze to her throat, where he could see the flutter of her pulse just above her sapphire necklace. In the depths of the gemstone, he spied a hint of his own reflection. It was like looking into a dark and dangerous mirror.

"Would *you* like it if I kissed you?" She lifted an impertinent brow.

Franco smiled in response. If she wanted to rattle him, she'd have to try harder.

"I'd like that very much. I see no need to pretend otherwise." He sipped his champagne. "I'd just prefer the kiss to be genuine."

"For your information, that kiss was more genuine than you'll ever know. Which is exactly why Artem is angry." Her gaze flitted toward her brother standing on the other side of the room.

Franco narrowed his gaze at Artem Drake. "Let me get this straight. Your brother wanted us to make everyone believe we were a couple, and now he's angry because we've done just that?"

Diana shook her head. "Not angry. Just concerned."

"About what exactly?"

She cleared her throat and stared into her champagne glass. "He thinks we've taken things too far."

Too far.

As irritating as Franco found Artem Drake's assessment of the situation, Diana's brother might be on to something.

He and Diana had crossed a line. Somewhere along the way, they'd become more to each other than business associates with a common goal.

Perhaps they'd been more than that all along. Every time Franco caught a glimpse of that massive billboard in Times Square he found himself wondering if they were somehow finishing what they'd started three years ago. Like time had been holding its breath waiting for the two of them to come together again.

He knew it was crazy. He'd never believed much in fate. Was it fate that he'd been born into the worst slum in Buenos Aires? No, fate wouldn't be so cruel. He was in control of his life. No one else.

But kissing Diana had almost been enough to make a believer out of him.

They weren't finished with each other. Not yet.

"And what about you, Diana? Do you think we've taken things too far?" He leveled his gaze at her, daring her to tell the truth.

Not far enough. Not by a long shot.

Chapter Twelve

When had things gotten so confusing?

A month ago, Diana had been bored out of her mind selling engagement rings, and now she was standing in the middle of the biggest society gala of the year being interrogated by Franco Andrade.

He shouldn't be capable of rattling her the way he did. The questions he was asking should have had easy answers.

Had they taken things too far?

Absolutely. That had happened the instant he'd fastened the sapphire around her neck. She should never have agreed to pose with him. That one photo had set things in motion that were now spinning wildly out of control.

Then she'd gone and exacerbated things by agreeing to be his pretend girlfriend. Worse yet, since she'd asked him to kiss her, she'd begun to doubt her motivation.

Did she really want to be co-CEO of Drake Diamonds? Had she ever? Or had the promotion simply been a convenient excuse to spend more time with Franco?

Surely not. She hated him. She hated everything about him.

You like it when I touch you.

Damn him and his smug self-confidence. She would have loved to prove him wrong, except she couldn't. She loved it when he touched her. The barest graze of his fingertips sent her reeling. And now she'd gone and admitted it to his face.

She lifted her chin and met his gaze. "Of course we haven't taken things too far. We're both doing our jobs. Nothing more."

"I see. And last night your job included kissing me." The corner of his mouth curved into a half grin, and all she could think about was the way that mouth had felt crashing down on hers.

"You seriously need to let that go." How could she possibly forget it when he kept bringing it up? "Besides, *you* kissed *me*."

"At your request." He lifted a brow.

Her gaze flitted to his bow tie. Looking him in the eye and pretending she didn't want to kiss him again was becoming next to impossible. "Same thing."

"Hardly. When I decide to kiss you, you'll know it. There will be no mistaking my intention." There was a sudden edge to his voice that reminded her of Artem's offer to end this farce once and for all.

Say the word, and your fake relationship with Franco can end in a spectacular or not-so-spectacular fake breakup. Your choice.

Her choice.

She'd had a choice all along, whether she wanted to admit it or not. And she'd chosen Franco. Again.

She was beginning to have the sinking feeling that she always would.

She'd tried her best to keep up her resistance. She really had. The constant onslaught of his devastating good looks paired with the unrelenting innuendo had taken its toll. But his intensity had dealt the deathblow to her defenses.

He cared. Deeply. He cared about Diamond. He cared about why she refused to ride again. That's why he'd forced her hand about the puppy. She'd known as much the moment that Mrs. Barnes had dropped the wiggling little pug into her arms.

Despite his playboy reputation and devil-may-care charm, Franco Andrade cared. He even cared about the kiss.

A girl could only take so much.

"What are you waiting for, then?" she asked, with far more confidence than she actually felt. She reminded herself that she knew exactly what she was doing. But she'd thought the same thing three years ago, hadn't she? "Decide."

A muscle tensed in Franco's jaw.

Then, in one swift motion, he gathered their champagne glasses and deposited them on a nearby tray. He took her hand and led her through the crowded lobby, toward a shadowed corridor. For once, Diana was unaware of the eyes following them everywhere they went. She didn't care who saw them. She didn't care about the Lambertis. She didn't care about the rest of the Drakes. She didn't even care about the press.

The only thing she cared about was where Franco was taking her and what would happen once they got there.

Decide, she'd implored. And decide he had.

"Come here," he groaned, and the timbre in his voice seemed to light tiny fires over every exposed surface of her skin.

He pushed through a closed door, pulling her alongside him, and suddenly they were surrounded on all sides by lush red velvet. Diana blinked into the darkness until the soft gold glow of a dimly lit stage came into focus.

He'd brought her inside the theater, and they were alone at last. In a room that typically held thousands of people. It felt strangely intimate to be surrounded by row upon row of empty seats, the silent orchestra pit and so much rich crimson. Even more so when Franco's hand slid to cradle the back of her head and his eyes burned into hers.

"This is for us and us alone. No one else." His gaze dropped to her mouth.

Diana's heart felt like it might beat right out of her chest. *You can stop this now. It's not too late.*

But it was, wasn't it? She'd all but dared him to kiss her, and she wasn't about to back down now.

She lifted her chin so that his mouth was perfectly poised over hers. "No one else."

He grazed her bottom lip with the pad of his thumb, then bent to kiss her. She expected passion. She expected frantic hunger. She expected him to crush his mouth to hers. Instead, the first deliberate touch of his lips was gentle. Tender. So reverent that she knew within moments it was a mistake.

She'd fought hard to stay numb after her fall. The less she felt, the better. So long as she kept the world at arm's length, she'd never have to relive the nightmare of what she'd been through. But tenderness—especially coming from Franco—had a way of dragging her back to life, whether or not she was ready.

"Diana," he whispered, and his voice echoed throughout the room with a ghostly elegance that made her head spin.

She'd wanted him to kiss her again since the moment their lips parted the night before. She'd craved it. But as his tongue slid into her mouth, hot and hungry, she realized she wanted more. So much more.

Was it possible to relive only part of the past? Could she sleep with him again and experience the exquisite sensation of Franco pushing inside her without the subsequent heartache?

Maybe she could. She wasn't a young, naive girl anymore. She was a grown woman. She could take him to bed with her eyes wide open this time, knowing it was purely physical and nothing more.

My choice.

He pushed her against a velvet wall and when his hands slid over the curves of her hips, she realized she was arching into him, pressing herself against the swell of his arousal. She could spend all the time in the world weighing the consequences, but clearly her body knew what it wanted. And it had made up its mind a long time ago.

Your body betrays you.

He'd been right about that, too, damn him.

"Franco," she murmured against his mouth. Was that really her voice? She scarcely recognized herself anymore.

But that only added to the thrill of the moment. She was tired of being Diana Drake. Disciplined athlete. Diamond heiress and future CEO. Perpetual good girl.

She wanted to be bad for a change.

"Yes, love?" His mouth was on her neck now, and his hands were sliding up the smooth silver satin of her dress to cup her breasts.

She was on fire, on the verge of asking him to make love to her right there in the theatre.

No. If she was going to do this, she wanted it to last. And she wanted to be the one in control. She refused to get hurt this time. She couldn't. Wouldn't.

But as she let her hands slip inside Franco's tuxedo jacket and up his solid, muscular back, she didn't much care about what happened tomorrow. How much worse could things get, anyway?

"Come home with me, Franco."

Franco half expected her to change her mind before they made it back to her apartment. If she did, it would have killed him. But he'd honor her decision, obviously.

He wanted her, though. He wanted her so much it hurt.

By the time they reached the threshold of her front door, he was harder than he'd ever been in his life. Diana gave no indication that she'd changed her mind. On the contrary, she wove her fingers through his and pulled him inside the apartment. The door hadn't even clicked shut behind them before she draped her arms around his neck and kissed him.

It was a kiss full of intention. A prelude. And damned if it didn't nearly drag him to his knees.

"Diana," he groaned into her mouth.

Everything was happening so fast. Too fast. He'd waited a long time for this. Three excruciating years. Waiting…wanting.

"Slow down, love." He needed to savor. And she needed to be adored, whether she realized it or not.

She pulled back to look at him, eyes blazing. "Just so you know, this is hate sex."

He met her gaze. Held it, until her cheeks turned a telltale shade of pink.

Keep on telling yourself that, darling.

He drew his fingertip beneath one of the slender straps of her evening gown, gave it a gentle tug and watched as it fell from her shoulder, baring one of her breasts. He didn't touch her, just drank in the sight of her—breathless, ready. Her nipple was the palest pink, as delicate as a rose petal. When it puckered under his gaze, he finally looked her in the eye.

"Hate sex. Obviously." He gave her a half smile. "What else would it be?"

"I'm serious. I loathe you." But as she said those words, she slid the other spaghetti strap off her shoulder and let her dress fall to the floor in a puddle of silver satin.

I don't believe you. He stopped short of saying it. Let her think she was the one in control. Franco knew better. "I don't care."

History swirled in the air like a lingering perfume as she stood before him, waiting. Naked, save for the dark, sparkling sapphire resting against her alabaster skin.

She was gorgeous. Perfect. More perfect than he remembered. She'd changed in the years since he'd seen her this way. There was a delicious curve to her hips that hadn't been there before, a heaviness to her breasts. He wouldn't have thought it possible for her to grow more beautiful. But she had.

Either that, or this meant more than he wanted to admit.

Hate sex. Right.

She gathered her hair until it spilled over one shoulder,

then reached behind her head to unfasten the sapphire-and-diamond necklace.

"Leave it." He put his hands on the wall on either side of her, hemming her in. "I like you like this."

"Is that so?" She reached for the fly of his tuxedo pants and slipped her hand inside.

Franco closed his eyes and groaned. He was on the verge of coming in her hand. As much as he would have liked to blame his lack of control on his recent celibacy, he knew he couldn't. It was her. Diana.

What was happening to him? To them?

"Diana," he whispered, pushing her bangs from her eyes.

He searched her gaze, and he saw no hatred there. None at all. Only desire and possibly a touch of fear. But wasn't that the way it should be? Shouldn't they both be afraid? One way or another, this would change things.

His chest felt tight. Full. As if a blazing sapphire like the one around Diana's neck had taken the place of his heart and was trying to shine its way out.

"I need you, Franco." Not want. *Need.*

"I know, darling." He grazed her plump bottom lip with the pad of his thumb. She drew it into her mouth, sucked gently on it.

Holy hell.

"Bedroom. Now." Every cell in his body was screaming for him to take her against the wall, but he wanted this to last. If they were going to go down this road together…again…he wanted to do it right this time. Diana deserved as much.

She released her hold on him and ducked beneath one of his arms. Then she sauntered toward a door at the far end of the apartment without a backward glance.

Franco followed, unfastening his bow tie as his gaze

traveled the length of her supple spine. She moved with the same feline grace that haunted his memory. He'd thought perhaps time had changed the way he remembered things, as time so often did. Surely the recollection of their night together shone brighter than the actual experience.

But he realized now that he'd been wrong. She was every bit as special as he remembered. More so, even.

He placed his hands on her waist and turned her around so she was facing him. She took a deep, shuddering inhale. The sapphire rose and fell in time with the beating of her heart.

She was more bashful now, with the bed in sight. Which made it all the more enticing when her hands found his belt. But her fingers had started trembling so badly that she couldn't unfasten the buckle.

"Let me," he said, covering her hands with his own.

He took his time undressing. He needed her to be sure. More than sure.

But once he was naked before her, her shyness fell away. She stared at his erection with hunger in her gaze until Franco couldn't wait any longer. He needed to touch her, taste her. Love her.

He hesitated as he reached for her.

This isn't love. It can't be.

The line between love and hate had never seemed so impossibly small. As his hands found the soft swell of her breasts, he had the distinct feeling they were crossing that line. He just didn't know which side they'd been on, which direction they were going.

He lowered his head to draw one of her perfect nipples into his mouth, and she gasped. An unprecedented surge of satisfaction coursed through him at the sound of her letting go. At last.

That's it, Wildfire. Let me take you there.

He teased and sucked as she buried her hands in his hair, shivering against him. He reached to part her thighs, and she let out a soft, shuddering moan. As he slipped a finger inside her, he stared down at her, fully intending to tell her they were just getting started. But when she opened her eyes, he said something altogether different.

"You have the most beautiful eyes I've ever seen. Like amethysts."

The words slipped out of his mouth before he could stop them. He loved her eyes. He always had. But this wasn't the sort of thing people said during hate sex. Even though he wasn't at all convinced that's what they were doing.

Still. This wasn't the time to turn into a romantic. If she needed to pretend this was nothing but a meaningless release, fine. He'd give her whatever she needed.

"There's a legend about amethysts, you know," she whispered, grinding against him as he moved his finger in and out.

"Tell me more."

He guided her backward until her legs collided into the bed and she fell, laughing, against the down comforter. He stretched out beside her and ran his fingertips in a leisurely trail down the perfect, porcelain softness of her belly.

Then he was poised above her with his erection pressing against her thigh, and her laughter faded away. Her eyes turned dark, serious.

"According to legend, they're magic. The ancient Romans believed amethysts could prevent drunkenness. Some still say they do."

Franco didn't believe it. Not for a minute. He felt

drunk just looking into the violet depths of those eyes. "Nonsense. You're intoxicating."

"Franco."

He really needed to stop saying such things. But he couldn't seem to stop himself.

If the circumstances had been different, he would have said more. He would have told her he'd been an idiot all those years ago. He would have admitted that this charade they'd both been dreading had been the most fun he'd had in ages. He might even have told her exactly what he thought of her breathtaking body...in terms that would have made her blush ruby red.

But circumstances weren't different. They'd been pretending for weeks. He'd just have to pretend the words weren't floating around in his consciousness, looking for a way out.

There was one thing, however, he definitely needed to say. Now, because come morning it would be too late. "Diana, there's something I need to tell you."

She shook her head as her hands found him and guided him toward her entrance. "No more words. Please. Just this."

Then he was pushing into her hot, heavenly center, and he couldn't have uttered another word if he tried.

What am I doing?

Diana's subconscious was screaming at her to stop. But for once in her life, she didn't want to listen. She didn't want to worry about what would happen tomorrow. Her entire life had been nothing but planning, practice, preparation. Where had all of that caution gotten her?

Nothing had gone as planned.

She was supposed to be on her way to the Olympics.

And here she was—in bed with Franco Andrade. Again. By her own choosing.

On some level, she'd known this was coming. She might have even known it the moment he'd first strolled into Drake Diamonds. She most definitely had known it when he'd kissed her at Harry Winston.

But the kiss had been her idea, too, hadn't it?

Oh, no.

"Oh, yes," she heard herself whisper as he slid inside her. "Yes, please."

It doesn't mean anything. It's just sex. Hate sex.

"Look at me, Wildfire. Let me see those beautiful eyes of yours." Franco's voice was tender. So tender that her heart felt like it was being ripped wide open.

She opened her eyes, and found him looking down at her with seriousness in his gaze. He kept watching her as he began to move, sliding in and out, and Diana had to bite her bottom lip to stop herself from crying out his name.

After months and months of working so hard to stay numb, to guard herself against feeling anything, she was suddenly overwhelmed with sensation. The feel of his body, warm and hard. The salty taste of his thumb in her mouth. The things he was saying—sweet things. Lovely things. Things she'd remember for a long, long time. Long after their fake relationship was over.

It was all too much. Much more than she could handle. The walls she'd been so busy constructing didn't stand a chance when he was watching her like that. Studying her. Delighting in the pleasure he was giving her.

"That's it, darling. Show me." Franco smiled down at her. It was a wicked smile. A knowing one.

He didn't just want her naked. He wanted her exposed

in every way. She could see it in the dark intent in his gaze, could feel it with each deliberate stroke.

This didn't feel like hate sex. Far from it. It felt like more. Much more.

It felt like everything.

It felt...real.

"Franco." His name tasted sweet in her mouth. Like honey. But as it fell from her lips in a broken gasp, something inside her broke along with it.

She shook her head, fighting it. She couldn't be falling for him. Not again.

It's all pretend. Just make believe.

But there was nothing make believe about his lips on her breasts as he bowed his head to kiss them. Or the liquid heat flowing through her body, dragging her under.

She arched into him, desperate, needy. He gripped her hips, holding her still as he tormented her with his mouth and his cock, with the penetrating awareness of his gaze.

This was all her doing. He knew it, and so did she.

They hadn't been destined to fall into bed together. Not then. Not now. She'd wanted him. For some nonsensical reason, she still did. Every time he touched her, every time he so much as glanced in her direction, she burned for him.

She'd made this happen. She'd seduced him. Not the other way around.

It wasn't supposed to be this way. It was supposed to be quick. Simple. But every time her climax was in reach, he slowed his movements, deliberately drawing things out. Letting her fall.

And fall.

Until everything began to shimmer like diamond dust, and she could fall no farther.

She began to tremble as her hips rose to meet his,

seeking release. Franco reached for her hands and pinned them over her head, their fingers entwined as he thrust into her. Hard. Relentless.

"My darling," he groaned, pressing his forehead against hers.

I'm not yours.

She couldn't make herself say it. Because if she did, it would feel more like a lie than any of the others she'd told in recent days. Whether she liked it or not, he held her heart in his hands. He always had, and he always would.

The realization slammed into her, and there was no use fighting it. Not now. Not when everything seemed so right. For the first time in as long as she could remember, she felt like herself again.

Because of him.

He paused and kissed her, letting her feel him pulse and throb deep inside. It was exquisite, enough to make her come undone.

"This is what you do to me, Diana." His voice was strained, pierced with truth. She felt it like an arrow through the heart. "No one else. Only you."

In the final, shimmering moment before she came apart, her gaze met his. And for the first time it didn't feel as though she was looking at the past.

In the pleasured depths of his eyes, she could see a thousand tomorrows.

Chapter Thirteen

Diana woke to a familiar buzzing sound. She blinked, disoriented. Then she turned her head and saw Franco asleep beside her—*naked*—and everything that had transpired the night before came flooding back.

They'd had sex. Hot sex. Tender sex. Every sort of sex imaginable.

She squeezed her eyes shut. Maybe it had all been a dream. A very realistic, very *naughty* dream.

The buzzing sound started again, and she sat up. Something glowed on the surface of her nightstand. Her cell phone. She squinted at it and saw Artem's name illuminated on the tiny screen.

Why was Artem calling her at this hour?

She couldn't answer the call. *Obviously.* But when she grabbed the phone to silence it, she saw that this was his third attempt to reach her.

Something was wrong.

"Hello?"

"Diana?" Artem's CEO voice was in overdrive…at six in the morning. Wonderful. "Why are you whispering?"

"I'm not," she whispered, letting her gaze travel the length of Franco's exposed torso. God, he was beautiful. *Too beautiful.*

Had her tongue really explored all those tantalizing abdominal muscles? Had she licked her way down the dark line of hair that led to his manhood?

Oh, God, she had.

She yanked one of the sheets from the foot of the bed and wrapped it around herself. She couldn't be naked while she talked to her brother. Not while the face of Drake Diamonds was sexually sated and sleeping in her bed.

"Diana, what the hell is going on?" She couldn't think of a time when she'd heard Artem so angry.

He'd found out.

Oh, no.

She slid out of bed, tiptoed out of the room and closed the door behind her. Her confusion multiplied at once when she saw heaps of feathers all over the living room. The air swirled with them, like she'd stepped straight from the bedroom into a snowfall.

A tiny black flash bounded out of one of the piles.

Lulu.

The puppy had disemboweled every pillow in sight while Diana had been in bed with Franco. Now her life was a literal mess as well as a metaphorical one. Perfect.

"Look, I can explain," she said, scooping the naughty dog into her arms.

Could she explain? Could she really?

I know I told you there was nothing going on between Franco and me, but the truth is we're sleeping together.

Slept together. Past tense. She'd simply had a bout of temporary insanity. It wouldn't happen again, obviously. It couldn't.

Hate sex. That's all it was. She'd made that very clear, and she'd stick to that story until the day she died. Admitting otherwise would be a humiliation she just couldn't bear.

"You can explain? Excellent. Because I'd really like to hear your reasoning." Artem sighed.

This was weird. And overly intimate, even by the dysfunctional Drake family standards.

"Okay...well..." She swallowed. How was she supposed to talk about her weakness for Franco's sexual charms to her *brother*? "This is a little awkward..."

Lulu burrowed into Diana's chest and started snoring. Destroying Dalton's apartment had clearly taken its toll.

"As awkward as reading about my sister's engagement in the newspaper?" Artem let out a terse exhale. "I think not."

Engagement?

Diana's heartbeat skidded to a stop.

Engagement?

Lulu gave a start and blinked her wide, round eyes.

"W-w-what are you talking about?" Diana's legs went wobbly. She tiptoed to the sofa and sank into its fluffy white cushions.

She hoped Franco was sleeping as soundly as he'd appeared. The last thing she needed was for him to walk in on this conversation.

"You and Franco are engaged to be married. It's in every newspaper in the city. It's also all over the television. Look, I know I gave you free reign as VP of public relations, but don't you think this is going a bit far?"

"Yes. I agree, but..."

"But what? The least you could have done was tell me your plans. We just talked about your relationship with Franco yesterday morning, and you never said a word about getting engaged." Artem sounded like he was on the verge of a heart attack.

Diana felt like she might be having one herself. "Calm down, Artem. It's not real."

"I know that. Obviously. But when are you going to clue everyone else in on that fact? While you're walking down the aisle?"

A jackhammer was banging away in Diana's head. She closed her eyes. Suddenly she saw herself drifting slowly down a path strewn with rose petals, wearing a white tulle gown and a sparkling diamond tiara in her hair.

What in the world?

She opened her eyes. "That's not what I mean. The announcement itself isn't real. There's been a mistake. A horrible, horrible mistake."

"Are you sure?" There wasn't a trace of relief in Artem's voice. "Because the article in the *Times* includes a joint statement from you and Franco."

"I'm positive. A statement? That's not possible. They made it up. You know how the media can be." But he'd said the *Times*, not *Page Six* or the *Daily News*.

The *New York Times* had fact checkers. It was a respectable institution that had won over a hundred Pulitzer Prizes. A paper like that didn't fabricate engagement announcements.

Now that she thought about it, the weddings section of the *Times* was famous in its own right. Society couples went to all sorts of crazy lengths to get their engagement announced on those legendary pages.

Her gaze drifted to the closed bedroom door. Ice trickled up her spine.

He wouldn't.

Would he?

No way. Franco would be just as horrified at this turn of events as she was. He wouldn't want the greater population of New York thinking he was off the market.

You and I are monogamous.

She'd actually laughed when he'd said those words less than two weeks ago. But she'd never pressed for an explanation.

This can't be happening. I can't be engaged to Franco Andrade.

Sleeping with him was one thing. Letting him slip a ring on her finger was another thing entirely.

Forget Franco. Forget Artem. Forget Drake Diamonds. This was her life, and she shouldn't be reading about it in the newspapers.

She took a calming breath and told herself there was nothing to worry about. There had to be a reasonable explanation. She didn't have a clue what that might be, but there had to be one.

But then she remembered something Franco had said the night before. Right before he'd entered her. She remembered the rare sincerity in his gaze, the gravity of his tone.

I need to tell you something.

The engagement was real, wasn't it? The statement in the *Times* had come from Franco himself. He'd even tried to warn her, and she'd refused to listen.

She hadn't wanted words. She'd wanted to feel him inside her so badly that nothing else mattered.

And now she was going to kill him.

"Artem, I have to go. I'll call you back."

She pressed End and threw her phone across the room. She glared at the closed bedroom door.

Had Franco lost his mind? They could *not* be engaged. They just couldn't. Even a fake engagement was out of the question.

Of course it's fake. He doesn't want to marry you any more than you want to marry him.

That was a good thing. A very good thing.

She wasn't sure why she had to keep reminding herself how good it was over and over and over again.

The tightness in Diana's chest intensified. She pressed the heel of her palm against her breastbone, closed her eyes and focused on her breath. She was on the verge of a full-fledged panic attack. All over an engagement that wasn't even real. If that didn't speak volumes about her attitude toward marriage, nothing would.

Breathe. Just breathe.

Maybe she was losing it over nothing. Maybe whatever Franco had wanted to tell her had nothing at all to do with the press. Maybe the *Times* wedding page had, indeed, made an unprecedented error.

She looked at the dog, because that's how low she'd sunk. She was seeking validation from a puppy. "Everyone makes mistakes. It could happen, right?"

Lulu stretched her mouth into a wide, squeaky yawn.

"You're no help at all," Diana muttered, focusing once again on the closed bedroom door.

There was only one person who could help her get to the bottom of this latest disaster, and that person didn't have four legs and a curlicue tail.

Franco slept like the dead.

He opened his eyes, then let them drift shut again. He hadn't had such a peaceful night's rest in months. He forgot all about the Kingsmen, Luc's ultimatum and the overall mess his personal life had become. It was remarkable what great sex could do for a man's state of mind. Not just great sex. Phenomenal sex. The best sex of his life.

Sex with Diana Drake.

"Franco!"

He squinted, fighting the morning light drifting through the floor to ceiling windows of Diana's bedroom.

Someone was yelling his name.

"Franco, wake up. Now." A pillow smacked his face.

He opened his eyes. "It's a little early in the morning for a pillow fight, Wildfire. But I'm game if you are."

"Of course you think that's what this is. For your information, it's not." She stood near the foot of the bed, staring daggers at him. For some ridiculous reason, she'd yanked one of the sheets off the bed and wrapped it around herself. As if Franco hadn't seen every inch of that gorgeous body. Kissed it. Worshipped it. "And I've asked you repeatedly not to call me that."

"Not last night," he said, lifting a brow and staring right back at her.

What had he missed? Because this wasn't the same Diana he'd taken to bed the night before, the same Diana who'd cried his name as he thrust inside her. It sure as hell wasn't the same Diana who'd told him how much she'd needed him as she unzipped his fly.

"I'm being serious." She tugged the bedsheet tighter around her breasts.

Franco pushed himself up to a sitting position, rested his back against the headboard and yawned. When his eyes opened, he caught Diana staring openly at his erect cock. *That's right, darling. Look your fill.* "See something you like?"

Her gaze flew upward to meet his. Franco was struck once again by just how beautiful she was, even flustered and disheveled from a night of lovemaking. He preferred her like this, actually. Fiery and flushed. He just wished she'd drop the damned sheet and climb back in bed.

"Cover yourself, please," she said primly.

"Sure. So long as I can borrow your tent." He stared pointedly at her bedsheet-turned-ballgown.

"Nice try." She let out a laugh. Laughter had to be a good sign, didn't it? "But I'll keep it, thank you very much."

Franco shrugged. "Fine. I'll stay like this, then."

Her gaze flitted once again to his arousal. If she kept looking at him like that, he might just come without even touching her. "Suit yourself. Naked or not, you have some explaining to do."

"What have I done this time?"

"I think you know." She titled her head and flashed him a rather deadly-looking smile. "My dear, darling *fiancé*."

Fiancé.

Shit.

The engagement announcement. He'd meant to tell her about it before it hit the papers. He'd even tried to bring it up the night before, hadn't he? "So you've seen the *Times*, I presume?"

"Not yet. But Artem has. He's also seen the *Observer*, *Page Six* and the *Daily News*. It's probably the cover story on *USA TODAY*." She threw her hands up, and the sheet fell to the floor. But she'd worked herself into such a fury, she didn't even notice. "Explain yourself, Franco."

"Explain myself?" He climbed out of bed, strode toward her and picked up the pile of Egyptian cotton at her feet. Pausing ever so briefly to admire her magnificent breasts, he wrapped the sheet around her shoulders and covered her again.

Her cheeks went pink. "Thank you." For a brief second, he saw a hint of tenderness in her gaze. Then it vanished as quickly as it had appeared. "You heard me. I can't believe I even have to ask this question, but why does everyone on planet Earth suddenly think I'm going to marry you?"

He sighed and rested his hands on her shoulders, a sliver of relief working its way through him when she didn't pull away. He reminded himself the engagement was a sham. Their whole relationship was a sham. None of this should matter.

"Because I told them we're engaged."

"Oh, my God, I knew it." She began to tremble all over.

Franco slid his hands down her arms, took her hands in his and pulled her close. "No need to panic, Wildfire. It's nothing. Just part of the ruse."

A spark of something flared low in his gut. Something that felt far too much like disappointment. He'd never imagined he would one day find himself consoling a woman so blatantly horrified at the idea of being his betrothed. The fact that the woman was Diana Drake made it all the more unsettling.

She wiggled out of his grasp and began to pace around the spacious bedroom. The white bedsheet trailed behind her like the train on a wedding gown. "What were you thinking? I can't believe this."

She took a break from her tirade to regard him through narrowed eyes. For a moment, Franco thought she might slap him. Again. "Actually, I can. I don't know why I thought I could trust you. About anything."

He nearly flinched. But he knew he had no right.

As mornings after went, this one wasn't stellar. He wasn't sure what he'd expected to happen after last night.

The line between truth and lies had blurred so much he couldn't quite think straight, much less figure out whatever was happening between him and Diana. But he was certain about one thing—he'd seen the same fury in her gaze once before.

Of course he remembered what he'd said. He'd regretted the words the instant they'd slipped from his mouth.

He'd known he needed to do something dire the moment he'd woken up beside her, all those years ago. She'd looked too innocent, too beautiful with her dark hair fanned across his chest. Too damned happy.

Strangely enough, he'd felt almost happy, too. Sated. Not in a sexual way, but on a soul-deep level he hadn't experienced before. It had frightened the hell out of him.

He didn't do relationships. Never had. Never would. It wasn't in his blood. Franco had never even known who his father was, for crying out loud. As a kid, he'd watched a string of men come in and out of his mother's life. In and out of her bed. When the men were around, his mother was all smiles and laugher. Once they'd left— and they always left…eventually—the tears came. Days passed, sometimes weeks, when his mother would forget to feed him. Franco had gotten out the first chance he had. He'd been on his own since he was eleven years old. As far as he knew, his mother had never come looking for him.

He wouldn't know how to love a woman even if he wanted to. Which he didn't. If his upbringing had taught him anything, it was that self-reliance was key. He didn't want to need anyone. And he most definitely didn't want anyone needing him. Especially not a diamond heiress who'd opened her eyes three years ago and suddenly looked at him as if he'd hung the moon.

He'd done what he'd needed to do. He'd made certain she'd never look at him that way again.

Come now, Diana. We both know last night didn't mean anything. It was nice, but I prefer my women more experienced.

She'd had every right to slap him. He'd deserved worse.

"You can breathe easy. I have no intention of actually marrying you," he said.

"Good." She laughed again. Too lively. Too loud.

"Good," he repeated, sounding far harsher than he intended.

What exactly was happening?

He didn't want to hurt her. Not this time.

"What you fail to understand is that I don't want to be *engaged* to you, either." She held up a hand to stop him from talking, and the sheet slipped again, just enough to afford him a glimpse of one, rose-hued nipple.

His body went hard again. Perfect. Just perfect.

Diana glanced down at him, then back up. There wasn't a trace of desire in her eyes this time. "I can't talk to you about this while you're naked. Get dressed and meet me in the kitchen."

She flounced away, leaving Franco alone in a room that throbbed with memories.

He shoved his legs into his tuxedo pants from the night before and splashed some water on his face in the bathroom. When he strode into the kitchen, he found her standing at the coffeemaker, still dressed in the bedsheet. Lulu was frolicking at her feet, engaged in a fierce game of tug-of-war with a corner of the sheet. The dog didn't even register his presence. Clearly, the two of them had bonded, just as he'd hoped. He should have been happy. Instead, he felt distinctly outnumbered.

Diana poured a steaming cup, and Franco looked at it longingly.

She glanced at him, but didn't offer him any.

Not that he'd expected it.

"I'm sorry," he said quietly.

She lifted a brow. "For what, exactly?"

For everything.

He sighed. "I should have given you a heads-up."

Her expression softened ever so slightly. "You tried."

"I could have tried harder." He took a step closer and caught a glimpse of his reflection—moody and blue—in the sapphire still hanging around her neck.

She backed up against the counter, maintaining the space between them. "Just tell me why. I need to know."

A muscle flexed in Franco's jaw. This wasn't a conversation he wanted to have the morning after they'd slept together. Or ever, to be honest. "My chances of getting back on the Kingsmen will be much greater if I'm engaged."

She blinked. "That doesn't make sense."

Don't make me explain it. He gave her a look of warning. "It matters. Trust me."

"Trust you?" She set her coffee cup on the counter and crossed her arms. "You've got to be kidding."

"For the record, it would be even better if we were married." What was he saying? He was willing to go pretty far to get his job back, but not that far.

Diana gaped at him. "I can't believe this. You're a polo player, not a priest. What does your marital status have to do with anything..." Her eyes grew narrow. "Unless... oh, my God..."

Franco held up his hands. "I can explain."

But he couldn't. Not in any kind of way that Diana would find acceptable. Even if he broke his promise to

Luc and told her the truth, she'd never believe him. Not in this lifetime.

"You did something bad, didn't you? Some kind of terrible sexual misconduct." She fiddled with the stone around her neck, and Franco couldn't help but notice the way her fingers trembled. He hated himself a little bit right then. "Go ahead and tell me. What was it? Did you sleep with someone's wife this time?"

He looked at her long and hard.

"You did," she said flatly. The final sparks of whatever magic had happened between them the night before vanished from her gaze. All Franco could see in the depths of her violet eyes was hurt. And thinly veiled hatred. "How could I be such an idiot? *Again?* Who was it?"

Less than an hour ago, she'd been asleep with her head on his chest as their hearts beat in unison. How had everything turned so spectacularly to crap since then?

A grim numbness blossomed in Franco's chest. He knew exactly what had gone wrong. The past had found its way into their present.

Didn't it always?

He'd written the script of this conversation years ago.

He wanted to sweep her hair from her face and force her to look him in the eye so she could see the real him. He wanted to take her back to bed and whisper things he'd never told anyone else as he pushed his way inside her again.

He wanted to tell her the truth.

"It was Natalie Ellis," he said quietly.

"Ellis? As in *Jack* Ellis?" She pulled the bedsheet tighter around her curves, much to Franco's dismay. "You had an affair with your boss's wife? That's despicable, Franco. Even for you. You must think I'm the biggest fool you've ever met."

"I'm the fool," he said.

She shook her head. "Don't, okay? Just don't be nice to me right now. Please."

"Diana…"

Before he could say another word, the cell phone in the pocket of his tuxedo pants chimed with an incoming text message.

Damn it.

Diana rolled her eyes. Lulu barked at the phone in solidarity. "Go ahead. Look at it. It's probably from one of your married girlfriends. Don't let me stand in your way."

Franco didn't make a move. Whoever was texting him could wait.

His phone chimed again.

Diana glared at him. "You disgust me, Franco. And I swear, if you don't answer that right now, I'm going to reach into your pocket and do it for you."

Franco sighed and looked at the phone's display.

See you at practice today at 10 sharp. Come ready to play. Don't be late.

The engagement announcement had worked. He was back on the team.

And back on Diana's bad side.

She hated him.

Again.

Chapter Fourteen

Diana didn't bother returning Artem's call. Instead, she decided to get dressed and go straight to Drake Diamonds and explain things in person.

But there was no actual explanation, was there? She was engaged. *Pretend* engaged, but still. Engaged.

She had no idea what she was going to say to her brother. If she admitted she'd known nothing about the engagement, it would look like she'd lost control over her own public image. And as VP of public relations, the Drake image was pretty much the one thing she was responsible for. On the other hand, if she pretended she'd known all about the faux engagement, Artem would be furious that she'd kept him in the dark. It was a catch-22. Either way, she was screwed.

She had to face him sooner or later, though. She desperately wanted to get it over with. Maybe she'd go ahead and tell him he'd been right. The charade had gone too far. She should end it. The Lambertis would walk away, of course. And she'd never be co-CEO. She might not even be able to keep her current position. Artem had told her she'd proven herself, but that had been before the engagement fiasco. Who knew what would happen if she broke up with her fake boyfriend now? She could end up right back in the Engagements department.

But that would be better than having to walk around pretending she was going to get married to Franco, wouldn't it?

Yes.

No.

Maybe.

The only thing she knew for certain was that she shouldn't have slept with him the night before. How could she have been so monumentally stupid? She deserved to be fired. She'd fire herself if she could.

He'd carried on an affair with a married woman. That was a new low, even for a playboy like Franco. And it made him no different than her father.

So, of course she'd jumped into bed with him. God, she hated herself.

"Is he in?" she asked Mrs. Barnes, glancing nervously at the closed office door. What was her brother doing in there? He rarely kept his door closed. He was probably throwing darts at the wedding page of the *Times*. Or possibly interviewing new candidates for the VP of public relations position. She shook her head. "Never mind, I know he wants to see me. I'm going in."

"Wait!" Mrs. Barnes called after her.

It was too late, though. Diana had already flung Artem's door open and stormed inside. Artem sat behind his desk, just as she'd expected. But he wasn't alone. Carla and Don Lamberti occupied the two chairs opposite him.

Ophelia was also there, standing beside the desk with what looked like a crystal baseball.

The diamond.

It was even larger than Diana had imagined. She paused just long enough to take in its impressive size and to notice the way it reflected light, even in its uncut state. It practically glowed in Ophelia's hands.

All four heads in the office turned in her direction.

Any and all hopes she had of sneaking out the door unnoticed were officially dashed. "I'm so sorry. I didn't mean to interrupt."

She practically ran out of the office, but of course she wasn't fast enough.

"Diana, what a nice surprise!" The brightness of Carla Lamberti's smile rivaled that of her diamond.

Diana forced a smile and cursed the four-inch Jimmy Choos that had prevented her speedy getaway. Why, oh why, had she worn stilettos?

Probably because there had been a dozen paparazzi following her every move all day, thanks to Franco's little engagement announcement. The doorman had warned her about the crowd of photographers gathered outside her building before she'd left the apartment. If her picture was going to be splashed on the front page of every newspaper in town, she was going to look decent. Especially considering that Franco's walk of shame out of her building earlier in the morning had already turned up on no less than four websites.

Not only had she made the terrible mistake of sleeping with him, but now everyone with a Wi-Fi connection knew all about it.

"It looks like you're busy. I just needed to talk to Artem, but it can wait." She turned and headed for the door.

"Don't be silly. Join us. We insist. Right, Mr. Drake?" Carla glanced questioningly at Artem, who nodded his agreement. "I want to hear all about your engagement to Mr. Andrade. I can't seem to pry a word out of your brother."

The older woman turned to face Diana again. Behind her back, Artem crooked a finger at Diana, then pointed to the empty place on his office sofa.

Okay, then. Diana took a deep breath, crossed the room and sat down.

"So, tell us everything. As I said, Artem won't breathe a word about your wedding." Carla cast a mock look of reprimand in Artem's direction.

Your wedding.

Diana did her best not to vomit right there on the Drake-blue carpet.

Ever the diplomat, Ophelia jumped into the conversation. "I'm sure Diana and Franco would like to keep some things private. It's more special that way, don't you think?"

Diana released a breath she hadn't realized she'd been holding. She owed Ophelia. Big-time.

Mr. Lamberti rested a hand on his wife's knee. "Goodness, dear. Leave Diana alone. She's here to join our meeting about the plans for the diamond, not to discuss the intimate details of her personal life."

Carla let out a laugh and shrugged. "I suppose that's true. Please pardon my manners. I was just so excited to read about your engagement in the paper this morning. I knew from the moment I saw you and Franco together at the Harry Winston party that you were destined to be together. The way that man looks at you..."

Her voice drifted off, and she sighed dreamily.

Artem cleared his throat. "Shall we proceed with the

meeting? Ophelia has drawn up some beautiful designs for the stone."

"Of course. Just one more question. I promise it's the last one." Mrs. Lamberti's gaze shifted once again to Diana. She prayed for the sofa to somehow open itself up and swallow her whole, but of course it didn't. "It's true, isn't it? Are you and Mr. Andrade really engaged to be married?"

This was the opening she'd been waiting for. She could end the nonsensical charade right here and now, and she'd never even have to set eyes on Franco again. All she had to do was say no. The papers had made a mistake. She and Franco weren't engaged. In fact, they were no longer seeing each other. The Lambertis would obviously be disappointed, but surely they wouldn't pack up their diamond and leave.

Would they?

Diana swallowed. *Do it. Just do it.*

Why was she hesitating? This was her chance to get her life back. It was now or never. If she didn't fess up, she'd be stuck indefinitely as Franco's fiancée.

Speak now or forever hold your peace.

She was already thinking in terms of wedding language. Perfect. She may as well climb right into a Vera Wang.

She glanced from the Lambertis to Artem to Ophelia. This would have been so much easier without an audience. And without that ridiculously huge diamond staring her in the face. It was blinding. Which was the only rational explanation for the next words that came out of her mouth.

"Of course it's true." She smiled her most radiant, bridal grin. "We're absolutely engaged."

* * *

All the way to Bridgehampton, Franco waited for the other shoe to drop. He fully expected to arrive at practice only to be ousted again. The moment he'd left Diana's apartment, she'd no doubt picked up the phone and called every newspaper in town to demand a retraction.

He wasn't sure what to make of the fact that she hadn't. His cell phone sat on the passenger seat of his Jag, conspicuously silent.

He arrived at the Kingsmen practice field at ten sharp just as instructed, despite having to break a few traffic laws to get there on time. He still hadn't heard a word from Diana when he climbed out of his car and tossed his cell into the duffel bag that carried his gear.

He needed to quit worrying about her. About the two of them. Especially since they weren't an actual couple.

It had only been hate sex.

He slammed the door of his Jag hard enough to make the car shake.

"And here I thought you'd be thrilled to be back," someone said.

Franco turned to find Coach Santos standing behind him. "Good morning."

"Is it? Because you seem pissed as hell." His gaze swept Franco from top to bottom. "A tuxedo? At ten in the morning? This doesn't bode well, son."

Franco was lucky he kept a bag packed with his practice gear in the trunk of his car. There hadn't been time to stop by his apartment. "Relax. I wasn't out partying. You caught me at my fiancée's apartment this morning. I'm a changed man, remember?"

"Let's hope so. Ellis isn't so sure, but he's willing to give it a shot. For now." Santos looked pointedly at Franco's rumpled tux shirt. "But try not to arrive at practice look-

ing like you just rolled out of someone's bed. It's not helping your cause. Got it?"

"Got it." Franco gave him a curt nod and tried not to
think about that bed. Or that particular *someone*.

He needed to have his head in the game, today more
than ever. But he hated the way he and Diana had left
things. He'd thought this time would be different.

If he was being honest with himself though, it was for
the best. Diana Drake had always been out of his league.
He didn't have a thing to offer her.

Time hadn't changed who he was. It hadn't changed
anything. He and Diana had ended back where they'd
begun.

"We've got a scrimmage in an hour. And don't forget
about Argentine Night at the Polo Club tonight. Ellis ex-
pects you there with your doting fiancée on your arm."

Franco's gut churned. Getting Diana anywhere near
the Polo Club would be next to impossible. It seemed as
though she hadn't gotten within a mile radius of a live
horse since her accident.

There was also the slight complication that she hated
him. Now, more than ever.

"What are you waiting for? Get suited up." Coach
Santos jerked his head in the direction of the practice
field, where the grooms were already getting the horses
saddled up and ready.

Before Franco had come to America—before all the
championship trophies and the late-night after parties—
he'd been a groom. He'd been the one who brushed the
horses, running a curry comb over them until the Argentine sunshine reflected off them like a mirror. He'd
bathed them in the evenings, grinning as they tossed
their heads and whinnied beneath the spray of the water
hose. Franco had lived and breathed horses back then.

When he wasn't shoveling out stalls, he was on horseback, practicing his swing, learning the game of polo.

Sometimes he missed those days.

But grooms didn't become champions, at least not where Franco had come from. He was one of the lucky ones. Not lucky, actually. Chosen. He owed Luc Piero everything.

"You did it, man." Luc greeted Franco with a bone-crushing hug the moment he stepped onto the field. "You're back."

"I told you there wasn't anything to worry about." Franco shrugged and fastened his helmet in place.

"Engaged, though?" Luc lifted a brow. "Tell me that's not real."

"Does it matter?" Franco planted one of his feet into a stirrup, grabbed onto the saddle and swung himself onto his horse's back. His grooms had gotten the horses to the field just in the nick of time.

"Yes, it matters. It matters a whole hell of a lot. I mean, you've never been the marrying kind."

"So I hear." He was being an ass, and he knew it. But he wasn't in the mood to discuss his marriageability. Not when he couldn't shake the memory of the hurt in Diana's gaze this morning.

He sighed. "Sorry. I just don't want to discuss Diana Drake. Or any of the Drakes, for that matter."

They had been the means to an end. Nothing more. Why did he keep having to remind himself of that fact?

Luc shrugged. "I can live with that. You're back. That's what important. Nothing else. Right?"

Franco shot him a grim smile. "Absolutely."

He rode hard once the scrimmage got underway. Fast. Aggressive.

By the close of the fourth chukker, the halfway point

of the game, the scoreboard read 11 to 0. Franco had scored each and every one of the goals. He managed four more before the end of the game. He was back, indeed.

His teammates gathered round to congratulate him. Ellis applauded from his box seat, but didn't approach Franco. And that was fine. Franco didn't feel much like talking. To Ellis or anyone. The urge he felt to check his cell phone for messages was every bit as frustrating as it was pressing. When he finally did, he had over forty voicemails, all from various members of the media.

Not a single word from Diana.

He shoved his phone in his back pocket and slammed his locker closed. What was he supposed to do now? Were he and Diana engaged? Were they over?

He had no idea.

He stopped by his apartment in Tribeca and packed a bag, just in case. No news was good news. Wasn't that the old adage? Besides, he couldn't quite shake the feeling that if Diana Drake had decided to dump him, he would have heard it first from the press...

Because that's how monumentally screwed up their fake relationship was.

But the mob of photographers outside Diana's building didn't say a word about a breakup when Franco arrived on the scene. They screamed the usual questions at him, along with a few new ones. About the wedding, of course. He kept his head down and did his best to ignore them.

The doorman waved Franco upstairs, just as he had before. That didn't necessarily mean anything. Diana probably wouldn't have broken the news first to her doorman, but Franco was beginning to feel more confident that he, indeed, had a fiancée waiting for him in the penthouse.

Sure enough, when Diana answered the door, there

was a colossal diamond solitaire situated on her ring finger. "Oh, it's you."

For some nonsensical reason, the sight of the ring rubbed Franco the wrong way. If their engagement had been real, he would have chosen a diamond himself. And it wouldn't be a generic rock like the one on her hand. He would have selected something special. Unique.

But what the hell was he thinking? *None* of this was real. The ring shouldn't matter.

It did, though. He had no idea why, but it mattered.

"Nice ring," he said through gritted teeth.

"I picked it up at Drake Diamonds today since my *fiancé* forgot to give me one." She lifted an accusatory brow. "What are you doing here, anyway?"

He gave her a grim smile and swished past her with his duffle and a garment bag slung over his shoulder. "Honey, I'm home."

She gaped at him. "I beg your pardon?"

Lulu shot toward him, all happy barks and wagging tail. At least someone was happy to see him. He tossed his bags on the sofa and gathered the puppy into his arms.

Diana frowned at Lulu, then back at Franco. *Someone looks jealous.* "What's going on? Surely you don't think you're moving in with me."

"We're engaged, remember? This is what engaged people do."

She shook her head. "Please tell me you're not serious. I've already taken in one stray. Isn't that enough?"

It was the wrong thing to say.

"You're comparing me to a stray dog now?" he said through clenched teeth.

She opened her mouth to say something, but Franco wouldn't let her. He'd heard enough.

"I've put up with a hell of a lot from you and your family in the past few weeks, Diana. But you will not speak to me that way. Is that understood, wifey?"

She blinked. "I…"

He held up a hand. "Save it. We can talk later. We have a date tonight, anyway. You should get dressed."

"A *date*?"

"We're going to Argentine Night at the Polo Club. If you have a problem with it, I don't want to hear it. I've accompanied you to every gala and party under the sun in the past few weeks. You can do one thing for me." He gave Lulu a scratch behind the ears. "Unless you'd like to kick both of the strays out of your life once and for all?"

She wouldn't dare. If she wanted him gone, she wouldn't be wearing that sparkling diamond on her ring finger. Franco honestly didn't know why she wanted to play along with the engagement, but he no longer cared.

You care. You know you do.

If he didn't, the stray dog comment wouldn't have gotten under his skin the way it had.

"Well?" he asked.

"I'll be ready in half an hour." She plucked the dog from his arms. "And Lulu isn't going anywhere."

She sauntered past him with the little pug's face peering at him over her shoulder and slammed the bedroom door.

Franco wanted to stay angry. Anger was good. Anger was comfortable. He knew a lot more about what to do with anger than about what to do with the feelings that had swirled between them last night.

But seeing her with the dog took the edge off. He'd been right to force the puppy on her. He'd done something good.

For once in his life.

Chapter Fifteen

Diana had spent the better part of her life around horses, but she'd never been to the Polo Club in Bridgehampton. Show jumping and polo were clearly two separate sports. She'd known polo players before, obviously. She'd certainly seen Franco at her fair share of equestrian events. But she'd never run in the same after-hours circles as Franco's crowd.

Even before the night she'd lost her virginity to Franco, she'd noticed a brooding intensity about those athletes that both fascinated and frightened her. They rode hard and they play hard. Deep down, she knew that was one of the qualities about Franco that had first drawn her toward him. He didn't care what anyone else had to say about him. He behaved any way he chose. Both on and off the field.

Diana had no idea what that might feel like. She was a Drake, and that name came with a myriad of expectations.

If she'd been born a boy, things would have been different. Drake men were immune to rules and expectations. At least, that had been the case with her father. He'd spent money as he wished and slept with whomever he wished, and everyone in the family had to just deal with it. Her mother included.

"You look awfully serious all of a sudden," Franco said as she stepped out of the Drake limousine at the valet stand outside the Polo Club. "What are you thinking about?"

"Nothing." *Marriage.* Why was she even pondering such things? Oh, yeah, because she was engaged now. "I'm fine. Let's just go inside."

"Very well." He lifted her hand and kissed it before tucking it into the crook of his elbow.

Diana looked around, expecting to see a group of photographers clustered by the entrance of the club. But she didn't spot a single telephoto lens.

"Good evening, Mr. Andrade and Miss Drake." A valet held the door open for them as Franco led her into the foyer.

"Wow," she whispered. "This is really something."

The stately white building had been transformed into a South American wonderland of twinkling lights and rich, red decor. Sultry tango music filled the air. Diana was suddenly very glad she'd chosen a red lace gown for the occasion.

She and Franco were situated at a round table near the center of the room, along with his coach and several other players and their wives. When she took her seat, the man beside her introduced himself as Luc Piero.

"It's a pleasure to meet you," she said.

"The pleasure's all mine, I assure you." Luc grinned from ear to ear. "I've known Franco for a long time, and

I've never seen him as captivated with anyone before as he is with you. I've told him time and again that I wanted to meet you, but he's been hiding you away."

"I've done no such thing," Franco countered.

"That's right. Your pictures have been in the newspaper every day for two weeks running. How could I forget?" Luc smiled.

Diana kind of liked him. She probably would have liked him more if she weren't so busy searching the room for Natalie Ellis. She had a morbid curiosity about the woman Franco had apparently considered worth risking his entire career over. Diana had seen the woman on a handful of occasions, but she wanted a better look. She wasn't jealous, obviously. Simply curious.

Right. You're a card-carrying green-eyed monster right now.

"I'm going to go get us some drinks, darling." Franco bent to kiss her on the cheek, which pleased her far more than it should have. "I'll be right back."

She reminded herself for the millionth time that she hated him, then turned to Luc. "You say you've known Franco a long time?"

"All our lives. We grew up together in Argentina."

"Really?" Franco had never breathed a word to her about his childhood. She couldn't help being curious about the way he'd grown up. "Tell me more."

"He's loved horses since before he could walk. You know that, right?"

She didn't. But she understood it all too well. "That's something we have in common."

"My father owned one of the local polo clubs in Buenos Aires. I used to hang out there when I was a kid, and that's where I met Franco."

"Oh, was he taking riding lessons there?"

Luc gave her an odd glance. "No, Franco's one hundred percent self-taught. A natural. He was a groom at my father's stable."

"I see." She nodded as if this wasn't stunning new information. After all, she should probably have some sort of clue about Franco's childhood since he was her fiancé.

But a groom?

In the equestrian world, grooms and riders belonged in two very different social classes. Not that Diana liked or condoned dividing people into such groups. But it was an unpleasant fact of life—she'd never known a groom who had gone on to compete in show jumping. Maybe things were different in the sport of polo.

Then again, maybe not.

"It's unusual, I know. But Franco was different, right from the start."

Indeed. Her throat grew tight.

She should be furious with him after the stunt he'd pulled. He'd strong-armed her into an engagement, plain and simple. An engagement she didn't want.

And she'd let him. She wasn't sure who she was angrier at—Franco or herself.

"Different. How so?" She glanced at Franco across the room, where he stood standing beside a man she recognized from equestrian circles as Jack Ellis, the owner of the Kingsmen.

Her breath caught in her throat. No matter how many times she looked at Franco—whether it was from the other side of a crowded room or beside him in bed— his physical perfection always seemed to catch her off guard. He was the most handsome man she'd ever seen. Ellis, on the other hand, appeared immune to Franco's charms. The expression on his face was grim. Even the woman on Jack Ellis's arm didn't seem to notice Franco's charming smile or dark, chiseled beauty. Natalie Ellis looked almost bored as she glanced around the room. When her gaze fell on Luc, her lips curved into a nearly imperceptible smile.

Odd.

"Well…" Luc continued, dragging her attention back to their conversation. "Like I said, he was a talented rider. Fearless. Instinctual. Even as a kid, I knew I was witnessing something special. He had a bond with the horses like nothing I'd ever seen. They were his life."

A chill went up Diana's spine. She had a feeling she was about to hear something she shouldn't.

"His life," she echoed.

"I found out he was sleeping in the stables and kept it a secret from my father for over year before he found out." Luc gave her a sad smile. "I thought he'd be angry and kick Franco out. Instead, he gave Franco a room in our family home."

She most definitely shouldn't be hearing this. Franco had never said a thing to her about his life in Argentina. Now she knew why. These were the sort of intimate details only a lover should know. A real lover.

She should change the subject. Delving further into this conversation would be an invasion of Franco's privacy. But she was so distraught by what she'd heard that she couldn't string together a single coherent sentence.

She'd called Franco a stray.

And he'd been homeless.

Oh, God.

"Are you all right, Diana?" Luc was watching her with guarded curiosity. "You look like you've seen a ghost."

No, just a monster. And that monster is me.

"Fine." She cleared her throat. "Is that when Franco

started playing polo? After he moved in with your family?"

Luc shrugged. "Yes and no. He was still working as a groom, but I'd begun playing. Franco was my training partner. In the beginning, he was just there to help me improve my game. That didn't last long."

"He's that good, isn't he?" She forced herself to smile like a doting bride.

What was happening? She was acting just like the nauseatingly sweet engaged couples she'd loathed so much when she worked in Engagements.

It *was* an act, wasn't it?

"He's the best. He always has been. His talent transcends any traditional rules of the game. That's why my father put him on the team." He smiled at Franco as he approached the table. "We've been teammates ever since."

A lump formed in Diana's throat. "I'm glad. Franco deserves a friend like you."

"He's more like a brother than a friend. He's always got my back. The guy's loyal to a fault, but I'm sure you know that by now."

Loyal to a fault...

Before Franco had walked through the door of Drake Diamonds a month ago, Diana would have never used those to words to describe him. Now she wasn't so sure.

She'd seen a different side to Franco in recent weeks. It all made sense now...the way he'd jumped at the chance to adopt a homeless puppy, his commitment to their fake relationship. Franco was a man of his word.

She was beginning to question everything she'd believed about him, and that wasn't good. It wasn't good at all. Their entire relationship had been built on a lie, and Diana preferred it that way. At least she knew where she stood. She operated best when she could look at the world in black and white. But things with Franco had blurred into a disturbing shade of gray.

She didn't know what she thought anymore. Worse, she wasn't sure what she felt. Because despite everything that had happened in the past, and despite the fact that just when she thought she could trust Franco he'd gone and announced to the world that they were engaged, she felt something for him. And that *something* scared the life out of her.

But he obviously had little or no regard for marriage, otherwise he wouldn't have bedded Natalie Ellis. Natalie Ellis, who seemed to have no interest in Franco whatsoever.

What was going on?

"Hello, darling. Sorry to leave you alone for so long." Franco bent and kissed her on the cheek again. "I hope Luc hasn't been boring you."

"No, not at all." Quite the opposite, actually.

She smiled up at him and tried to forget all the things she'd just heard. But it was no use. She couldn't shake the image of Franco as a young boy, sleeping on a bed of straw in a barn. What had happened to him to make him end up there? Where was his family? So many unanswered questions.

The air between them was heavy with secrets and lies, but somewhere deep inside Diana, an unsettling truth had begun to blossom.

She had feelings for Franco. Genuine feelings.

"The tango contest is about to begin." He offered her his hand. "Dance with me?"

She stared at his outstretched palm, and words began to spin in her head.

Do you take this man to love and to cherish, all the days of your life?

She was losing it.

"Yes." *I do.* She placed her hand in his. She didn't even know how to tango, but she didn't much care at this point. "Yes, please."

The music started and Franco wrapped his right arm around Diana until his hand rested squarely in the center of her back. When he lifted his left arm, she placed her hand gently in his.

"I should probably mention that I don't exactly know how to tango." She blushed.

"Not to worry. I'm a rather strong lead."

"Why am I not surprised?" she murmured. He took a step forward, and she moved with him in perfect synchrony. "Luc had some lovely things to say about you just now."

They reached the end of the club's small dance floor, and Franco spun her around. "He's probably had more than his fair share of champagne."

"Don't." Diana shook her head and slid one of her stilettos up the length of his leg. "I'm being serious. He loves you like a brother."

Franco nodded. Her leg had traveled nearly up to his hip. He pulled her incrementally closer. "You're right. He does. And I'd do anything for him."

He deliberately avoided glancing in Natalie Ellis's direction.

This wasn't the time or place for a heart-to-heart, but something about the way Diana was looking at him all of a sudden made it impossible for him to keep giving her flippant responses.

She slid her foot back to the floor and they resumed stalking each other across the floor to the strains of the accordion music.

"I had no idea you could dance like this, Franco." Diana swiveled in his arms. "You're full of surprises."

"It's an Argentine dance." He lifted her in the air, and her legs wrapped around his waist, then flared out before she landed on the floor with a whisper. For someone who claimed not to know how to tango, Diana was holding her own. Someone had clearly been watching *Dancing With the Stars*.

This was beginning to feel less like dancing and more like sex. Not that Franco was complaining.

"Tell me more about your life in Argentina," she whispered as her hand crept to the back of his neck.

Should he be this aroused at a social function? Definitely not. He was a grown man not a horny fifteen-year-old kid. "Other than the dancing?"

"Yes, although I'm a little curious about the dancing, as well."

He pulled her closer, but kept his gaze glued in the opposite direction. The quintessential tango posture. Convenient, as well, since he never discussed his family upbringing. But he'd witnessed a staggering amount of Drake family dynamics over the past few weeks. Hell, he was beginning to almost feel like a Drake himself. If she was asking questions, he owed her a certain degree of transparency.

"I grew up with a single mother in Barrio de la Boca. I never knew my father."

"I see," she murmured.

He cast a sideways glance in her direction, hoping against hope he wouldn't see a trace of pity in her gaze. Having Diana Drake look at him in such a way would have killed him. She wasn't, though. She seemed more curious than anything, and for that, Franco was grateful.

"My mother was less than attentive. I ran away when

I was eleven. Luc's father took me in. The rest is history, as they say."

They reached the end of the dance floor again, but instead of turning around, Diana slid her foot up the back of his calf. "I wish I would have known about this sooner."

He reached for the back of her thigh and ground subtly against her before letting her let go. "Would it have changed anything?"

"Yes." She swallowed, and he traced the movement up and down the elegant column of her neck. "I'm sorry, Franco. I should have never said what I did earlier."

He lowered her into a deep dip and echoed her own words back to her from the night before. "You're forgiven."

"Ladies and gentlemen, the winners of the annual tango contest are Franco Andrade and Diana Drake."

The room burst into applause.

"I can't believe this," Diana said as Franco pulled her upright. "We won!"

Franco wove his hand through hers and held on tightly as Jack Ellis approached them, holding a shiny silver trophy.

His mouth curved into a tight smile as he offered it to Franco. "Congratulations."

"Gracias." The fact that Ellis was so clearly upset by his presence probably should have bothered Franco to some extent, but he couldn't bring himself to care at the moment.

Diana was speaking to him again. They'd only exchanged a handful of words since their engagement had been announced, and somehow he'd managed to get back in her good graces. Better than that, it felt genuine. He was starting to feel close to her in a way he seldom did with anyone.

Don't fool yourself. It's only temporary, remember.

"Miss Drake, it's a pleasure to make your acquaintance." Ellis shook Diana's hand. "Will you be joining us at tomorrow's match?"

Diana went instantly pale. "Tomorrow's match?"

"The Kingsmen have a game tomorrow. Surely Franco's mentioned it." Ellis frowned.

A spike of irritation hit Franco hard in his chest. Ellis could talk to him however he liked, but he wasn't about to let his boss be anything but polite to Diana. "Of course I have. Unfortunately, Diana has a previous engagement."

She nodded. After an awkward, silent beat, she followed his lead. "I'm afraid Franco's right. I have a commitment tomorrow that I simply can't get out of."

"That's too bad," Ellis said. "Another time, perhaps."

"Perhaps." She smiled, but Franco could see the panic in her amethyst gaze. She had no intention of watching him on horseback. Not tomorrow. Not ever.

Ellis said his goodbyes and walked away. The band began to play again, and Franco and Diana were swallowed up by other couples.

"Come with me." He slid his arm around her and whispered into her hair.

"Where are we going?" She peered up at him, and he could still see a trace of fear in those luminous eyes.

Franco would have given everything he had to take her distress away. But no amount of money or success could replace what she'd lost the day she'd fallen. He'd never felt so helpless in his life. Nothing he could do would bring Diamond back to life.

But maybe, just maybe, he could help her remember what it had been like to be fearless.

If only she would let him.

* * *

"Close your eyes," Franco whispered. His breath was hot on her neck in tantalizing contrast to the cool night air on her face.

Franco's voice was deep, insistent. Despite the warning bells going off in Diana's head, she did as he asked.

"Good girl."

A thrill coursed through her and settled low in her belly. What was she doing? She shouldn't be out here in the dark, taking orders from this man. She most definitely shouldn't be turned on by it.

She inhaled a shaky breath. *Open your eyes. Just open your eyes and walk away.*

But she knew she wouldn't. Couldn't if she tried. Something had happened out there on the dance floor. She felt as if she'd seen Franco for the first time. She'd gotten a glimpse of his past, and somehow that made the dance more meaningful. Not just their tango…the three-year dance they'd been engaged in since they'd first met.

"This way." His hand settled onto the small of her back. "Keep your eyes shut."

He started walking. Slowly. Diana kept in step beside him, letting him lead her. Unable to see, her other senses went on high alert. The sweet smell of hay and horses tickled her nose. The light touch of Franco's fingertips felt decadent, more intimate than it should have.

She licked her lips and let herself remember what it had felt like to take those fingertips into her mouth, to suck gently on them while he'd watched through eyes glittering like black diamonds. She wanted to feel that way again. She wanted *him* again, God help her.

"Be careful." Franco's footsteps slowed. She heard a door sliding open.

"Can I open my eyes now?" He voice was breathy, barely more than a whisper.

Franco's hand slid lower, perilously close to her bottom. "No, you may not."

How close was his face? Close enough to kiss? Close enough for her to lean toward him and take his bottom lip gently between her teeth?

She swallowed. This shouldn't be happening. None of it. The sad reality of Franco's childhood shouldn't change the ridiculous truth of their situation. The only thing they shared was a long string of lies. This was the same man who'd called the newspapers and told them he was marrying her. It was the same man who'd so callously dismissed her the morning after she'd lost her virginity.

They were pretending.

But it no longer felt that way. Not now that she'd seen the real him.

"Franco," she whispered, reaching for him.

He caught her wrist midair. "Shhhh. Let me."

She waited for a beat and wondered what would come next. Franco slid her hand into his, intertwining their fingers. Then her hand made contact with something soft. Warm. Alive.

She stiffened.

"It's okay, Diana. Keep your eyes closed. I'm here. I've got you." Franco's other arm wrapped around her, pulling her against him. He stood behind her with his hand still covering hers, moving it in slow circles over velvety softness.

A horse. She was touching a horse. She knew without opening her eyes.

I'm here. I've got you.

Did he know this was the closest she'd come to a horse since she'd fallen? Did he know this was the first time she'd touched one since that awful day? Could he possibly?

Of course he did. Because he saw her. He always had.

She felt a tear slide down her cheek, and she squeezed her eyes shut even harder. If she opened them now and saw her fingers interlocked with Franco's, moving slowly over the magnificent animal in front of them, she wouldn't be able to take it. She'd fall apart. She'd fall…

But this time, Franco would be there to catch her.

Or not.

How could this man be the same one who'd slept with Natalie Ellis and gotten himself fired?

It didn't make sense. Especially now that she knew his background. She could see why he pushed people away. She could even see why he'd said such awful things after she'd slept with him three years ago. Intimacy—real intimacy—didn't come easily to Franco. It couldn't. Not after what he'd been through as a boy.

If anyone could understand that, Diana could. Hadn't her own childhood been filled with a similar brand of confusion? They'd each found their escape on horseback. Which is why nothing about his termination made sense.

Polo meant everything to Franco. More than she'd ever imagined. Why would he risk it for a meaningless romp with his boss's wife?

There had to be more to the story. She wished he would tell her, but she knew deep down he never would. And she didn't particularly blame him.

"I lied, Franco." She kept her eyes closed. She couldn't quite bring herself to look at him. "It wasn't hate sex."

"I know it wasn't." He pulled her closer against him. When he spoke, his lips brushed lightly against the curve of her neck, leaving a trail of goose bumps in their wake.

"I don't hate you. I never did." She was crying in earnest now. Tears were streaming down her face, but she didn't care. She was tired of the lies. So very tired.

"Don't cry, Wildfire. Please don't cry." He pressed an openmouthed kiss to her shoulder. "It kills me to see you hurting. It always did, even back then."

Her heart pounded hard in her chest. There were more things to say, more lies to correct. She wanted to set the record straight. She *needed* to. Even if she never saw him again after next week.

You won't. He's going away, and he's not coming back.

"For three years, I've been telling myself I chose you because I knew you'd let me down. It's not true. I chose you because I wanted you. I wanted you back then. I wanted you the other night. And I want you now." She opened her eyes and turned to face him.

They were standing in a barn. She'd known as much, and she'd expected to feel panicked when confronted with the sight of the horses in their stalls. But she didn't. She felt right, somehow. Safe.

She'd dreaded coming here tonight, and now she realized it had been a gift.

"How did you know this is what I needed?" she asked.

He cupped her face, tipped her chin upward so she looked him in the eyes. "I knew because, in many ways, you and I are the same. I want you, too, Diana. I want you so much I can barely see straight."

"Take me home, Franco."

Chapter Sixteen

Franco didn't dare touch Diana in the backseat of the limo on their ride back to New York. If he did, he wouldn't be able to stop himself from making love to her right there in plain view of the driver and every other car on the long stretch of highway between Bridgehampton and the city.

It was more than just an exercise in restraint. It was the longest ninety minutes of his life.

They rode side by side, each trying not to look at the other for fear they'd lose control. An electric current passed between them. If the spark had been visible, it would have filled the lux interior of the car with diamond light.

As the dizzying lights of Manhattan came into view, he allowed his gaze to roam. It wandered down Diana's elegant throat, lingering on the tantalizing dip between her collarbones—the place where he most wanted to kiss her at the moment so he could feel the wild beating of her pulse beneath his lips. He wanted to taste the decadent passion she had for life. Consume it.

Diana felt each and every one of her emotions to its fullest extent. It was one of the things he'd always loved about her. Being by her side these past weeks had caused Franco to realize the extent to which he avoided feelings. Since he'd moved to America, he'd done his level best to forget the world he'd left behind. His memories of Argentina were laden with shame. The shame of growing up without a father. The shame of the way his mother had all but abandoned him.

He'd tried to outrun that shame on the polo field. He'd tried to drown it in women and wine. But it had always been there, simmering beneath the surface, preventing him from forming any real sort of connection with anyone. At times he even kept Luc at arm's length.

Luc knew the rules. He knew not to bring up the past. He knew not to push. Why he may have done so this evening was a mystery Franco didn't care to examine too closely.

He thinks this is different. He thinks you're in love.

This *was* different.

Was it love? Franco didn't know. Didn't want to know. Because what he and Diana had together came with an expiration date. He'd known as much from the start, but for some reason it was just beginning to sink in. The date was growing closer. Just a matter of days away. And now that he was a member of the Kingsmen again, he'd be leaving just as soon as their arrangement came to an end.

He should be happy. Elated, even. This was why he'd gotten himself tangled up with the Drakes to begin with. This was what he'd wanted.

But as his gaze traveled lower, past the midnight blue

stone that glittered against Diana's porcelain skin, he had the crippling sensation that everything he wanted was right beside him. Within arm's reach.

Screw the waiting.

He pushed the button that raised the limo's privacy divider and slid toward her across the wide gulf of leather seat in under a second. Diana let out a tiny gasp as his mouth crushed down on hers, hot and needy. But then her hands were sliding inside his tuxedo jacket, pulling him closer. And closer, until he could feel the fierce beat of her heart against his chest.

Not here. Take it slow.

But he couldn't stop his hands from reaching for the zipper at her back and lowering it until the bodice of her dress fell away, exposing the decadent perfection of her breasts. He stared, transfixed, as he dragged the pad of his thumb across one of her nipples with a featherlight touch.

The gemstone nestled in her cleavage seemed to glow like liquid fire, burning blue. On some level, Franco knew this wasn't possible. But he'd lost the ability for rational thought. All he knew was that this moment was one that would stick with him until the day he died.

He'd never forget the feel of Diana's softness in his hands, the way she looked at him as the city whirled past them in a blur of whirling silver light. Years from now, when he was nothing but a distant memory in her bewitching, beguiling mind, he'd remember what it had felt like to lose himself in that deep purple gaze. He'd close his eyes and dream of radiant blue light. God help him. He'd probably never be able to look at a sapphire again without getting hard.

"Diana, darling." He groaned and lowered his lips to her breasts, drawing a nipple into his mouth.

He was being too rough, and he knew it, nipping and biting with his teeth. But he couldn't stop. Not when she was arching toward his mouth and fisting her hands in his hair. His hunger was matched by her need, which didn't seem possible.

It was like falling into a mirror.

How will this end?

Badly. No question.

He couldn't fathom walking away from Diana Drake. But he knew he would. He always walked away. From everyone.

"Mr. Andrade." The driver's voice crackled over the intercom.

Franco ignored it and peeled Diana's dress lower. He was fully on top of her now, spread over the length of the backseat. He was kissing his way down her abdomen when the driver's voice came over the loud speaker again.

"Mr. Andrade, there are photographers at the end of the block, just outside the apartment building."

Diana stiffened beneath him.

"It's okay," he whispered. "Don't worry. Everything will be fine."

He gently lifted her dress back into place, cursing himself for being such an impatient idiot.

What were they doing? They weren't teenagers on prom night, for crying out loud. He was a grown man. The choices he made had consequences. And somehow the consequences of his involvement with Diana seemed to grow more serious by the day.

Diana sat up and brushed the chestnut bangs from her eyes. Her sapphire necklace shimmered in the dark.

Franco looked away and straightened his tie from the other end of the leather seat.

"We're here, Miss Drake, Mr. Andrade," the driver announced.

"Thank you," Franco said, squinting through the darkened car window.

The throng of paparazzi gathered at the entrance to the building was the largest he'd ever seen. The press attention was getting out of hand. The wedding would be a circus.

Get a grip.

He shook his head. There wasn't going to be a wedding. Ever. The engagement was a sham, despite the massive rock on Diana's finger.

The ring was messing with Franco's head. He was having enough trouble maintaining a grasp on reality, and seeing that diamond solitaire on Diana's hand every time she reached for him, touched him, stroked him just added to the confusion.

The back door opened, and he and Diana somehow managed to find their way inside the building amid the blinding light of flashbulbs. The photographers screamed questions at them about the details of the wedding. Would it be held at the Plaza? Who was designing Diana's wedding dress?

It occurred to Franco that he would have liked to see Diana dressed in bridal white. She would look stunning walking toward her man standing at the front of a church in front of the upper echelons of Manhattan society. A lucky man. A man who wasn't him.

They managed to keep their hands off each other as they navigated the route to Diana's front door. When had touching each other become something they did in private rather than for show? And why did that seem so dangerous when that's the way it should have always been?

Diana slid her key into the lock. She pushed the door open, and they paused at the threshold.

Franco caught her gaze and smiled. "I'm sorry about what happened in the car and the close call with the photographers. That was…" He shook his head, struggling for an appropriate adjective. *Careless. Intense. Fantastic.*

They all fit.

The corners of her perfect bow-shaped lips curved into a smile that could only be described as wicked. "I'm not sorry."

Franco swallowed. Hard.

Like falling into a mirror.

But mirrors broke when they fell. They ended up in tiny shards of broken glass that sparkled like diamonds but cut to the quick.

He didn't care what happened to him next month. Next week. Tomorrow. He just knew that before the night was over, he would bury himself inside Diana again. Consequences be damned.

The moment they stepped inside the apartment and the door clicked shut behind them, Diana found herself pressed against the wall. Franco's mouth was on hers in an instant, kissing her with such force, such need that her lips throbbed almost to the point of pain.

A forbidden thrill snaked its way through her. This was different than it had been the night before. They'd been somewhat cautious with each other then, neither of them willing to fully let down their guard. But she knew without having to ask that tonight wouldn't be like that. Tonight would be about surrender.

"Take off your dress," he ordered and took a step backward. His gaze settled on her sapphire necklace as he waited for her to obey.

She stood frozen, breathless for a moment, as she tried to make sense of what was happening. She shouldn't enjoy being told what to do, but this was for her pleasure. His. Theirs. And the molten warmth pooling in her center told her she liked it, indeed.

She reached behind her back for her zipper, but her hands were already shaking so hard that they were completely ineffectual. Franco moved closer, his face mere inches from hers. Her neck went hot, her knees buckled and she desperately wanted to look away. To take a deep breath and calm the frantic beating of her heart. But she couldn't seem to tear her gaze from his.

The corner of his mouth lifted into a barely visible half smile. His eyes blazed. He knew full well the effect he had on her. In moments like this, he owned her. He knew it, and so did she.

It should have frightened her. Diana had never wanted to belong to anyone, let alone him. And she wouldn't. Not once their charade was over and they'd gone their separate ways.

But just this once she wanted it to be true. Just for tonight.

"Turn around, love." His voice was raw, pained.

She did as he said and turned to face the wall. With excruciating care, he unzipped her gown. Red lace slid down her hips and fell to the floor. Franco's hands reached around to cup her breasts as his lips left a trail of tantalizing kisses down her spine.

"*Preciosa,*" he murmured against her bare back. *Lovely.*

His breath was like fire on her skin. She was shimmering, molten. A gemstone in the making.

She sighed and arched her back. Franco's hands slid from her breasts to her hips, where he hooked his fingers around her lacy panties and slid them down her legs. She stepped out of them, turned to face him, but he stopped her with a sharp command.

"No." He took her hands and pressed them flat against the wall, then whispered in her ear. "Don't move, Diana. Stay very still."

This was like nothing she'd ever experienced before. She'd never been with anyone besides Franco, but this was even different than the times they'd been together. The brush of his designer tuxedo against her exposed skin made her consciously aware of the fact that, once again, she was completely undressed while he remained fully clothed. She couldn't even see him, but that seemed to enhance the riot of sensations skittering through her body. She could only close her eyes and feel.

He brushed her hair aside and kissed her neck, her shoulder. His hands were everywhere—on her waist, her bottom, sliding over her belly. She was suddenly grateful for the wall and the way he'd pressed her hands against it. It was the only thing holding her up. Her legs had begun to tremble, and the tingle between them was almost too much to bear. She was so overwhelmed by the gentle assault of his mouth and the graceful exploration of his hands that she didn't even notice he'd nudged her legs apart with his knee until his fingertips reached between her thighs and found her center.

"I could touch you forever," he said and slid a finger inside her.

Forever.

It was a dangerous word, but this was a dangerous game they were playing. For all practical purposes, they were playing house. Living as husband and wife. And to Diana's astonishment, she didn't hate it.

On the contrary, she quite enjoyed it.

Especially now, bent over with Franco's fingers moving in and out of her. She moaned, low and delicious. She needed him to stop. Now, before she climaxed in this brazen posture. But she'd lost control of her body. Her hips were rocking in time with his hand, and she was opening herself up for him like a flower. A rare and beautiful orchid. Diamond white.

"Franco," she begged. "Please."

"Come," he whispered. "For me. Do it now."

Stars exploded before her eyes, falling like diamond dust as her body shuddered to its end. She collapsed into his arms, and he carried her across the apartment to the bedroom, whispering soothing words.

She'd gone boneless, yet her skin was alive. Shimmering like a glistening ruby. The King of Stones. And as he gingerly set her down and pushed inside her, she felt regal. Adored as no woman had ever been.

She was a queen, and Franco Andrade was her king.

Chapter Seventeen

Diana took her place at a reserved table situated near midfield, where Artem and Ophelia sat beneath the shade of a Drake-blue umbrella. She tried not to think too hard about the fact that this is what life would be like if she and Franco were together.

Really together.

Sundays at the Polo Club, sipping champagne with her brother and his wife, surrounded by the comforting scents of fresh-cut grass and cherry blossoms. A real family affair.

It wouldn't be so bad, would it?

Her throat grew tight. It felt quite nice, actually. Far too nice to be real.

Surrender.

It would have been so easy to give in. The past month had been more than business. It had been such a beautiful lie that she wondered sometimes if she actually believed it.

I could touch you forever.

Forever.

The word had branded itself on her skin, along with Franco's touch.

"Here he comes," Ophelia said.

Diana dragged her attention away from the night before and back to the present, where Franco was riding onto the field atop a beautifully muscled bay mare. The horse's dark tail was fashioned into a tight braid, and the bottoms of its legs were wrapped with bright red bandages. These were protective measures, necessary to guard against injury during play, rather than fashion statements. But the overall effect was striking just the same. The horse was magnificent.

But not as magnificent as its rider.

Diana had never seen Franco in full polo regalia before. Riding clothes, sure. But not like this…

He wore crisp white pants and brandy-colored boots that stretched all the way above his knees. The sleeves of his Kingsmen polo shirt strained at his biceps as he gave his mallet a few practice swings. She couldn't seem to stop looking at the muscles in his forearms. Or the way he carried himself in the saddle. Confident. Commanding. The aggressive glint in his eyes was just short of cocky.

He winked at her, and she realized he'd caught her staring. Before she could stop herself, she wiggled her white-gloved fingers in a tiny wave.

Beside her, Artem cleared his throat. "Are you ready for this, sis?"

She dropped her hand to her lap and nodded. "I am."

He was talking about the horses, of course. As far as Artem knew, she hadn't been this close to a horse since the day of her accident. She thought about telling him what Franco had done for her, but she couldn't find the words. She wasn't even sure words existed to describe what had happened when he'd taken her hands and placed them on the warmth of the gelding's back.

But the main reason she didn't try and explain was that she wanted to keep the grace of the moment to herself. To preserve its sanctity. Almost every move she and Franco had made for the past month had been splashed all over the newspapers. Every touch. Every kiss. Every lie. The truth between them lived in the quiet moments, the ones no one else had seen. And she wanted to keep it that way as long as she possibly could.

Because so long as no one knew how much he really meant to her, she could pretend the end didn't matter. She could hold her head high when the gossip pages screamed that she and Franco were over.

Right in front of her, the players were clustered together in the center of the field. The two teams faced each other, waiting for the throw-in—the moment when the umpire tossed the ball into play. Diana forced herself to watch, to concentrate on the present rather than what hadn't even happened yet. But as the bright white ball fell to the ground, she couldn't help but feel like time had begun to move at warp speed. And, with a resounding whack of Franco's mallet, it did.

The ball sailed across the grass, a startling white streak against bright, vivid green. Franco leaned into the saddle, and his horse charged forward. The ground shook beneath Diana's feet as the players charged toward the goal.

Franco led the charge, and when he hit the ball with such force that it went airborne, her heart leaped straight to her throat.

She held her breath while she waited for the official ruling. When the man behind the goal waved a flag over his head to indicate the Kingsmen had scored, she flew to her feet and cheered.

Franco caught her eye as his horse galloped toward the opposite end of the field. He smiled, and her head spun a little.

God, she was acting like an actual fiancée. A wife.

But she was supposed to, wasn't she? She was just doing her job.

It was more than that, though. There was no denying it. She wasn't acting at all.

Oh, no.

Her legs went wobbly, and she sank into her white wooden chair.

You're in love with him.

"He's amazing, isn't he?" Ophelia clapped and yelled Franco's name.

"He is, indeed." Diana felt sick.

How had she let this happen? Sleeping with Franco again—*twice*—had been stupid enough. Falling in love with him was another thing entirely. Off-the-charts idiotic.

The players flew past again in a flurry of galloping hooves and swinging mallets, and Diana's gaze remained glued to Franco. She shook her head and forced herself to look away, to concentrate on something real. The silver champagne bucket beside the table. The feathered hat situated at a jaunty angle on Ophelia's head. Anything. She counted to ten, but none of the little tricks she'd once used to stop herself from thinking about Diamond worked. She couldn't keep her eyes off Franco.

In the blink of an eye, he scored three more goals. It was a relief when the horn sounded, signaling the end of the first chukker. The break between periods was only three minutes, but she needed those three minutes. Every second of them. She needed a break from the intensity of the action on the field. Time to collect herself. Time to convince herself that she wasn't in love with the high-scoring player of the game.

Artem refilled their champagne flutes. "Franco's on fire today."

Diana watched him trot off the field toward a groom who stood by, ready and waiting, with Franco's next horse and mallet. By the time the match was finished, he'd go through at least seven horses. One for each chukker.

"Diana?" Artem slid a glass in front of her.

"Hmm?" she asked absently.

Franco had removed his helmet to rake his hand through his hair, a gesture that struck her as nonsensically sensual. Even from this distance.

"Could you peel your eyes away from your fiancé for half a second?" There was a smile in Artem's voice.

Sure enough, when she swiveled to face him, she found him grinning from ear to ear. Ophelia's chair was empty. Diana hadn't even noticed she'd left the table.

"Fake fiancé," she said. The back of her neck felt warm all of a sudden. She sipped her champagne and wished Artem would find something else to look at.

"You can stop now," Artem said. "I know."

"Know what?" But she was stalling. She knew exactly what he'd meant. He *knew*.

"About you and Andrade." His gaze flitted toward Franco climbing onto his new horse. This one was a sleek, solid-black gelding. Just like Diamond.

Diana's heart hammered in her chest. "Who told you?" Franco? Surely not.

But no one else knew.

"No one." Artem let out a laugh. "Are you kidding?

No one had to. I'm not blind, sis. It's written all over your face."

She shook her head. "No. We're not… I'm not…"

I'm not in love. I can't be.

"Don't even try to pretend it's an act. I'm not buying it this time." His gaze flitted from her to Franco and back again. "How long?"

Diana sighed. She was suddenly more exhausted than she'd ever been in her life. So many lies. She couldn't tell another one. Not to her brother. "I don't know when it happened, exactly."

Slowly. Yet, somehow, all at once.

Was it possible that she'd loved him all along, since the first night they'd been together, back when she was twenty-two?

"This is awful. Artem. What am I going to do?" She dropped her head into her hands.

Artem bent and whispered in her ear. "There are worse things in the world than falling for your fiancé."

She peered up at him from beneath the brim of her hat. "You seem to be forgetting the fact that we're not actually engaged. Also, I know for certain that you hate the thought of Franco and me."

His brow furrowed. "When exactly did I say that?"

She sat up straight and met his gaze. "The day of the Lamberti diamond announcement. And the morning the engagement was listed in the newspaper. And possibly a few other times over the course of the past four weeks."

He shook his head. "Clearly you weren't listening."

"Of course I was. You're not all that easy to ignore, my darling brother. Believe me, I've tried." She gave him a wobbly smile.

She felt like she was wearing her heart on the outside of her body all of a sudden. It terrified her to her core.

The giddy, bubbly feeling that came over her every time she looked at Franco was probably the same thing her mother had experienced when she'd looked at Diana's father. His long list of mistresses had no doubt felt the same way about him, too.

Fools, all of them.

Artem reached for her hand and gave it a squeeze. "I never said I didn't like the idea of you and Franco having a *genuine* relationship."

Could that be true? Because it wasn't the way she remembered their conversations. Then again, maybe she'd been the one who found the idea so repugnant, not Artem.

He leveled his gaze at her. "I was concerned about your pretend relationship. It seemed to be spinning out of control, far beyond what I intended when I make the mistake of suggesting it. But if it's real…"

If it's real.

That was the question, wasn't it?

She would have given anything in exchange for the answer.

Ophelia returned to the table as the next chukker began. Diana redirected her attention to the field, where Franco cut a dashing figure atop his striking black horse. Seconds after the toss-in, he was once again ahead of the other players, smacking the ball with his mallet and thundering toward the goal.

But just as he reached the far end of the field, a player from the other team cut diagonally between him and the ball.

"That's an illegal move," Artem said tersely.

Diana could hear Franco yelling in his native tongue. *Aléjate! Away!* But the player bore down and forced his horse directly in front of Franco's ebony gelding.

Somewhere a whistle sounded, but Diana barely heard

it. Her pulse had begun to roar in her ears as Franco and his horse got lost in the ensuing fray. She flew to her feet to try and get a better look. All she could see amid the tangle of horses, players and mallets was a flash of dazzling black.

Just like Diamond.

Her throat grew tight. She couldn't breathe. Couldn't speak. She reached for Artem, grabbed his forearm. The emerald grass seemed too bright all of a sudden. The sky, too blue. Garish. Like something out of a nightmare. And the black horse was a terrible omen.

No. She shook her head. *Please, no.*

There was a sickening thud, then everything stopped. There was no more noise. No more movement. Nothing.

Just the horrific sight of Franco lying facedown on top of that glaring green lawn. Motionless.

Franco heard his body break as it crashed into the ground. There was no mistaking the sound—an earsplitting crack that seemed as though it were echoing off the heavenly New York sky.

The noise was followed by a brutal pain dead in the center of his chest. It blossomed outward, until even his fingertips throbbed.

He squeezed his eyes closed and screamed into the grass.

Walk it off. It's nothing. You've been waiting for this chance for months. You can't get sidelined with an injury. Not now.

He moved. Just a fraction of an inch. It felt like someone had shot him through the left shoulder with a flame-tipped arrow. At least it wasn't his playing arm.

Still, it hurt like hell. He took a deep breath and rolled himself over with his right arm. He squeezed his eyes closed tight and muttered a stream of obscenities in Spanish.

"Don't move," someone said.

Not *someone.* Diana.

He opened his eyes, and there she was. Kneeling beside him in the grass. The wind lifted her hat, and it went airborne. She didn't seem to notice. She just stared down at him, wide-eyed and beautiful, as her dark hair whipped in the wind.

For a blissful moment, Franco forgot about his pain. He forgot everything but Diana.

If she was putting on an act, it was a damned convincing one. Something in his chest took flight, despite the pain.

"You're a sight for sore eyes, you know that?" He winced. Talking hurt. Breathing hurt. Everything hurt.

Especially the peculiar way Diana was looking at him. As if she'd seen a ghost. "Why are you sitting up? You shouldn't be moving."

"And you shouldn't be on the field. You're going to get hurt." She was on her hands and knees in the grass, too close to the horses' hooves. Too ghastly pale. Too upset.

She remembers.

He could see it in the violet depths of her eyes—the agony of memory.

"*I'm* going to get hurt? Look at you, Franco. You *are* hurt." She peered up at the other riders. "Someone do something. Get a doctor. Call an ambulance. Please."

Luc had already dismounted and stood behind her with the reins to his horse as well as Franco's in his hand. He passed the horses off to one of their other teammates and knelt beside Diana. "The medics are coming, Diana. Help is on its way. He's fine. See?"

She blinked and appeared to look right through him.

Franco wished he knew what was going on in her head. Which part of her horrific accident was she remembering?

He'd known she was having trouble coming to terms with what had happened to her...with what had happened to Diamond. But he'd never once suspected that she remembered her accident. She'd had a concussion. She'd been unconscious. Those memories should have been mercifully lost.

No wonder she'd had such a hard time moving on.

"Diana, look at me." He reached for her, and a hot spike of pain shot through his shoulder. He cursed and used his right arm to hold the opposite one close to his chest.

A collarbone fracture. He would have bet money on it.

It was a somewhat serious injury, but not the worst thing in the world. With any luck he'd be back on the field in four weeks. Six, tops.

But he didn't care about that right now. All he cared about was the woman kneeling beside him...the things she remembered...the fear shining in her luminous eyes.

He'd been such an idiot.

The list of things he'd done wrong was endless. He shouldn't have pushed her to overcome her fears. He shouldn't have ridden a jet-black horse today. He damn well shouldn't have pressured her into watching him play.

He wished he could go back in time and change the things he'd said, the things he'd done. He would have given anything to make that happen. He'd never set foot on a polo field again if it meant he could turn back the clock.

If that were possible—if he could step back in time, he'd walk...run...all the way to the first moment he'd touched her. Not last night. Not last week.

Three years ago.

"Diana, I'm fine. Everything is fine."

But his assurances were lost in the commotion as the medical team reached him. He was surrounded by medics, shouting instructions and cutting his shirt open so they could assess his injuries. Someone shone a light in his eyes. When the spots disappeared from his vision, he could see the game officials clearing the horses and riders away. Giving him space.

He couldn't see Diana anymore. Suddenly, people were everywhere. Jack Ellis loomed over him, his expression grave. The emergency medical team was carrying a stretcher out onto the field.

Franco looked up at Ellis. "Is all of this really necessary? It's a collarbone. I'll be fine."

"Let's hope so," Ellis said coldly. "We need you on the tour."

Luc cleared his throat. His gaze fixed on Franco's, and Franco felt...

Nothing.

For months this was all he'd wanted. Polo was his life. Since he'd left home at eleven, he'd lived and breathed it. Without it, he'd been lost. The thought of losing it again, even for a few weeks, combined with the look on Ellis's face should have filled him with panic.

He wasn't sure what to make of the fact that it didn't.

"Diana," he said, ignoring Ellis and focusing instead on Luc. "Where is she? Where did she go?"

"She's with her brother." Luc jerked his head in the direction of the reserved tables.

"Go find her." Franco winced. The pain was getting worse. "Bring her to the hospital. Please."

Luc nodded. "The second the game is over, I will."

The game.

Franco had all but forgotten about the scrimmage. He'd turned his life upside down to get back on the team, and in a matter of seconds it no longer mattered.

Slow down. This is your life. She's a Drake. You're not. Remember?

Diana would be fine.

She was a champion. She'd come so far in conquering her fears in recent weeks. She was close. So close. His fall had been nothing like hers. Of course she'd been rattled, but by the time he saw her again, she'd be okay.

He clung to that belief as the paramedics strapped him to a stretcher and lifted him into an ambulance.

But the look on Diana's face when she walked into his hospital room however many hours later hurt Franco more than his damned arm did. The person standing at his bedside was a ghost of the woman he'd taken to bed the night before. Memories moved in the depths of her amethyst eyes.

Painful remembrance.

And stone-cold fear.

Franco had seen that look before in the eyes of spooked horses. Horses that had been through hell and back, and flinched at even the gentlest touch. It took years of patience and tender handling to get those horses to trust a man again. Sometimes they never did.

"You're here." He shifted on the bed, and a spike of pain shot from his wrist to his shoulder. But he didn't dare flinch. "I'm glad you came."

She gave him an almost invisible smile. "Of course I came. I'm your fiancée, remember? How would it look if I weren't here?"

So they'd gone from making love to just keeping up appearances. Again. Marvelous.

"Sweetheart." He reached for her hand and forced himself to speak with a level of calmness that was in direct contrast to the panic blossoming in his chest. "It's not as bad as it looks. I promise."

She nodded wordlessly, but when she quietly removed her hand from his, the gesture spoke volumes. He was losing her. It couldn't happen again. He wouldn't let it, damn it. Not this time. Not for good.

"Diana…"

"I'm fine." There was that forced smile again. "Honestly."

He didn't believe her for a minute, and he wasn't in the mood to pretend he did. Hadn't they been pretending long enough? "You're not fine, Diana."

She stared at him until the pain in her gaze hardened. *Go ahead, get mad. Just feel something, love. Anything.* "Be real with me."

She shook her head. "We had an agreement, Franco."

"Screw our agreement." She flinched as if he'd slapped her. "There's more here than a fake love affair. We both know there is."

"Stop." She exhaled a ragged breath. "Please stop. The gala is in two days, and so is the Kingsmen tour."

"Do I look like I'm in any kind of condition to play polo right now?" He threw off the covers and climbed out of the hospital bed. There was too much at stake in this conversation to have it lying down.

"You're going on the tour. Luc said Ellis is insisting that you come along. As soon as your injury heals, you'll be right back in the saddle." Her gaze shifted to his splint, and she swallowed. Hard.

"I'll always ride. It's not just my job. It's my life." Using his good arm, he reached to cup her cheek. When she didn't pull away, it felt like a minor victory. "It's yours, too, Diana. That's one of the things that makes us so good together. You'll ride again. You will. When you're ready, and I intend to be there when it happens."

She backed out of his reach. So much for small victories. The space between them suddenly felt like an impossibly vast gulf. "Go on tour, Franco. You'll be fired again if you don't."

Franco sighed. "I highly doubt that."

"It's true. Ask Luc. Apparently your coach wants to keep an eye on you." Her gaze narrowed. "I guess he doesn't want to leave you behind with his wife."

Shit. That again.

"Natalie Ellis means nothing to me, Diana. She never did."

"That's not such a nice way to talk about a woman you slept with. A woman who was *married*, I might add."

Franco followed her gaze to her ring finger, where her Drake Diamonds engagement ring twinkled beneath the fluorescent hospital lighting. He watched, helpless, as she slid it off her hand.

No. Every cell in his body screamed in protest. "What do you think you're doing?"

"I'm breaking up with you." She opened her handbag and dropped the ring inside. Her gaze flitted around the room. She seemed to be looking anywhere and everywhere but at him.

"Why remove the ring? It's not as if I actually gave it to you." Would she have been able to remove it so easily if he had?

He hoped not, but he couldn't be sure.

"I still think it's a good idea to take it off. You know, in case the press…"

"You think I still give a damn what the press thinks? Here's a headline for you—I don't. This isn't about our agreement. It's not about Drake Diamonds or Natalie

Ellis. It sure as hell isn't about the press. What's happening in this room is about you and me, Diana. No one else."

He'd fallen off his horse—something he'd done countless times before with varying degrees of consequences. Over the course of his riding career, he'd broken half a dozen bones and survived three concussions. But never before had a fall caused so much pain.

"Diana, you're afraid. But I'm fine. I promise. Now stop this nonsense. We have a gala to attend in two days."

She shook her head. "We had a deal, and now it's over. We both got what we wanted. It's time to walk away."

"Don't do this, Wildfire." His voice broke, but he couldn't have cared less. The only thing he cared about was changing her mind.

He wasn't sure when, but somewhere along the way he'd stopped pretending. He had feelings for Diana Drake. Feelings he had no intention of walking away from.

"Marry me."

Her face went pale. "You're not serious."

"I am. Quite." He'd never wanted this. Never asked for it. But he did now. The future suddenly seemed crystal clear.

She saw it, too. He knew she did. She could close her eyes as tightly as she wanted, but it was still there. Diamond bright.

"I'll marry you right now. We could go straight to the hospital chapel. Just say yes." They could have a fancy ceremony later on. Or not. Franco didn't care. He just wanted to be with her for the rest of his life. "Come on the tour with me, Diana. I don't want to do this without you."

"No." She shook her head. "You're not. You're just confused. I am, too. But it's not real. *We're* not real. You know that as well as I do."

"All I know is that I'm in love with you, Diana."

"Is that what you told Natalie Ellis? Were you in love with her too?" Diana's gaze narrowed. "You slept with a married woman, Franco. Your boss's wife. Do you even believe in marriage?"

What was he supposed to say to that?

I never slept with her.

I lied.

She'd never believe him. "There's never been anyone else, Diana. Only you."

"That doesn't exactly answer my question, does it? I can't marry you, Franco. Don't you see that? I might be a Drake, but I'm not my mother. She stood by the man she loved, even as he slept with every other woman who crossed his path. It killed her. It would kill me, too."

Then Diana turned and walked right out the door, and Franco was left with only the devastating truth.

He knew nothing.

Nothing at all.

Chapter Eighteen

The Met Diamond gala was supposed to be the most triumphant moment of Diana's fledgling career as a jewelry executive, but she dreaded it with every fiber of her being. She should have been walking up the museum's legendary steps on Franco's arm. She couldn't face the possibility of doing so alone. Not when every paparazzo in the western hemisphere would be there, wondering what had happened to her famous fiancé. She'd rather ride naked through the streets of Manhattan, Lady Godiva-style. But she'd made a promise, and she intended to honor it.

Thank God for Artem and Ophelia. Not only did they ride with her in the Drake limo, but they also flanked her as she climbed the endless marble staircase. She didn't know what she would have done without them. Artem slipped her arm through his and effectively held her upright as she was assaulted by thousands of flashbulbs and an endless stream of questions.

"Diana, where's Franco?"

"When's the wedding?"

"Don't tell us there's trouble in paradise!"

She wanted to clamp her hands over her ears. She could hear the photographers shouting even after they'd made it inside the museum.

"Are you okay?" Artem eyed her with concern.

God, she loved her brother. This night was every bit as important for him as it was for her, but his first concern was her broken heart.

She forced a smile and lied through her teeth. "I'm fine."

"No, you're not," Ophelia whispered. "You're shaking like a leaf. Artem, call our driver back. Diana should go home."

As good as that sounded, she couldn't. She'd made it this far. Surely she could last another few hours. Besides, she couldn't hide forever. The world would find out about her breakup eventually. It was time to face the music.

She was shocked no one had learned the truth yet. Two days had passed since she'd ended things with Franco. He hadn't breathed a word to the press, apparently. Which left her more confused than ever.

"Diana, I'd like you to stay." Artem glanced at his watch. "At least for half an hour. Then you can go straight home. Okay?"

"Artem…" Ophelia implored.

He cast a knowing glance in his wife's direction, one of those secret signals that spouses used to communicate. Diana would never be on the receiving end of such a look. Obviously.

"Thirty minutes," he repeated. "That's all I'm asking."

"No problem. I told you I'm fine, and I meant it." For the thousandth time since she'd walked out the door of

Franco's hospital room, the pad of her thumb found the empty spot where her engagement ring used to be.

A lump sprang to her throat.

She wasn't fine. She hadn't been fine since the moment she'd seen Franco fall to the ground at the polo match.

She'd thought she'd been ready to be around horses again, but she hadn't. She'd thought she'd been ready for a real relationship, one that might possibly lead to a *real* engagement and a *real* marriage, but she'd been wrong about that, too.

She couldn't lose anyone again. She'd lost both her mother and her father, and she'd lost Diamond. Enough was enough. She couldn't marry Franco. Not now. Not ever. If she did and something happened to him—if she lost him, too—she'd never be able to recover.

She shouldn't even want to marry him, anyway. The man had zero respect for the sanctity of marriage. He'd been fired for sleeping with his boss's wife, which meant that Diana had somehow fallen for a man who was exactly like her dad.

She'd have to be insane to accept his proposal.

Even though she'd almost wanted to…

"Excuse me." A familiar voice broke into their trio.

Diana turned to find the last person in the world she ever expected to see. "Luc?"

What on earth was Luc Piero doing at the Met Diamond gala? Had Franco not even told his closest friend that the engagement was off?

"Luc, I'm sorry. There's been a change of plans. Franco's not with me tonight." *Or any other night*.

He shook his head. "I'm not here for Franco. I came to talk to you."

"Me?" She swallowed.

What could she and Luc possibly have to talk about?

"Yes. You." He looked around at their posh surroundings. The Met was stunning on any given day, but tonight was special. Faux diamonds dripped from every surface. It was like standing inside a chandelier. "Is there someplace more private where we can chat?"

She shouldn't leave. She had a job to do. She had to speak to the Lambertis and pose for photos. And just looking at Luc made her all the more aware of how much she missed Franco.

She shook her head, but at the same time she heard herself agreeing. "Come with me." She glanced at Artem and Ophelia, who'd been watching the exchange with blatant curiosity. "I'll be right back."

She led Luc past the spot where the Lamberti diamond, which had just been officially rechristened the Lamberti-Drake diamond, glowed in a spectacular display case in the center of the Great Hall. Her stilettos echoed on the smooth tile floor as they rounded the corner beneath one of the Met's sweeping marble archways. When they reached the darkened hall of Greek and Roman art, her footsteps slowed to a stop.

They were alone here, in the elegant stillness of the sculpture collection. Gods and goddesses carved from stone surrounded them on every side. Secret keepers.

Diana was so tired of secrets. She'd spent her entire life mired in them. No one outside the family knew the circumstances surrounding her mother's death. Diana hadn't been allowed to talk about it. Nor did the public know the identity of Artem's biological mother. To the outside world, the Drakes were perfect.

So much deception. When would it end?

She turned to face Luc. "What is it? Has something happened to him?"

She hadn't realized how afraid she'd been until she uttered the words aloud.

Luc wouldn't have sought her out if what he had to say wasn't important. The moment he'd asked to speak to her in private, her thoughts had spun in a terrible direction. She remembered what it had felt like to find her mother's lifeless body on the living room floor...the panic that had shaken her to her core. It had been the worst moment of her life. Worse than her accident. Worse than losing Diamond. Worse than watching Franco's body break.

Every choice she'd made since the day her mother died had been carefully orchestrated so she'd never feel that way again. And where had it gotten her?

Completely and utterly alone.

But that wasn't so bad. She could handle loneliness. What she couldn't handle was the way her heart had broken in two the moment she'd seen Franco's lifeless body on the ground.

She'd fought her love for him. She'd fought it hard. But she'd fallen, all the same.

"No, he's fine." Luc's brow furrowed. "Physically, I mean. But he's not fine. Not really. That's why I'm here."

Her heart gave a little lurch. "Oh?"

Franco couldn't possibly love her. Not after the way she'd treated him. He'd been real with her. Unflinchingly, heart-stoppingly real. And she'd refused to do the same.

Worse, she'd judged him. Time and again. She'd acted so self-righteously, when all along they'd both been doing the same thing—running from the past. She'd chosen solitude, and in a way, so had Franco. Neither one of them had let anyone close. Until the day Franco asked her to marry him.

He was ready to leave the past behind. He was moving

beyond it, and he'd offered to do so hand in hand with Diana. But she'd turned him down.

She'd spent years judging him, and now she knew why. Not because the things he'd done were unforgivable, but because it was convenient. So long as she believed him to be despicable, he couldn't hurt her.

Or so she'd thought.

But he hadn't hurt her, had he? She'd hurt herself. She'd hurt them both.

"He's in love with you, Diana," Luc said.

She shook her head. "I don't think so."

She'd made sure of that.

"You're wrong. I've known Franco all his life, and I've never seen him like this before." The gravity in his gaze brought a pang to her chest. "He misses you."

She shook her head. "Stop. *Please.*"

Why was he doing this? She'd nearly made it. Franco was leaving with the Kingsmen in less than twenty-four hours. Once he was gone, she'd have no choice but to put their mockery of a romance behind her and move on. She just had to hold on for one more day.

A single, heartbreaking day.

She swallowed. "I'm sorry, Luc. But I can't hear this. Not now."

She needed to get out of here. She'd thought she could turn up in a pretty gown and smile for the cameras one last time, but she couldn't. All she wanted to do was climb into bed with her dog and a pint of ice cream.

She gathered the skirt of ball gown in her hands and tried to slip past Luc, but he blocked her exit. He jammed his hands on his hips, and his expression turned tortured. "You're going to make me say it, aren't you?"

Diana was afraid to ask what he was talking about. Terrified to her core. She couldn't take any more. Refusing Franco had been the most difficult thing she'd ever had to do.

But she couldn't quite bring herself to ignore the torment in Luc's gaze. "I don't know what you're talking about."

Luc shook his head. "Franco is going to kill me. But you deserve to know the truth."

The truth.

A chill ran up Diana's spine. She had the sudden urge to clasp her hands over her ears.

But she'd been turning her back on the truth long enough, hadn't she?

No more secrets. No more lies.

"What is it?" Her voice shook. And when Luc turned his gaze on her with eyes filled with regret, she had to bite down hard on the inside of her cheek to keep from crying.

His gaze dropped to the floor, where shadows of gods and goddesses stretched across the museum floor in cool blue hues. "Look, I don't know what happened between the two of you, but there's something you should know."

Diana nodded wordlessly. She didn't trust herself to speak. She couldn't even bring herself to look at him. Instead, she focused on the marble sculpture directly behind him. Cupid's alabaster wings stretched toward the sky as he bent to revive Psyche with a kiss.

A tear slid down her cheek.

"Tell me," she whispered, knowing full well there would be no turning back from this moment.

Luc fixed his gaze with hers. The air in the room grew still. Even the sculptures seemed to hold their breath.

"It was me," he said.

Diana began to shake from head to toe. She wrapped

her arms around herself in an effort to keep from falling apart. "Luc, what are you saying?"

"I was the one who had an affair with Ellis's wife, not Franco." He blinked a few times, very quickly. His eyes went red, until he stood looking at Diana through a shiny veil of tears. "I'm sorry."

Diana shook her head. "No."

She wanted him to take the words back. To swallow them up as if she'd never heard them.

"No!" Her voice echoed off the tile walls.

Luc held up his hands in a gesture of surrender. "It wasn't my idea. It was Franco's. I left my Kingsmen championship ring in Ellis's bed. He found it and knew it belonged to one of the players. Franco confessed before I could stop him."

"I can't believe what I'm hearing." But on some level, she could.

Franco loved Luc like a brother. He wanted to protect him, just as Luc had protected him when he'd been living in his barn and then his home.

She should have figured it out. From the very beginning, she'd suspected there was more to Franco's termination than he'd admitted. Then, at Argentine Night at the Polo Club, Natalie Ellis had looked right through him.

And Diana had known.

Franco had never touched her.

But Diana had been so ready to believe the worst about him, she'd pushed her instincts aside. What had she done?

"He never anticipated being cut from the team. He was too valuable. But Ellis couldn't stand the sight of him. I tried to tell the truth. Over and over again. Franco wouldn't have it."

She wanted to pound her fists against his chest. She wanted to scream. *You should have tried harder.*

But she didn't. Couldn't. Because deep down, she was just as guilty as he was. Guilty of letting the past color the way she saw her future.

I should have believed.

Franco wasn't her father. Loving him didn't make her into her mother. And she *did* love him, despite her best efforts not to.

She'd spent every waking second since her accident trying to protect herself from experiencing loss again, and it had happened anyway. She'd fallen in love with Franco, and she'd lost him. Because she'd pushed him away.

"Tell me this changes things." Luc searched her gaze. His eyes were red rimmed, but they held a faint glimmer of hope.

"I wish it could." Her heart felt like it was going to pound out of her chest. She pressed the heel of her hand against her breastbone, but it didn't make a difference. She was choking on her remorse. "He asked me to marry him, Luc. And I turned him down."

Luc's brow furrowed. "What do you mean? I thought you were already engaged. It was in all the papers."

"He didn't tell you?" Her voice broke, and her heart broke along with it. "It was never real."

"He never said a word."

The fact that Franco never told Luc their relationship was a sham meant something. Diana wasn't sure what… but it did. It had to. He'd been willing to sacrifice everything for Luc, but he'd let his closest friend believe he was in love. He'd let him think he was going to marry her.

And that made whatever they'd had seem more genuine than Diana had ever allowed herself to believe.

It was real. It had been real all along.

She needed to go to him. What was she doing standing here while he was preparing to leave? "Sorry Luc, there's something I need to do."

She turned and ran out of the sculpture gallery, her organza dress swishing around her legs as she ran toward the foyer. But when she rounded the corner, she collided hard against the solid wall of someone's chest.

A hard, sculpted chest.

She'd know that chest anywhere.

"Franco, you're here." She pulled back to look up at him, certain she was dreaming.

She wasn't. It was him. He was wincing and holding his arm in the sling where she'd banged against it, but it was him. She'd never been so happy to see an injured man in all her life.

"I am." He smiled, and if her heart hadn't already been broken, it would have split right in two.

It felt like a century had passed since she'd walked out of his hospital room. A century in which she'd convinced herself she'd never see him again. Never get to tell him the things she should have said when she'd had the chance…

"Franco, there's something I need to say." She took a deep breath. "I'll go with you on tour. Please take me with you."

His smile faded ever so slightly. "Diana…"

"I just want to be with you, Franco. *Really* be with you." She choked back a sob. "If you'll still have me."

She felt as if she'd just taken her broken heart and given it to him as an offering. Such vulnerability should have made her panic. But it was far easier than she'd expected. Natural. Right. The only thing making her panic was the thought that she'd almost let him leave Manhattan without telling him how she felt.

She took a deep, shuddering inhale and said the words

she'd tried all her life not to say. "I love you. I always have. Take me with you."

Around them, partygoers glided in the silvery light. The air sparkled with diamond dust. They could have been standing in the middle of a fairy tale.

But as Franco's smile wilted, Diana plunged headfirst into a nightmare.

"It's too late." He took her hands in his, but he was shaking his head and his gaze was filled with apologies that she didn't want to hear.

She'd missed her chance.

She should have believed.

She should have said yes when she'd had the opportunity.

"I understand." She pulled her hands away and began gathering her skirt in her fists, ready to run for the door. Just like Cinderella.

The ball was over.

Everything was over.

"It's okay." But it wasn't. It would never be okay, and it was all her fault. "I just really need to go…"

"Diana, wait." Franco stepped in front of her. "Please."

She couldn't do this. Not now. Not here, with all of New York watching. Couldn't he understand that?

But she'd fallen in love while the world watched. She supposed there was some poetic symmetry to having her heart broken while the cameras rolled.

"I can't." It was too much. More than she could take. More than anyone could.

But just as she turned away, Franco blurted, "I quit the team."

Diana stopped. She released her hold on her dress, and featherlight organza floated to the floor. "What?"

"That's what I meant when I said it's too late. You

can't go with me on the road because I'm not going."
His mouth curved into a half grin, and Diana thought
she might faint. "Did you really think I could leave you?"

He's not my father.

She'd turned him down, sent him away. And he was
still here. He'd stuck by Luc, even when it had come at
great personal cost.

Now he was sticking by her. He was loyal in a way
she'd never known could be possible.

"You're afraid," he said in a deliciously low tone that
she felt deep in her center. "Don't be."

He moved closer, cupped her face with his left hand.
She'd missed him. She'd missed his touch. So, so much.
She could have wept with relief at the feel of his warm
skin against hers.

"I'm not afraid. Not anymore." She searched his gaze
for signs of doubt, but found only rock-solid assurance.
His eyes glittered, as sharp as diamonds.

He dropped his hand, and her fingertips drifted to her
cheek, to the place where he'd touched her. She hadn't
wanted him to release her. *Too soon*, she thought. She
needed his hands on her. His lips. His tongue.

Everywhere.

"Wildfire." Franco winked, and she felt it down to
the toes of her silver Jimmy Choos. "I have something
for you."

He reached into the inside pocket of his tuxedo and
pulled out a tiny Drake-blue box tied with a white satin
ribbon. It was just like the ones she'd once sold to all the
moonstruck couples in Engagements.

Diana stared at it, trying to make sense of what was
happening. For as long as she could remember, she'd
hated those boxes. But not this time.

This time, the tears that pricked her eyes were tears of joy.

"Franco, what are you doing?" How had he even gotten that box? Or whatever was inside of it?

Her gaze flitted over Franco's shoulder, and she spotted Artem watching from afar with a huge grin on his face. So her brother was in on this, too? That would certainly explain where the tiny blue box had come from. It also explained his insistence that she stay for the beginning of the gala.

Is this really happening?

"Isn't it obvious what I'm doing?" Franco dropped down on one knee, right there in the Great Hall of the Met.

It *was* happening.

A gasp went up from somewhere in the crowd as the partygoers noticed Franco's posture. Diana could hear them murmuring in confusion. Of course they were baffled. She and Franco were supposed to be engaged already.

Let them be confused. For once, Diana didn't care what anyone was saying about her. She didn't care what kind of headlines would be screaming from the front page of the papers tomorrow morning. All she cared about was the man kneeling at her feet.

"It occurred to me that I never asked properly for you to become to my wife. Not the way in which you deserve. So I'm giving it another go." He took her hand and gently placed the blue box in it.

Her fingertips closed around it, and their eyes met. Held.

"I love you, Diana Drake. Only a fool would walk away from something real, and I don't want to be a fool anymore. So I'm asking you again, and I'm going to keep asking for as long as it takes." But there would be no more proposals, because she was going to say yes. She could barely keep herself from screaming her answer before he finished. *Yes, yes, yes.* "Will you marry me, Diana Drake?"

"I'd love to marry you, Franco Andrade."

The crowd cheered as he rose to his feet and took her into his arms. Diana was barely conscious of the popping of a champagne cork or the well-wishers who offered their congratulations. She was only aware of how right it felt to be by Franco's side again and how the tiny blue box in her hand felt like a magic secret.

She waited to open it until they were back at her apartment. The time between his proposal and the end of the party passed in a glittering blur. She needed to be alone with him. She needed to step out of her fancy dress and give herself to him, body and soul.

After they left the gala and finally arrived at her front door, Diana wove her fingers through Franco's and pulled him inside.

"Alone at last," he said, gazing down at her as the lights of Manhattan twinkled behind him.

"Sort of." Diana laughed and lifted a brow at Lulu, charging at them from the direction of the bedroom.

Franco scooped the puppy into the elbow of his uninjured arm and sat down on the sofa. Lulu burrowed into his lap, and he gave the empty space beside him a pat. "Come sit down. Don't you have a box to open?"

She sat and removed the little blue box from her evening bag. She held it in the palm of her hand, not wanting the moment to end. She wanted to hoard her time with Franco like a priceless treasure. Every precious second.

"Open it, Wildfire."

She tugged on the smooth satin ribbon and it fell onto her lap, where Lulu pounced on it with her tiny black paws. As the puppy picked it up with her mouth, she fell over onto her back between them, batting at the ribbon with her feet. The comical sight brought a lump to Diana's throat for some strange reason.

Then she realized why…

The three of them were a family.

She lifted the lid of the box, but the large rose-cut diamond solitaire nestled on top of the tiny Drake-blue cushion inside was unlike any of the rings in the shiny cases of the Engagements section of Drake Diamonds. Jewelers didn't typically style diamonds in rose cut anymore. This ring was different. Special. Familiar in a way that stole the breath from Diana's lungs.

"This was my mother's ring." She hadn't seen this diamond in years, but she would have recognized it anywhere. When she was a little girl, she used to slip it on and dream about the day when she'd wear sparkling diamonds and go to fancy black-tie parties every night, just as her parents did.

That had been in the years before everything turned pear-shaped. Before they'd all learned the truth about her father and his secret family. Back when being a wife and a mother seemed like a wonderful thing to be.

Diana had forgotten what it was like to feel that way.

Now, with breathless clarity, she remembered.

"How did you get this, Franco?" It was more than a stone. It was hope and happiness, shining bright. Diamond fire.

"I went to Artem to ask for your hand, and he gave it to me. He said it's been in the vault at Drake Diamonds for years. Waiting." Franco took the ring and slid it onto her finger. Then he lifted her hand and kissed her fingertips.

The diamond had been waiting all this time. Waiting for her broken heart to heal. Waiting for the one man who could help her put it back together.

Waiting for Franco.

At long last, the wait was over.

Epilogue

A *Page Six* Exclusive Report

Diamond heiress Diana Drake returns to New York today after winning a gold medal in equestrian show jumping at the Tokyo Olympics. The win is a shocking comeback after Drake suffered a horrific fall last year in Bridgehampton that resulted in the death of her beloved horse, Diamond. Drake's new mount—a Hanoverian mare named Sapphire—was a gift from her husband, polo-playing hottie Franco Andrade.

Andrade was on hand in Tokyo to watch his wife win the gold, where we hear there was plenty of Olympic-level PDA. We can't get enough of Manhattan's most beautiful power couple, so *Page Six* will be front row center this weekend when Andrade returns to the polo field as captain of the newly formed team, Black Diamond, which he co-owns with his longtime friend and teammate, Luc Piero.

All eyes will certainly be on Diana, who is returning to the helm of her family's empire Drake Diamonds as co-CEO. Rumor has it she declined a glass of champagne at the party celebrating her Olympic victory, and we can't help but wonder...

Might there be a baby on the horizon for this golden couple?

Only time will tell.

* * * * *

LET'S TALK
Romance

For exclusive extracts, competitions
and special offers, find us online:

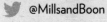 facebook.com/millsandboon

 @MillsandBoon

@MillsandBoonUK

Get in touch on 01413 063232

For all the latest titles coming soon, visit
millsandboon.co.uk/nextmonth